MW00477738

his pretty little burden

his pretty little burden

NICCI HARRIS

also by nicci harris

Copyright © 2022 by Nicci Harris

All rights reserved.

No part of this book may be reproduced in any form or by any electronic or mechanical means, including information storage and retrieval systems, without written permission from the author, except for the use of brief quotations in a book review.

ISBN ebook: 978-1-922-492-13-5

ISBN print: 978-1-922492-14-2

ISBN Hardback: 978-1-922492-20-3

Edited by Writing Evolution. @writingevolution.

www.writingevolution.co.uk

Edited by Mostert-Seed Editing

www.mostertseedediting.com

Internal graphics by Nicci Harris

Cover design by Books & Moods

This is a **work of fiction**. Names, characters, businesses, places, events, locales, and incidents are either the products of the author's imagination or used in a fictitious manner. Any resemblance to actual persons, living or dead, or actual events is purely coincidental.

his pretty little burden

this is my darkest novel yet.

Please be aware that His Pretty Little Burden explores themes of severe trauma, taboo topics, age-gap dynamics that can be confronting, lots of steam, heart-breaking loss, and brutality.

Nothing fades to black.
Side effects may include: excess discomfort and pressure between the thighs, a throbbing sensation that beckons any kind of relief so please avoid sharp objects,

—also crying, shaking, drooling, growling, nightmares, daydreams, and, finally, *divorce*. **I take no responsibility** for any of the above mentioned. And think about the children before you leave your husbands. The Butcher Boys are fictional.

If you need more details on said triggers please feel free to reach out to me on my social media platforms - *your friend and writer of random things, Nicci Harris.*

For Detailed Triggers And Spoilers
visit my website. authornicciharris.com

song list

Kids of the District
His Pretty Little Burden

1. Take me home - Jess Glynne
2. You should know where I am coming from – BANKS
3. Mad world – Michale Andrew
4. Deer in headlights – Sia
5. Take me to church – Hozier
6. Heaven – Julia Michaels
7. Come as you are – Imaginary Future
8. Human – Christina Perri
9. Demons – Boyce Avenue
10. The sound of silence – Simon & Garfunkel
11. Here comes revenge – Metallica
12. Feeling good – Muse
13. Control – Halsey
14. Knocking on heavens door –Raign
15. Dear Society –Madison Beer

16. Happiness is a butterfly –Lana Del Rey
17. Whispers in the dark –Skillet

Go to Spotify to listen.
His Pretty Little Burden

happiness is like a butterfly

"Happiness is like a butterfly, the more you chase it, the more it will elude, but if you turn your attention to other things, it will come and sit softly on your shoulder." –Henry David Thoreau.

Clay

12 months earlier

SITTING IN THE FRONT PEW, under the stained-glass windows crowning the District's oldest church, alongside the daughters of the man in the polished mahogany casket before me, I feign my attention. My eyes set ahead, but my muscles tighten as vengeance rolls through the room.

It's not that I do not grieve this man.

I do.

I grieve alongside his family—my family—the council officials, and hundreds of members of the city who saw Jimmy Storm as a kind of philanthropist.

Grieving him was always a certainty.

My jaw clenches in a solemn smile as I feel something is amiss.

I stare respectfully forward while behind me the presence of my father, brothers, and their partners is ripe with sadness, bitterness, and betrayal. Jimmy would be proud he still affects them so.

Despite the fact my brother and I executed him ourselves, it isn't problematic grieving with his admirers as we shared a kind of affection for this man.

He was a second father to us.

But that is the way it goes.

His time was up the moment he betrayed the *Cosa Nostra*. Stole one of our own. Lied to another made-man. Spent money he had no right to spend.

Greed and hubris were his biggest sins.

Still, he had loyal followers...

In the adjacent pew, the Family heads from Sicily listen like devout Catholics as the priest recites psalm after psalm, their conscience is as clear as mine, their minds without shame, but surely, they too feel the electrified air. See the side-eye glances.

Usually, I am the most powerful man in the room, but today, I'm matched by many. This is the first and last time this number of Family members will be in Australia.

Caporegimes and Bosses from Sicily and from across the country are spread throughout the room. Between these four walls is the most dangerous place in the world; a gathering like this rarely happens. The last time was probably back in '57 at the Apalachin meeting, where my American Family was raided and arrested by the feds. It's bad business bringing everyone to one location, but for Jimmy Storm's funeral... they came anyway.

We stand to pray.

The fact my six-foot-five frame towers above most is not lost on me as right now a shot to the back of my head would be child's play. Even so, I stay at my full height. They wouldn't dare. If someone did, they better aim true because I'll have him gutted while his heart still beats.

Aurora, Jimmy's eldest daughter and my wife, stands quietly beside me, her whiskey-coloured eyes misted over but not a tear to be seen—for she is no fool either. She is *Cosa Nostra* royalty. So, her father's death came as no surprise to her. I've never kept a secret from my wife, and she has never made me regret that stance.

When we sit again, Aurora holds her hands in her lap, and I tear my eyes away from the priest at the altar to watch her worry her wedding band around her long, elegant finger. A piece of jewellery equal parts a platinum shackle and a crown. We do not have a traditional relationship—nor a sexual one—our union is based on business. Being my wife is the last claim she has to this empire now that her father has been overthrown.

Still, she is my partner.

Exhaling hard, I reach for her hand and hold it, stilling her nervous fidgeting.

She squeezes my fingers.

Beside her, her younger sisters share muted sobs while wafting black silk hand fans at their flushed faces. Despite the millions we give this church, air-conditioning doesn't seem to be a priority in the midst of a scorching Australian summer.

The ceremony runs for hours.

Each time we stand to pray, the back of my neck prickles under the eyes of Jimmy's beloved citizens. The narcissist in him was very skilled at playing Gandhi, disturbingly so. A skill I have honed as my own, but Jimmy still sails through this procession like a phantom. Even now, the guests that idolised him breathe life back into his corpse.

Jimmy Storm was the heart and teeth of the District, enlightening and adoring his followers while gnashing and shredding those who challenged him.

He and my father built this city from the ashes of poverty. They nourished it. Fed it. They cleaned the streets and secured previously unattainable tenders for employment. They saw our residents hold gold and green in their fists. Jimmy and my father are businessmen, and they sank their claws so far into the heart of the District that if anyone was to rip the *Cosa Nostra* from it, the entire city would bleed to death.

Alceu and my father deliver speeches and condolences as the heads of the Family in the District.

Solemn nods.

Tight smiles.

Grief thick in the air.

The procession ends. But the eerie current coursing through the very fibres in the air does not dissipate as the bodies filter from the pews. I clasp my hands in my lap, waiting. My father and the four most formidable men in the world also linger to speak with me, alone in this house of God.

Aurora leaves my side, knowing the ritual to be had is not for her to witness. As members of the city leave alongside her, she takes her time to console them in a flawlessly elegant manner. Pride moves through me. She is just like Jimmy.

The church doors echo as they shut. The silence surrounding us is woven with superiority and expectation.

With tension.

I'd know it anywhere.

I sigh roughly, the sound breaking the quiet.

"Rest in peace, my boy," Alceu states, his words

projected towards the corpse of the man he raised as his own back in the old country. I stare ahead at the garlands and polished wood of his coffin, my attention not straying from the stage.

"Now is the time, Clay," he says. "We are all here to see you take your place."

The most dangerous man in this room by my measure—my father—waits respectfully quiet behind me. Significance moves through my bones. I've been bred for this moment my entire life, and now that it is here, I'm ready.

I dig into my pocket, retrieving the card I have carried with me since I was twenty-one. Spinning it in my hand, I approach the coffin.

The priest hovers nearby.

I still when he moves. Quick. Jerky. Pulling a gun from his robe, he points it between my eyes, his hand shaking violently.

I slide the card between my newly growing smile; my instincts are very rarely wrong. Darting from his line of fire, I draw my Glock before he can take a breath and blow the priest backwards into his pulpit, the gun still braced in his rigid right hand. I don't look behind me at the four men on the bench.

I approach the priest, my shadow creeping up his trembling form as I tower over him. *So, it was you.* The man whimpers, hisses, gurgles on blood and saliva; the helpless sounds of a dying man fill this sacred room.

My heart pumps hard. Steady. Strong.

The gaping wound at the priest's stomach puddles and pools. His hand vibrates around the poorly held gun; the other clumsily holds the hole while viscous fluid, stomach contents, and toxins bubble through split flesh and infect his whole fucking nervous system.

A stomach wound means a slow death. Sepsis first. Then his organs will shut down.

At least he is in *His* house.

Humidity gathers in the air, causing my skin to mist, for sweat to slide down my forehead. The shift is immediate. Control seeps through me as the threat that hung in the air now dwindles with the man choking on his own fluids. I expected a final present from Jimmy.

The priest was a nice touch.

Dropping to my haunches, I stare indifferently into the wide haunted eyes of God's representative, wondering how much Jimmy paid for his soul.

"*Please*," he begs, his voice rattling in his throat. His eyes drop to the gun, as he tries to lift it to his temple. He wants me to show him mercy. Blow his brains out. His crooked fingers twitch around the gun, before finally weakening, dropping the metal piece to the stage.

Reaching for his mouth, I enclose it, silencing the gurgling and sobbing beneath my iron-tight grip. He flails around. My bicep twitches as I hold him still. Hold him until the life leaves his fearful grey eyes. *I am merciful.*

I wipe the card on his wound, smearing Saint George—my saint—with holy blood spilled—*desecrated*—at *His* altar.

Standing, I approach the coffin and casually flick the card on top before slowly making my way down the aisle, the sound of my father and the four Dons from Sicily flanking me as I do.

So, it begins.

CHAPTER ONE

Three months earlier

THE TELEVISION FLICKERS ON, but it is one of those old-school boxes, thick and bordered in a kind of wood-look laminate. Static brings it to life, lighting the basement with flickering colour and then the glow of a black-and-white movie.

The girl and the boy on the screen are naked, but the girl isn't moving, and then I realise it's because she's unconscious. It isn't in English. Despite the disturbing content, I find it hard to look away from the hypnotic way her body shakes as he takes her without consent.

I glance from the screen and meet Benji's soulful gaze. In my mind, I smile, and yet, my lips won't form the curve.

Still, I'm almost certain he winks at me.

Subtle. Just for me to see. And even in this strange state

of intoxication, I feel my heart soar in response to that gesture.

When the girl on the television screams, my eyes cut across to watch as she wakes up with the boy inside her. It's not a nice film. But Benji likes cult movies, and I like him...

Dotted in the light from the standing lamps and the monitor, his room in the basement looks plucked straight from the set of an 80s show. On his wall, retro pin-up girls pose, their pear-shaped physiques tightly covered in short jumpsuits, taunting my skinny frame. He likes his girls curvaceous, confident, and dominant. Everything I'm not.

A cough drags my attention back to my brothers, back to the cannabis and cocaine sprinkled carelessly on the glass coffee table. My eyes scan their faces, naturally landing on Benji's once more, and he gives me *that* grin. I think I successfully smile back this time.

A whooshing fills my ears, my heart rate slow but shuttering, nonsensical. I go to stand but wobble, dropping back down onto the couch.

No one notices.

My mouth is suddenly dry.

I go to talk, but the words don't reach my tongue, yet I know they are in there. My bare thighs are like ice below my palms, and I wonder if I'm wet or sweating or if it's just the sensation of being cold.

"She looks fucked."

Benji moves beside me and wraps an arm around my shoulders. I lean into him, seeking comfort as the inebriation climbs into my consciousness and warps my reality. His scent covers me like a blanket fending off the awful helplessness my condition brings with it.

We watch the horrible movie play.

My eyes shift from the rape scene ahead, slicing through the air to a blinking red dot.

...flash...flash...flash...

CHAPTER TWO

Present Day

MY MUM TOLD me that bad things come in threes.

Her death: number one.

His murder: number two.

Yep, murder.

Not an accident like they reported.

A murder.

A collection of crows.

Stop stalling!

So, while I look across the street at the imposing, steep white gates, knowing I have mentally and physically prepared myself for this afternoon, wearing a nice pair of jeans, tan ankle boots, and a cute crop top, the swarm of butterflies in the pit of my stomach reminds me that I have number three looming. And that I'm out of my depth here...

Stupid, even, for considering reaching out to a man who doesn't know I exist. Which, according to my mum, isn't exactly a bad thing.

She'd said he's a dangerous man.

But I need a dangerous man.

I peer out at the enormous walls that seem to go on forever to my right and left, a sprawling white barrier for an enormous estate. He needs the walls. He's a crook. Well, *Mafia* is the word she used, although it's hard to stomach such a serious accusation. In the Mafia? A Mafia man?

Sighing, I wrinkle my nose. No, I don't even know how to phrase it in my head, but he's damn dodgy. I worry my bottom lip while reaching for my right plait, untangling the freshly washed strands before starting on the left.

Just cross the street.

Knock.

My feet don't move.

I shake my hair free, the long straight blonde curtain falling down my shoulders and over my breasts. I try to calm my nerves, reminding myself that Mum also believed mattress factories are warehouses harbouring secret alien research laboratories. *"Five mattress factories in this town, baby. Five. We only buy a mattress every ten years. Who is buying all these mattresses?"*

Forcing my feet forward, I take the first step and then watch a camera set above the wall come to life, stalking me the entire way up to the intercom.

When I face the speaker, my eyes widen, reality reaching into my chest and squeezing the air from me. I fiddle with the ends of my hair. It's not too late to just walk away. I could do a little wave, mouth 'whoops, wrong house,' and run like a lunatic back to the bus stop. Maybe no one saw me, maybe the camera has a sensor, maybe no one is actually—

"Miss, please state your business."

Fuck. I step backwards, then forwards, then backwards because that step was way too big before forcing the words out. "I'm looking for my father."

Smooth.

I grimace at my outburst, locking my jaw to cease the verbal diarrhoea. When silence circles me, butterflies start to breed inside me, plotting to escape straight through my stomach lining. "Did... did you hear me?"

"What is the name of the man you wish to see?"

"Right, sorry." I lean into the speaker, my voice a stammering mess. "Jimmy Storm. He lives here, right?" I swallow. "He knows my father, I think. At least that's what my mum said. I was hoping he would help me find him."

"What is your father's name?"

"Ah, Dustin Nerrock... They're friends. I've been trying to track him down for months." That's a lie. It's been exactly eleven weeks, four days, and thirty-seven minutes. I knew from that moment this was my only choice. The only option left. And despite hating asking favours, even more so from privileged people, I'll do anything for Benji.

Startling me, the gate to my left opens. I'm surprised by the soundless way it slides across the silver driveway. A big breath puffs out my cheeks. I've come this far. Before I can wander through, the man on the intercom says, "Wait on the bench by the pond. We will send someone to collect you, Miss. It is quite a walk to the main house."

I nod, wrapped in awe, as I walk over the threshold. He is going to think I want money. I'm prepared for that assumption. It's not like these people would miss a small amount, though.

Gazing at the rippling lily pond directly to my left, surrounded by perfectly sculptured hedges, I wish Mum had at least told my dad about me. Wish that she had asked for help, so she could have put food on the table more often. Maybe she wouldn't have killed herself trying to be a mother when she clearly had no idea how to be one... maybe she wouldn't have killed herself.

I stroll over to the black-and-white marble bench beside the pond. Sitting, I marvel at the hedges, rolling parallel to the driveway and disappearing off into the distance. I feel as though I have tumbled down a rabbit hole. The hedges are almost too large, the greens too vivid. It reminds me of the movie *The Labyrinth*, and that, of course, reminds me of *Benji*.

A sad sigh leaves me. This place is far removed from my foster mother's little red brick house in Storm River, with her dry, dusty backyard littered with my foster brother's bikes and broken-down vehicles.

I shuffle nervously when a shiny black car comes into view, the sleek elegance of it an odd sight amongst the vast greenery, the car's metallic paint glittering under the sun's gentle touch. It slows to a stop, and I stand, smoothing my shirt down my stomach. Blinking at the ominous black vehicle, I wait.

A man in his early forties, black suit and black tie, steps from the driver's seat before wandering around to the passenger door. He looks like a butler on steroids. "You won't be seen for a few hours. The man you need to speak with is busy. Please,"—he gestures politely to the backseat—"I'll take you somewhere you can wait."

The formalities stir me. "I'm sorry. I don't want to impose. If he's busy, I can come back?"

"It's fine, Miss. Please." He nods towards the open passenger door.

I swallow my need to hightail it and run as the big arse butterflies inside me fight for space. "Okey dokey."

Climbing into the passenger seat, I shuffle to the opposite window to take in the sights. As the car takes off, rolling smoothly up the driveway, I realise there is nothing to be seen except hedges. An elegant solution to any privacy problem. Private people have things to hide... I would know.

Rising as we climb a hill, I see an extended roofline with multiple chimneys, and then the house comes into view. No. Understatement. A mansion. "Woah," I mutter in wonder. It's three storeys, at least, with a wide, imposing frontage. Large colonial-style pillars tower from the ground floor to the top.

A gentle breeze brings the Australian flag to life, waving it from atop a white pole. I shuffle around the backseat to watch a gardener water the lawn—it appears newly laid with the roll lines still visible, the blades not having weaved together yet.

As we pull into the turning circle, I blink my surprise from my eyes. The boundary netting of a tennis court is visible behind large palm trees. My mouth drops open as I stare up the front steps to the pillars and double doors.

The passenger door is opened for me, and I step out. *Fuck me...* My nerves are twitching. I look at the flag. He's patriotic. That's a good sign, surely?

"I'll take you around to the pool, where you can wait," Henchman Jeeves says, indicating for me to follow him.

Passing the four armed guards at the door, I tail him into a parlour and spin around to take in the grandeur, unapologetically stunned.

While walking backwards to not miss a single detail, I peer up the staircase. The sun seems to flood the space, light rolling up the glossy porcelain flooring. Mr Storm's cleaner must be very good at her job; I can't see a single blemish.

"Come along."

I hurry after him.

Entering a room on the left, I watch Henchman Jeeves open double French doors to reveal a large wrap-around stone veranda with marble steps cascading like a waterfall down to the poolside.

"Woah," I say again, stopping at the top of the steps, the breeze skimming the water surface and rising to tousle my hair around. The aqua water glows within a border of manicured gardens.

"You can wait out here," he says, and before I can ask him a question, he is on the other side of the French doors, striding away. Shrugging, I ignore the wrought-iron table and tiny chairs because they don't look comfortable at all.

Knowing the person who owns this house decided to buy them despite having plenty of money, makes me suspicious.

Surely, they are ornamental.

I sit down on the second step, cuddle my knees, and gaze at the pristine gardens and pool with canals disappearing under bridges and around corners.

Drumming my fingers on my leg, I try to redirect my mind while my stomach twists in hunger. The peanut butter sandwich I had back in the motel wasn't enough after the train, two buses, and two kilometre walk here. *Fucksake.* I don't want to ask for anything here, though. I hate owing people shit. I'll feel that tether of debt regardless, but for Benji, I can handle it.

"Here's a sandwich."

I laugh out loud, spinning to find Henchman Jeeves approaching with a plate. "Thank you, you are fantastic at your job, but I can't accept that."

He sets the food down despite my refusal. I peer at a toasted Caesar sandwich, my stomach growling, my mouth salivating. *That smells epic.*

"Your empty stomach just had a conversation with me in the car. So, yes, you can accept it," he notes, his words circled in humour, his tone surprising me.

I chuckle, snubbing out my embarrassment with a joke. "Well, thank you. But you know what they say, malnourished is the new sexy."

I lift the sandwich. The toast crunches as I sink my teeth in. Salt and creamy dressing explode in my mouth. It's so fucking good. I chew it, twisting to watch the view of the pool. As I moan around a bite of bacon, someone comes up behind me, clearing their throat. I turn, expecting to see Henchman Jeeves, but instead, I crane my neck even further, dragging my eyes over the crisp, fitted charcoal suit of a man who is clearly not a butler or a henchman.

Piercing blue eyes trained on me with unapologetic inference. Behind him, a henchman with an emotionless face stands with his hands by his sides, not looking at me, but appearing ready for anything.

I jump to my feet, dusting the toast crumbs off my jeans and straightening my shirt.

"Hi," I say, the word skating down a heavy breath. Arching my neck further, I feel as though I am withering beneath his gaze. I attempt to control the budding of my anxieties, inhaling fresh air. An attempt to zero fucking avail.

Now, I don't believe in God, never have, but if God made *man* in his image, then I think the tall, dark, thirty-something-year-old in front of me was the prototype. Being beautifully tanned, handsome, with that perfect masculine jawline, and broad chest filling out his expensive black suit to perfection—he's a damn work of art.

Kudos, God.

And while I have you, you're an a-hole.

Amen.

My pulse kicks up when his dark brows weave in contemplation, reminding me who he is. What my mum said he is. What I hope he is... *Mafia.* It's unmissable too. The suit and polished outward appearance do nothing to gentrify him. I see it within his aura—the phantom of darkness, a no bullshit, no excuses, takes-what-he-wants kind of energy that is very at home within him. My heart shudders with unease because maybe I'm wrong about him being designed by God.

Maybe he's the creation of the Devil.

I shuffle in his shadow.

"You believe you're Dustin Nerrock's daughter?" he says, projecting a tone of smooth, effortless authority. Dropping his gaze to my feet, he scrutinises me slowly, leisurely trailing the length of my body. Settling on my face, his eyes narrow. "You bear no resemblance."

Not sure why, but that hurts. I'd rather look like the predator than the prey, but I admit, "I look like my mum."

He nods towards the chair that I refused to sit on earlier, holding his hand out to insist I precede him. And although I immediately walk over to it, my gaze is snagged on the size of his hand. I wonder how many dirty deals he's signed with them, how many men he's beaten to death. "Take a seat."

Doing as I'm told, I slide into the chair, still holding my sandwich tightly. The Devil's prototype sits down opposite me, leans back, and settles his ankle on top of his knee. He's all smooth and casual, while wearing a suit that drips wealth, that screams he is anything but a casual man. "I'm afraid I have some bad news for you. The man you came to see died twelve months ago."

"Oh." My heart sinks, feeling as though I've missed my opportunity, as though the three buses here were a waste of time, and the money spent just a waste in general.

"Your father..." A hint of a grin tugs at his left lip, the charismatic curve lighting a flame in the lowest part of my abdomen. I don't like that reaction. "If he is, in fact, your father, is very much alive."

My eyes widen. "Really? Do you know where I can find him? Where is he?"

"Firstly,"—he motions to me, a piercing blue gaze sliding across my face with intent—"your name?"

"Fawn." My eyes dart to the sandwich, which I instinctively place on the table instead of holding it in my lap like a dog afraid her master will take away her bone. "I'm Fawn."

"You understand I need to make sure you are Dustin's daughter, don't you?" When the words leave his mouth, I sink further down onto the cold, hard chair because I have no proof. Just a dead woman's bedtime stories. I glance to my lap, worrying my lip.

"Fawn," he says, and as though he has a direct line to my chin, my head rises to meet his stern gaze. "When I talk to you, you look me in the eye."

Fuck me.

Forcing the dryness from my throat, I swallow and nod. His glowing blue eyes dart to watch the roll of my throat. "And you answer me. Do you understand?"

"Yes," I say straightaway, his tone stoking the little flame in my abdomen to a full-blown fire. "I understand. It's just... I have no proof."

He twists his knees to face away from me. "Come over here. Let me get a good look at you."

I blink at him.

Once.

Twice...

Oh my God, he's serious.

When I stand, my legs tremble, nerves racketing through me. I take the two steps to stand by his side, waiting for instruction. He opens his legs. "Kneel."

My heart scrambles right into my throat while my body does exactly as he commanded—I'm a puppet and he wields the strings. I swear I didn't give my legs permission to kneel, but I'm between his thighs now, and he's looking down at my face with a measuring gaze.

I hold his stare, watching the way it traces the curves of my features, the way it flicks from one of my eyes to the other, an action I'm familiar with, given I have one green eye and one blue-grey.

Captivated by him, my breath catches when his fore-finger touches my chin, lifting. And *God*, his smell moves around me, into me. He doesn't smell like Benji. His scent is like his aura: deep, rich, powerful, and just so very... *masculine.*

When the French doors open, a man walks through them, and I peer at him without turning my head, my chin still controlled by the gentle touch of *his* finger. He taps the side of my chin, drawing my attention back to his intense stare that seems to have never left my face. Under his gaze, everything seems strange. Dizzying, yes. But also... like I want to make damn sure I don't disrespect him.

The man beside us hands him something, and I catch the flash of a thin white column. My breathing instantly becomes shallow. He notices, his eyes dropping to my chest, watching my nervousness play out through the weighted rise and fall of my breasts. His gaze drags back up to my face as he says, "Now. Open these lips."

When I don't instantly respond, too busy contemplating

his words, bewilderment squeezing my lungs, his hand moves to my jaw. I gasp as he digs his fingers into my cheeks, parting my teeth, forcing my lips wide apart. I wince at the harsh hold, but don't show any resistance, don't recoil either, too focused on breathing, on staying very still. He's dangerous; that much is damn clear. A mob boss? My mind drifts to the feel of his hands, to how those hands have probably taken a life... or two. How he could probably throw my head to the side, snap my neck, and not break a sweat.

And no one will miss you.

He stares at my open mouth, the vulnerability I feel set ablaze by his unwavering attention. I peer down through my lashes as he puts what looks like a white Q-Tip between my lips. A whimper of fear drifts up my throat, feeling utterly helpless. His eyes shift at the sound, now both a cool, crystal-clear blue ocean and a dark, tempestuous sea.

The fire in my abdomen billows into my veins.

A tickle caresses the inner flesh of my cheek, a gentle stroke that moves up and down inside me, the action and sensation forcing a tiny mewl from my throat. A zap of awareness rushes between my legs. I curl in, squeezing my eyes tight, squeezing my thighs together, fending off the warmth making me want to rock my body.

The Q-Tip leaves my cheek.

His hold on my jaw softens. Fingertips caress my sore cheek muscles in a soothing way, making small circles around the harsh dips his thumb and forefinger left, completely replacing the discomfort with... I don't know, but I think a soft smile plays on my lips at the sensation, an action so incongruous with the weight of indecency in the air.

"Good girl." In my dazed state, I barely hear him say, "Stand. Go back to your seat."

I place my palm in his, the size comparison instantly dragging me back to a place of sanity. And while I have it, I use his hand to stand and then drop it quickly, as though something may happen if I feel its warmth a moment longer.

Needing to shift my focus, I grab the sandwich as I slide onto the cold iron chair. Taking a huge bite, I swallow the bacon and chicken, along with the feel of him inside my mouth. Chewing, I ignore the way my body prickles and swoons beneath his gaze.

"Does Dustin know about you?" he asks, his voice taking on a gravelly timbre, a more virile edge. I shake my head, still chewing to avoid anything else. "*Fawn*," he warns. The demand for my words, not a simple nod, sails through the air between us and rattles my resolve.

I swallow chunks of the sandwich, finding his gaze again. "No. He doesn't know."

"Why now?"

Dread finds a place amongst the fire in my stomach. I wince, glancing at my ankle boots to avoid the perfect blue gaze scrutinising me so thoroughly I feel bare. "That's private."

Silence prickles the air between us, and when I look back at him, a slow smile moves across his lips, both daring me and warning me not to be disrespectful. "I asked you a question, Fawn. I expect the right answer."

Shifting, I work my lower lip between my teeth. I don't want to lie. I'm a terrible liar. But I don't know him. And he's not the person I came to see... I decide to tell him a half-truth, admitting, "I'm pregnant." A heavy exhale leaves me, and I meet his eyes, seeing his jaw respond with the slightest of tics. I'm not sure why, but that twisted truth seems to annoy him. And I don't like how I now care about how he perceives me.

Not that it should matter what he thinks.

Not wanting to make this about money, I follow this half-truth, pressing, "I don't want money. I just thought that maybe Dustin would want the baby. His grandchild."

Another tic from him.

Another sinking feeling for me.

Why do I care?

Why do I care that he's now looking at me like a silly girl for having gotten knocked-up, for not having a home, for being so vulnerable?

The quiet is painful, stretching between us for too long. I can't handle it. With a nervous chuckle, I blurt out, "I can't keep it. I'm eighteen. I've got very little money. Nowhere to go. I'm... I just can't look after a baby."

I'm not made of the right stuff.

It's not a lie. But it still hurts. I feel my eyes pool, my composure slip, but keep them on him as he asked, keep them submerged in his calculating blue gaze that is somehow unreadable no matter how intensely I feel it tunnelling beneath my skin.

"Good," he finally says, and I gape at him. "If you're Dustin's daughter, then you will stay here." He stands, smoothing down his black tie. "Until Dustin arrives to collect his property, that is."

As he turns to leave, I shoot up. "Wait. Here? In this house? How long for?"

"Logistics, Fawn. Your father is a busy man. A..." He considers his words. "Tiresome man to track down. Bolton will show you to your room."

Then he disappears through the grand French doors to the mansion that is now my place of residence, flanked by his emotionless henchman.

Fuck me.

Not what I was expecting. I want to exhale with the utter relief I feel about having a free place to sleep for a few nights, for being that much closer to my dad and answers, but I'm also acutely aware that nothing in this life comes without certain expectations.

And kindness usually has a cost.

CHAPTER THREE

.

THE OLD TELEVISION BOX MOVES, *the entire unit slowly gliding towards me, in a way it might if on wheels.*

It's upon me.

Then I'm inside it.

"Wake up."

My back arches off the bed, rising me with it, pulling me from my tormented slumber as my muscles fight to flee but barely move at all. A nightmare, I think.

"Wake up."

I sit up with a start, clutching at the sheets, endorphins and fear like a spiralling entity consuming me, eyes wide with panic, mind lost while trying to comprehend the day, the time, reaching for my most recent memory so that I can place myself somewhere. Anywhere. Desperately, I search the large unfamiliar space around me. Where am I?

As my eyes land on a girl sitting beside me, I scoot to the opposite end of the enormous bed, kicking the sheets as I go to create a barrier between me and the stranger. "Who are you?"

She holds her hands up by her face. "It's okay. I'm Jasmine. I won't hurt you."

"Why, why are you in here?" Here? Where is here? I dart my startled gaze around the room, bouncing it off the lamp dotted walls, the reverie of yesterday slowly tumbling into my tired, confused mind. I'm staying *here* a few nights, I remind myself. The mansion. Henchman Jeeves brought me to this room. I laid down on the bed for a moment and then... I fell into the television again.

"Mr Butcher told me to sleep in here with you," she says, a soft English drawl to her accent. "On the roll-out."

My heart slows to a normal rhythm once I remember I'm safe, that my father will be here soon to collect me. *"His property,"* is what the man said. I didn't mind that at all. No one has ever wanted to own me before... And most people look after their property, find a place in their world for it, and take responsibility. I like that a lot. "Mr Butcher?"

"Yes, my boss." She nods. "Didn't you meet him?"

"I, ah, yes," I recall, rubbing my dry eyes to life and relaxing my offensive stance, sliding my knees up and hugging them, the sheets like a little fort around me. "The man with the blue eyes?"

She laughs, a hue of pink lighting the pales of her cheeks. A blush, in fact. I get it; he's hot. "He *does* have particularly striking eyes, doesn't he? Don't you know who Clay Butcher is?" She slides further onto the bed, crossing her legs, settling in. I drop my gaze to her pink button-up sleep shirt and drawstring shorts, outwardly young and hip apparel. I think she is about my age, perhaps a year or two older.

"What time is it?" I squint around the room again, scarcely able to see much beyond the lamps emitting a low glow on the walls. The shadowed corners are pitch-black; the curtains are blackout. It is seemingly night-time. "Wait,"

I say, meeting her hazel eyes again. "What do you mean, '*Do I not know who he is*?' Should I know who he is?"

Finding her drawstring, she fiddles with the ends. "Well, yeah. I guess you don't watch much television. His brothers are like the District Kardashians. They're rich and beautiful. Everyone wants to know their business, ya know? And Mr Butcher has recently been..." She ponders the correct wording. "Knighted? Crowned? I dunno, become the mayor of Connolly."

"Mayor?" Surprised by that, my mind reaches for understanding. *"He is in the Mafia, Fawn."* My mum's words throw me further into bewilderment. So my mum was being her eccentric self when she thought my father was associated with the Mafia. His involvement in the political world instead makes far more sense as to why she didn't want to reach out to him, a man whose image I imagine is pristine. A bastard daughter is probably the worst kind of publicity. I feel pride skip through my heart, imagining my father giving speeches and organising citizens. A man of impeachable character—

Fuck.

The skip abruptly halts. The main reason I'm here is not possible if he *truly* is a man of impeachable character. I remember the way darkness lurked below Mr Butcher's practised veil of professionalism; he can't just be a politician.

That's not what I want.

I shake my head, deflating.

Still, taking the baby and giving him a place to belong, with food and love, will release me of that burden. The rest, I can figure out on my own... Even in theory, it's laughable. Or maybe one day, I'll just remember.

"Who are you?" Her words draw me from my thoughts,

planting me back onto the bed with the strange girl. "To be able to stay here, in his house?"

Startled by her question, I say, "He never said?"

"He told me you were his guest and to stay by your side until he comes for you. But Bolton is outside your door, so that means you're not *just* a guest."

Given her tone, I suppose that isn't usually done. If my father is an influential man, then it would make sense that Mr Butcher would want to keep me out of the media and prevent me from conversing with other people. I don't mind. I don't want attention, anyway. "I'm trying to find my dad. Dustin Nerrock. Do you know—"

"Yes. I know him," she confirms, sweeping her long chocolate-coloured hair to the side. "He was an associate of Mr Storm. I met him a few times when Mr Storm was still alive before his son-in-law, Clay, erm, sorry, Mr Butcher and his daughter Aurora came to live here."

I beam, wanting to know more about the man who is partly responsible for my existence. "You know him? My dad? What's he like?"

"Rude," she says with a laugh that isn't malicious, but I still feel my spine tighten, not liking her admission. "I know powerful people, been around them my whole life, and they are all rude. Mr Butcher can be very... curt, but he is kind in a cold way too."

She can't know him that well. She's young. "You're my age? How long have you worked for them?"

"Since I dropped out of high school, so like, three years. I'm a maid, usually, but this is just for now because I need something to do. But I suppose he wanted someone your age to be with you. See, that was thoughtful. Sort of."

I nod, liking that I didn't wake up alone in here, but still unsettled given she's sitting on the bed with me. "So you're being paid to just hang out with me?"

"I'm being paid *a lot* to hang out with you."

Not a bad gig.

My hollow stomach contracts, a groan reaching out, the sound outward and loud. A blush hits my cheeks. *"Hunger is unbecoming."* My foster mother's words sound in my ears.

"You're hungry," she says, jumping to her feet, eager to act. "You missed dinner. What do you want?"

"I'm fine," I say, the gurgle of my stomach fighting against my words, rendering them lies dangling in the air. "Okay, sorry. I *am* hungry, but I don't want to eat his food."

She clicks the side lamp on, lighting the room further, allowing my eyes visibility. She shimmies her slippers on. "Don't be silly. You're a guest. Want ice cream?"

I slide from the mattress, looking down and seeing I'm in the same shirt and jeans, reminding me that I really should go back to the motel and collect my things. I adjust my clothes because the material feels rough compared to the luxurious, soft sheets I was touching with my fingers. "Ice cream?"

"Yeah! You're pregnant, though. Do you feel like ice cream? Or cake. They have the best cakes downstairs. I sneak slices when I'm on the late shift, cleaning up after a party or something." Her bright eyes and beaming smile cause the corner of my lips to twitch upwards and a flake of excitement to settle inside me. I lock away my wariness.

"Yeah. Cake sounds amazing."

"Cool." She twists around, bounding towards the door. "I'll go get us some."

"Wait," I blurt out, stepping towards her and the door. "Can I come?"

"Ah..." She pauses, her eyes wide in thought. "I don't see

why not. Everyone is asleep anyway. It's past midnight." I trail her from the room, and she makes a little hmm sound in her throat. "Looks like Bolton has ducked out. I thought I'd have to convince him to let us go to the kitchen."

I sneak after her down the shadowy hallway where most of the lights are off or dim. The walls are bare, with not a picture frame in sight, no indoor trees or ornaments.

Twisting around to view the direction we came from, I see several doors heading in that direction. We turn and she descends a wide staircase with another hallway continuing in the opposite direction. I would most definitely get lost if I were alone.

At the bottom of the stairs, we take a door behind them, and Jasmine flicks a switch. The room comes to life under the strip lights on the ceiling. *Woah*. It's a kitchen. A large commercial-style kitchen, set in chrome, sterling silver, glass, and white splashback tiles. Nothing like the small kitchenette in my foster family's house, but I suppose that is to be expected as I imagine Mr Butcher has a full house of staff.

His staff probably have staff.

I stay by the door as she bounces towards the double fridge. Gripping a cake box, she appears, bringing it towards me. She cuts two pieces and then lifts herself onto the work-bench, sitting up there and taking a bite. "Come have some. It's orange and macadamia."

I slide up beside her, eagerly grabbing a slice of cake and taking a bite. My tastebuds burst under the sweet and tart flavours, the playful but delicate tones. "Fuck, this is so good. I feel like we're being naughty or something."

"Nah. Bolton has a camera on him at all times, so he knows we are in the kitchen and Mr Butcher told me to make sure you eat, and, anyway, I can get away with pretty much anything." She takes another bite, talking around her mouthful. "So, you're trying to find your dad? Why? Because you're knocked-up?"

Her lack of a filter only brings a bright smile to my lips, liking the friendly, no-bullshit approach she has with me. We share this flaw in tactfulness. I stare at the cake, wishing I could create something this magnificent. Wish I had a skill. Wish I was worth more than my appearance. *"You may feel good about yourself now, while you're young and pretty, but when you're my age, you'll be nothing."* The bitter words of my foster mother fill my mouth with bile, the truth in them hard to keep down. I'm not good for much, not good enough to be a mother, that's for sure. I won't let this baby struggle with me through life like my mother did, and I can't let it be raised by the system like I was after her suicide. So, giving Dustin the baby makes sense... "I want to give Dustin the baby. I can't look after it. I'm not made of the right stuff to be a mother."

"What about the father?" she asks, finishing her slice and staring longingly at the remaining wedge, her internal debate clear in her eyes. "Doesn't he want the kid?"

The reverie of an old black-and-white television show flickers behind my eyes, provoking my heart to shudder, to move low into the pit of my stomach with the surprise baby and the delicious cake. Benji... I want to say it's Benji's. That the baby was made in a loving moment, but then she might ask questions. Want details. Then I would have to lie, and I've twisted the truth enough today. I'm exhausted by the weight of all my omissions. "I don't know who the father is. Not for sure," I admit, taking another bite, filling my mouth with more joy and coating the bile with sweetness. The word *slut* is probably echoing in her ears.

"Oh." She dusts the sugary shaving from her fingers. My

confession thickens the air, an awkward silence hangs between us.

Slut. Slut. Slut.

"What about you?" I say, finishing my slice before sliding off the countertop, needing action and a distraction from, well, *slut*. Cringing inwardly, I walk to the fridge and open the door. As the frosty air radiates out, I ask, "What's your story?"

"My story? Where do I start?" She laughs, before bouncing to her feet, outwardly indifferent to my predicament. I sigh my relief. "I have so many stories to tell. My parents are always travelling for business," she says. "They are really important. I've been to almost every country with them. But when I turned eighteen, I wanted to experience something real. I'm sick of stuffy galas, ya know?"

I blink at her. "Um... *Sure.* I know."

"The house looked different when I started. Mr and Mrs Butcher have slowly been renovating."

I lean my hip on the counter, thinking about the way Mr Butcher made me kneel between his knees, about my body's response to his scent, proximity, and domination. I shake the memory away, as the words *Mrs Butcher* repeat. He has a wife, and I'm little more than a stray pet who might be growing someone worth something to someone important, maybe.

"How did Jimmy Storm die?" I ask.

"Cancer, but it was sudden," she says, walking over to the kitchen, a subtle indication for us to head back to the room. "Like, one minute he was breathing and the next"— she chokes herself, making a theatrical gagging sound—"his lungs gave out. Just like that."

As I wander past her, she flicks the light off, engulfing my back in black as we exit the kitchen.

Approaching the room, I feel my face burn, shame like a furnace heating my cheeks. Under the unimpressed gaze of Henchman Jeeves, I trail Jasmine. She adds a prance to her step, proving his scrutiny is ineffective, to one of us, at least. He straightens, waiting for us, his arms folded over his chest, foot tapping slightly. I've never been minded like this before. Most of the time, my presence goes unnoticed.

He raises an eyebrow at her. "Next time, a heads-up would be nice before you go wandering around."

She laughs. "Why? You hungry?"

"A little, yes."

Back in the room, I strip down to my underwear and make myself comfortable on the king-size bed while Jasmine snuggles into the roll-out mattress.

I think about our conversation. One part, actually.

Mrs Butcher.

Images of a beautiful, graceful woman taunt me, while the thought of him creates a warm pool low in my stomach, too low to be anything but indecent.

Clay Butcher.

He's not old enough to be a *Mr Butcher.* How old is he, anyway? Mid to late thirties? Beneath that flawlessly fitted suit, I can tell he has a powerful body, but I can't picture it. Does he have a light dusting of grey hair on his chest? I groan at my own mind, rolling onto my side. Squeezing my eyes shut, I count inappropriate sheep with piercing blue irises.

And feel guilt move into my stomach because they should be hazel, just like Benji's were.

CHAPTER FOUR

THE GLOCK PULSES in my palms, its rounds unloading into the organs of the distant canvas swaying at the end of my shooting range.

Stomach.

The image of my brother, Bronson, tied to a metal chair rattles my resolve. The following bullets rattle the room.

Left knee.

Right knee.

Blood pissed from Bronson's forehead, snaking in rivulets down his cheek.

Left shoulder.

Right Shoulder.

I was drinking whiskey in first class on the way home from Sicily while he was bleeding...

Left iliac

Right iliac

All to take down Jimmy, step into his shoes, fight my way from beneath his ever-growing shadow with an entire city watching my every move. With my brothers depending on me.

Left eye.

It's all on me.

Right eye.

To hunt down Dustin, to give Max his revenge. To keep them clean. For once. Like I promised. To keep them out of this business. Out.

Left lung

Safe.

Right lung.

Peaceful.

Pressing down on the pedal with my foot, I activate the belt, dragging the target further down the lane. As the canvas recedes, I focus on two holes, like eyes. Like betrayal that turned Bronson's blue gaze to slits that night in the chair. That crazy heart of his was ready to take vengeance for his family—my family—he actually believed I'd betray him. Betray my family. He'd have mauled me like a Rottweiler for my part. I should have never let it get so far. I had no idea Jimmy would take him without consulting me—

Fucker.

Stepping back, bracing the Glock, I narrow my eyes on the distant mark.

Heart

I drop the spent magazine and snap in a new one in quick succession and then unload the rounds, the sound of each blast contained as they bounce around the padded basement walls. While above my head, the rest of the house remains in early morning silence, in peace. In the peace I'm fighting to give them while the echoes of all that it takes to deliver such a lifestyle thrash within these concrete walls with me. Alone. But a leader, well... a leader is always alone.

I lower my arm, the muscles shaking from the power, the back thrust, the weight...

I exhale hard all this *bullshit*.

There is no place beyond this range for my frustrations. For my uncertainties. Guilt. Burdens.

The dawn is barely gathering outside these concrete walls, yet the room is already stifling, peak summer humidity clinging to my bare torso, perspiration misting along my skin. The only clothes I have on are a pair of jeans and my headgear.

I place the Glock down on the ledge and pull the head-gear off before activating the chain, bringing the canvas-human forward until it stops just shy of me. I inspect the holes, fingering the blown openings. Straight through. Perfect shots. For a man who is plagued by insomnia, I still never miss a mark.

Retrieving my gun, I tuck it down the front of my blue jeans. My shooting jeans.

Exiting the basement, I take the steps up to the ground floor. Tomorrow night I'll be back to blow more pieces of that canvas apart.

When I enter the kitchen, Aurora is standing at the breakfast bar drinking her latte while Maggie works over the stove to have a banquet prepared for my entire staff to graze on throughout the day.

Aurora and Lorna enjoy the leisure of mealtime while, for the most part, I eat on the go. I step into the kitchen, helping myself to a glass of water, the smell of gun powder and sweat clinging to my chest.

My man, Que, appears from behind me, handing me a towel, being both my first guard and my assistant.

"Thank you, Que." I give him a quick once over. His every line is immaculate, every crease ironed and steamed to almost fabricated perfection, like a tin soldier in a black suit. Yet, only a fool would consider him anything short of lethal. I smile smoothly at him. "You know, you can stop dressing like you're serving the Queen of England."

He merely straightens, cocking a greying brow at me. "The queen is more relaxed than you are, Boss. I feel the attire is suitable," he advises with the gentlemanly grace his London accent provides him.

Aurora clears her throat. I can see her in the corner of my eye, but I pat myself down before acknowledging her. As I throw the towel over my shoulder, I turn to face my awaiting wife. "Good morning."

She sets her coffee down on the table but tightens her hold on it, her long nails like red bars around the white china mug. "How did you sleep?"

"Well," I lie. Making my way over to her, I take in her tall womanly form wrapped in a dark business blouse and skirt. Take in her long dark hair twisted into a bun on her crown, not a strand out of place. My perfect wife.

"You're a fantastic liar, Clay. I have always thought so," she says, arching a thin dark eyebrow, exasperation in every inch of her flawless face. *Madonna Mia*, even if she wasn't so transparent, I would still see straight through her. I know her almost as well as I know myself. "This week is ridiculous. I wish you would delegate more. Ever since..." She doesn't continue.

She doesn't have to.

Ever since Jimmy's death. I don't want to delegate. I'm the damn Don of the *Cosa Nostra* in the District at thirty-five, and I didn't work my way up the political ladder to run things the way past bosses have—with a front-man paid to do our biddings. I'm the damn front man, the face, and the boss, the entire top level of this organisation, reaching new heights of control. *Control the streets; control the people.* It's a message from the old country, and one I'll make a reality.

Ignoring her statement, I kiss her on the cheek, inhaling her perfume, a scent straight from Chanel's limited-edition range, I'm sure. "You look beautiful. Are you staying for the meeting about the girl?"

The girl...

Dual-coloured eyes.

Too pretty.

Too eager to drop to her knees as if coached how to please me...

"I'm available for the first half of the day, then I have five senators from Indonesia to meet for lunch and show around Connolly, remember? Your less than reputable Indonesian associates? That is unless the Lord Mayor himself wishes to accompany them around?" She smiles, her mauve painted lips curving teasingly. "I hear Mr Kampa leans more towards your brand of company."

I stroll off towards the foyer, talking as I go. "Bronson would say it's because I'm so pretty. Show them the cable bridge. I'll be checking in on the warehouse, and then I'll be at the club to meet them this evening."

"Well, it's a good thing you have your dutiful wife to oversee everything before you make your appearance."

I halt mid-step, spinning to face her, realisation finally gripping hold of me. "Are you feeling unappreciated?"

She glances to the side, a little action that offers much insight into the softer layers beneath her composed exterior. I see a lot of myself in her. A lot of Jimmy too. She is the most powerful woman in the city, but her power only holds weight because it is bound to my own. And I often forget how much she needs my appreciation, especially since losing her father. Knowing we dethroned him has cut into her sense of place in our organisation. His existence and our marriage are the only claims she ever had to this legacy; Aurora isn't the blood of the Family. This, I never cared about, but she does. There isn't a slither of Family blood in the name Storm and what dismay that causes my perfect wife.

My confidant.

We share a life of servitude. Me to the *Cosa Nostra*. She to me. It's all she has ever known, but without me, she's out — her and her sisters. Deported to Sicily where the Don can keep an eye on them, as he did their father.

I would never take this legacy from her. We share it. That is what we agreed to decades ago, and I trust no one more than her.

"A little," she admits through pursed lips.

I take easy steps towards her, stopping so close she has to crane her neck to catch my gaze as I scan her smooth olive skin and large whiskey-hued eyes. She's stunning. "The past year has not been easy. I know. I'm very proud of how you have handled it. I'm very proud of *you*," I say, and her gaze drops under mine.

Pulling herself together, she regards my words with feigned indifference, but the satisfied softening of her body can't be veiled. I continue, "If you ever need me for anything, you know you need just ask, don't you?"

"I need you to sleep," she deflects. "I worry about you."

I grin. "What a waste of your time."

Turning, I make a note of her mood. She clearly needs a little more attention than I can provide at this point. I take the tiled steps to the fourth floor instead of utilising the lift, eager to stretch out my muscles with the incline. The sun from the east floods the side of the house, inviting its warmth and a view of the horizon and gardens. I'm certain it was Jimmy's way of showcasing his wealth. An addition for guests of the parties he often held. On the contrary, to showcase *The Family's* wealth. Such terminological inexactitude sealed his death sentence.

In my suite, I drag my gaze over the beautiful redhead sprawled out naked on top of my black silk bedding. She may wake to join me when she hears the spray, although she indulged in a few too many wines with Aurora last night before I ordered her to sober up, so perhaps she's in a deep alcohol sleep, *again.*

It's not often I allow her to sleep in my room, but last night, after seeing that sweet teenage girl so willingly drop to her knees, I needed more attention. Aurora, of course, didn't care less that I monopolised our shared woman for the night.

Removing my jeans, I walk into the marble shower and wash the guilt from my skin. Massaging my taut muscles, I release the tension in my thighs, among other places.

After dressing in a charcoal two-piece suit, I stare at myself in the mirror, fixing my tie with a silver clip. Scowling at the blue eyes staring back at me, I move away from him before self-indulgent bullshit ghosts into my mind and the lingering image of my brother, beaten and bloody, changes the course of this day. Such thoughts should stay in the basement. I brush the lapel of my jacket, straighten, and casually stride down the hallway.

I enter Jimmy's office—*my office*—and head straight for the cabinet, finding a small smile for my impending company.

Within seconds, *good man*, there is a knock at my door. "Whiskey, Marius?" I ask as invitation to enter. Preparing two despite having no answer, I pour generously.

He walks in. "No, it's a bit early—"

Cutting him off, I set the glass down as he sits before

moving around to my wing-back chair. He accepts the whiskey, of course.

Taking a seat, I lean back, lift my calf to my knee, and sip the liquor. "It is never too early. What have you found out about our little Fawn?"

He dips down below the desk before pulling out a file as thick as the damn bible, and my forehead tightens immediately at its ominous presence. Marius runs his hands through his sparse greying hair, a habitual movement, I imagine, as he has so little left to muse.

He flicks through the file, and I nurse my glass in wait. "Well, I got the results back and found her," he confirms. "Her name is Fawn Eva Harlow. She is eighteen. She *is* Nerrock's daughter, Mr Butcher. There was a lot to work through, though. More than I had time for last night, but she lived with her mother, hippy type, living in a caravan. Then she was moved into foster care."

I lean across the desk and retrieve a photo of the girl from when she was approximately my nieces' age, four or so, towards me. I scan the image of her tiny frame, shoulders curled in on herself, making her body smaller than it should be.

A memory from long ago, its recall strange, flashes behind my eyes. It hasn't accosted me in many years. I guess this young girl reminds me of her, of someone who once haunted me. I touch the time-healed scar on my collarbone, now tattooed with vines. As I raise my whiskey to my lips, the fumes somewhat draw me from that reverie.

When I really study Fawn's young face, she doesn't bear any resemblance to the face that now blurs around the edges with that dissolving memory. I shut that bullshit right down before giving it any more attention.

I focus on Fawn's dual-coloured irises—*sceptical.*

Me too, my girl. Me too.

I sip my whiskey.

He continues talking as I study this tiny girl, who may be the key to hunting down the man we have been searching for since he organised the attack on my sister-in-law. My brother deserves his revenge.

But then, Fawn wandered through my gates. I sneer at the name. "*Hippy type,*" Marius said. Goddamn mother named her sweet baby girl *little deer.*

Well, this little deer strolled right into the mouth of the wolf. A pretty slice of bait with Dustin's blood. Not enough to bring him out of hiding as he cares more about himself than his four daughters—five now. But alas... a baby is growing in her young womb. If that child is a boy—Dustin's heir—I think we may have ourselves bait that is too appealing for him to pass up, too important, forcing him out of the shadows, where my brother can finally cut him from ball-sack to skull.

"There are recordings too," Marius says, interrupting my thoughts. He slides a USB drive towards me. "Recordings from statements by the police. It seems her mother shot herself while the girl was at home. I haven't watched the footage."

Her mother shot herself.

Her father is absent.

I can use this.

Use her neglect to my advantage. "Anything from the past twelve months?" I ask.

He shrugs nervously. "I haven't got to them yet."

"I will look them over," I state, placing the photo on the desk and leaning back with my whiskey in hand, the idea of keeping her close, flirting with my mind.

He looks at me strangely, and I return his gaze with a

smile, the kind that is calm but not kind. "There are hours and hours of footage," he presses, sipping his drink, feigning enjoyment with a hum as the liquor probably scorches his untrained throat. "I am more than happy to—"

"I need it done soon. The girl is living in my house. I won't be letting her out of my sight, but I need to know everything about her. So, I'll work through half. You work through the other. How does that sound?" It wasn't a question, and he knows that. I eye the extensive file.

We need to be sure of her intentions.

Suspicion is the pillar of control. The thing that keeps me several steps ahead. After Jimmy's execution, my team spent months going through his affairs. We found files of operations I had no part in. No knowledge of. No control of. Human trafficking. A weapons deal with Indonesia, managed by Fawn's long-lost father. We took Dustin's warehouse and gained control of the operation, but it was a shitshow, and we have been trying to keep our relationship with the *Preman* solid, which is why I will be entertaining them this week... but I feel their alliances are with him. Suspect they are safe-housing him in Jakarta right now.

This girl could be working for them...

A distraction and a burden.

Finally, in Jimmy's suite, the suite I now occupy, I found documentation outlining a self-funded and managed facility for lung cancer research. It appears our Jimmy had stage three Adenocarcinoma.

I sip the whiskey, the scent and taste somewhat a reminder of him. A man I have both affection for and imagine digging up and slaughtering all over again.

I remember how eager he was to go down fighting, classy, and proud to the moment my little brother drove his nose bone into his brain. He was never going to let a common nuisance such as cancer bring him to his knees. Then comes the images of my brother tied to a chair, blood streaming down his face, the talons of betrayal wrapping around his eyes.

Ignoring the images and the man in front of me now flicking through Fawn's stack of documents, I open my laptop and insert the USB drive, intent on sourcing information about her foster family, the people around her, anyone who could be traced back to an association with my syndicate.

Within a few moments, I'm staring at her—at Fawn. At a recording from a witness room, the view of her tiny frame, maybe ten, captured from a camera opposite and above her. She fidgets with the long ends of her hair, and even in the sepia-toned footage, it still looks like snow—so light it's almost white.

THE OFFICER *opposite her tilts his head, pen braced and ready against a notebook. "Where were you when the gun went off?" When she doesn't reply, he tries again, "Fawn?" She looks up from her hair. "Where were you, sweetheart?" he repeats.*

"With my mum," she whispers. "With the butterfly."

He leans back in his chair as he says, "The butterfly? And where is the butterfly kept?" She raises an eyebrow at him. "Is it in your room?"

"Butterflies live in trees. They come out of cocoons. They get to live two lives. One as a caterpillar and one as a butterfly," she says in an almost schooling tone, a hint of surprise he asked such an obvious question.

· · ·

HER TONE FORCES a quick chuckle from me, seeing strength in her before I decide this is mostly useless information. I don't need to know how her mother died. I crack my knuckles before finding a document detailing her family situation *before* her mother's suicide.

I lift my whiskey glass, inhaling the fumes before swallowing the liquor, a burn chasing the cool.

After two hours of perusing, I know the girl lived in a caravan on the ocean in Carnarvon. Her mother had several arrests for trespassing. It seems she was quite the activist, living on the dole and setting her pretty daughter up to be wolf bait.

Fucksake, *Fawn.*

Terrible name.

"I have footage here from three months ago," Marius says, spinning his laptop to face me.

I gaze at the footage of Fawn—looking the same age as she does now—in a similar witness room. However, this time, the man opposite her has his arms folded across his chest as he sits, swaying impatiently, slumped back in his chair, its rear legs taking most of his weight. He clearly doesn't give a shit what she has to say.

"LET ME GET THIS STRAIGHT. *They're not your drugs?"*

She plays with the ends of her hair. "They aren't mine, as in I didn't buy them."

"You didn't buy them?" He chuckles, condescension clear in his tone, his posture. "But your pretty little nose snorted them."

She shakes her head slowly, in a way that might suggest the information isn't there, and she is trying to shake it free. "I told you, I don't remember." A slight hint of anger flares through her when she slams her palm on the table. "Are you seriously grilling me about the drugs? What about fucking Benji?"

He stops swinging on his chair. "You're high now."

She shrinks back. Wraps her skinny arms around her middle, cuddling herself tightly. "Yes."

MY FISTS SUDDENLY ACHE. My fingers are balled tight, my previously broken knuckles taut and shifting with the intensity of my grip. I relax them. Crack them.

This is distasteful business.

Something niggles at the boundaries of my resolve, an emotion I rarely indulge for strangers—disappointment.

The questions now are... *Is she an addict?*

Who the hell is Benji?

Is this footage fake? Planted by Dustin.

Perhaps for a moment, her slight resemblance to that girl from my past caused hints of concern for her. A misguided, misplaced feeling. Or perhaps her mother's downfall reminds me of my own. Or the rotten luck she has encountered in her young eighteen years on this Earth made me give a shit.

Or her body language in that footage.

It fucking screams victim.

She could easily be an addict, being paid handsomely to *act* the victim, to distract me. "She's an addict," I say, no, spit out, startling Marius.

"This surprises you?" he asks. *Now, that assumption isn't polite.* I raise my eyes slowly to meet his, watching him shrink down into his seat. He murmurs, "I only mean that she is—"

Finished with him, I say through a warning smile, "Did little Lucy get my birthday card?"

If eyes could blanch, his just did. "Yes. She said thank you. You know we appreciate everything you do for our family."

"Of course." I gesture to the door. "Thank you for your time, Marius." He'll be at the bottom of Stormy River if he ever glances at me like that again. As he collects the documents, I demand smoothly, "Leave them." He drops the paperwork, but the confusion shifting through his eyes is obvious. "You look confused."

"Ah, no. Have a nice day, Mr Butcher," he says as he quickly leaves the room.

"And you." Leaning back in my seat, I stare at the paused screen, at Fawn gripping herself protectively. *So fragile. So uncertain.*

And yet, there is a small snap to her, too.

A hint of Cosa Nostra blood.

Between the women I call mother, the one I call wife, and the one who sucks my dick, I am surrounded by the strongest, most powerful female creatures on two legs. Powerful women are all I have known. Yet, here I am distracted by this fragile thing...

What to do?

I'm not a soft-hearted man. Not particularly generous, either. My predecessor was far more giving. So, what is this? Disappointment in her perhaps, because of her bloodline? Because she is a *Cosa Nostra* princess, whether she was brought up in this world or not—that stands for something. She should have more control. More... *Fuck*. Honour.

Glancing at the clock, I note that I have a few hours before I should be at the warehouse. A better mood is called for. I hit the intercom. "Que, send Lorna up."

I down the rest of my whiskey. Butchers have hotter heads than most, but my temper is mostly mastered. There is simply no place for it in my position. My brothers aren't quite as schooled. So, while Max is a slave to anger and Bronson embraces it, I, for the most part, command it.

One thing that sits like salt on my gums, though, is being *wrong*. Tricked. Lied to. And I didn't peg her as an addict. So, she is either a spy, or she royally fucked-up—got high, got pregnant, and now needs help.

Or someone hurt her.

That's not a pleasing consideration.

My hands twitch.

Her entire life displeases me.

The mother shooting herself.

Taking drugs and putting herself in danger.

The police's response to her—*disrespectful*.

Lorna draws my attention towards the door as she walks through it, still in only her pink robe. Her presence resonates in my cock, her mouth and body has been used in so many ways to please me. I stroke the growing bulge that delights in her. A better mood is definitely needed.

Squeezing my erection hard, I hiss at the image of the little deer. Bare feet move across the carpet and circle my desk, coming to a stop in front of me. Lorna releases the cord on her robe, the silk curtains falling apart and revealing her long creamy body, full womanly breasts, and bright-red pussy hair that matches the wavy, long locks flowing over her shoulders.

Lowering her hooded hazel eyes to watch as I palm my cock, she flirts, "What has you so wound up, my Lord Mayor?"

I widen my knees expectantly, and she drops to hers in an instant, and all I can now imagine is how willingly Fawn did the same for me just yesterday.

Too willing.

Lorna's hands replace my own as she draws my zipper down and releases my cock. She licks up the underside, sending teasing heat that causes my muscles to twitch. It's not enough. I don't want to be fucking teased right now. Gritting my teeth, I inhale through my nose, trying to relax.

A fucking addict.

Someone hurt her.

Fisting Lorna's hair, I work her head down my entire length. She presses her palms to my thighs, trying to control the pace, but I push through her resistance. I rip her up and force her down, flicking my attention to the monitor, momentarily fuelled by the image of the fragile deer cradling herself. I groan as I use Lorna's head to my liking, ignoring her small whimpers of uncertainty, focused on pumping the disappointment straight from my balls.

Her throat and tongue pulse, squeezing my cock as I drive it into her mouth. As the taut muscles in my thighs tense up, my balls prickle and squeeze.

Lorna moans around my cock, and the reverie of the small sound that slipped from my little deer's lips when I stroked inside her cheek, flashes in my mind.

Madonna Mia.

Tearing my gaze away from the image on my laptop, I stare heatedly down at Lorna's watery eyes, black puddles of makeup clinging to her lashes.

She closes them under my stare, focusing on her task. She starts to suck me like a fucking machine, hollowing her mouth as I drag her up and loosening her throat as I plunge her deep. I take her mouth and throat until my balls slap her chin. *Fuck.* So deep.

"*Good girl*," I hiss approvingly, feeling the smallest relief at her obedience. I release my tight hold on her hair, stroking the strands down her crown. "Such a pretty mouth." She cups my balls and fixes her pink lips around the tip of my cock, working the ridge. I buck as sensation pools like molten lava in my abdomen. "Take every drop. Lick me clean. Don't disappoint me," I state, unable to stop my gaze from drifting to the monitor, instantly feeling heat fire into my veins, billowing through me.

I shudder, my cock exploding into the warm hole of her mouth. She works every drop out until my thighs contract and I groan, sucked to the point of near discomfort. I pull her away from my cock and drop my head back, breathing in and out roughly.

She's quiet, waiting until I'm ready to praise her. I lift my head to find her face, her red, puffy lips, and big hopeful eyes. Caressing her cheek with my knuckles, I soften my expression. "That was perfect."

She beams.

I grab her jaw, inspecting it, and she squirms with pleasure. I imagine her cunt dripping at the feel of my tenderness. Staring at her lips, I say, "Is your jaw sore?"

She shakes her head slowly, seemingly delighted she can manage my needs. "No. How do *you* feel?"

"Better. Are you on call today?"

She nods, her words strained as she struggles to talk with her face still in my grip. "Yes. But it's been quiet of late. Thanks to the efforts of our Lord Mayor."

A hint of a grin hits my mouth. "You enjoy calling me that, don't you?"

"The three of us have worked hard for it," she says, a pink blush hitting her cheeks. It is such an interesting colour on her, every inch of her skin a slight rosy hue, the softest of the colours—perhaps second to white. To be the fool who views those traits as humble and compliant, who attempts to lead her. She would end their career within seconds. She's a fox, her red hair and beauty drawing in her prey only to maul them the instant they go in for a pet.

"Yes. You have worked very hard." I release her jaw, rolling my gaze over the strip of flesh between her parted robe. "You may stay here next weekend," I offer. "Aurora and I will both show you our appreciation. Thirty representatives from Indonesia are joining us this week, and they will surely misbehave."

A salacious grin hits her lips. "And we know how much you like seeing people behave inappropriately."

I narrow my eyes in warning. "You know how hard it makes me, so have your pretty holes ready. I won't be gentle with you." Smoothing her hair down her crown, I say, "Aurora can kiss you all better after I'm done."

My words seem to cause a shiver to rush up her spine, excitement in each little shudder. She climbs to her feet, revealing the criss-cross pattern on her knees. Leaving me to my business, she sashays as she goes. I twist back to the monitor briefly before slamming the laptop shut.

A fucking addict.

Well, not under my roof.

CHAPTER FIVE

WAKING up to the lavishly soft sheets surrounding me is like arising from a place on a cloud. Still, with my eyes shut, I focus on my toes, curling them, feeling them caress the blankets. Then I concentrate on my fingers, gliding across the mattress. *Fuck me*, this is how the other half lives.

Touching my lower stomach, I chuckle and shake my head. This kid could grow up in this world, and for the first time since the strip turned pink, I'm excited for the life inside me. Yeah, it won't know me, but it will be in sheets as soft as clouds, eating cake that tastes like the gods made it.

"Good morning," I say to no one in particular before seeing Jasmine is already up and pulling her clothes on.

Immediately, a knock at the door causes me to sit up and grip the sheets high under my neck, concealing my underwear.

"Morning," she chirps. "Don't worry, that's just Bolton. He's waiting for us."

I sit up straighter, saying, "For us to do what?"

"To head to room twenty-four."

If I didn't already grasp the size of this house, the mention of a room referred to by a numeral—like in a hotel —really cemented that reality.

I get dressed quickly, cringing as I slide on day-old clothes before following Jasmine and Henchman Jeeves through the warren of halls and parlours. We pass too many henchmen to count; they seemingly become part of the furniture, like tall sturdy hat racks with bullet-proof vests and handguns instead of... well, *hats*.

Do politicians have this many henchmen?

No, this all screams organised crime to me.

The house seems to have a U-shaped footprint, with one side—the side my room is in—used minimally, whereas the other side is busy with staff. I scan the open-plan living area, my brows drawing in, seeing no sign of actual *living*. This mansion could be a movie set, not a cushion out of place. No sign anyone has ever sat on the cream-coloured leather sofas.

As I turn a corner, the French doors and entrance to the pool come into view. Through the glass windows, I can see two guys in their twenties working in the gardens. They both look up as I pass, and I offer them a small smile before trailing Henchman Jeeves and Jasmine into a room at the rear.

My feet grip the tiles as we enter, bringing me to a complete stop. The sight of one of those high hospital-style beds, two women I don't know, an older man in his late fifties perhaps, and ... *Clay Butcher* in all his intimidating glory, throw those damn butterflies straight back into my stomach, fighting for room around the growing human. I step backwards and hit a body—Henchman Jeeves.

"Don't be nervous," a pretty woman with shiny near-obsidian hair says as she switches on the monitor. "I'm Dr

Adel. You can call me Shoshanna. We just want to check on the baby. Slide up here, Fawn."

Still not moving...

The other woman approaches, glancing at Jasmine and Henchman Jeeves, saying, "You can leave." She places her hand on my shoulder. I peer up at her. She is at least half a foot taller than me. The way she carries herself, the commanding yet charismatic cadence to her voice, screams this is the lady of the house—*Mrs Butcher*. "I'm Aurora. Come, Fawn. Have you seen the child yet?"

A breath escapes me as she leads me further into the room. I get that they need to make sure I'm not full of shit, and actually, full of, well, a baby. But this is a lot. I'm not a monkey! Not an exhibition. But my rebuttal is frozen on my tongue.

Pick your battles, Fawn.

Deciding this isn't one; I pretend there aren't so many spectators and avoid looking at them. "No," I finally answer. "I just did the strip test from the chemist."

She smiles softly as I climb onto the mattress; it is hard and shakes slightly as I mount it. "Well, let's take a look. This is Clay's father, Luca Butcher. He's a very close acquaintance of your father's and will personally see that the news of your arrival gets into the right hands."

An acquaintance? "You know my father?" I ask, eyeing him as I lie back on the bed. Shoshanna hovers over me. She pulls my shirt up to reveal the small mound—barely even noticeable yet—at my lower stomach, basically merely taut skin stretched from one hip to the other.

Luca nods once, folding his arms over his chest, the thickness of his biceps bulging beneath his hands. "For a very long time."

He looks scary as shit.

If not for the powerful gaze and expensive black suit, he could easily be a henchman. The scars across his face and undeniable bend in his nose are enough to warn most people with any sense of caution.

I wriggle around as Shoshanna tucks my shirt into my bra, my fingers finding the ends of my hair, twisting them around each digit. She squeezes a blob of cool gel on the centre of my stomach, causing me to shuffle more.

"Fawn, lay still." The distinct timbre of Clay Butcher freezes my spine, my body instantly doing as he commands. *I didn't give it permission to do that.* Heat rises the length of my neck, prickling along the skin, vines of nervousness reaching for my cheeks.

I look up at the monitor, realising it's been turned to face Luca and Clay.

Of course.

This isn't for me.

This is because they don't *trust* me.

The screen covers the lower parts of their faces, leaving me staring into Clay's narrowed blue eyes instead of the monitor. Shoshanna slides the pen along my abdomen until a beat crackles like an old radio.

"There is the heartbeat. Nice and strong."

I close my eyes, wanting to disregard my situational circumstances and not being able to see the monitor anyway, and instead listen to the second heart inside me for the first time. I crack a smile.

This is really cool.

Lasting evidence that something happened that night between Benji and me.

"He's about twelve weeks," she says, but I barely absorb her words, lost in the sound of new life. Sadness flitters through me that Benji isn't holding my hand, touching my hair softly. Not that he ever did that while he was alive. But, he wanted to. Our situation stopped him. I'm sure of it.

And now I'm kinda hopeful, for the first time since that day. This kid is going to have a great life. *Belong.*

Many beats of his heart later, Shoshanna stops moving the pen around my stomach, and holds it still, pressing firmly, pointedly, just to the left of my hipbone.

Forcing my eyes open, I gaze up at her. Shifting across her soft gaze is something strange, a message to the men I don't understand. I inhale quickly, holding my breath, white noise crackling between my ears. What's wrong? Shoshanna nods at Clay, who narrows his clear blue eyes on the monitor.

Shoshanna turns back to me. "Well, he is still small, but the nub between his legs is facing vertically, Fawn. That means it is likely you are having a boy. Congratulations."

A boy.

A boy who might look like Benji...

I thought that I would forever be looking for his smile, seeing it in crowds, seeing it behind me in the reflection of a store window. But now, I'm hoping I'll see it in the boy we made. It'll be nice knowing that a smile like his is still shared with the world even if I don't get to experience it firsthand.

"Very good," Luca states, tapping Clay on the shoulder before leaving the room with a stiff nod.

Shoshanna watches him leave, and then stares at Clay expectantly while I dart my eyes between them, wondering what I'm missing. "Maybe she'd like some privacy for the next part of this, Clay?" she says firmly.

He shakes his head once but creates the illusion of discretion, by stepping into a corner of the room and sitting down on a chair. "Privacy is a privilege."

"Well, I'm her doctor. So, you need to move up by her

head." He stares at her, a subtle smile on his face but a pulse beneath his jaw. Shoshanna rolls her eyes. The exchange is familiar, as though they are related. She looks back at me as she says, "Have you had a Pap smear since you had intercourse, Fawn?"

My world tilts, and I glance at Clay but he's cool as a cucumber, as though watching a pelvic exam is just in a day's work for him. The tips of my ears burn as I dart my gaze to the ends of my hair, shaking my head slowly.

"No worries. I'll do it now."

CHAPTER SIX

clay

THE GIRL IS INVALUABLE.

Aurora and I enter the boardroom to find my brothers awaiting the news. Butch, my father, flanks us. The chair at the head of the polished black oak table is empty, waiting for me, while Butch moves straight to the position to the right. Eager to hear the verdict, my youngest brothers, Max and Xander, are already seated.

A meeting of this importance would usually require at least two of our capos, but this is a family issue. I have left my brothers out of most business affairs for the past twelve months, but this... this is personal. The other families in the District accept Dustin's time is up but are staying on the sidelines of this situation.

Dustin is a boss, with his own loyalties and alliances, and they don't need targets on them while we finalise this matter.

Across the room, Bronson is at the bar, helping himself to a coffee, working the machine and harmlessly flirting with Sofia as she offers to prepare it for him.

As is her job.

"I got it, darlin'," he says with a wink that is all for show. That is one Butcher who has never been available to women. He's been lost in the ocean of Shoshanna since he was a teenager. The coffee is probably to combat the fatigue my nephew Stone is causing him. Knowing my little brother, he probably takes the night feeds so Shosh can sleep.

I hide my own fatigue well.

The memory of what they lost all those years ago, the conversation I had with Bronson's woman, assurances I gave her that they would be happy, protected... but I didn't keep them—*couldn't*. I lock my jaw and smile smoothly at my company. Aurora pulls my chair out slightly, her hands squeezing the leather head, an edgy reaction that displeases me. Offends me, even.

This is her family too.

Being Jimmy Storm's daughter does not make her any less a Butcher, and she shouldn't be pulling out my goddamn chair. I nod at her, my eyes cutting, delivering a message of disapproval before I take my place as the head of my family. A position twisted with expectation, given to me, burned into my soul the moment I was born.

I lean back, the wing-back declining slightly. Lifting my ankle to my knee, I nod and smile at Max. "We have Dustin's daughter and grandson."

The energy thickens. Max almost smiles, but it is anything but fucking pleasant, vengeance in the subtle curve of his lips. He deserves his revenge, but this was too easy. "I'm not eager to dive into this manhunt yet, mate." I shake my head. "I raided Dustin's warehouse and five million dollars' worth of weaponry. All from deals Dustin had made with the Indonesian *Preman*. The exchange of management has not been easy. They left me with crates full of unboxed live rounds to sort. Weapons in pieces. This shipment was a mess.

"So I now have five senators involved in this corrupt shit-show and thirty members of their party in the District to meet with, to get a better feel for where their loyalties lie. And the same week they arrive, a little deer walks into my house." Leaning forward, I focus my attention completely on him. "I don't like coincidences."

Butch sighs roughly. "Before our rivalry started, Dustin and I had an understanding. He wanted me to arrange a union between one of my boys and one of his daughters. Not having a son of his own weakens him."

"Dustin doesn't know about the girl," my youngest brother Xander states adamantly. "He might offer up his daughter as a spy, but he wouldn't risk his grandson." He shifts his gaze between Max and me. He may be the youngest of us, but that kid's a damn genius. If only he would spend more time studying and less time in the ring, he'd have taken the bar by now. "If Dustin does have an alliance with any of the members visiting from Indonesia, then we should make sure they all meet the girl."

I nod my agreement. "I'll have her attend dinner on Saturday. If they are in alliance with him, we won't have to go anywhere to get the news to Jakarta. They'll take it to him. And then, he'll come to *us*."

I glance at my father, a quiet perceptive man who speaks when necessary or not at all. Still, he's stronger than most men his age, having been raised in the ring. To this day, he could beat the life from any of us with his fists. In that respect, he and Max are basically carbon copies.

Max cups his fist, cracking his knuckles—a Butcher habit that runs innately in us from years of boxing out our frustrations. Before our heads even heat, the fists and jaw prepare, indicating our brewing irritation.

He levels me with a stare. "And if they are not safe-housing Dustin, we hunt the bastard down."

I feel Aurora's presence behind me, her unsaid advice and whisperings scoring down my neck. Exhaling roughly, I focus on Max, knowing he will understand the need for caution, but hating that I must make him wait longer. If this was Bronson's revenge, I'd have a far harder time encouraging him to see reason. That is one Butcher whose hot head explodes rather than bubbles. "We watch the girl for a while first. Let her get comfortable. Make damn sure she is here for the reasons she says."

Bronson settles into the seat beside Max, sipping his coffee, his tattooed fingers a stark contrast to the china teacup in his hand. A shiny Glock flashes from his holster as he shrugs off his jacket.

"Then..." I clasp my hands together on the table, setting my eyes on our father. "You take some men and the news to the streets. Get the prick out of hiding."

Aurora's breath all but demands my attention, but there is still not a word from her beautiful mouth. I spin in my chair to face her, my back to my family. "Aurora, speak. What do you have to say on this?"

She squares her shoulders, standing strong like the woman I know she is at her roots, beneath this apprehensive façade. "I agree on all fronts," she says, her voice even and velvety. "It is too risky to react hastily and fly to Indonesia with this message. But I think we can move the process along." She directs her words over my head, eyes trained on my brothers. I swivel in my chair to face them, looking at my hands in contemplation while my wife offers her advice. "The girl is quite enamoured by you, Clay." I twist to see her wandering around to meet my rising gaze. A soft smile sets on her lips. "She blushed when you spoke to her."

"That's not surprising, Aurora, sweetheart. Look at him. He's a handsome son-of-a-Butcher," Bronson says, ever the comedic mask in place to hide his true darkness.

Of course, I noticed her pinkening cheeks. I noticed her pulse in her throat, the heavy beat of her chest, the sparks of her arousal when I made her kneel at my feet, when I held her pretty face in my hand. I enjoyed it a little too much myself. "What are you suggesting?"

"I think you should make yourself available to her. Be present. Befriend her. She has daddy issues." I meet her knowing eyes, and there's no hint of jealousy within their whiskey-coloured depths. It is not an emotion that plagues my wife, at least not in relation to me. Our legacy, perhaps, but our relationship doesn't extend to the bedroom, despite us sharing a woman. Aurora has always leaned towards curves, soft lines, and I can't say I blame her, but since her father's death, she has been far more liberal with her delight in the female persuasion.

Her sexual preference means nothing to me, but I feel she favours the dominant role. A role she simply cannot play with me. And Jimmy wouldn't have allowed such behaviour from his eldest daughter, not with the twin pillars of our existence—the *Cosa Nostra* and the church—a constant shadow.

Reaching up, I rub the short bristles along my jaw as the idea she's presenting, one I had already considered, plays in my mind. Befriending an eighteen-year-old girl who undeniably attracts me is riddled with issues. But they are hers, not mine.

I could gain her trust.

Fuck her, maybe.

Use her, and eventually spit her back out into the world that was so brutal to her. One less person to trust. One more betrayal... I'd be the damn catalyst. She'll probably end up like dear old mum—bullet sailing through her brain. I don't know why I care so much.

"I don't know who the father is," she'd told Jasmine. Flashing in my mind, the image of her across my knee, bare arse and pussy exposed, while I spank her red raw for such behaviour. Teach her a lesson or two. Spank the addiction, the promiscuity, the fragility out of her.

And yet, I'm not convinced that is her.

Not convinced she wasn't hurt in some way. I have seen a lot of violence, a lot of victim behaviour, and that is exactly what her body language screamed in that witness room, even when her mouth said nothing of the sort.

Nodding slowly, I state, "I have Jasmine to befriend her, but I will be keeping her close."

"The girl... is she just collateral damage? What happens to her and the child when all is finished? Dustin in the ground. The girl homeless again?" Bronson asks, that demon of his riding each word. A warning that he won't let me use or hurt her. His heart beats with pure intent for women and babies, despite the mist of pitch-black volatility circling it.

"She is ultimately a *Cosa Nostra* princess. And that stands for something. Hopefully, she plays bait and not martyr. If all goes smoothly, we send her on her way with a cheque and an ironclad NDA, but if it doesn't..." I look at him, noting the pulse of his jaw muscles. "We kill her before the boy is born and grows up wanting *his* revenge."

"Now, now, darling," Bronson says, that dark smile forming on his lips. "You know I won't let you kill them."

"I'd prefer not to, Bron," I say, watching his body still, like a mine waiting under the pressure of this conversation. "We will send her off with a cheque then, shall we? Betrayed. Angry we used her to kill her precious father."

"And if the boy seeks his revenge in years to come, if he comes for his grandfather's cut of the diamonds, of the deals he cut with Indonesia, what then?" Xander asks, playing the devil's advocate, I'm sure. There is no way he wants me to kill them.

"He won't," Max states, siding with Bronson on this front. The girl is pregnant at eighteen, blonde, sweet, probably reminds him of his wife, although I see nothing of Cassidy in those dual-coloured eyes. This girl hasn't lived a life of luxury nor been offered opportunity. "But if he does, we deal with the little shit then."

"Do we agree then?" I ask, locking my gaze on Butch, wanting him to have the last say in this room, every room for that matter. The man has sat by the head's side for most of his life, earning the right to finalise our agenda. I am here in lieu of him, because I was bred for this role, a singular path crunched beneath my shoes.

A path paved by the *Cosa Nostra*.

I'm ruthless with this business. Focused. And well, he's getting soft in his old age. He's not the cutthroat boxer he was in his youth; he's a man making amends for years of absence. A family man now solely invested in his sons, daughters-in-law, and his grandchildren. Still, I offer him the esteem he deserves.

Butch nods slowly, eyeing us with straight eyebrows cut above a stern blue gaze. "Show her off at the dinner on Saturday. Let's hope one of the senators takes the news to Nerrock, but if he doesn't, then I'll have our men spread the word that I have his grandson, and the bastard will come to me." He looks over at Max. "I will bring him to you, son. He's yours, as agreed upon."

We settle into lighter matters.

While Xander leads the conversation, being my legal aid in this business, I find my attention drifting to the girl who sat on the counter in my kitchen last night, eating cake as though it was her first and last meal. I'd watched from the camera above; she doesn't have a corner in this house to go undetected.

Something doesn't sit right with me... She doesn't seem to want anything for herself, purely here for her child. But what teenage girl doesn't want anything? Doesn't seem likely.

And she's pretty.

Dropped to her knees so willingly as though someone schooled her on my preferences, and she has this odd reasoning for being here... Why not adoption? Why now? Of all times, months after I took her father's warehouse... I don't want to kill her, but if she's a spy, if she's lying to me about why she's here... I will.

A little deer.

One grey eye.

One green.

I'll kill her if I must.

CHAPTER SEVEN

"IT'S OKAY, FAWN. JUST BREATHE."

Like a splash of icy cold water, I'm dragged from my slumber by those words spoken in Benji's voice. I jerk upright, the gruff tone a distant reverie or conjured up in my own desperate brain—I can't tell which, but they strangle me to the point I can't breathe.

Panicked, I concentrate on my surroundings for several long seconds, willing my mind to return to the present, the external information to settle back into order.

"It's okay, Fawn. Just breathe."

Okay, Benji.

I inhale through my nose, steadying my exhale, controlled and unhurried. To my left, I recognise the curtains that blackout the clusters of stars and the bright white moon.

Twisting to gaze at the hemp dreamcatcher hanging on the left post of this bed—my temporary bed—I once again wish my mother had instilled more scientific remedies for my afflictions. Nightmares: dreamcatcher. Not therapy or sleeping pills... No, a fucking dreamcatcher.

"Baby, the Native Americans used dreamcatchers well before we started using drugs for every problem."

Thanks, Mum.

I always wanted to point out that many drugs were widely accepted for medicinal and spiritual use by the natives in countries across the world, but never did. There was no point.

Either way, I like the dreamcatcher there, simply because that's where it has always been. So I'm thankful Henchman Jeeves retrieved my backpack from the motel yesterday. I have all my belongings however sad the compilation may be.

They are mine.

Twisting onto my knees, I shuffle up the mattress to touch the little notepad under my pillow. Pages of nonsensical lines. Unrelated words. That maybe, I hope, combined will create a picture one day.

I grab it and flick it open before sliding the miniature black pen from the plastic ring binding. It is the smallest pen in the world, barely fitting in my palm as I set to write my newest edition to this senseless tale.

I write,

"It's okay, Fawn. Just breathe."

Those words further convince me that we had made love that night. I imagine him saying them right before he took my virginity. It was a sweet moment. And slow. I'm sure of it. I would have enjoyed it... my heart double taps.

I just wish I remembered...

Then I close the notebook, stuffing it under the cushion once more.

Finding Jasmine asleep on the mattress, a little niggling feeling knots in my stomach. Is she really here to help me settle in or to monitor me? I'd monitor me, too.

Sliding from the mattress, I decide to look at the moon and get some fresh air. Another ridiculous remedy my mother instilled in me from a young age. The moon and the stars can cure anything, even insomnia. *Fucksake, Mum.*

Still, ten years' worth of bohemian ideologies don't simply dissolve, and if the alternative is my foster mother's bitter words and obtuse insights, I'd rather embrace the former.

After wrapping myself in a small robe, I open my bedroom door to find Henchman Jeeves outside on a stool. This is his job. To watch over me. But then, what is Jasmine ultimately here to do?

"You are very good at your job," I say, startling him slightly. I tie my robe in a neat bow at my navel as I step from the bedroom and close the door.

He raises an eyebrow. "Watching over teenage girls doesn't challenge me like it did when I was a teenage boy."

"And why are you watching over me?" I cross my arms over my chest. "I'm not going to steal anything."

He shrugs. "I'm just following orders, Fawn. I have no idea what he thinks you might do."

I hum, not convinced. "Well, can I go for a walk? Am I allowed or is it forbidden or something? Ya know, like Belle from *Beauty and The Beast*? Will I find a magic rose? Enchanted crockery, perhaps?"

"No enchanted inanimate objects here." He nods to the hallway as way of invitation. "You can go for a walk. It's only in your room that there are no cameras. Which is why I'm here. The rest of the house is covered in them. And men watch them around the clock. I'm basically rendered obsolete by the technology in this house. Don't tell the boss."

"I think he knows." I walk down the corridor, guessing the direction to the pool, hoping my sense of space and my muscle memory serve me well.

I follow the lights that sporadically light the halls and main rooms.

When the French doors to the pool come into view, I realise this is the first moment I've shared alone in this house with just the kid in my stomach. Sighing softly, I press my hand to him, and indulge, while in my solitude, in the idea of this kid growing up in a house like this.

The dimly lit space, so quiet in its night-time state, is incredibly beautiful even if it's a little staged.

A little soulless.

Through the glass, the pool glows a brilliant blue, darker than *Mr Butcher's* eyes, but just as vivid. I shake the comparison from my mind, groaning at myself for allowing the thought in.

Across the glittering pool and into the horizon, the first sign of dawn lights up the gaps between the tree foliage. It must be early morning. Around 4:30 a.m., perhaps.

If I had grown up in a house like this, I think I'd watch the sun rise over the pool every morning. Maybe I would have breakfast outside on the stone balcony. Read a newspaper. Not on that horrid wrought-iron table, though. I'd get an outdoor daybed and sprawl across it like a cat.

I'd also get a cat.

Opening the doors, the balmy air sweeps around me, my hair and robe swaying around my body. My mother was right about the fresh air. It may not be the remedy for everything, but it does seem to carry energy.

As I inhale the breeze, a shadow moves behind me, causing my heart to lurch. My smile to fall. And I press my hand against my chest, feeling the rapid beating beneath.

I spin around to find a man staring at me.

And God...

I do a double-take.

It's Clay Butcher standing in only jeans, seemingly just thrown on, hanging low around defined hips.

Dark tattoos that I can't quite distinguish span his chest and dip low beneath his jeans. His perfectly virile physique is cut into trim, defined muscles coated in perspiration, the lingering scent of sweat and something musky surrounding him.

Fuck me.

If my ovaries still operated, they'd be popping eggs out like a tennis ball machine.

In a suit, the man is a powerhouse of intimidation, a handsome mystery, but in very little, he's... overwhelming, alarmingly breathtaking, masculine, sexy as sin, and if my brain blood wasn't between my legs right now, I would be able to think of other synonyms.

Butterflies take flight inside me.

I've never wanted to lick a man before, but right now, I want more than anything to know what his sweat tastes like. Power probably; if power had a taste, that's what his sweat would taste like.

My eyes drop to the light dusting of hair on his abdominals, following the trail between the thick V-shaped muscles leading beneath his pants, where I am now staring at the dense bulge between his thighs, a shape hard to hide due to the size and girth. I can't look away.

Stop looking at his cock, Fawn.

But I don't.

I press my thighs together.

Bouncing my eyes up from the thick channel of his cock, I meet his searing blue gaze. His eyes are locked on me like he is imagining tasting me the way I am imagining tasting him, which can't be true because I'm a nobody.

An obligation.

His gaze falls to my bare feet before sliding up, a slow pursual of the entire length of my body. Like, it's his turn to make a show of checking me out. Being alone with him, in the quiet, surrounded by shadows and darkness, is even more intimate under his attention.

Shuffling, I manage to whisper, "*Sorry*." I don't manage to elaborate, but that's okay. Sorry will suffice. Sorry for being in the same space as you. For catching you half-naked. For being here. For—

"Sorry for what?" he says, his voice unaffected.

I'm trying to work that out. "Um, for... being here?"

Staring at me, a soft grin moves across his lips, and it startles me, because he's calm in our encounter and I'm ready to explode. "She doesn't eat. Hardly sleeps." He pauses, and my heart becomes an erratic drum between my ears. "If you were my property, I'd bend you over my knee."

In shock, my lips part.

Then he walks off, and I'm left speechless. Wordless, confused, with a barely functioning body that is uncomfortable and wrapped in burning skin.

"*Sorry*," I whisper as he disappears.

I head towards my room, dashing around the hallways, hoping I find a direct path while the spindling shame reminds me how inappropriate my arousal is. I'm pregnant. Here for my dad. Here for Benji.

But that man is brutally hot.

Of course, I'm going to look, appreciate even.

I find my door, deciding I'll stay on the other side of it and forget all about the way his voice was outright erotic when he threatened to take me over his knee—

Yep, I'm going to forget all about that.

CHAPTER EIGHT

STAYING in my room was good in theory.

In practise, the idea lasted half a day before encountering a huge, *always-hungry* problem—*Jasmine* and her perpetual need to coax me into things she so desires.

She is hungry.

We get food.

She wants to swim.

Here I am, tiptoeing down the stairs, but I have no idea why because Jasmine's feet hit each step like lead hooves.

I cringe, saying, "So, you're sure it's okay we hang out by the pool?"

She jumps the final two steps and peers up at me as I hover awkwardly in the middle of the staircase. "You're his guest. It'd be weird if you just stayed holed up in your room all day and night."

But I'm not on holiday here.

When I don't respond, she says, "What exactly happened that has you all nervous now?"

The image of his torso, slick with sweat and carved with

muscles, comes tumbling to mind. Front and centre, actually. It's been there all night, this morning, in the shower. Too often. That, and his words, *"If you were my property, I'd bend you over my knee,"* seem far too eager to monopolise my brain space.

She lifts a brow at me, and I relent. My knees wobble slightly as I follow her out to the poolside.

Outside, we slump down on the pool loungers. The thick breeze tousles the blonde strands around my shoulders while the sun strokes my flesh, a light mist of perspiration forming a film over my skin. The pool's surface is like a rippling metallic silver sheet beneath the rays.

Three-Months-Ago Fawn would not believe Present-Fawn if she was to describe this sight. I try not to allow my mind the luxury of finding too much comfort in my current lifestyle. Although, it is hard not to enjoy it.

And Jasmine is relentless.

The white bikini I have on is the only one I own, but it's pretty, with a square-shaped neckline, thin straps, and a tube style coverage across my chest. The bottoms sit high on both cheeks and hips, the design making the sight of the taut skin at my lower stomach barely distinguishable, offering a little too much of my arse to the breeze and world, but I've never been a prude, and I like my body.

Benji liked this bikini.

"Don't forget this." Henchman Jeeves appears, passing Jasmine a white paper sheet, before walking up the stone-step waterfall and sitting on the horrible wrought-iron chair. He's overlooking the garden, as well as me. My own personal watchdog. *A guest, my arse.*

I nod to the sheet Jasmine is staring at. "What's that?"

She passes it to me. "A menu. Pick what you like. You need to eat. Yesterday you skipped two meals."

Clay Butcher's words find their way into my mind again. *"She doesn't eat. Hardly sleeps."*

It's not something I ever noticed, but three meals a day wasn't on my radar. As for the perpetual insomnia, that's a new ailment.

Sitting up, I cross my legs on the pool lounger, staring at the menu. I worry my lower lip while Jasmine waits impatiently, longingly. It makes me want to recoil, feeling like an imposture. I scan the menu even with discomfort twisting up inside me. I never wanted this kind of treatment, and I don't trust free shows of generosity, but I also cringe at being seen as ungrateful. Basically, I have no stance to take that will ebb this feeling. So, I touch my stomach, imagining the kid growing inside me, reminding myself this is about him.

It isn't about you, Fawn.

I can deal with that.

Jasmine scoots in closer to me. "Come on, they make pretty great food here. I mean, not like missile stars, but pretty close if you ask me, and I've eaten at a lot of fine restaurants."

Henchman Jeeves makes himself known by shuffling the chair on the stone veranda above us. "*Michelin Stars.*"

"What?" she calls up.

"I'm not being picky." I hand her the sheet. She wants it, can't stop looking at it, as though her longing gaze has telekinetic powers. "I'd foam at the mouth over two-minute noodles."

Henchman Jeeves laughs. "Please don't foam at the mouth; it involves a lot of paperwork."

When Jasmine lets a quick chuckle break free, taking the menu and studying the options, I relax.

"I don't know what two-minute noodles are," she says. "But I doubt they are on the menu."

"I lived off two-minute noodles for three months," I admit.

"Well, Mr Butcher said you're to have three meals a day here," Henchman Jeeves states. "And I don't think he would approve of two-minute noodles."

Here. How long will I be here? I look back at Jasmine, catching a little roll of her eyes in response to Henchman Jeeves's comment.

"Well, you pick for me then," I say to her, watching her face light up like New Year's Eve fireworks over the bridge at Storm River.

"Okay! Well, you should alternate between honey oats and an omelette for breakfast, but it looks like he won't let you have bacon—"

"It's processed," Henchman Jeeves calls down.

I gaze up at him, lifting my hand to umbrella my eyes, the sun overhead creating a glowing hue around us. "Do you like that I have a mandated feeding schedule?"

"Oi, you up there, you're missing your calling as a housewife." She tries to dodge a tablecloth that comes hurtling at her, but it hits her shoulder. She brushes it to the side.

I smile, liking their playfulness. We are an odd threesome. We'd make a good joke. A teen mum, a thirty-year-old butler on steroids, and a peppy maid walk into a bar—

"As I was saying," she continues. "Right, lunch. Alternate between sandwiches. They are all good. *Dinner,* I'd go with..." She clicks her tongue in contemplation, flipping the page over to view the other side, before realising it's blank and flipping it back again, the skin on her nose slowly bunching up on the bridge. "*Eww.* He is making you have fish. Salmon or Cod."

"High in omega threes," Henchman Jeeves chimes in again, still the hint of amusement dancing through his words. "And I think a feeding schedule is a good thing for you. I read in a magazine the other day that malnourished is *not* the new sexy."

I laugh a little at that, slumping back on the pool sunbed, stomach down and arms cushioning my head. Twisting my face to the manicured gardens, I find the two cute gardeners I saw a few days ago trimming roses, both their eyes meeting mine, small smiles playing on their lips. They exchange words, eyeing me intermittently while they slice the ends of the roses off, leaving woody stems. Perfectly good roses, too. I wonder if they will end up in a vase inside, or if they are simply lessening the load, allowing lower branches to fill out. I stare a little too long. When the one with blond hair catches my gaze again, a blush creeps up the nape of my neck, squeezing the column with warmth.

From here, he sort of looks like Benji.

"That's Robbie and Lee," Jasmine says, causing me to dart my eyes in the opposite direction, her perceptive demeanour a bit unnerving at times.

"Oh." My voice is too high to not be completely obvious. "Who the gardeners?"

Smooth.

A clammer of noise comes from above us, the sound of serious voices sailing down the stone steps to where I lay by the poolside. Sitting up immediately, not feeling comfortable half-naked on my stomach in someone else's house unless that someone else isn't around, I watch as Clay and a film crew head down the steps. Beside him, a tall, elegant, red-headed woman in a sheer navy suit-dress is deep in discussion with him. She reads from a clipboard in an almost informative way, while he nods as they navigate the garden to the other side of the pool. The camera crew trails them, seamlessly checking their equipment before they all stop and the crew begins to set up.

I peer over at Jasmine, who sits on the other sunbed, just as interested as I am in what is taking place. "Are they filming something?"

"He is probably doing a press release. Maybe something has happened." She tugs her phone out from her bag. She swipes her finger along the black display, bringing the screen to life and begins searching the internet. She hums before saying, "Yep. There's a fire. Looks big too. We had one a few years back, and I volunteered to help with the animals. Ya know, koalas and things." She suddenly cracks up, bracing her phone tightly as she rolls forward a little with the spasm of her laughter. "The headline is calling him 'The District Daddy.'"

Brushing my long straight blonde hair over my shoulder, the ends tickling my lower back, I scoot in beside her. Sharing her lounger, the sides of our bodies press together so I can peer at her phone.

At the sight of Clay on the screen, a little awe spirals within me. *He really is a politician...* And I've never had anyone to admire before. This warmth in my chest definitely feels like admiration. That explains my mild obsession. It's just admiration. *Good.* I'm glad that's sorted out.

She reads from the display, nudging me slightly and talking in a hushed tone. "Daddy Butcher has called for all citizens on the north side of Stormy River to evacuate, but the state government won't sanction such a drastic move, saying it's too early, and will affect the trade through the Stormy River docks." She makes a face, her smile tight with a suppressed giggle. "He wants to wrap us in cotton wool. I guess that's why they are calling him daddy."

A scorching hot sensation rolls up my spine, causing my

gaze to lift, finding Clay staring at me from across the garden.

We lock eyes.

It's. Just. Admiration.

The redhead is straightening his tie, the glossy curve of her lips moving, but his attention roams the length of me, his piercing blue stare sliding down my body for what feels like an entire heady minute.

I part my lips under his gaze, feeling the heat of sparks within me, the heat building every second his eyes—

Then he snaps his head towards the gardeners as though he sensed them. They both drop their line of sight but not soon enough, having caught him watching me. Their unease is noticeable even from this distance.

Clay Butcher looks on with a subtle smile that is more menacing than nice. *Like he's angry, but what about?*

When his gaze finds me again. The blacks of his eyes have widened, the darkness he carries within them like a shadow consuming the piercing blue that makes him so beautiful to look at, unmasking a different kind of raw, virile beauty that is even harder to tear my eyes away from.

I hold my breath, but then his devastating gaze dissolves as he looks at the redhead before him, nodding as though she had his attention the entire time.

I breathe out in a rush.

What was that?

Clearing my throat, the entire column arid and thick, I force a smile even though nerves skip through the gaps between all the butterflies and the kid in my stomach. "I don't think we should be out here while they're filming, right?"

When I peer across my shoulder at Jasmine again, she is fixed on me, stone-faced with uncertainty. I chew my bottom lip, not grasping what that was or what she saw or thought she saw. *Fuck.* The entire silent interaction between me and *Clay Butcher* was probably in my head. The intensity between Clay and the gardeners, too. All my body's manifestation of some kind of meaningless crush.

No, Fawn.

Not a crush.

Admiration.

It's just admiration. The first person to impress me has scrambled my brain, jumbling the appropriate response. So, he didn't look condescending for a moment but instead looked... irritated, possessive, protective, I don't know!

No big deal.

"Ah, okay," Jasmine mutters, snapping me from my thoughts and standing with the menu in her hand. "Let's get this to the kitchen then. Maggie will want it."

I head up the steps, flanking Jasmine. Each rise of my thighs, each steady placement of my bare feet, seem intensely exaggerated. He wasn't looking at me when I left, but, boy, can I feel his eyes on me now.

The thick air circles my scantily dressed physique like the cloak I wish I had on, a veil for the blaze of my vulnerability.

My skin prickles, but I don't turn around despite the palpable tug on my body to do so.

CHAPTER NINE

"SHE'S FUCKED, MAN."

I bounce out of bed, onto my feet, the words striking hot pokers into my chest, stealing slumber from me again.

Searching the room, I settle on Jasmine as she snores lightly from the mattress in the corner. Wanting to bleach the words from my mind but dead set on remembering them long enough to log. I glance at the clearly ineffective dream-catcher hanging from the wooden post.

Squinting at it, as though my peaceful slumber is meant to be within its delicately woven web, I grumble under my breath. "Where were you just now?"

After adding,

"she's fucked, man"

to my notebook, I pull a white dressing gown over my nude-coloured silk sleep shorts and singlet. Slipping out to stretch my legs for a moment, I know that lurking in the back of my reasoning is the misguided hope he is awake again.

When I open my bedroom door, Henchman Jeeves isn't outside, so I navigate my way down the stairs and stop before the French doors. Through the window, the moon illuminates the sky above the rippling water.

A light catches the corner of my eye.

Twisting, I glance down a dark hallway to my side at the white glow cutting through the gaps framing a door.

"It's too close to the warehouse," I hear a man say before a deep voice mutters something inaudible. The preceding silence curls around me, sending my pulse into a steady gallop in my neck. I didn't really want to see him, anyway. My feet take a step backwards, my mind deciding it's time to retreat to my room, my legs agree they are adequately stretched.

"Fawn, come in here."

Fuck.

I gape at the closed door ahead. Is he a fucking X-Man or something? Can't one of them see through walls? I swallow down the knot in my throat as my bare feet guide me towards the rectangular beaming light.

The door opens for me before I can reach for the handle. Within the doorframe, a gorgeous young man in his twenties grins at me. A small cut below his eye betrays the youthful, almost angelic features. His intense blue eyes, tousled dark hair, and strong body resemble the man sitting behind the desk opposite me. I feel safe presuming they are related in some way. I remember Jasmine's words: *"His brothers are like the District Kardashians."*

"So, you're Fawn. I'm Xander, the grumpy prick behind the desk's smarter and cuter brother." He steps back to allow me access to the room while my feet once again move forward of their own accord.

I smile politely. "Xander, like from Buffy? He was always my favourite."

He grins. "I'm going to pretend I don't have a female best mate who made me watch every episode growing up and say, *who?*"

I laugh a little as I take another small step into the room, giving it a quick perusal. It's a large office with a huge rich wooden desk and seating for several people.

My heart fills with airy arousal when I settle on Clay Butcher's powerful gaze, seeing him more relaxed than he's previously been, and yet, no less intimidating.

Leaning back in one of those massive boss chairs with his tie loosened, his top button undone, his hair deliciously mussed, and the black veins of a tattoo peeking out from his chest, he looks decadent in the most indecent way.

Kudos, Satan.

Warmth pools low inside me, lower than it should, and I wriggle at the knowledge of what lays beneath his suited professional façade.

"I'm sorry. I wasn't snooping," I say, holding his gaze like he requested I do. "I was just stretching my legs."

He smiles softly, a trained smile not unlike the one I saw on his ridiculously handsome face in that news article. *The District Daddy.* "Your apology implies you haven't been making yourself comfortable here?"

His words shake me slightly. "Ah. Should I be?"

"You may be here for a while, Fawn. Your father isn't in the country." I clutch at my stomach as it growls. I mutter, "Fuck," under my breath. The sound is so loud that his eyes drop to where I nurse the area. My cheeks ignite, embarrassment wrapping itself around my every wince, every curve of my lips. I cringe. "*Sorry.*"

Xander laughs, moving over to the small couch in the

corner of the room. Sitting down, he says, "Sorry? For what? Being hungry?"

"You didn't eat your dinner," Clay mentions pointedly. "Don't you like fish?"

Feeling defensive and ungrateful, I impulsively say, "I don't need you to feed me. I'm here to see my dad. That's all. I'm not your responsibil—"

He stands and my words freeze on my tongue as his eyes narrow. Towering above me even from the other side of the desk, he liquifies my knees and legs.

"I'll indulge this conversation once and once only," he states, closing the gap between us before leaning back on his desk, dropping slightly to just above eye level. He grips the polished wood either side of his hips and looks me dead in the eye while I try to remember how lungs work. "You *are* my responsibility. While you are under my roof, you will eat three meals a day. You will make yourself comfortable. If you don't like something, use your voice, say it. You will not apologise unless you have done something wrong. The word *sorry* carries no significance when it's used to hide a lack of confidence."

I swallow. Where I should feel shame or anger over being schooled, I actually feel ... *noticed?* My mother used to tell me I apologised too often, whereas my foster mother made the word my soundtrack.

I nod, stiffly. "I understand, Mr Butcher. Thank you."

A smile builds across his masculine features, and God, it's not a practised smile, but a real one. This one soars into my heart. I like it too much. The curve of his lips—subtle and confident. The way his eyes respond—softening, flittering with small amounts of praise.

"*Sir,*" he purrs. The word carries weight as his tone drops, hitting me with a gravelly aftershock that creates a pulse in places it really shouldn't. Places that cause me to shift, squirm. His eyes drop to watch my feet.

He has a wife.

"May I be excused, *Sir*? I'd love some orange juice." I exhale fast, somehow breathless, feeling his energy around me, too intoxicating, too close. The strands of his attention and the dizzying affliction of being held accountable are addictive.

Ignore this feeling.

To him, you're an obligation.

This is just hospitality—fucked-up, controlling hospitality.

Nothing else.

I back up.

His mouth is now a provocative tick, tilting at the corner as though he can read my body language. "Absolutely." Forcing myself to turn from him, I go to leave, but his voice stills me. "No cake, Fawn. Not without having had dinner."

I sink my teeth into my bottom lip—where there should be shame, annoyance, I feel immensely *seen*. I wrap my arms around myself. "That seems fair."

"I'm glad you think so."

With that, I stride away from him. Air like a gale-force wind beats into my lungs, expanding them to aid my shallow breaths.

CHAPTER TEN

I WATCH Fawn as she wanders away, down the hallway, before turning to my brother, catching his eyes scrutinising me.

Smug little shit.

"She's... *distracting*," he says with a smirk.

I move back to my desk, smiling with feigned indifference as though he's alone in his assessment. "Plenty of pretty girls in this world, Xan. Which reminds me, go home. You need your beauty sleep."

"I'm young, mate, those kinds of issues are reserved for men your age." He fights back an inevitable yawn as it surfaces. "But I do have a hot chick in my bed. Wouldn't mind waking her up early with my cock."

Sitting down, I shake my head through a long sigh. "Charming."

"Absolutely." A grin twitches on his lips as he collects his backpack and file. "I'm smooth as fuck. She won't even wake up until I'm balls deep."

It's a front. I know this. A small chuckle leaves me

anyway, amused by his youthful demeanour, be it a mask for whatever ails him or not. I've still always enjoyed his unrestrained banter. "You spent far too much time with Max growing up."

I know... because he was available.

Where I wasn't. It's an unfortunate truth.

He heads towards the door, his backpack braced over his shoulder, looking every bit a young man without the kind of weight that my predetermined path bestowed upon me. Looking it, yes, but he isn't fooling me. He's hiding so much. But aren't we all? If I were a better brother, I'd ask him about it. If I were a better brother, I'd know. "Thanks for your help, Xan. Drive safely."

Something taps on his tongue, but then he nods, squashing it. "Always. Night, mate."

"Night, buddy."

I exhale a long breath as he closes the door behind him. As always, regret for my absence, for being just like Butch and Jimmy and finding business more important than them, whatever it is that keeps him a fort for his true emotions, settles inside me.

Being neglectful, it seems, is a family trait.

Which brings my mind back to my little deer.

Glancing back at the monitor, I go to the USB drive and open it up, clicking on the footage of Fawn from three months ago in that witness room. Marius recently confirmed the information on the footage. The mother's death, the boy she spoke of, Benji, is also dead, all leading me to believe her reasoning for being here. She is alone.

I press play.

· · ·

"YOUR MOTHER SEEMS *to think the drugs are yours,"* *the officer says, sliding a photo over to her. "Lots of illegal contra-* *band found."*

"Foster mother," Fawn corrects, staring at the photo. Her *confidence, bite, is nearly non-existent. "And she's lying. I don't* *do drugs."*

"You're high, Fawn." He grins, her state humorous to him. *"That would make you the liar. Not her."*

She looks up to find him smiling, her eyes glossy, confused. *"Have you spoken to Landon and Jake?"*

He sighs, exasperated, uninterested. "Do you know that you *could be charged with manslaughter for providing the drugs?* *Causing the boy's accident?"*

Fawn straightens. "How do you know it was an accident? *Who said that?"*

He folds his arms over his chest. "Your brothers said he fell, *Fawn. The three of you were in the basement, and the boy fell on* *the table. Stabbed himself with the leg. They both gave the same* *statement."*

She lets that sink in before saying, "They told me they didn't *remember. So, you spoke to them separately then? Landon away* *from Jake? Jake's a bully."*

"You seem suspicious," he taunts, and she visibly loses her *resolve—sinking back. "You know the people who are the most* *suspicious usually have the most to hide."*

She shuts down. "I'm sorry. I'm not thinking properly."

I PAUSE THE SCREEN.

So, the boy died in front of her only three months ago. That is not something normal people just walk away from unscathed. She's scathed—

I've watched the life dissolve from within men's eyes, a

few women and one girl, too. Only one person, though, that I would consider a kind of family member. *Jimmy Storm*. And his passing is always thick in the air around me.

Death doesn't usually affect me.

But his *lingers*. It is in my pores, that sweet whiskey and cigars. It's in my mind that suspects everyone. In the shadow atop all of my dealings as I move several steps ahead of everyone else while he moves four ahead of me. *Fucker*.

How do their deaths linger around young Fawn?

What actions are driven by their passing? What do their emotional phantoms guilt her into feeling, doing? Is she here because of what happened that night... or is she simply retreating, vulnerable, trying to find any semblance of family she can latch onto?

Neglected.

Like my brothers were...

That fucking realisation hits me hard, bringing regret, consideration, fucking pity, perhaps, down on me. And that girl from so long ago slams back into my mind. The one she reminded me of. The one who was just business. A casualty of the Family. A job to be done.

Just like Fawn.

I stand and head towards the kitchen.

Slowly making my way towards the light, I loosen my tie further, feeling warmth on my skin from the humidity, from the half bottle of whiskey I've ingested.

When I enter my kitchen, I'm stilled by the sight of Fawn bowed at the hips, peering at a lower shelf in the fridge.

She's oblivious to my presence.

I lean my shoulder against the door frame, intrigued by her as she analyses the contents of my fridge. She moves nervously, every action hesitant. Her previously questionable submission, the dropping to her knees, it's not an act.

I can see that now.

Just like in the witness room. She relented. Decided she couldn't win. So, she's either smart or weak; I think the former.

But her use of the word sorry... it has no meaning to her. She is casually sorry for everything. A little people-pleaser. I don't like it—at all.

My eyes drop to her small, petite feet before trailing up the length of two perfectly formed legs. I frown when my view is interrupted by the silky material lightly grazing the skin at her upper thigh. I know what it hides. A masterpiece of a figure, seamlessly feminine in a sweet girlish way. Not the kind you can create by visiting the gym and eating healthy, the kind that is soft skin moulded around a perfect frame—the kind that is genetic.

"I look like my mother," she said.

No wonder Dustin had an affair with her mother. It would take a damn army to drag a body like that away from any man with a pulse. Away from her hair, near white, long, and thick, it drapes across her like a shield. Away from the lower curves of her arse in that bikini. Away from her long legs. Legs I should demand to fold, to kneel above me while she sits on my face... I ball my fists in tight.

She's too slim, though.

A soft sound surrounds her. Is she talking to herself? She scoops her long blonde hair to the side, laying it down one shoulder. I smile. Watching her in her own company, not pleasing anyone but herself, is insight.

Well, I did tell her to eat.

So, she is pleasing me.

She touches the cake container, her fingers tapping the lid softly, contemplatively. My cock twitches as she considers defying me. She pauses. Then twists to the door and retrieves the glass bottle of freshly squeezed orange juice.

I wish she had gone for the cake.

Seemingly in her own mind, she walks the glass bottle over to the counter, carelessly placing it down too close to the edge. It slips off.

Fucksake, Fawn.

I'm upon her just as it careens to the floor, smashing around her bare feet and ankles. Startled by the smashing sound, then by me, her breath hitches.

Glass pops beneath my shoes as I scoop her into my arms, cradling her against my chest. Her warm, weightless body heats that Butcher head of mine.

Her hesitation makes her clumsy.

Her lack of confidence is a damn issue.

I despised Dustin before I knew he had a daughter he never cared for... like him even less now she is in my arms and smells like... I lock my jaw.

Natural.

Feminine.

Sweet. Not a scent I often get from skin alone. It makes me consider Aurora's advice, overlooking the damage my temporary affection could have on her. I could spread her wide open and taste her sweat as it drips between her pussy lips.

Needing her out of my arms before that becomes a very real, raw reality, I plant her arse on the countertop and stare deadpan at the glass wading in the orange liquid marring the kitchen tiles.

"God, I'm sorry." She groans to herself. "I'll clean it up. And I'll squeeze more oranges tomorrow... if they'll let me squeeze them," she says, attempting to amuse me.

Gripping the marble edges on either side of her body, I

sigh roughly. Then lift my attention, finding her wide-eyed gaze. "What would you have done if I wasn't here?" The question mocks me, *loaded,* annoyingly so. Images of her in the witness room plague me, of her arms holding her waist, her relenting to their interrogation.

At her neglect.

She glances at the glass, then back at me. "I'd survive. It'd just be a cut."

She'd survive. My blood pumps heatedly through my body, scorching every cell. It's the onset of a possessive sensation. Mis-fucking-placed as it is, but right now, every muscle inside me wants to protect her.

This girl is getting to me.

CHAPTER ELEVEN

HE NARROWS his eyes on me as I say, "I'd survive. It'd just be a cut." The glass particles sparkling within a pool of orange juice would probably cut me, but I've seen worse done with glass—a lot worse.

My nonchalance is seemingly annoying him, so I get a strike of urgency to clean the sparkling orange chaos. As I shuffle to jump down, his heat circles me, his proximity to me suddenly enveloping, and I become acutely aware that I am literally caged by his arms. Locked in place. His presence a wall of muscle I am unable to move past.

He's *close.*

And my head is dizzy again.

My need to clean is incinerated in a fire lit by his warmth and scent, and—I swallow. The heat radiating between us, filling the gaps, moves around me as if it owns me. Within a few seconds, I'm able to memorise this moment, bank it away. I map the black ink that decorates the slip of chest between his open collars. Map the veins in his forearms, exposed below the shirt rolled up to his elbows. Map the metallic icy flames in his eyes when I peer up to find them tunnelling into mine.

Is he upset about the glass?

Doesn't seem likely.

Suddenly, my attention is drawn to a sensation in my abdomen. Startled, I curl in slightly.

A fluttering inside me steals my breath. It's not butter-flies. Unless they have managed to break from my stomach and into my uterus... I press my hand between my hipbones. My face stills, my eyes losing focus while my mind becomes attune to the whooshing—no, rolling sensation.

Then I realise what it is.

Squeezing my eyes shut, I hone in on the feeling, forget-ting about Clay for just a moment so I don't miss this. I thought it was too early, but I'm small so maybe... I think, the baby is moving inside me. I can feel something strange.

"What's happening, Fawn?" he orders, his voice finds me in my daze, pulling me from my focus.

I open my eyes to his full of a kind of stern interest—on anyone else's face, it may be considered *concern*. I smile at him, training my eyes on his devilishly handsome face, ignoring the fact that he's little more than a stranger, inti-mating, all that, and just eager to see if he feels it too. "I feel something."

Without thinking, I throw the silky lapels of my gown open. Pulling his much bigger hand away from where it has a death grip on the counter, I press it firmly to my lower stom-ach. His hand almost flinches from me, stiff and defiant, but then he stills with my hand on top of his. Exhaling heavily, his long fingers span out to cradle my abdomen with a protective dominance that causes a rabble of butterflies to take flight inside me.

I stare into his eyes as the strange sensation happens

again, but it's too early to be movement... isn't it? His eyes narrow to the sensation. Then meet mine. I smile wider, breathing with excitement and rapture, knowing he feels it aswell.

He smiles too.

That. Is. Everything.

And for the first time, the mystery in his usually impassive gaze dissolves in a deep pool of sentiment, meeting my soul on an equal plane, no longer the enforcer.

I see him a little raw.

Hi, Clay.

I feel like there is a single moment in time while holding eye contact with someone that can change a relationship forever. The moment has risen for us. We both are met with the choice to look away. It's an itch in my throat, a shudder in my heart—*it's time to look away, Fawn.*

It's time to stop smiling at him.

To remove his hand from my stomach.

Yet... I don't.

And neither does he.

But then his fingertips glide around the outline of the swelling between my hipbones, as something inside him switches. *Visibly.* He leans closer, his breath a warning as he says, "Who put this inside you, little deer?"

My heart sinks.

Hating the question, wishing it had never been asked, but wanting more than anything to confide in him, to be honest, I merely shake my head with regret a spiralling pit I'm balancing on the cusp of. A tear pinches from the corner of my eye. He looks at the bead, tracking it as it glides down my cheek and drops off my lip. "I don't remem —" My voice falters, trembles. The emotions don't make sense; I haven't cried over this. Not once. I was angry. And

I've been on a mission to find out what happened... but I never cried.

Right now, admitting I don't remember feels like a shredder to my heart. But I want to tell him the truth. And I don't try to understand why, maybe simply because, like me, he wants to know. And that matters... Someone else wants to know, and thinks I *deserve* to know. "I don't know for sure. I was cuddling this boy and that's the last thing I remember. I think it's his, but I can't be sure."

"You were high," he states, displeasure dripping from each and every syllable, his tone almost a growl. I hate the sound. My heart starts to sting. "Was the boy who touched you high too?"

I gasp. "How did you know I was h—"

"Do you take drugs?"

"No!" I bite out. The memory of the interrogation room, the officer who sneered at me, confused me, rains down frustration and fear and helplessness. I hate assumptions. Hate being questioned. I hate even more that I don't blame any of them. I was a fucking mess that day. *I had just lost Benji.* "I only ever touched drugs that once. *That night.*"

Something dark and angry consumed the thin blue rings around his large pitch-black pupils. It's there. But it doesn't scare me. I don't think it's for me... He leans in closer, his lips just above my ear, his whiskey scented breath floating down my throat, forcing my spine to steel with the intensity pulsing from him and into me. "Are you lying to me, Fawn?"

"No! *Fucksake.*" My head gets dizzy. My heart desperate to stop the unfettered disappointment in his voice. "I swear it. I swear. I'm not lying to you. I don't want everyone to think I'm this drug-addicted tramp—"

"Everyone?" he says smoothly, but the warning his tone

carries causes me to flinch. "The only person you need to concern yourself with is *me*. Only me."

"I thought I heard a glass smash," Aurora says from the kitchen doorway. While my body instinctively wants to separate from his, he simply glances over at her, leaving our closeness and the position of his hand on my lower stomach for her to witness.

It feels daring.

Possessive.

As if he's staking a claim.

My pulse runs riot in my throat. The word wife fills my head with white noise. She is right there, looking like a goddess even in a nightgown, even with the soft hooded eyes of a woman who was pulled early from slumber.

Oh God.

What am I thinking?

What am I *even* doing?

When we say nothing, she smiles. "Sorry. Didn't mean to interrupt." Her lips are an elegant tick on her flawless features. "Careful when you get down, Fawn. You might cut yourself." Then she turns and sashays away from us. I stare at the space she disappeared from, lost in confusion.

When I look back at him, the silver lining that was *Clay* has disappeared behind his mask of professionalism despite his wife's indifference to our intimate position.

Clay removes his hand from my lower stomach, leaving a lingering warmth that seeps deeper than skin. He lifts me from the countertop and walks me away from the broken orange juice jug.

He places me gently on the ground; his height at this close distance makes me feel like a daisy in a great tree's shadow. I want to ask so many questions about Aurora and whether he felt that moment between us, too, that they are crawling up my throat wanting freedom. *"Silly girl. You're reading into things."* My foster mother's anthem chants inside my mind.

Hail the queen of gaslighting.

In this case, she's right, though.

Dragging my foolish reality of the situation down my throat, away from my waiting tongue and mouth, I lock my jaw.

When he reaches down, covering my body with the silky gown, lacing it up himself, I chant her words and close my eyes. *"You're reading into things."*

Ignore the way you feel seen.

Ignore the way his eyes narrow, his lips look good enough to kiss.

Ignore your heart. What concerns him is not the same thing as what it beats so violently in your throat for!

It isn't.

I let him tie the knot at my waist, wordless, confused. My hands don't know what to do, so I coil my blonde ends around my fingertip.

"Go back to your room."

CHAPTER TWELVE

SLEEP HOVERS IN THE DISTANCE, my mind alert with the image of his hand on my stomach. The way his fingers flexed against me. I can still feel them. God, I wish the moment with him in the kitchen wasn't the closest I have come to feeling important to someone.

"Love, baby, is feeling invincible." My mum told me as she ran out the door after her fourth husband. I was only seven. Left alone that night and so many before because love is a drug with a mighty grappling high and a brutal bludgeoning low—and she was an addict.

I know nothing of that kind of love, but for the first time in my life, I think her perpetual desire to seek it out makes sense. *Invincible.* Not a fleeting sexual desire. Not a childish game of cat and mouse. True commitment. For a moment in the kitchen, I felt as though belonging to someone—to that man—would be the sweetest of existences.

When the image of his wife, Aurora, flashes behind my eyes, I wince. Guilt battles my jealousy, while my silly crush takes score. With any luck, there'll be no survivors.

I may be single and inexperienced with men, but if my gorgeous husband was cradling another woman's baby and staring intensely into her eyes, seemingly considering whether to eat her or kiss her, I'd be ropeable. Self-hate slithers into me, because I'm either concocting this intensity in my mind or ... *no.*

That is what is happening.

I envy his wife for the right to say she belongs to him. For her last name. Her elegance. Jealousy is like a bitter taste tingling my gums. Even her attitude towards our closeness was graceful. My mind wanders... Perhaps they're in an open marriage? Or maybe I'm grasping at straws, or maybe she just knows a man like him would never be interested in a scrawny, uneducated girl like me.

Little deer.

I scowl; his nickname for me is woven with condescension. He sees me as a weak animal, as merely a meal and bones to pick his teeth with.

I swallow that thought before it manifests.

"Who put this inside you, little deer?"

As the memory of his possessive and gravelly voice thrums between my ears, I roll to the side, cuddling the large pillow into my chest, willing this restlessness to ebb.

Covering my face with the pillow, I breathe it in, identifying the subtle fragrant notes of the fabric softener, recognising the scent from his shirt, too.

God, I'm a glutton for punishment.

Why are you here, Fawn?

For Benji.

I groan to myself. "Haven't you learnt your lesson?"

"You're awake?" Jasmine says softly from her spot on the roll-out in the corner of the room. "Are you hungry?"

I chuckle softly. "Do you ever think about anything besides food?"

"Hey, you made a noise that sounded like you're hungry, okay? Then you said, 'Haven't you learnt your lesson' or something." She goes quiet, and I blink through the dense soundless void between us. Then she says, "You have nightmares, huh? Is that what the dreamcatcher is for? You know they don't work, right?"

I sigh long and slow. "Yeah. It's fucking useless, but I still need it."

"What do you dream about?"

Ringing between my ears, Clay's words add emphasis to her question. *"Was the boy who touched you high too?"*

So, he must have presumed I was high. When I said I didn't remember, I completed the image of the homeless teen mother with an addiction problem.

The perfect cliché.

I *was* high, but Benji has—*had* this smile, and he was wearing it when he offered me the smoke. He flashed it again when he held the straw to the cocaine for me... And then cuddled me against him... I forgot the rest. The smile was all that sticks, and then the rest is an abyss.

"Do you have a boyfriend?" I ask, redirecting our conversation from my nightmares and her eagerness to probe that particular subject, hoping she will go on a long tangent about the boy she likes.

"Yeah. He's six foot two. Short, military-cut, dark hair. Super-hot," she sings his details, and ends with a dreamy sigh. "What about you?"

That derailing went full circle quickly. I squint ahead at the dark ceiling, finding his memory easily, a *perfect* picture of him with that *perfect* Hollywood smile. How to explain such a thing. A non-existent relationship that still ended in a baby. "There's this boy... I liked *him*... and I think he liked me, too. We had known each other for years, but he always had a girlfriend. A different one each month, but *I* was a constant in his life. And there was never any proof he liked me except ... when we were out, he'd always offer things to me first before any of his girlfriends.

"At the movies, it was the popcorn, a sip of his Mountain Dew. At dinner, he'd pass me the pizza box first, or he..." I frown as I talk, sorting the information in my mind, reaching for the outcome I want even as the reasoning is pathetic. Sadness slips into me. My voice wobbles as I think about him and all the things we will never say or feel. "He always offered me everything first as though to say to his girlfriend that I am his first choice, only, it wasn't appropriate."

She hums in thought. "Or he was using you to make his girlfriend jealous because he knew you liked him. You know, the whole 'treat em mean to keep em keen' thing."

I despise that explanation.

Flipping to the other side on a small groan, I stare at the ribboning blackout curtains, wishing for a peaceful sleep away from Benji and everything else. "No," I press, needing to fight her annoying insight. "He'd risk looks at me. He'd give me this... *smile*... but being together would be inappropriate because he *is*"—I swallow the word *was*, not needing more questions about that—"my foster brother."

I hear her confused pause. "You're not related, though. Is he the dad?"

I answer honestly, because fuck it, why not? "I think so."

Yes. He has to be.

Giving up on the charade of sleep, I crawl from the bed. "I'm going for a walk. Do... Do you want to come?" I offer. *Please say no.* I like her, but I want to see if Clay is awake again but only so I can stare at his blue eyes and manly hands that can snap necks, and not think about Benji using me to *'keep his girlfriend's keen.'* Or the way his body looked impaled on the leg of the coffee table—

"Nah. I'm going to *sext* my boyfriend while you're gone. We used to do it every night, but it feels awkward typing, "I'm dreaming of your manhood," when someone else is tossing and turning in their sleep."

Okey dokey.

Too much information.

I leave the room, waving at Henchman Jeeves as I meander off, without saying a word, down the hallway. Not caring about feigning my pretence to see the moon, I search the house to see if he is awake. I follow the lights again until I am in a new area of the house, looking down a dimly lit hallway.

At the end of it, a door opens. As he walks through it, his chest sweaty and bare, on instinct, I almost turn to dart off in the other direction.

This was a bad idea.

Crush and jealousy for the win.

Goddamn it.

Amidst my own scolding session, I do a strange stop, turn, shuffle, and then turn back to face him, looking sheepish and awkward. No cool person has ever done that dance in the face of their completely inappropriate crush.

His dark brows pinch in. "Do I need to instruct Bolton to keep you in your room at night?"

Bolton? Oh right—HJ.

I square my shoulders, feeling naïve strength for a moment because, under that unaffected façade, I think he's hiding something. He gives a shit. It doesn't have to be much. A tiny crumb of consideration is like gold to me. "You don't sleep either, though."

"Excuse me?" He walks towards me, slow, measured strides that are meaningful; his every action has purpose and power. And when he stops close, I can feel the heat from his powerful bare torso.

I arch my neck, keeping his blue gaze locked to mine. Somehow, I find my confidence, whispering to him, "He doesn't eat. Hardly sleeps. If you were my property, I'd bend you over my knee."

Oh. My. God.

I'm dead.

A soft smile ticks a corner of his mouth. "You amuse me. Do you use humour to deflect?"

"Sometimes..." I admit as he strolls past, heading away, but my heart doesn't want our interaction to end so quickly. "Why don't you sleep?" Spinning to chase him with my gaze, I watch him stop midstride as my question sails across the dark space between us.

He turns to face me, his features hard to see in the dense low light. "No one has asked me that before."

That makes me sad, and I wonder how that can be. Doesn't his wife ask why he isn't in bed? "Well... *I* am."

A small stream of light glows around his silhouette as he states plainly, "I have nightmares."

I chuckle once, but when his indifferent gaze doesn't shift, I realise he's not joking. Shocked at his candid response, I pause. How can a man like him admit to having something as vulnerable as a nightmare? How can he be so honest and still somehow manage to make this normal human condition sexy? Tortured. Real. "What could *you* possibly be afraid of?"

That perfectly charming and practised smile settles on his face. "Failure, Fawn."

I nod, understanding that fear but still not able to grasp

how the most impressive man I have ever met can be afraid of such a thing. He has never experienced true failure. "I have nightmares, too," I say, reaching up to twirl my hair around my finger. "And I'm afraid of failure... *too*." I laugh contemptuously, opening my arms to display the little mound between my shirt and sleep shorts. "You'd think I'd be used to it, huh?"

He clasps his hands in front of him, and even in the dark, I can identify stern brows weaving above a serious expression. "What have you failed?"

"Um. Just, like, *everything.*"

Darkness whirls around him, as he is seemingly displeased with my ambiguous response. A ball forms in my stomach under his gaze. "Let me rephrase the question, Fawn. What have you *tried* and then failed?"

My mouth gets dry because I don't really understand the question, and he's smarter than me. When he talks, it always feels like he is several steps ahead of the conversation. "I've never really had a chance to try anything," I admit. "I just... ya know... *survived.*"

"And yet, you're not dead," he says, his voice a rumbling purr. Stepping close, he moves until he is with me in the dimly bathed space in the hallway. My eyes adjust to enjoy all the masculine details of his face. Lifting his hand, he strokes my jaw, sending blissful warmth coursing along my skin.

His wife...
Red flags everywhere.
Look at them!

Then he slides his hand lower and circles the small column of my throat, and I ignore the flags even as they wrap around my neck. I swallow against his palm.

My eyes grow wide.

His gaze studies me, rolling down my face as he says, "So, you haven't failed, sweet girl." He smiles, softly. "You are resilient despite all odds. And you'll *survive* what's to come."

Tears burn the backs of my eyes.

His words twist inside my chest like a corkscrew in my heart, making me hot and happy and uncomfortable and needy. Neediness hurts. It is the worst feeling in the world. It is at the core of my every action.

Squeezing my throat in a wonderful, dominant way, he dips his head, and I lean up, reaching to be closer to him, sucking in a breath, feeling his intention to kiss me like a wave I need to catch.

Then he straightens. His hand slips from my throat. And I drop back to my heels, his intent dissolving immediately.

"Go back to your room, little deer."

CHAPTER THIRTEEN

"GOOD MORNING, FAWN," Xander Butcher says, striding into the quiet dining room and joining me at the empty table, completely casual and friendly as though our relationship predates the awkward introduction from a few nights ago. My eyes shoot to Henchman Jeeves, who. is quietly reading the paper on the far side of the room, before gazing at Xander over my half-eaten spinach and three-egg omelette. Still chewing the salty, creamy concoction, I work the food faster in my mouth and set the fork down on the placemat.

Xander rests his hands on the table. His eyes are trained on me expectantly, but his right one is puffy, painted in blues and greens from bruising that wasn't there the other night. It doesn't seem to faze him. He flashes a bright white smile at me that makes my stomach do flips. He looks like a younger, softer version of *Clay*... The man who hasn't left my brain alone since I met him.

"Ah." I swallow the food in my mouth, clearing my throat

after. "Hi, Xander." I play with the ends of my hair at my waist, coiling them around my finger.

He squints, his gaze assessing. "You have killer eyes, Fawn. One green? One, like, cloudy blue? And you know what?" He nods slowly, saying, "I *can* see Dustin in you. Good looking man. It's not an insult."

I beam at him. "Thank you. I always hoped I had a little bit of him, enough that maybe he'll recognise himself in me. Do you think?" I'm surprised by my candour, feeling the hope sparkling through my face, unable to stifle it. Kindness makes me dumb, too. He shouldn't be so friendly. It's odd.

His lips close, pursing on the same smile that flashed brilliant white teeth before. "Sure he will." I like Xander. He chuckles in a deep cadence before saying, "So, do you like the movie, *Pretty Woman*?"

I raise a blonde brow at him, not wanting to jump to conclusions about the random question, but not really being a great swindler of tactful responses. "Are you comparing me to a prostitute?"

Smooth.

He laughs out loud, and it's hard not to let my own smile break free, refreshed by him. Sceptical of his motivations, but refreshed, nonetheless. He is nothing like his big brother; no stoicism to him at all. "No, Fawn. My best mate Stacey loves that film. And her favourite bit is the shopping montage. You know that bit? *'Big mistake.'* It's a thing, right? And well..." He leans back casually, retrieving a card from his wallet. Holding it up for me to see, he says, "I got big Butcher's credit card, and I thought you, me, and her can go rack up some mad dollar signs and give him a headache. What do you think?"

And there it is.

I shrink a foot.

Humiliation snaps at the heels of my pride. I don't like

the idea of accepting clothes at all. Not one bit. It sounds like swallowing a boulder of debt. "Ah. No, *thank you*."

Again, smooth.

"What?" Thrown by my answer, his brows weave tightly. "Why not?"

I stand up and walk over to the dishwasher, bending to stack my plate inside and hide my pathetic, *ungrateful* face from him. Ungrateful maybe, but I'm not a charity case. "I can't accept any—"

"Fawn," he cuts in, "he wants to buy you clothes. He has guests tonight, and he wants you to have a dress at the very least."

"I have clothes," I mutter to the contents of the dishwasher, where even the dirty plates seem to pity me. With their shiny surfaces and scratch-free coating, they are a bunch of obnoxious, privileged dishes.

No enchanted crockery, my arse.

"*Right*," he says, playing with the word, his response sailing over the countertop to where I frown at inanimate objects. "You know it's okay to accept help."

Inhaling courage, I straighten to look at him, finding knowing cool-blue eyes. "I *am* letting him help me, and I'm really grateful, but I'm just here to see my dad. I don't need to be dressed. Or fed. Or—" I run out of things to say.

Jasmine appears from the lounge room, her maid uniform on and a bottle of Spray and Wipe clutched in her hand. "You are letting him help the baby," she chimes in, and I deadpan. "You're taking the absolute minimum even then."

Contempt, whether misplaced or not, crawls its way up my spine, a sensation I'm unable to flick from my fingers. "I'm going for a swim." My words come out curt as I stride straight for the French doors of the mansion I live in for free, because I am a baby bird pushed from the nest, trying to fly but not able to and having everyone notice every fall and collision. My reality and efforts are merely failings in my spectators' eyes.

I lock my teeth, bend to pull my shorts down my thighs, and wrangle my shirt over my head, my long blonde hair flicking free as I hurl it onto the lounger.

I dive into the pool in my underwear, the cool arms of her silky body enveloping me, smothering me, and for a few seconds, no one can watch me barely existing.

Watch me beg for the truth about that night. The crazy girl with no memory of how she got knocked-up. Improbable.

Watch me beg for an autopsy. The stupid girl who challenges the words of her two foster brothers, only to have the police sneer at her.

Watch the silly girl being coddled by a stranger twice her age who makes her warm and uncomfortable and all the while having another person's kid growing in her uterus and no memory of how it happened.

Watch a lost cause.

Then it's over.

Surfacing, I breathe in as the water slides down my face to return to the pool.

Laying on my back, I make water angels. As I close my eyes, the water muted trees clap to an otherworldly cadence. I never asked for handouts. Not for me. I've felt alone since I was ten, before that, really. Now, I may not have done a good job raising myself on judgemental words from my foster mother or the perpetual humility forced on me to the point of soul-crushing emptiness, but I kept myself alive on it. I didn't give up. I didn't shoot myself in the head like *she* did.

"Hey."

Within my watery self-therapy session, I hear the muted words of a man reach me. Opening my eyes and coming to my feet on the concrete pool floor, I glance up and see a pitiless gaze filled with interest.

I smile at him.

One of the gardeners has come over to the poolside, a mist of perspiration clinging to every muscle his singlet exposes. He's cute. Young. Probably Benji's age.

"Hello." I splash water at him, a small amount hitting his skin. "You look hot." *Oh my God*. I inwardly groan but pretend the only interpretation of that was a literal one.

"Thanks for the shower." He pauses with hesitation. "I've never seen you before, and I've worked here for years."

"I'm not staying long, just a friend of the family."

He smiles easily at me.

Easy would be nice.

CHAPTER FOURTEEN

clay

"*APAKAH ANDA MENYEBUT SAYA PEMBOHONG*?" I ask casually as the Statesman pulls into the garage. I grip my jaw, rubbing the short bristles along my chin and cheek, feeling the insomnia I fight all night, testing my patience with the fucker on Bluetooth. The morning sun hangs low in the sky, but its heat is already burning through the black tinted windows.

The Indonesian prick on the other line jumps right in, his anger flaring through the speaker at my accusation that he has shorted us nearly a hundred thousand worth of ammunition and weapons.

Vinny, my capo, twists in the front passenger seat, his dark Italian gaze meeting mine. He shakes his head in reference to the discussion. He understands a bit of Indonesian but not enough to speak it. Being an ex-military man, Vinny follows orders seamlessly and respects the hell out of everyone who earns it. His word is solid. If he tells me there is missing stock, then there is missing stock.

I lean back in my seat as the man yells down the phone.

"Kami mengirim apa yang Anda pesan, Anda bajingan," He ends the call with a slam. *Well, then.* There may be an awkward interaction on Saturday night.

"I think he just called you an arsehole, Boss," Vinny says with a chuckle in his tone.

"Yes, I believe he did."

Despite the car being parked with its ignition switched off, I don't move. Pulling my phone out, I check the satellite image of the fire burning through the national park in Stormy River. I release a gruff sigh. "I'm not happy with how damn close it is to the docks, to my warehouse."

Vinny opens his arms. "You think it's a pointed attack?"

Que hums from the driver's seat; his knowledge of my business is thorough, his loyalty absolute, and his shot, almost as direct as mine. "It could bring a fair amount of unwanted attention to the docks, Boss."

I stare at the glowing red mass as I rub my jawline. "Another coincidence or..."

"Or arson," Que says what I'm thinking before stepping from the car.

Yes, or arson.

Vinny scoffs. "They wouldn't dare light up your city, Boss. Are they fucking mad?"

"Lots of mad-men out there, Vinny. Go home. Sleep. You need it." I nod towards the door, and he understands, leaving me alone in the vehicle.

I stare at the satellite image of my city. It has always been my intention to run it from the top and, as we have since the seventies, from the underground. We have so much power in this city. And since stationing ourselves in powerful roles, scattering our influence across industries—Max in the building industry, Xander moving into law—we are in every crevice of her, every deal. I run this city, so this fire is for me.

My finger taps the phone gently as I fight the urge to open the home security application and flick through the rooms to find her whereabouts. Over the past few days, I've spent far too much time fighting that particular urge. If something happened to her or the baby, I'd get a call within seconds, so my desire to monitor her isn't rooted in necessity, and yet the thought of my men watching over her sends displeasure climbing up my spine.

Staring at the phone, I imagine one green eye and one grey, sparkling with awe as her baby flips around inside her. She shared that moment with me, in a way she might her friend. Silly girl.

I think about the sensation of her stomach pulsing softly beneath my palm. Aurora and I decided long ago we would never have children. Bronson and Max will continue this legacy, and their children after them. Producing an heir to our empire was never essential. Neither she nor I tolerate children well, and yet, when I felt that ripple, when I saw my little deer's eyes mist over with emotion, I felt a kind of feral possessiveness.

My little deer.

Christ.

And some *fucker* put that inside her while she was high. I grit my teeth, fending off the volatile heat sweeping over me, threatening to become me.

I shove my phone into my pocket.

Exit the car.

Que waits by the garage entrance to my house, opening the door for me to enter. I'm fucking hot with exhaustion as I head into the kitchen, finding Bolton, Xander, and Jasmine conversing, but my little deer is nowhere to be seen.

"She is by the pool, Boss," Bolton states immediately. His

entire career—life—depends on his ability to pinpoint her exact whereabouts.

Xander turns to acknowledge me while Jasmine straightens, twisting her arm behind her back, hiding the slice of cake she was carelessly scoffing when I strolled in.

Not giving a damn about the cake, I look at my brother. My brows knot in tight at the sight of his ballooning eye, at the raw slice a knuckle surely inflicted.

I sigh roughly. "Who got the hit on you?"

"Oh." He grins with not a hint of concern in his expression. "The eye? Drazic, of course. I gave him a good shiner, too."

"You know Butch has MRIs once a year." I pause, scanning the youthful face of my youngest brother, beaten and stupidly smiling. Drazic would be at the bottom of the river if this happened outside the ring. Yet, I know my brother probably coaxed him into a bare-knuckle fight. It's how our father trained—a means to make the comps less impactful, less intimidating. Gloves don't hurt when you have had ninety kilograms worth of bare fist thrust into your face. "You keep this up—"

He scoffs. "Yeah, I know, Clay."

"Don't interrupt me," I state, clasping my hands together in front of me. "Is that what you want for your future? At the moment, you make us all look like fools, but you keep taking hits like that, and you won't be taking the bar; you'll be taking food through a straw."

He releases a quick chuckle, dripping in derision. "I appreciate the concern, but I was beaten up enough as a kid... Still smarter than you. At least now I get hit by choice. Now I can fight back. I win, too."

I frown at that lie. Even though I wasn't home for most of his childhood, I know my brothers. "No one ever dared touch you as a kid, Xan. Bronson and Max wouldn't allow it."

"Sure, mate. You know everything," he says, standing up. "Fawn doesn't want any clothes, by the way." He laughs once, his amusement striking hot pokers into that Butcher head of mine. "She doesn't like being told what to do either... She said *no*. Well, actually, she is very polite, so she said, *'No thank you.'*"

"Like hell she did."

Xander's smile shifts from amused to measuring. *Little shit.* I'm usually far more neutral, but she's in my care, my responsibility, pregnant and being fucking...*Fuck.*

Prideful.

She should just say yes. Not even thank you. And she shouldn't deny my offerings. I don't need her to tell me how to care for her, which, despite how it came about is now my duty. And I'm a busy man; I don't have time to convince her to comply.

Christ, she's getting to me.

Dual-coloured eyes are in my head. Her questions about *me*, not the business—*me*. Asking about my insomnia. Giving a shit, and then not letting me give a shit in return.

Frustration circles me.

Striding away before my perceptive little brother can analyze my tone further, I head towards the pool. Still before the French glass doors, the sight of a perfectly shaped figure dripping with water comes into view.

I watch as she climbs from the pool. The swell of her arse stretches her knickers. My brows tighten as she stands in full view of everyone, the guards, cleaners, everyone.

Her underwear is clearly too small for her now, her having put on a few kilograms since she's been under my care, but she refuses new clothes. My little people-pleaser is eager to charm everyone with her pleases and thankyous but she doesn't want to charm me?

Veins of heat rush up my arms.

My breathing becomes shallow, my eyes glued to the lower curve of each cheek, the material dipping into the gap between them, stuck to her like another layer of skin. Blood pumps to my cock, lengthening it across my leg to agony.

Past Fawn, Lee grins nonchalantly as though she isn't damn near naked in front of him. This is not acceptable. She knocks his shoulder with her fist in a playful gesture, comfortable in his presence.

The heat in my arms begins to hurt.

Twisting to the lounger, she bends over to grab her clothes, and I inadvertently ball my hands into fists, the heat curling my fingers at the sight of her soft wet thighs, and the curves of her pussy lips visible between them, the tight wet material translucent.

Perfect.

Then Lee tilts his head and peers down, seeing what I'm seeing.

And I don't even think.

I stride through the doors, drawing my Glock from the holster around my belt. Upon him before he can even blink those wandering eyes, I take a fistful of his hair, shadow him, and press the Glock to his lips, demanding entry to his mouth.

His eyes gape with terror.

The metal clinks as I scrape it along his teeth.

"Mine," I hiss. *Mine. Mine.* A word I didn't know I would use, but now that I have, it takes root inside me. My responsibility. Mine to protect. Mine to care for. To clothe. To look at. *Mine.*

A trembling little boy stares up at me, and I realise I'm

out of my goddamn mind, plagued with fatigue and in need of a fuck, but that changes nothing. I want to remove his eyes, but I fight that dark impulse.

Panic drains the blood from his cheeks as he nods violently. I release him. Lowering the Glock, I watch him bolt across the grass and disappear into the trees in the direction of the staff parking bays. There is only silence surrounding me, but I can feel her close. I stare at the tree he vanished behind, a tension-releasing shiver rushing along my skin.

That's better.

Holstering my Glock, I retrieve my phone and text Que.

> Butcher: Get Lee. He needs to sign an NDA before he can leave the grounds.

I slide my phone into my pocket.

Turning around, I narrow my eyes at the most beautifully stunned dual-coloured gaze—my deer in headlights.

"You *will* let me buy you anything I so *please*, little deer," I state smoothly. "Part of resilience is not secretly rotting behind your bullshit pride, my girl. Accept opportunities. Grab them by the balls despite how they arise." I hear Jimmy Storm in my words, in my tone and realize how much of my deceased boss has rubbed off on me.

Stepping towards her, I reach up and grab her jaw with one hand, puckering her lips, holding her startled mouth open, the pink of her tongue flashing at me deliciously. "Now be a good girl, and let me see these lovely lips say, '*Yes, Sir.*'"

My gaze drops from the pink insides of her mouth to watch her rub her thighs together. She's turned on by what just happened, at least her body is screaming such a truth. And I'm too tired, too horny, to think straight.

Fuck.

"Yes, *Sir,*" she mutters, a whisper of a growl weaving

through the word *Sir,* surprising me, exciting me too. Her eyes find mine, awash with a hint of a challenge. My little deer, daring and determined, having listened and obeyed me, now reaches up and wraps her hand around my wrist, pulling my grasp from her face.

I don't let her.

"*Please,*" she begs, fighting against my hold. I let go of her jaw. "You're not just a politician," she mutters, stepping backwards, putting space between us. That's a good move, but not hers to make. As her throat rolls, she takes another step away before whispering, seemingly to herself, "My mum was right."

I step towards her, closing the gap she just made, my body hovering over hers, my narrowed gaze anchoring in beautiful uncertain eyes. "Put your clothes on or I will do it for you," I order, the threat forcing more blood to my cock.

She does as I asked, sliding her tiny denim shorts on and pulling her shirt over her head as I watch her closely. My hands twitch with the desire to do it myself.

As soon as she is clothed, I tear my gaze away from her and walk inside with one thought in my mind—bending Lorna over my mattress.

I have denied myself a lot to get to the position of power I now hold. Denied myself the search for a marriage based on love. Yielded to serving the *Cosa Nostra.* I continuously give up the luxury of time to control every aspect of my legacy, but I have never denied myself the soft, warm body of my choosing.

Until now.

CHAPTER FIFTEEN

HOURS LATER, I huddle in the shower, cuddling my knees to my chest, staring blankly at the large marble tiles opposite me. The entire bathroom is royal. A gilded space for the dumb pregnant girl who willingly stepped into a household of corruption. Willing and thankful.

This is it, Benji.

Politicians don't carry guns, don't draw them on gardeners, don't—I squeeze my knees, feeling wet from the perfectly warm spray of the shower faucet, and between my legs as the possessive grasp of his fingers lingers on my cheeks. I think about his searing blue eyes tunnelling deep into my cells, making my body his home.

I want desperately to ease the pressure rolling through me, but I've never been able to do it. Not once.

"Am I afraid?" I whisper to myself, the echo of my voice bouncing off the walls. "This is what you're looking for."

I'm not afraid of him. I want my dad to help me with the baby, but I also want a dangerous man and all that entails. A man who may feel he owes me something for his absence, for his part in putting me on this Earth to barely get by. Owes me a small favour.

I squeeze my eyes shut under the warm sensual spray... *Mine*. Many misguided feelings spar inside me, making me question my reality. *"Mine."* He said that loud and clear, but for what purpose?

The word is an elixir, dousing me with a burning neediness. Dropping my legs to the tiles, the water pooling around my body, creating a rippling, fluid outline, I spread my thighs and feel a blush hit my cheek. I press my palm between my legs to ebb the ache. Rolling my hips off the floor, I grind myself against my palm, hearing that word.

Mine.

Mine.

God, it sounds so good. A moan vibrates in my throat. Rocking wantonly onto my hand, I whimper again, louder this time. It just isn't enough pressure, not right, not deep enough. I need so much more.

With a soft growl, I crawl to my feet, angry this primitive sensation is controlling me, making the world hazy at the edges. I pull a towel from the rail, wrap the soft white material around me, and pout my way into the bedroom.

Fuck.

My eyes hit Clay.

I fist the towel at my chest, holding it high, feeling my heart a frantic tattoo vibrating on the other side. I stare wide-eyed at him sitting on the edge of the mattress, intensity consuming his gaze.

Dressed in a black suit and smooth black silk tie, he continues to stare at me as though his gaze was drilling holes through the door moments before I entered.

"You didn't finish," he says, his tone strained and rough.

I gasp.

He can't mean... Did he hear me?

Blood pumps into my cheeks, the heat radiating like fire directly beneath my thin layers of skin.

He rises, and I sidestep from the blazing trail his eyes have me marked in. What is he doing in here? I will my mouth to tell him to get out. *Fuck*, what am I thinking? It's his house... I can't just tell him to leave.

Walking slowly to my backpack on the floor, I hold my breath along with any protests. My mind a siren of white noise while my sanity hides in the drone of it all. Ignoring the thick clouds of indecency closing in on me, I frantically search for clothes inside the blue canvas. Clothes. I need clothes.

I feel him come up behind me, and I immediately straighten, before the expensive material of his suit touches my shoulder, and a big warm hand feeds up through my hair.

It wasn't in my head.

I'm not just an obligation.

Not just his responsibility.

I gasp at the sensation of his touch. Flutters rush from my toes to my scalp, as he fists the strands tightly.

God, air.

I need it.

His shoes hit my heels as he walks me to the seating area in the corner of the room.

My bare feet slide across the floor. His shoes rap menacingly. When my shins touch the cushion, he stops me from falling forward with his hold on my hair.

His breath blankets the nape of my neck. "I want to touch you, but I won't," he states while his grasp tightens and tugs on my hair, pulling my chin to the ceiling. A warning sting of sensation rushes along my crown. "You're a very naughty girl for showing me your body by the poolside. For letting me hear your sweet moans."

"Why can't you touch me? *Why?*" I breathe the last word, a panting sound that is now my chorus.

Remember those red flags, Fawn?

He has a wife.

He's twice your age.

He's dangerous...

God, I could write an extensive list, and yet, I don't give a shit. "Because of your wife?"

He chuckles, the rumble deep and delicious, and God, I love that sound more than any other. "No, Fawn. Aurora doesn't care who I touch. We don't have a physical relationship."

I squeeze the towel, holding it in place, as though it is ready to drop to the floor of its own accord in response to his statement. Even inanimate objects obey him. *Yep, enchanted house. I knew it.* The enchanted towel believes his word to be infallible... But do I believe him? *'Do I'* and *'should I'* seem to be duelling concepts here.

The memory of his wife's soft, unaffected smile as he cradled my unborn baby, flashes behind my eyes. How can that be? Is that just a line? He doesn't strike me as the kind of man who endures or offers lies.

He's making the decision for you.

For us both.

Find comfort in that.

He sees you. Knows what you desire.

Unravelling his fingers from my hair, he leaves it a mussed mess around my shoulders and back, the ends dancing below my waist. He reaches around me and grips my hands, still clutching the towel for dear life, pulling them away from the soft cotton towel. The material glides down my body and puddles at my bare feet.

He hisses, and I tremble.

I try to stifle my humming and whimpering, but my nipples harden to aching beads, forcing the insolent little sounds from me.

"I came here to gift you a dress to wear tonight. To check you were... feeling better. But now I need you to finish what you started in the shower."

Is this really happening?

Fear and arousal compete for dominance inside me. We stand a few inches apart, and he doesn't lay a finger on my skin, but I can feel his presence, potent and dangerous, rich in this room. "Do you want me to help you come?"

Panting fiercely, I nod my head.

"Do I accept a nod as an answer?"

"No. Sorry, Sir."

"Kneel," he orders, and I hear him sit down on the opposite couch, feel his eyes all over me. "Do as I tell you, or I won't be able to control what I'll do to you."

I swallow hard. A sick, sadistic part of me wants to explore what *'I won't be able to control what I'll do to you'* really means, but I drop to my knees for him as nerves gather inside me, preventing my defiance.

"Bend over. Press your pretty tits to the cushion."

My stomach swarms with my friendly eagle-sized butterflies as I lean forward, bending at the hips to lay my torso on the cushion.

I fist the soft material by my head. My hair makes a blonde wing beside my face as I turn it to stare at the armrest, waiting for his voice to carry me away, to direct me.

I can't think of anything.

Braced and hanging on for his voice.

Heat mars my body bright crimson, a physical coat of embarrassment I can feel sizzling as he stares at my exposed body bent over, his eyes on my bare arse, on the wetness sliding down my inner thighs as my pussy grasps around nothing. I'm not sure whether to fight it? To enjoy it? If it's normal to be this wet?

I just want the swelling to stop, want the distraction that is him, the late nights, and restless sleep, to culminate in something. Anything.

"*Pretty*." He hums his approval from behind me. "You're dripping down your legs, little deer. You shouldn't have let yourself get so desperate. Let me fix this for you," he says, restraint deepening his words to a near growl. "Now, be a good girl and reach between your thighs. Stroke the length of your pussy lips... *slowly*. I want to see your flesh quiver as you do."

"I'm scared," I find myself whispering, before squeezing my eyes shut and hoping he didn't hear that confession.

"Don't be. Do as you're told."

His gravelly voice soars around the room, his demand an undeniable entity. I decide that I like the way he says, little deer. I found it patronising before, but now, I want him to say it again and again in that dark, husky, authoritarian voice.

As I remember the way his eyes held me as I walked through the bathroom door, like he was on the brink of detonating, I know this isn't just about me.

He wants me too.

Like I want him.

With that realisation encouraging confidence in me, I reach between my thighs and find my soaking lips, doing as he asks. The plump skin feels soft and supple. The touch of my finger like the beginning of a tickle.

"Tell me how that feels?"

I suck a sharp breath in. "*Good. Strange.*"

"Back and forth, sweet girl. Don't be embarrassed by what you're doing. You have no idea how pretty it is to watch."

I arch involuntarily when a buzz of sensation flares through me. I almost stop to allow my mind time to comprehend it, but don't. Instead, I glide my fingers through the slick valley, wrestling the embarrassing hum that vibrates in my chest.

"*Relax*... And now that your fingers are beautifully wet, be my good girl, and slide them inside so I can see your pussy open and swallow them."

I moan at his words, now leaping off the edge of respectable decorum without reservation, with little reprieve, not caring how wrong it is to be doing this in front of him. He makes it feel okay.

He makes it feel safe.

And I'm fuelled by the need to feel the simmer turn to a boil. Sliding a finger inside, I feel the clasping of muscles inside me. I didn't know they did that. It's as though I don't have any control. As though I'm fighting with my own body.

"Twist against your pussy, sweet girl. That is where you'll find your pleasure."

I turn my fingers and mewl and wriggle my backside, not caring that he's behind me, watching. A shiver of thrill prickles up my spine, up my neck. My nipples chaff on the cushion, the friction like little electric shocks, the sensation rushing down my inner thighs to my clit.

"Swallow two fingers."

As I slide a second finger inside, rocking back and forth, my mouth opens, expelling the strained moans I am fighting to suppress.

"*Fuck*. Sit back on them. You'll like that."

I sit backwards on my hand, taking both digits inside, circling them as the sensation grows. Then I lift my hips, pulling them out but as soon as they are, I'm desperate for the feel of them filling me again.

I start to ride my fingers for him. It feels primal—innate —to do this. Like my body knows what I don't. And in my mind, I imagine they are his fingers pushing into me, taking me, bringing me pleasure.

"*God, oh God,*" I whimper the words aloud, but inside my head I moan *his* name. *Clay.* My fingers lose precision as my body shudders, pleasure building.

"Don't you dare stop. You'll feel like you want to, but don't... That's a good girl. You're doing so good. Twist your fingers. Curl them. Explore. When you find a little tongue inside you, rub it until you feel it beating back. That is where you will find your release."

I do as he tells me, seeking the place that'll finish this extraordinary growing sensation. I find the muscle, thrusting deeper on a groan and stroking it hard.

"Good girl. You're such a good girl for listening. Do you enjoy fucking yourself in front of me, my pretty deer?"

"Yes," I whisper, wishing he would take me from behind, steal the control from me so I can relent and collapse and just feel.

"Yes, what?"

I moan, my sex rippling. "Yes, *Sir*," I say, filling the room with my panting, my whimpering, the sound of my fingers sliding in and out.

Somewhere inside my hazy edged mind, I hear him shuffle. "Look at you. I have never seen such a *pretty little thing.* And here you are under my roof." His tone drops. "While you're in my house, you are to touch no one, and you best not let anyone touch you, or you'll be mourning them from the banks of Stormy River. Have I made myself clear?"

I cry out as wave upon wave of pleasure moves up my body in response to his possessive utterance. Pleasure blooms in my toes, my thighs. I want to stop because it's in my ears, too, everywhere. "I'm so hot." *Is this normal?* "Is this normal?"

"Completely natural, little deer. Don't stop."

"*Yes, Sir.*"

"Come for me. Now."

At his command, a pulse of sensation explodes around my fingers. A torrid surge crashing together as I rub and rub and mewl and shamelessly grind.

It's scary.

It's incredible.

Then it dies down, and I immediately mourn it.

I still on the cushion, panting.

Fuck me.

Emotion and gratitude and affection fill me. I float through a few minutes of silence, and then feather down as slithers of embarrassment weight me, riding the tails of my returning sanity.

Bit late to be embarrassed, Fawn.

Whimpering, I pull my fingers from inside me. I sit back on my heels, listening as he stands, as he takes meaningful steps, circling the couch until he is a formidable tower hovering above me.

He stops, and I crane my flushed face to see him, but I feel so weak, so tired, so completely overwhelmed. Inundated with feelings, some forcing tears to my eyes and some provoking a smile to dance on my lips.

Utter confusion.

I struggle within the clutches of muscular fatigue. He

must notice, dropping to his haunches, so I don't need to arch so far. His piercing blue gaze drops to my wet hand before reaching for it and pulling it to his face. Sinking both my forefinger and middle finger into his mouth, he closes his eyes, sucking my wetness from my skin.

God, this man is walking sin.

His mouth is hot, his tongue aggressive against my fingers, forcing more moans to vibrate within my throat.

His eyes open. He drags my fingers slowly from his lips and smiles—a charming, dangerous curve that could cause nuns to simultaneously clutch their rosaries and drench their panties.

"I am very proud of you for listening," he says, and his words carry warmth into my heart.

The tears lying in wait now force themselves to the surface of my eyes. I don't know how to handle all the praise, don't know how to react.

It. Is. *Everything.*

He continues, "For not being ashamed to show me how beautiful you look and sound when you come." He reaches up and smooths my messy blonde mane down my crown, causing me to move into his touch, to chase it. A pet eager for his tenderness. *His little deer.* "There is a dress on the bed for you. Put it on."

When he stands, I shiver, mourning his closeness, needing it in this time of vulnerability. My body trembles as the comfort I felt having him attentive, disappears.

I want someone to hold me—want him to hold me—but he's standing over me, indifference a circling phantom. Misplaced disappointment seeps through me—such a familiar feeling, I'm surprised that it still stings.

I stare blankly ahead at his pristine black pants. The outline of his erection is a thick, menacing bulge that pulses, battling for room in his pant. He's *big*. He rubs his palm over the material covering his thick shaft, hissing slightly as he does. "And Fawn, remember," he says through a deep groan, still palming his length up and down. "*Stormy River."*

Then he strides from the room.

Leaving me on my knees.

Wrecked from my very first orgasm.

"YOU LOOK SO BEAUTIFUL," Jasmine says longingly, gazing at the slim-line gold floor-length garment. The sleeveless bodice has an oriental inspired collar with a little satin button at the divot in my neck. The gold silk, adorned with shimmering clusters of tiny beads, clings to my every curve, shaping me down to my toes.

Turning on my side, I roll my hands from the start of the small swell at my navel to the end at my pubic line. The presence of the baby is a small lump that could be mistaken for food or beer but unlikely.

Squaring my shoulders, I stare at the pretty girl in the mirror; her body doesn't suit her unsettled mind. She is physically perfect, with lush blonde hair pulled into a messy bun, a plait around the dome, glowing skin, and a slim but softly curved physique. She's comfortable in her skin. Inside though, she is riddled with self-doubt.

Did he enjoy watching me?

Will we do that again?

Warmth spreads beneath my skin as the scene half an hour ago plays back in my mind. He desires me, of that I am absolutely certain. That, though, is possibly where his affections start and end.

My stomach twists.

I should have never relented to the fantasy that he may want to hold me... just for a moment.

I wish I understood him.

But I doubt a girl like me has any business understanding a man like him.

"Mine?"

Fuck me.

I gave him something today.

Invincible. My mother was wrong. Falling for someone does not make you feel invincible; it makes you feel the opposite: fragile, transparent, cut open.

Quite frankly, the feeling sucks.

"Why am I in this?" I shake my head to see if the girl in the mirror can be controlled by my mind. She can.

"They have guests over tonight. I won't be here for it. It's closed house, so only certain staff are invited." Her voice is a little tight, as though her words are being forced out when they don't want to be uttered at all. "Doesn't matter," she chirps quickly. "It'll be boring anyway. I went to a function with my dad once when he won a medal, and the President of Australia was there, so these things don't really impress me much," she says, turning to grab the matching shoes from the dresser. Her high-pitched tone, tight smile, and quick evasive movements betray her entire nonchalance.

"You mean the prime minister, right? We don't have a president," I say, wishing I hadn't because she freezes like I just pulled a loose string, and she's about to tumble into a heap of messy yarn on the floor.

She shrugs. "Yeah, the prime minister. Not very impressive at all."

I decide not to pull any more string. "Well, the whole thing, him, the house... *everything* impresses me," I say. "I've never even been in a store that sells clothes like this."

Dropping to the floor to help me put the small shimmery ballet flats on, she mutters, "You'll have only the most beautiful clothes, the best food, the whole royal service while you're here. Your dad is loaded, too." She stands, smiling that tight, almost false smile that I dislike so very much. Now it's all I can see. "You're like Cinderella."

She's jealous, I think.

Great, another one.

I haven't really had many female friends, having moved often. That, at least, is my excuse for other females not being drawn to me. Truth is, something about me evokes scowls and sneers instead of greetings. I may have had more conversations with her than any other girl... ever. And, well, she's being paid to hang out with me, so I'm not sure this relationship can be considered a kind of friendship.

I doubt it.

Still, it's what I'd like.

I grip her hand, and her brows draw in. "I'm not Cinderella. She becomes a princess. I'm the pumpkin. At the stroke of midnight"—I touch my lower stomach—"It'll all be over."

My own words sadden me, knowing them to be true, contradictory to the feelings I have. Hopeful. For me, not just for the kid inside me. It's silly. The last time I thought someone cared, that someone might want me as their own.

Well, that person is dead.

I'm the pumpkin.

She squeezes my fingers, her eyes softening on mine, her smile relaxing. Honest. A little sheepish. I like that smile. I feel like it matches mine. "Well, you better make the most of it then, Pumpkin. I'm probably wrong. Clay Butcher is way richer than the *president* anyway. I bet it will be impressive."

I don't know why I'm invited, why I am wearing this

pretty dress, or what to expect. A familiar sensation—Paranoia—creeps into my mind.

I'm on show again.

The monkey, right?

What does he get out of having me here? I want to trust his intensions—a rich man extending the hand of hospitality for a friend's daughter... I snort inwardly, because even if it started out like that, I doubt part of that generous offer was to help her experience her first-ever orgasm.

The betrayals I've endured at the ignorant hands of my mother, the bitter hands of my foster mother, the police... my foster brothers, have culminated in a kind of thick fog that sits forever in my mind. So, trust from me is as rare as the loyalty I have endured from the people in my world.

"Time to go," Jasmine says, cutting into my thoughts.

Nodding stiffly, I stroll slowly from the bedroom with my paranoia biting at my heels.

I immediately bump into Henchman Jeeves. He grins at me. A dapper tuxedo has replaced his usual henchman attire, transforming him into Bond Jeeves.

He holds his arm out for me to take, and I stare at it for a moment, its presence confounding. "Ahh?"

"You put your hand over it," he states seriously.

I arch an eyebrow at him. "I know what to do with it. I just don't know why it's in front of me."

"It is there to hold on to."

I roll my eyes. "Seriously, Henchman Jeeves? I know it's there to hold on—"

"Wait," he splutters the word out on a single short chuckle, and I blush like a drag queen with an unskilled makeup artist. "What did you just call me?"

My cheeks prickle. "Ah... I've been calling you Henchman

Jeeves in my head." I cringe a little, an apology all over my face. "Sorry. I should sto—"

"It's perfect. I might make it official. Now, take my arm, Miss Harlow," he orders softly, straightening, a quirked grin etched on his mouth.

Ignoring the shadow of mistrust behind me, I circle his forearm with my hand, holding tightly as we stroll down the hallway, my dress confining my legs, making my steps shorter than usual.

Music sails up the grand staircase, a flute and drums, flirty and oriental. The sound matches my dress and I wonder whether tonight is themed. My heart starts to skip along with the flirty notes as waiters in all white, balancing canapés set with shiny crystal glasses filled with sparkling gold fluid, careen around below us.

We descend the staircase carefully.

Entering a ruby-hued room that overlooks the glowing pool from the east side, I slow my steps a little, not eager to join the fifty or so powerful looking strangers.

Swooping in to capture my breath, my butterflies make an appearance in my stomach where I am sure they plan on staying for the entirety of the party—event? Gathering? Whatever, they're here to stay and make me uncomfortable.

Immediately, I understand the garment, the music, as the guests are nearly all men from Indonesia. The rest are beautiful girls filtering through the congregation.

Aurora stands out, looking tall and elegant in a silver dress similar to mine, and that makes me feel strange. Did she choose one for me? Or did he pick one for each of us? She is shaking a man's hand, offering him a practised smile that they all seemed to have nailed. They must have gone to the same School of Sophistication and Etiquette, majoring in confusing the hell out of people. I wish I had gone to that school so I could understand him better. Wish I was skilled at shaking hands without my palms sweating, smiling politely, not having my filter-less mouth open and dropping some ridiculous comment.

That would be nice.

Clouds fill the room. Hanging above lit cigars, the sailing smoke illuminates the glow of the side table lamps. As Henchman Jeeves nudges me forward, the smoke creates ribbons of white as we part the mass. A game table is set up in the left and right corners. Men crowd around to watch the silent play while across the table, chips pile up.

What am I meant to do?

I dig my nails into Henchman Jeeves's arm.

"Fawn," he murmurs, stopping to unclamp my tight clutch. I stare ahead at the guests, my eyes wide, my muscles frozen. "Mr Butcher said for you to eat. And then for me to take you back to your room in an hour."

Suddenly, I feel him; my breathing slows as sensation crawls up my spine and circles my throat. I swallow within the phantom grip.

Searching the space, I'm stilled by the sight of him in all black, standing beside a tall red-headed lady, the same lady from the day on the lawn with the news crew. Confidence and charisma exude from her as she flaunts a long red dress, the sleek material hugging her frame, the tail falling from her curvaceous thighs to the marble floor beneath. The skirting looks weighted. She exchanges words with him and another man while he displays that easy grin.

For a moment, I only watch the way others interact with him. Lowered gazes. Bowing heads. They fear him. He nods at the waiter; he is offered a drink. He glances at his watch, so another man tells him the time. He peers at the redhead, and her breasts swell as a quick breath fills her lungs.

The fact he is physically breathtaking bears no significance in this control he possesses over everyone. The power is like electricity sparking in every inch of space around him. My mum once said, *"We are all just atoms, no more superior than the dirt."* Well, she never met Clay Butcher. Some things can't be explained in words. They need to be felt. And what I feel is that his atoms are far more superior than anyone else's.

The Devil's prototype.

His eyes shift through the air, locking on me. I part my lips beneath his gaze, and his eyes drag along my body as he bites down on a cigar, hollowing his cheeks around the column, the ember radiating as it crackles under pressure.

Fuck me.

This man is a whole world of intense.

Blunting out his cigar in an ashtray on the high table beside him, he utters something to the man next to him before leaving his companions, taking easy, unhurried strides towards me. I worry my bottom lip to stop my mouth's predisposition to smile at him as if we are lovers.

Which we aren't and yet... there is intimacy now.

Far more intimacy than I've ever felt with anyone, and it's not just that hours ago he watched me come—made me come. It's the small conversations while the rest of the world sleeps.

The looks.

Touches.

The butterflies go berserk. My heart feels as if it doubles in size and my petite body cannot cope with everything taking up real estate inside it.

A man steps in front of him to get his attention, and I gape as Clay swipes him out of the way; the man merely a web hanging in his path.

My line of sight leaves the now shocked face of the man, focusing on Clay as he stops an arm's length away. His eyes dart to my hand on Henchman Jeeves's forearm, his brows weaving in.

"I think that is unnecessary now," he states smoothly. I drop my hand to my side while Henchman Jeeves nods and steps backwards, offering us some space. His curt words throw me, hurt me a little as I expected more gentleness. I *needed* a bit of gentleness after... *that happened, right?*

As hurt flares, I ask, "When is my dad coming?" The question tumbles from my mouth, suddenly feeling as though that is the only conversation we should be having right now, or at all, really. The words put a barrier between us, a good solid construction made with *reality*.

I reach up to find the ends of my hair, only to realise they are bunched on my head. *Dammit.* So, instead, I fidget with the material of my dress.

The oriental music sweeps around us, mingling with the chatter. I peer across the room, and see side-eyes from guests, but I doubt anyone can hear us over the conversation and music.

"In a few weeks," he answers smoothly, lifting his thumb to his lower lip and dragging it along the swell, his eyes licking me in a way that screams he has seen me bent, bare, and exposed. The action, riddled with indecency, forces my thighs together to fend off the pressure—the discomfort. And I only just quelled it. Is this a never-ending desire? *Goddamn it*, how do sexually active people get anything done with this perpetual urge?

"So—" I clear my throat. "You have spoken to him?"

"Eat something, then go back to your room."

"Is that a yes?"

His lips twitch and his eyes darken, his pupils swallowing his blue irises like dark mist rolling over a still ocean. "I don't need to."

I blink at him, needing a moment of reprieve from the conflicting messages barrelling from him in hot waves. "You shouldn't look at me like that."

His jaw clenches, and my heart stops beating as he leans down, his lips a whisper away from my ear. "I like looking at you. I'll look at you however I please, and you will like it, too. If you ever tell me what I shouldn't do again, I'll spank that perfect arse of yours until it's raw."

I exhale in a rush, unable to stop myself from turning into his mouth, causing his lips to skate along my hair. "Is part of your hospitality to also help me come because that is definitely something you should put on the brochure."

Oh. Fuck.

Kill me.

The breath from a small chuckle hits my ear, his lips skating my flesh as he says, "You need to stop that pretty head from overthinking. I don't offer such an itinerary for all my guests, but your perfect little body is hard to ignore."

There it is. He acknowledges it. I don't know why I needed that so much, but I did. My fingers tingle. "What would my dad say?" I mutter, a slither of volume.

He steps back, putting space between us. "Are you besotted by him? By a man you don't know."

"I am. He's the only person in my life who impresses me," I lie, but the person who actually impresses me is regarding me, my words displeasing him, and it feels all wrong... and right. I can't think straight. "Even if he is a bad man," I bite out, observing his reaction to my words, "he's better than my mother, than my foster mother. I bet he's never been the victim."

He smiles, but it's unfriendly. "Your father doesn't know

your dress size. Or that the only time you clean your plate is when you're given sweets. That you use humour to deflect. That you have nightmares about the television."

Air catches in my throat.

How did he know that?

"Hello there," a man with a thick Indonesian accent says, approaching and appearing like a little boy next to the towering broad physique of Clay Butcher. "So many pretty, young girls. Who might this be?"

"Dustin Nerrock's beautiful young daughter," he says, deadpan.

"Ah." He nods, eyeing me with the skilled intensity a seamstress might when measuring me for a fitting. "Are you expecting? Mr Nerrock must be excited."

He knows my dad. I want to ask questions, but I'm still reeling from the insight about my nightmares. Waves of dizziness flood my mind, breaking my balance.

I stumble.

"Woah," the Indonesian man says, leaning in to help me, but Clay steps forward, grabbing my elbow, holding me to my feet and away from the man.

"Sorry," I say to no one in particular, instigating a light squeeze to my arm, a warning not to use that word.

Smoke from the man's cigar drifts around between us, the dance hypnotic, but the fumes twist nerves in my forehead, inducing a dull ache behind my eyes.

Clay drops his gaze to my stomach with a possessiveness that causes my heart to shudder in my throat. I like it. It terrifies me. It also confuses me. He rips the cigar from the pinched fingers of the other man, tosses it to the marble floor and walks me from the room.

"*Madonna Mia,*" he mutters to himself.

As he drags me outside by my elbow, guilt and frustration over the entire scene spar inside me. I groan to myself. "I'm sorry if I disappointed you by falling over in front of that man, but I didn't ask to be invited to the party, or dressed, or anything. I just want to find my dad. But I'm here, and I don't know what to do or say from one moment to the next, and you are confusing me."

We stop by the poolside, Clay dropping my elbow immediately. The glow emitting from the cool rippling water lights him up as he stands in silence looking at it. Across the yard, the trees are darkened by shadows.

He puts his hands in his pockets with his back to me, and I shuffle nervously, waiting to be schooled.

I continue, "I'm not a clumsy person at all. The smoke was really—"

"That was poor judgement on my part. I apologise for that," he states, and my eyes widen as he says sorry without saying sorry, despite his dislike for the convention. "I didn't consider the tobacco... and your condition. I'm very rarely careless with my property. It won't happen again."

His property.

Tears form behind my eyes, and they sting. I don't like their presence or what they imply. Why is he like this? I feel as if he's playing games with me. Playing at the caring, over-protective authority figure while confusing me with his words. Dangling affection like a carrot, and I'm the stupid bunny—no, *deer*, that trots after it.

What is he to me?

A kind of uncle?

No, just another temporary carer.

God, what is this feeling inside me? Does he know what he's doing to me? Making me vulnerable and needy when I need to be anything but to survive. The indecision over what to do or how to react to him is taking up so much space in my mind—there is very little room for anything else.

I close my eyes, safe with them in blissful darkness. I don't want his sorry, but I definitely don't want to disregard his sense of right and wrong, so I say nothing more about it.

Opening my eyes again, I step a little closer to him. "How did you know about my nightmares?"

"You talk in your sleep. Jasmine was concerned."

Oh. I nod slowly, absorbing his words. Hating them, too. So, she's not my friend. Well, that's fucking fine. And he doesn't trust me? Well, I don't trust him, either.

I feign indifference, but the words come out in an irritated cadence. "I don't know why you invited me today, but whatever. It was hospitable of you. So, thanks, I guess. Your home is beautiful, by the way. I've never really had a home."

"You have," he says while staring ahead, ignoring my tone, which only makes the mild tantrum dwindle when I kinda wanted to have it out with him. He continues, "But I understand you are being contextual with the word home, so in that light, neither have I."

I blink in confusion, feeling interest replace my irritation. *Dammit.* "You have a home now."

He laughs but it's sad, and I dislike that sound even more than the cold cadence his words are often uttered in. Even more than the condescension, more than the pity. "This is not my home."

"What about your family home?" I ask, taking another step towards him and rolling my eyes at my feet's preference to be close to him. I sigh, saying, "Your brother seems like great company—"

"My family home is where my brothers grew up, Fawn. I didn't grow up with them." He turns to face me, and my heart grows so big I feel it may burst. He's so handsome, so... *royal*.

It irritates me how breathtaking he is, how perfect his face is. How badly I want to stroke his jaw and feel the short hairs that create a perfect shadow. I want to touch him—so badly my fingers flex—but then he talks again.

"Don't mistake me for that man," he says. "I'm not the family man you imagine me to be or the man the District paints. I didn't grow up in a family. I went to boarding school. I was only around them summers, the occasional weekend. So, like you, I had to make the place I set my head down a *home*."

This doesn't surprise me at all. He seems... institution-alised, in a way. "Why not make this home?" I ask. "Why aren't there pictures on the walls? Why aren't there books left on couches and towels draped over sofas, comfortable seating outside?" I glance quickly at the wrought-iron table that now symbolises so much about this man; I hate it more than I did a week ago when I first saw it. "Why do you have this horrible wrought-iron table?"

"You have a problem with my table?"

"It's horrible."

He almost smiles. "I don't want to get comfortable."

That's crazy. My brows pinch as I ask, "Why not?"

He steps closer to me. Now, I can smell him—cigars and whiskey, earthy and sweet. "It's what I'm used to."

I laugh once. "Discomfort?"

"We operate best under a level of duress."

"If that's the case, then I've been operating at my best my entire life," I say with a cynical laugh.

His eyes soften on my face, and as his hand reaches up to stroke my jaw, I close the gap by leaning into him. His fingers are warm and dominant on the sides of my cheeks. His gaze, narrowing in contemplation, follows their movement. "You're so young. So very pretty." He sighs with an easy smile. "We are such different and yet such similar creatures, my little deer."

He finally gives me the gentleness I needed, and it somehow manages to douse the irritation. His caress forces weight into my eyelids. I flutter them shut, feeling his sincerity in his touch defy the contradictory ways he treats me. The balmy air sweeps around us, tussling the rogue strands of my hair. In this moment, everything inside me races. My heart. My lungs.

I swallow, content with my eyes closed, solely focused on the feel of him. There was never a moment in my life when I felt quite so seen, so special. I wish that wasn't the case. Wish I had more stories of great loves, warm cuddles with a parent... I have none. Not one single moment compares to this.

"You told me to make *myself* comfortable here. Can I really do that?"

"Yes."

Suddenly, his hand slips from my face as the sound of heels approaching grows. I open my eyes, taking a moment to adjust to reality, to settle my ballooning hopeful heart, and steady my silly lavish breaths.

"You're needed back inside," the red-headed woman says, a wide unauthentic smile curved across her stunning face. "Who is this? I haven't had the pleasure."

"A colleague's daughter," he states simply, turning his back on me, turning the warmth he showered down on me into icicles in the air.

He walks towards her. Placing his hand on her lower back, he says over his shoulder, "Go to your room, Fawn."

CHAPTER SIXTEEN

LEANING BACK IN THE CHAIR, drawing the Romeo Y Julieta into my lungs, I watch my Indonesian associates drink my cognac liberally and flirt with my female staff. It's nearly eleven p.m., and the volume has escalated with alcohol-induced confidence.

Scattered around the room, members of the *Cosa Nostra* discuss business, showing an interest in our foreign guests.

Beside me, Vinny prattles on about his cousin who has been hitting big numbers in crypto currency, the conversation vaguely reaching me.

The warm fumes circle within my mouth and throat before I exhale them slowly, watching the sweet brown vapour cloud my vision. I blunt it out in the crystal tray before spreading my arms wide across the back of the sofa.

Good hospitality was taught to me in boarding school but instilled in me by Jimmy Storm. That man had impeccable manners. He went from warm and inviting to Reaper in less than a second. I smile, imagining him now in this room.

A large presence, who enjoyed a far sultrier vibe, but I was always going to move our association away from its sexist origins. Women no longer used as commodities, was one thing Aurora held fast with when we negotiated our business. I allowed it.

For now.

Still, as I gaze across the room, there are plenty of pretty things to watch move and share a drink with. For a moment, I miss Jimmy. Not for the women he made sprawl across my lap for my drink to rest on. But for his guidance and assurance.

It is all on me now, though.

Every decision.

Every order.

Every execution.

The cognac heats my head, not a feeling I often allow. I usually cut myself off before letting any unpredictability take root, but not tonight. Not after seeing my little deer near faint from the fumes in this room. I sneer to myself. Dolled up and on show for them to gawk at, just as discussed with my family.

At risk.

She is always at some kind of risk, not having a man to care for her while she is the most vulnerable she will ever be. I glance over at Aurora as she entertains Bulan, then across to Lorna, who leans in close to Arif. I don't know anything about vulnerable women.

The Indonesian fucker who approached Fawn and myself earlier drops a glass, and I watch as he carelessly steps on the shards, further grinding them into little pieces. I don't know him. He must be a low-level member of their party.

My stare zeroes in on his shoe.

Feeling their eyes, I glance at the five guards around the room, letting them know not to react to the accident, for now.

"Let's discuss the shipment, shall we?" I state softly, but the entire room falls quiet with even my whispers.

Vinny stops talking.

Some look at their glasses. Some at the floor. But Eka and Bulan walk confidently over to me with wide, fake smiles and white teeth that I would like to rearrange. "Have you spoken to your storeman about the missing product?"

Eka speaks, his words short and mispronounced but understandable. "We thought business could wait until tomorrow, Mr Butcher—"

"Please," I say, still not inching from my sprawled-out position on the couch, "call me Clay tonight, seeing we are such good friends now." *Or maybe you'd like to call me an arse-hole again?* I dare him with my stare.

They share an amused glance, and I don't miss the way Vinny shifts under the disrespectful interaction, ready to call them out on it.

Heat wraps around my shoulders.

Sitting down on the chair opposite us, Bulan says, "Count again. All the stock is there." That alone is a mockery of the highest sort because it has taken Vinny twenty people and two weeks to sort this most recent shipment.

"I counted it twice," Vinny states, sucking air through his front teeth.

Wanting to offer them a polite way to conclude this conversation, I say, "Let me make a deal with you. Let us stop this miserable back and forth right now, and I offer you twenty percent of Dustin's cut of the diamonds in exchange for your business. No more loose crates. No more missing weapons." I pause, watching my proposal sink in, knowing they will rebut, but the polite Sicilian blood in me finds it necessary to offer. "And your loyalty, eyes, and ears in Indonesia."

Eka stares at me with that large mocking curve set into his lips. "What might you need eyes and ears in Indonesia for?"

Vinny huffs. "That is not how to talk to a boss—"

"Vinny." I raise my hand to stop him.

I smile softly at Bulan and Eka, but the fire in my head starts to singe my nerves. "I think you know."

Bulan waves his hand dismissively. "We don't do business with Mr Nerrock anymore."

Another glass smashes to my side, the sound like a shorting circuit in my head, but I hold their eyes, fighting through the internal Butcher habit to beat the table with my fist until they all drop their unconcerned grins.

Eka looks at his associate and laughs before finding my gaze again. "Count the crates again. It is all there."

Vinny is getting more and more agitated, moving in place to keep from jumping to his feet while I stay perfectly still and relaxed. Stoic.

"I would very much like some hospitality of the female kind," Bulan says, drawing my eyes to him as he licks his thin, tanned lips and peruses the room. "The girl from before, the little blonde one. She is pregnant, no? I thought I saw a small bump... such a sexy thing, and I have to admit I have a... How do you say it, a *fetish*? I get hard for pregnant women, especially little ones like her." His eyes twitch daringly. Is he challenging me? "Did you know that pregnant women have tighter pussies? It is a fact; the lovely flesh between their legs is swollen with all the blood pumping to that area."

I still don't move.

He continues, "They are far more sensitive down there. I would make sure she enjoyed it. I'll be very gentle with both her and the baby."

They look at each other and exchange another meaningful laugh. I share in the amusement, chuckling softly as my head burns in molten lava. My mirth gets louder, drowning theirs out, and their faces fall.

Across the room, my other capos and associates, brazenly watchful, measure the situation closely.

Then Vinny flips the table over, sending it and the glasses on top, hurtling to their feet, liquor splashing across their clothes, the glasses shattering on the marble tiles.

I stop laughing and tsk my friend and colleague for his outburst. "*Vinny*, please. That's not how we treat our guests."

He walks through the glass to get another drink, muttering, "Sorry, Boss."

I rise to my full height. The silence in the room is so crisp now, a bullet hurtling through the air would be explosive. I do nothing for a moment, while their muscles shake against the fight not to show any emotion.

Exhaling calmly, I smooth down my jacket. "I'm glad to hear you don't do business with Dustin Nerrock anymore, Bulan. I know you two were very close. Your wife and his wife are related, no?"

Bulan's eyes are wide. "Half-sisters."

"Well, I doubt you want to fuck the girl then. She is your niece. Nerrock's daughter, with Nerrock's grandson inside her womb. As for cutting ties with him, I hope it hasn't affected your family too much, not with the news of your wife's very ill father," I remind. "That is a tragedy."

I walk around the broken table, over the glass, the

crunching beneath my shoes like an echo of consequence, and I can't help remembering the night in the kitchen when I mindlessly scooped her into my arms.

Fucksake, I care.

I care about her.

Everyone's attention is on me. My guards have their hands hovering above each weapon. "I am beginning to feel offended, and you don't want me to feel offended. So perhaps you don't know why you are here. Not to use my wife as a tour guide. Not to drink my liquor or to ask me for my girl." The *my* wasn't a mistake. I mean it to my core. *Mine.*

I continue, "Not to ask me for anything. You are here—" I grip the arm rest either side of Bulan's chair and lean down until I am inches from his face. "To *woo* me. Do you know what that small word means? It means to persuade, to gain my love. Sicilians are full of love. And in case you have forgotten, this is the *Cosa Nostra*. Not the *Preman*. We are the federal police. The taxi drivers. We are the pilot who flies you back to Indonesia. The man who delivers your fruit on his bicycle every day. We are everywhere.

"And this here, in Australia, is *my thing*. So, you, my friend, are here to make certain I trust you. To convince me to do business with you in lieu of going straight to Saudi Arabia where you attain the stock for half the price you charge me." I smile at him. "A kindness on my part, but now that we are such good friends, I feel the rate should drop considerably."

My message seems to sink in, his entire demeanour changing, stooping, like a puppy when it meets a full-grown dog for the first time, stomach to the floor, simpering expression.

He exhales. "Let's start again."

Vinny sits back down, nursing his newly poured scotch. "Now, that's better."

I nod. "What a good idea."

After our discussions, where deals are met and agreed upon, I am still not convinced I have Bulan on my side, given his family ties, but I do believe their organisation will be working for mine. If not, if I get one more unorganised crate, I'll cut them off and dispose of a few party members for good measure. It means little to me as I have a connection in New Orleans. The Bratva. Jimmy would have never worked alongside the Russian Bratva, but I'm not the elitist Sicilian he was. Dimitri seems every bit the businessman I am. A man of his word. And he is keen to try his hand at the diamond trade, of which I have an abundance of stock that needs clearing.

He has weapons.

We will see.

I retire after the last black limousine rolls down the driveway to escort them back to their hotels. Instead of strolling to my room, I find myself stopping outside hers.

Bolton is stationed beside it, but he bears me no attention, as is his directive. I have become banner blind to most of the soldiers in this house, having them everywhere and silent, seemingly nowhere.

It's two a.m. now. Insomnia, my old friend, doesn't leave me tonight, and I seem to be eager for her company again. For her caring little questions that I answer honestly for whatever damn reason, I do not know.

"You know, for a man that never wanted children, you make a very attentive father," Aurora says from beside me. Bolton stands up and walks further down the hall, out of earshot.

I turn to face her, shaking off her statement. She knows that isn't what is happening here... "Where is Lorna?"

"In my bed, waiting for me."

Knowing we are alone, I shake my head once. "Bulan will race straight back to Jakarta with the news of Dustin's heir... *This*"—I nod at the door—"is a bad idea. For—"

"For you, " she cuts in with a meaningful smile. Leaning on the wall beside me, Fawn's door in front of us, she says, "I've seen you with women, Clay. For the past two decades, I have seen every aspect of your affection for them. I've seen you swoon them, *eye-fuck* them—"

"Charming."

A husky chuckle leaves her. "*Charm* them. I have seen you almost, *almost* love them." Aurora's face softens. "But I have never seen you look at a girl the way you looked at her tonight."

"And how was that?"

She touches my cheek. "Like you couldn't bear not to."

I breathe out roughly before redirecting the subject completely, not able to feign this one with the women I share my legacy—my life— with. "She needs clothes."

"Well, I will have my store bring them to her room. She'll need just pick them from the rack. *Unless*... you take her to my boutique tomorrow and spend some time with her. I think she will prefer your presence in this. It will seem less military to her and more..."

"Intimate."

"*Yes*." She turns to leave, then says over her shoulder, "And you could use real intimacy in your life, Clay."

I put my hands in my pockets, my black jacket fanning out behind my arms, my eyes glued to the silver handle, willing myself not to take it, not to turn it.

Not to fuck her.

Not to touch her.

But to have her ask me again why I can't sleep.

Relenting, I push open the door. Meeting me instantly is

the sound of Jasmine's breathing, even but loud. I stop. If I wasn't so damn obsessed with this girl, wasn't nursing half a bottle of whiskey in my mind, that sound would stop me. I will remove her from watching Fawn. Leave her alone in this room so I can... visit.

Jasmine's presence doesn't seem necessary anymore. The girl isn't a spy. She isn't. She's a stray. My stray. Could she think that little of herself that she would honestly give her child to a stranger, be him her blood or not?

Her father is a fucking stranger.

I walk up to Fawn's bed side, my body casting a shadow over her petite form as I lean down to get a better look at her.

On her back, with the sheets around her waist, her body is a thing of perfect proportion. And yet, it is when she opens those doe eyes, a perfect green and a distressed blue, meeting mine that chips away at my stone soul.

Her eyes dance beneath their lids—dreaming.

Leaning down, I blow softly on her nipples, and they begin to grow to tight peaks beneath her silk nightgown. It takes every ounce of strength I have to not wrap my mouth around those exquisite tiny beads and suck on them through the silk. Another... perfection.

This girl is too damn pretty.

I grip the top of the white sheet laid across her waist and drag it down her hips, past where her little gown lies across her upper legs.

My fingers skim across her knee, panning upwards, nothing more than the slightest of touches but enough to drag her gown up to her waist, revealing the prettiest bald pussy lips in the triangle gap between her thighs. I know what they look like when they open and swallow what they are given to swallow.

Fuck.

I pull the sheet back up.
Walk from her room.
Away from sweet temptation.

CHAPTER SEVENTEEN

I STROLL into the house just after ten p.m. Sunday night, having seen the Indonesian fuckers off at the airport for their redeye flight back to Jakarta. The press stopped me from making a timely exit, wanted a spontaneous interview about the fires while my illegal weapons partners checked in across the terminal.

All in one room.

Lorna is the queen of propaganda, and she has set me on a pillar for the residents to worship. A place I can operate without their eyes, too focused on the right or left of me to stare straight at the obvious. They all know. They knew when Jimmy ran this city, his influence in every department, and deep down in their guts, they know the same about me.

But while I protect them.

While I stand for them.

They just don't care.

When I enter the main living room, I expect to see the house bathed in a low hue of orange, allowing the night staff and security visibility as the rest of the house sleeps. What I don't expect to see is the lights turned up to blinding levels, five books face down on my cream-coloured leather sofa, the cushions stacked in a kind of pyramid on the floor, and a little deer sitting crossed legged staring at a crystal vase filled with freshly cut red roses.

I frown.

She catches me off guard, not twisting to face me when she projects her voice over, saying, "You know, roses are the most uncomfortable of flowers, Sir. Even your choice of floral bouquet is painful to touch, pick, hold, even to look at if you really stare long enough. At first, I thought, how pretty. I saw them being cut and wondered what would happen to them. Now, though, I'm looking at them like... thorns and spiny stems... not nice at all. Only the petals themselves are soft. Might as well just pluck them and sprawl them over the television unit."

This is about my admission to not making this house a kind of *home*. That isn't how I relax. I relax when I fuck. I relax when I shoot. I don't need décor to do that for me.

I stop at the entrance to the lounge room, loosen my tie, and run a hand through my hair. "The thorns and stems are what protected them. Roses are only able to be so soft and beautiful due to that protection."

Her pupils dilate, and I hate that she's letting ridiculous concepts like this get to her. "They wouldn't last long without the stems. The thorns. It's funny, isn't it?" she says, without a hint of mirth. Climbing to her feet, she stares at the roses as though they are responsible for everything wrong with the world. Perhaps, by design, they are. It's a shame that something so soft and beautiful needs so much protection to survive. "Without the spiny stems and thorns, they'll slowly wilt and die. Pretty things need ugly defences.

Kinda like Monarch Butterflies. They're poisonous, did you know that?"

This isn't about the fucking roses.

Although a twitch moves through my knuckles, heat through my forehead, her sad metaphor agitating me, igniting something in me, I bite it all back.

Releasing a long jagged sigh, I say, "I did know that... Are you feeling dramatic today, little deer?"

She finally looks at me, those wide dual-coloured eyes firm, deep in thought, until they meet my face, and she swallows thickly, as always, visibly anxious in my presence.

It's fucking delicious.

She mutters, "All last night, I thought about making this room more comfortable." Bouncing her tired eyes around the space. Lashes beating slowly. Her lips thin in her disappointment. "I played with the pillows." She motions, with a careless hand, towards the sofa. "I turned them askew. Fluffed them. Made them look used, enjoyed. But they didn't look any more comfortable. In fact, I wanted to put them back into their perfect diamond-shaped positions, so instead, I stacked them because it didn't make sense and that made sense..." She sighs. "Then I read a book about that war in Timor—even your reading material is *uncomfortable*. I read it just so I could put it face down on a cushion, thinking the space would look like someone was just here. A ghost of warmth welcoming the next person. One book didn't look any less staged. Two neither. So, I put five out and now it looks ridiculous just like the stack of pillows."

My jaw tightens, even though this is beyond eccentric behaviour. Beyond what I would consider normal. It reminds me why I didn't mourn the leisure of dating or relationships after I married Aurora—married the business. Besides my family, I have no relationship that isn't related to this business.

That is how I like it.

Liked it...

Fucksake, I solve problems.

I make things happen.

In her case, in this teenage girl's conundrum, I have nothing. I rub the muscles in my jaw, watching her, fascinated by her, wanting to fix this issue that has her sleepily rearranging my living room. Give her something. Anything. *Fuck.* "It's not something you can force, sweet girl. You'll know what makes you comfortable one day. You're still young."

A bullshit line is not my usual approach. She tilts her head at me, her blonde brows weaved, her lips making a heart shape for a moment in her confusion. "I didn't do this for me. I did this for you."

Madonna Mia.

Her sweetness resonates in my cock; it is the first part of me that responds, wants to act. "What a waste of your time. Think of yourself. Now go to bed."

She obeys me, walking towards the staircase, and I chase her with my gaze, following that sweet scent and warmth, and ignoring my cock as it beckons me to throw her face down and sink inside her.

She stills with one foot on the first step. "I *couldn't* think of anything, though. I just realised something tonight. That I really have been operating under a constant level of duress. To the point I have no idea what makes a house feel like a home. I thought I knew. Hence, the rearranging. I thought it was that simple. I was wrong. But I never had the opportunity to find out. You have. You do."

I think about my brothers. My obligations. But also, the

fact that this is who I am, who I wanted to be—fuck—*want* to be. "I don't."

She glances at the ground, sadness flittering across her face. It pisses me off that she cares because, right now, I'm anticipating Bulan is on his way to Indonesia to tell Dustin I have his daughter. Right now, I'm using her.

She shouldn't care about me.

She nods slowly before wandering up the stairs.

Watching her leave, I can't tear my eyes from her until she turns the corner. Sighing roughly, I twist to scrutinise the dishevelled room, books butterflied open, including a first edition copy of *To Kill a Mockingbird*, the spine creased, the cushions on the floor. I shake my head with a small smile forcing its way onto my lips. I pull out my phone and text the housekeepers not to clean this room, before heading to my shooting range.

CHAPTER EIGHTEEN

ON THE FLOOR in my temporary bedroom, my avocado, bacon, and tomato sandwich sits half-eaten on the plate beside me as I hunch over with my notepad in my lap so I can list all the things that make me comfortable. The pen, annoyingly small, makes it harder to control—at least, that is my internal reasoning for why my print isn't elegant and cursive.

And why I'm writing very little.

The truth is, I still have no idea what makes a person comfortable in their space.

Without knocking, the door opens. Jasmine always knocks, so I'm not entirely surprised when I lift my head to see Clay. What drops my mouth to the floor is the sight of him in navy pants forming perfect coverage over his muscular thighs, a white dress shirt tucked in casually, and a tan belt, that for reasons I can't quite fathom reminds me of a certain threat involving my arse.

I haven't seen him since the mild stroke I had last night when I decided to be an anti-Marie Kondo and throw his neatly organised living room into chaos. He didn't make me feel crazy, though. He understood.

He understood *me*.

My heart pitter-patters. His eyes coast across the room, stopping over the top of my head, glued to the seating area where he... and I... I take a big breath, forgetting for a slip of time about my little log, then close it quickly and stand, unable to be on the floor while he stands at over six foot.

"How tall are you?" I ask, holding the notepad by my thigh, hoping he finds its presence unintriguing. A notepad? Oh, it's just a dream log... love letters... Ignore the hearts with little *B's* in them. I swallow thickly as the B for Benji turns into a B for Butcher.

"Six-five," he states, his eyes doing a quick perusal of my waist-high short shorts and the slip of skin between the pink crop top, landing briefly on the item in my hand before settling on my face. "Do you want to please me?"

My cheeks are not warm; they are icy cold as blood leaves them. I don't know what to say to that. "How would I... I mean... Yes... but—"

He chuckles softly at my paling face, and the deep timbre moves into my soul to be stored away with the crashing of waves and early morning bird song.

"I'm taking you shopping," he states, his phone coming to life in his pocket. "Get ready. I'll meet you in the car." He answers the call, "Butcher," before strolling from my room.

He's taking me shopping?

He's taking me shopping!

Don't smile.

I shrug at his retreating back. "Sure, whatever."

Then dart around the room to get ready. I slide my tan ankle boots on, pull my hair into a high ponytail, the blonde lengths dangling halfway down my back, and grab my boho geo-print silk jacket, which tickles my calves, being much longer than my shorts.

As I dash from the room under a wave of nerves and excitement, the butterflies create a nice stir in my stomach while my brain tries to rein in my heart's eagerness. *This is just shopping*, my brain scolds. *Yes,* my heart thinks, *but it's shopping with him.* Real, quality time that doesn't involve a chance encounter at midnight.

Passing the living room, I halt for a second to see my pillow pyramid and books still plopped open on the cream sofa. The roses are gone, though. I groan at myself, blaming the hormones and the fatigue and the goddamn confusion this house and that man inflict. Stupid, really.

I stare at the messy room.

He left it...

No, not just *left* it. No. His house staff would have been down here at the crack of dawn to tidy this up, so that can only mean... He must have deliberately asked them not to stage it again.

But why?

Does he like the ruins of my silly moment?

And now that I'm looking at it in the glow of day, I think the space does look more comfortable. *Strange*, but... *welcoming* somehow.

Ha. I spin and head for the door.

At the front steps, a fleet of shiny black cars idle. Two SUVs and a central car, a long sedan of some sort. Only when a greying man, who still looks capable of cracking someone's spine in half, steps from the driver's side of the sedan, rounds it and opens the passenger door, do I know which car is his.

As I step inside, the rich scent of leather surrounds me. My heart does strange flutters that mimic the butterflies set to a chaotic flight down low. There are two couches in the back that face each other, and he is on one, with his legs man-spread like he owns the city—which, I suppose, he does —and his phone to his ear.

I sit still, folding my fingers together, fiddling with them. He scans me, his brows pinching in when they still on my head.

"No. I'll be out of the office," he states to the man on the other end of the call and then mutters, "Take your hair down," to me before continuing to talk through the phone. "It's simple. If he wants the building permit, he'll need the approval, and for that, he'll need to have Max's signature on those documents. Now, I'm busy today. He will accept the commission, or he can kiss his permit goodbye and that land will remain dirt until he dies. Are we clear?" He nods, listening. "Good. Don't call me again today."

Then he hangs up.

God, power is sexy as hell.

His eyes pin me to the seat. "Take. Your. Hair. Down."

My hands refuse to do as they are told, thrown by his tone on the phone, unaffected and commanding, and by his brazen demand. "Why?"

He stares at me expectantly, a soft smile settling on his handsome face. "Because it will please me if you do."

I reach up and pull the band from my ponytail; the long blonde curtain falls around my shoulders. "Are we spending the day together?" I ask pointedly. "Just the two of us?

He relaxes further into his seat. "Why?"

I try to hide my smile as I say, "Because it will please me if we do, Sir."

The car moves, and he looks as if he is about to leap across the console and make good on his threat to drag me across his lap and spank me raw.

I shuffle as he stares.

With a tight jaw hidden beneath a cool smile, he says, "You aren't afraid of me, are you?" He doesn't wait for an answer. "After what you have seen. Heard. What happened with the fucking gardener? You still aren't afraid. Tell me why."

I stare out the window now, unsure how to answer that question given the reason for my being here is still a purposeful omission of sorts. "My mum told me my dad was dangerous. I'm not surprised that you are too." There is silence as I watch the white dashes down the road blur into a continuous line, feeling his eyes on me but too hesitant with where to settle mine to look away.

He hums, carrying a hint of disapproval through the air. "Your mum, like your dad, failed you. Did she make this life-style seem worthy of awe? It isn't."

"I know that." Twisting, I find his face again. "I know what you are." *Say it, Fawn.* "You're in the Mafia."

"*No*," he purrs, his tone an auditory tonic of lust and danger. "In the District, I *am* the *Cosa Nostra*."

I inhale deeply. Hearing it from his own lips for the first time, I run my brain in circles, trying to find fear or resistance or nervousness within it but find only relief. I'm *relieved* he is who my mother said he was. That *they* are the dangerous men I wanted to speak with. I think about my silly fascination with the roses last night. My father could have been my thorns, could be this boy's thorns, allowing him to be soft and beautiful. "And my father?"

"An associate... Yes, also in this *thing of ours*... But you, little deer,"—he shakes his head once, his piercing blue eyes arrow on me, pinning me to the seat—"have no place in this dangerous world."

Rejection spindles through me, but I grit it back. I'll let my father be the judge of that. "Well, I never planned on staying, you know that. So, I'm sorry if I'm putting you out, Sir. I'll be out of your hair the moment my father comes for his *property*," I say, noting the tic in his jaw.

The blue in his devasting gaze shrinks to nothing as the blacks expand to consume them in darkness. "What did you just say?"

"Sorry?"

My heart and head and the butterflies all agree for once, shuddering and hazing and diving for cover, all on the same page but a little too fucking late.

"Stop the car," he states, raising two fingers to the driver, who closes the dividing screen while the vehicle rolls to a stop. I take shallow breaths as he frowns at me, his gaze feverish, not only angry, but hot with warning. "Take your shorts off. Lay over my knees."

With a shaky hand, I sweep a piece of hair from my face. "What?"

He taps his thigh. "Underwear. Face down. Over my knees.

There is no denying the gravity in his fixed blue stare—an icy haul, nearly palpable as it demands I comply. My body buzzes with adrenaline, never having been spanked. Not once.

I actually, kind of—*fuck,* what am I thinking? I fight against the distant voice of argument, the one that says this is inappropriate, and indecent, and— I drown that voice.

I want this, want to know what it feels like to have him spank me, to have him care.

Breathing deeply, I peer around the car, the black tinted windows, the sleek, elegant design offering privacy.

He leans back, lifting his hips slightly as his cock spans across his thigh, creating a thick bulge in his pants. I shrug off my jacket and shimmy out of my shorts before crawling across his lap on shaky limbs. I can feel him pulsing beneath me. "I wonder if Dustin's little girl likes it when I spank her," he says, his tone twisted, strained. I quiver when his hand caresses my plump curve. "You are not allowed to say sorry anymore. Ever. It's your default response. It means nothing now."

His fingers slide my underwear into the seam of my back-side, exposing more flesh. He hisses as he strokes me like he might the fur on a pet, then his hand comes down, the sound piercing. I cry out, bucking over his erection, the sting shooting through my veins, tightening every muscle. The shock resonates along all the sensitive nerves between my legs; my pussy ripples and swells. I become slick. I cover my face as two fingers trace the material bunched between my cheeks, stopping to touch the lower dampening spot. "Did you like that, sweet girl? Don't lie. The truth is right... here." His feather-light touch creates subtle circles over the wet fabric, alarming me, shaming me, and all the while sending my mind reeling with pleasure.

My cheeks burn. "Yes."

"Do you want more?"

Slowly I nod. "Yes."

My pulse is like a drone in my ears as his hand meets my burning flesh again. I cry out, then moan uncontrollably, grinding my hips into his leg.

He does it again.

Each slap creates a pulse of shock in my clit. Vibrating on his lap now, the sensation is like dropping through a hole in the ice, shock—paralysing and confusing. This doesn't seem normal. Natural. Sane. I don't know whether to hide my face as I drip from between my legs or beg him to please never stop the punishing pleasure.

He rains down slap after slap, until I drag my nails down

the leather seating, carving into the material as my orgasm carves into me.

I pant, face down, tears dripping from my eyes but not from sorrow. I'm all wrong. This is all wrong.

Everything I want from him is *all wrong*.

Then he lifts me from his lap, dipping down to scoop me up, and cradles me in his arms. He kisses my temple, and I think I might die, my heart skipping off its tracks, no longer on the same trajectory. Lost in him.

"That's my good girl." He strokes my hair, and I nuzzle into his chest. "Don't be ashamed. That was beautiful. You're safe..." He pauses for a moment, but I want more words, so I lean up to see his face. His intense blue eyes collide with mine, and he repeats, "You're safe here. You have no place being here, yes, and you will leave once it's all done, but for now, you're under my care. You have my word."

"Why do I feel like this?" I ask him, feeling incomprehensibly wrapped in content.

"You trust me."

My eyes widen in shock while my head nods in slow acceptance. "*Yes.*" I inhale steadily, and his mint-laced breath mingles with mine. While holding his gaze, I become willingly lost in the lines and swirls of the crystal-clear blues in his irises. "I don't do that often, Sir. I've had a lot of bad luck."

"I'm surprised you believe in luck. It's only real to those who hang on to it for every move. You have raised yourself. All your achievements are on account of you."

I snort contemptuously. "And that's why I have so many of them."

I feel the brunt of his stare intensify. "You're stronger than that, my girl. You're better than that thought." His hand comes to my lower stomach. "You are better than them. You don't need anyone," he states, his tone deepening with severity. The cadence of his voice sends tingles inside me, forcing me to really concentrate on the words while my head spins in the wonder of his affections, of his attention. "You will survive everything the world throws at you because you have learned how to adapt. You will survive. Just like you have survived everything else in your life. You're a very brave girl. Wilful. Stop apologising for being you."

I like his lessons... Still, I chuckle softly and pretend they don't mean the world to me. "You're bossy." A little flitter of euphoria dances beneath my skin, through my blood and bones, a little high off him, light-headed, and hopeful —*invincible.*

Gah, Mum was right.

"Yes." He smiles at me. "I am."

With that, he grips my hips and slides me to stand in front of him. Ducking, I manage to avoid the roofline. Not that my short arse—my *throbbing* arse—has to dip much at all.

He reaches for my shorts, and I place my quivering hands on his shoulders before stepping into them. It's the endorphins. A constant buzz at the tip of every cell.

When he taps the seat beside him, I instantly comply, sitting down. As he leans across me to buckle me in, I barely notice the way my arse stings under my weight.

He belted me in.

It's the little things. The small actions. Such a tiny gesture, but *oh my God*, I'm not sure anyone in my past would have even noticed if I was fastened in or not, let alone taken it upon themselves to secure me like a fragile item.

The car starts again.

As he looks out the darkened windows, I stare at *him*. He drags his thumb over his lower lip in a contemplative way, his distant gaze narrowing in thought. For a moment, just a split second, a flitter of exhaustion crosses his eyes. I think about his admission to having nightmares. Such a seemingly common issue for such a powerful man to be bothered by.

Failure...

I imagine him frowning when he's pulled from slumber. *Do you know who I am? Clay Butcher, that's who. I don't have time for your insolence, little nightmare.*

I chuckle at my own inner monologue.

Though, if *I* fail—I look down at my stomach—inconvenient things happen, but if *he* fails, does the whole city fall apart? Do people die? What is at stake if he fails?

After the past ten minutes, our distance feels wrong. Reaching out, I grab his hand and place it on my thigh because I want him to touch me, want to know that the attachment we shared won't vanish and challenge my sense of reality. Is this the first time I've touched him? It feels like the first time, because like with any first, I'm worried I'm doing it wrong.

Too firm.

Too soft.

Too early.

I just want to know what it feels like to have someone strong and dependable put their hand on my thigh like they do in the movies when the relationship gets real, gets emotional, and now they are in comfortable silence in the car.

"You'll survive too," I whisper. "You won't fail."

Then he squeezes my thigh.

The rest of the drive is like that.

His hand on my thigh

My heart on the line.

CHAPTER NINETEEN

I GUIDE her towards the store, flanked and surrounded by my men as we filter through the people on the street muttering my name. Offering them a gracious smile, I touch her lower back as we pass through the sliding doors.

The service staff lock them behind us, sealing the entire section off to the public, leaving my little deer to wander around without interruption. Awe circles her. It's adorable.

In the corner of my eye, I see people line the glass, peeking in, but I ignore them. I'm used to this. District residents eager to ask me questions about the fire, bored or, being the prying lot that they are, wanting to know who the pretty girl is.

Mine.

"Woah," she mutters, opening her arms wide and spinning in a circle, the long strands of her white-blonde hair skirting out as she takes in her surroundings. I look at the time on my cell. Today is an inconvenience.

Yet, I wanted to give her something.

After last night, I needed to.

Aurora would have had hundreds of pieces of clothing sent to her room to choose from had I agreed to it, but I didn't, and I'm still not sure why. An entire day wasted —*shopping*.

Lifting my hand, I rub my jaw. My cock twitches as I smell the lingering scent of her pussy on my fingers, as I remember her damp lips, the cries that fell helplessly from her throat, the way she said, 'You won't fail,' and I put my phone back into my pocket.

I stalk her with my eyes, watching the prettiest thing I have ever seen—a sight that makes my chest ache, my mind torrid—the thing I dare not throw down and claim despite my every muscle convulsing to do so, stroll nervously around, stopping to touch the fabric on a mannequin.

I'm a possessive man and fucking her will be the start and end of something. My urges have already undermined my controlled lifestyle, the decisions I've made regarding her have shown to be uncharacteristic...

What is it about her?

I see a lot of myself in her, but where I have spent every day attempting to step from Jimmy Storm's shadow, she has spent every day clutching at life, merely trying to exist. We are both the perfect product of our institutionalised circumstances.

Moving forward, she will be my responsibility, and after, when we gut her father, she'll still be mine to watch over— however, from afar.

It is better that way.

Could I keep her after it is all done? She will hate me. Would that stop me? I don't have the answers to those questions. Had this vendetta not been for my brother, but my own, I may lay it to rest for *her*... Such a self-indulged and pathetic consideration. As I know, I won't choose a soul over them again...

But I won't allow her to merely survive. I doubt she'll know what to do with herself...

Try something, perhaps.

She leans down, peering at the price tag.

She blanches.

I smile.

Her eyes train to a small clothing display, her feet taking her towards it hesitantly as though drawn to the unknown. She stops beside the small table, shuffling her feet coyly. Then she lifts a baby onesie from the pile of folded clothing. Across the white cotton vest is a blue and green print of some native American-looking symbol, a web with feathers, a hanging ornament of sorts.

A dreamcatcher, I think.

I straighten, watching her. Then I'm on my feet. I stop beside her because I need to know what about this item has her attention, has her hands trembling.

Barely noticing my presence, Fawn circles the print with her fingertip, careful not to touch it too much. When her eyes mist over and her throat rolls, I frown at the piece of cotton, ready to shred the thing to pieces for that response.

Her lips try to smile. "My mum would have loved this."

"Get it for him then."

"We shouldn't be buying him anything. I'm not keeping him. I'm not made of the right stuff to be a mother. I don't even know how to cook."

"You learn on the job, little deer," I state, my words forcing a shaky breath through her lips. "You have the luxury of time before you give birth. Use your time. Think hard about whether you want to give him up."

I know I'm going to set her up and send her on her way.

Hell, I'll give her enough money to never work, to never just survive. I consider it her payment for my brother's revenge. I'll trim the wage straight from Dustin's cut of the diamonds. I'm not worried about her—*financially*—and yet... there is this fucking burn in my chest that surges every time I remind myself that her presence is temporary, that she may give that boy up for adoption, limiting my access to him. Not that it'd stop me—*Fucksake.* What am I thinking? "We should buy it for him," I say, gritting my teeth as I do, her short inhales finding their fragile way into my chest.

We?

Madonna Mia.

She looks up at me, her dual-coloured eyes glossy with tears, her green eye so bright beneath the rising pool. "I like the sound of that. You said to take the opportunities; however, they arise. I think I can do that today."

She is far more compliant, sweeter, after a good spanking. *Eager to please me now, are we?*

I touch her jaw and look down at her wide-eyed hope. "Then get it."

My thumb moves over her mouth as she parts her lips. I want to lick the length of that pretty soft flesh, so I release her. Strolling slowly over to the large white ottoman, I make myself comfortable.

I nod at her, drawing the service girls into action. Leaning back on the couch, I observe them sycophantic to her needs. Her inexperience against their enthusiasm to please is just so damn entertaining. Women approach me, one after the other, displaying clothes, and I nod at a few, shake my head at more, but offer Fawn most of my attention.

They flash her my approved pieces. Her smile lights up the darkest crevices of my stone soul. But even a rock can be worn down when affected the right way. By persistence. By determination. By another rock.

She ducks into the dressing room to try them on.

Below the curtain, I see her shorts drop to the floor, followed by her panties and her bra. My phone buzzes in my pocket, and I sigh, frustration tumbling down my breath.

Retrieving it, I prepare to fire someone until I see it's a text message from my mother. My forehead tightens as I read the message. She is another person who relies entirely on me, as there is nothing but dislike and distrust for her in her own household.

She was never a good mother.

But she is, still, our mother.

> Victoria: Did I just see you in town? Come share a drink with me, darling. We haven't had a drink in weeks.

> Butcher: We discussed your sobriety last time I saw you.

> Victoria: Clay, I am out with the girls. They want to meet you. I am so proud of you, sweetheart. I want to show you off.

> Butcher: Another time.

I pocket my cell as Fawn walks from the dressing room in jeans worth more than all her collective belongings. They're tight and purposely faded around the curviest part of her legs, adding accentuation to her perfect pins. It would be wrong to leave teeth marks on them, and yet... I rub my jawline.

With a stunning wide smile that reaches her eyes, she gestures towards the new shirt.

A print. A little deer—Bambi.
She grins at me.
Well fuck.

CHAPTER TWENTY

"I should ask them all their names," I murmur to myself as two henchmen clutch plastic bags neatly packed with an entire new wardrobe, each item individually wrapped in tissue paper. They head towards the rear SUV while a few others circle us. I can't keep calling them all henchmen.

My dress twirls around me, reminding me of its pretty presence. Looking down at it, I smile. I slipped on a white summer dress that skirts thigh-high, exposing my legs to the faint tapping of the warm breeze. I love it. And all the other pieces, but most of all, I love the way Clay watched me, as though missing a single outfit would be simply unacceptable.

"They wouldn't answer you," Clay states, and I gaze at him as his deep gravelly cadence hits me.

"Why?"

"Because they have been instructed not to."

"Don't you trust what I'll say?"

"Get out of your head, little deer." He places his palm at

the lowest part of my back, his fingers spreading out to touch more, to control more, and it is all so smooth, so dominant.

A flutter sweeps to the delta at my core, thinking about how that hand smacked my bare arse in the car and how he made me feel vulnerable and accountable. It seems strange, but I think I understand it. The spanking thing. The scolding. It is the infliction of caring. It's caring so much you hold a person accountable, push them to be stronger, to notice their weaknesses.

It's being cruel to be kind.

He cares.

Escorting me towards the central black sedan, I try to control the way his touch fills my lungs with a kind of airy bliss that freaks me the hell out.

Passing a few drifters lingering near, eager to catch a glimpse of their mayor, I cast my gaze low, not wanting the attention.

Their mayor...

Do they know who he really is?

Is the District like Gotham City and Clay a villainous Batman? Corruption is a steady heartbeat that ensures pockets are filled and people stay employed. I arch my neck to see the tall man, gripping in his appearance, a magnet to every gaze. He's so handsome. He's almost agonising to behold, his appearance inducing feverish skin, a galloping pulse, overwhelming faintness.

He is basically a virus.

The henchmen have a perfect formation, seemingly well versed in curtaining their boss from perusal. I can't even imagine what every day must be like for him, being the subject of permanent intrigue. Always on. The city's charismatic leader.

"Fawn?"

I freeze when I hear that unmistakable voice. A voice I didn't expect or prepare for. My hand falls to the slight bump between my hips, hiding it with the small span of my tiny palm.

No!

Not now.

I peer around, my gaze bouncing between the shoulders of Clay's men, frantic to convince myself the voice was in my mind but then—

I see him cross the street.

Oh God.

He calls over, "Where have you been?"

Stop. I don't want to see you.

He is jogging towards me now.

As he closes the gap, I shuffle backwards, adding more space before bumping into a hard, warm body that should bring me comfort but only reminds me that I'm a pumpkin. My reality is this boy from my past, and the fairy-tale is the man who consumes my every waking thought.

Clay gently swipes me to the side, tucking me behind a six-foot-five wall of muscle. I peer around him.

The henchmen break apart slightly to allow him room to address Landon, but he speaks to me instead. "Do you know this boy?"

"Yes," I whisper as Landon gets within a few metres of us. I step out from behind Clay, taking a few shaky steps to face my foster brother, but I can feel his torrid, wild, and powerful energy crashing into my back.

Landon stops mid-stride, his eyes dropping to my stomach. "*Fuck.*"

My heart fights for freedom within my ribcage like a hysterical baby bird in a tight fist. "I couldn't—" I stammer on the words, reaching for a reason to why I couldn't, shaking my head frantically. I don't need to give him a reason! "I just couldn't do it."

"You kept *it?*" Horror swallows his features. Blood drips from his cheeks. His judgemental gaze infuriates me. I have thought this through. I want to tell him my son won't know me, won't ask what happened or be burdened by the gruesome incident that took place the day he was conceived. He'll be fine. As for me, I'm going to find the truth! The truth he and Jake kept from me!

He continues, "Why would you keep it? I never want to think about that night, Fawn. And you fucking kept it?"

What?

I step forward, nausea washing through me, threatening to fill my throat. "What? You and Jake said you didn't remember that night." *I knew it!* I knew they remembered. I saw the phantom of their betrayal moving through their meaningful glances when we were separated by the police to give our testimonies.

They knew something.

They know what happened to Benji!

Gritting my teeth, I ball my hands into fists, yelling, "Don't lie to me again!" I hear my voice crack as the words expel. "You remember! What happened? Who hurt him?"

"I—" He fumbles on his lying tongue, suddenly tearing his eyes away from my stomach and pinning them to someone over my shoulder, then to my right, left, to all the powerful bodies surrounding me, supporting me.

For once, I'm not alone.

A large shielding hand slides across the bulge at my lower stomach, gripping with a possessive intensity that nearly scorches my skin.

Landon drops his gaze, eyes paling as he stares at Clay's hand. He stumbles backwards a few steps and smiles. Spitting out a nervous chuckle, he addresses Clay. "She always gets like this." Heat scorches the tips of my ears. "You don't know her like I do." *A-hole.* The boy I cared about only four months ago looks back at me, alarm widening his brown eyes. "I don't remember, Fawn. I meant to say, I don't want to remember the morning after. Finding Benji like that. I don't want to remember that."

Heat blankets my spine as Clay presses me back into his body. As I peer up and over my shoulder, my breath stalls when I see his unreadable gaze shift. His practised charming smile slides into place.

Eyes softly on Landon, he states, "She *is* a bit eccentric." Landon grins triumphantly, I nearly vomit, and Clay nods at his men—*the nod.* The effortless mannerism the most powerful man in the city uses to summon the actions of many. "Take her home."

What?

No!

"*Sir*!" I scramble to stay close to him, but a henchman grabs me as I reach out for his arm. "Let me go!"

"*Gentle.*" Clay tsks as I'm manhandled into the rear passenger seat of the waiting car. I try to keep my eyes on Clay and Landon as they exchange friendly words. *Friendly!* Bile fills my throat, my old friend betrayal wrapping around me like a serpent, squeezing the hopefulness from my pores.

"Please, Clay. *Please!*" I cry out, panicked that Landon will twist the situation, telling him all the details I've omitted— turn Clay against me. Make a liar out of me.

Suddenly, I'm surrounded by bodies in suits—circled— and then basically stuffed into the back seat of the idling car.

The door slams with me inside.

Through the thick glass, the world is muted. The privacy of this space, its sanctuary, is now a prison. I tug on the handle, fighting against the mechanism as if my tiny grip can somehow dislocate the pins and latches, breaking my way out of this car to ask him what is happening, to not listen to what Landon has to say about me.

About that night.

About the drugs that weren't mine.

About how Benji fell, and I'm crazy and have a silly crush and need someone to blame.

About how I trashed my foster mother's house trying to find that goddamn camera! The one I saw flash moments before my memory fades to black. The one I know has my answers, my first time and Benji's death on it.

About all the reasons I am really here.

About all my eccentric actions.

Eccentric...

He called me eccentric.

My throat tightens, but I fight the internal sobs, picturing myself talking about thorns and roses and pillow stacks, and I thought for a moment he understood me. I choke within the clutches of betrayal. I thought we connected in a way I've never felt with another living soul, despite our age gap, despite our power divide, despite it all.

I *trusted* him.

What a fucking joke.

Releasing the handle when my fist aches, I pull my knees up and cuddle them—alone again.

Eccentric.

Just like your mum, Fawn.

CHAPTER TWENTY-ONE

AFTER BEING DRAGGED to my room, I rush to my pillow with the awareness of my notebook and the truth in those pages my only thought. My entire reality of that event is logged by nonsensical words and drawings. I didn't lie. I withheld a very personal truth from a stranger.

There's a difference.

With the chilling scene of Clay's friendly smile tightening the hold betrayal has on me, I scramble along the mattress and retrieve my tether to that night, to Benji's murder. I look at it, wishing I had told Clay the absolute truth yesterday or the day before that. Wishing I had told him when he was asking for it while cradling the kid in my stomach.

He cared about us then.

He wanted to know.

But he smiled...

At Landon.

"No, it was a practised smile," I lie to myself and rush back to the bedroom door.

When I grab at the handle and turn, it resists, unmoving

and stiff and—those *a-holes* have locked it. The fist around my notepad shakes violently with fear and anticipation and guilt, and all those feelings combined with about a thousand others. They locked me in!

"Bolton! Let me out!" I scream, beating the door with the brunt of my clenched hand over and over. "Anyone!" My mind suddenly jumps to Jasmine. "Jasmine! Can you hear me? Let me out."

The pad of my fist starts to ache, so I kick the door a few times before stepping back and testing the strength in my shoulder. Hitting the wooden door, the hinges barely rattle. I try again. The image of an old cult film where a group of men used their shoulders to burst into a woman's house, flashes in my mind. Then the memory of Benji's smile as he handed me the popcorn during said movie, crumbles my knees, and I drop to the carpet. I failed. If Clay believes Landon, then I've failed Benji. He's dead. He's fucking dead, and those manipulative arseholes are going to get away with it.

Jake gets away with it.

The truth dawns on me like the sky falling, and I feel its weight on my back. I lay down on the carpet, pulling my knees up as the thought knocks me around. I think Jake hurt him to get to me. I feel it in my bones. The way he used to watch me was unnatural. He would tease me relentlessly.

Mock me.

And watch...

But Clay won't believe me after he finds out I lied. Why would he? The police didn't. My foster mother didn't. Why would he when I've given him every reason not to trust me by omitting the truth.

My body shakes.

Landon is going to serve him twisted lies. I fucked-up by keeping this from Clay.

I fucked-up by... *falling* for him.

My heart tightens as I pull the notepad to my chest and rub the place over the frantically beating organ with my knuckles. I let my mother's romantic genetics win, instead of the powerful blood my father filled me with.

I have feelings for Clay. Lose my mind when he was around. Forgot the entire reason I'm here.

God. I'm so stupid.

He doesn't care.

He was *friendly* with Landon.

Friendly...

I groan as lumps of betrayal clog my throat, making it hard to breathe past them. The smile on Clay's face, so perfectly set, so patronisingly pointed at me. They are talking about me right now. They are laughing at me. At my stupidity, my gullibility, naivety, silly, stupid—*eccentric*—self.

A sob escapes me, and I curl in tighter.

CHAPTER TWENTY-TWO

FOOTSTEPS SAIL INTO MY SUBCONSCIOUS, and then I'm floating through the air and placed on the mattress. Before I'm able to react, able to provoke my body into action, my mind is drifting back out to slumber's wide arms.

The scent of sweet smoke encloses me.

A soft caress on my thigh taps at my consciousness.

Desire builds in my core as soft material slowly slides down my thighs, my body shuffling even as my mind lags to what is taking place. My underwear...

I flutter my eyes open, finding Clay a dark shadow hovering over me. Glowing blue eyes are fixed on my face. His hand is beside my head on the cushion, his other gliding my dress over my torso.

He's undressing me. Wait. I'm angry at him. What's happening? My heart wakes up with a start, throwing my pulse into a wild rhythm that moves between my ears and rattles within my throat. My anger, the betrayal, it all turns to ash as the reality of what's happening ignites.

"Sir?" Is all I can say beneath his dark gaze, his eyes never leaving mine as he undresses me. I let him. Aid him. Lifting and wriggling and using my own hands to remove everything until I'm lying naked beneath his formidable, suited wall of muscles.

Then he plants his hands beside my head, creating a cage with his big powerful arms.

Breaking our connection, his eyes pan down my body and his cheek muscles pulse once. I don't know what it means, but that small action crawls inside me with a warning.

I blink up at him, not able to catch up, can't seem to refocus my mind on the moment. His shoulders are taut, coiled, and ribbed with muscles protruding like wings either side of his neck. My eyes catch on his tongue, tracking its slow movement as he traces his lower lip. It's full of meaning. Full of intention. *Say something, Fawn.* "You had no right to drag me away from him. You had—"

His eyes snap to mine again. "You lied to me."

I think about his smile. The one he gave Landon, and an angry sob fills my throat. "You chose him over me."

"I did nothing of the sort," he says as his head dips towards me, his heavy breath heating my cheeks. We have never been this close before, the intensity not sweet and gentle but volatile, battering my frenzied heart. The mattress vibrates beneath me as his arms contract, his muscles flexing within the fitted shirt sleeves. He's shaking. *Angry?* Glowing predator-like eyes pin me to the mattress. "Has that boy been inside you, little deer?"

My stomach flips. "No."

"You said you didn't know who the father is."

"I don't," I assure him, that I didn't lie to him—about *that* at least. "I mean... I think... Did he say something to you?" *God, Fawn. Think. Think of questions. What did Landon say?* The heavy, distracting cage of his arms begins to shake harder, drawing my focus from Landon, the questions, the betrayal, that smile, to this moment. "*Sir*," I whisper, gazing into his fierce eyes, "you're shaking."

"You have been keeping your intentions from me, my girl. That disrespects me."

"You disrespected me by pulling me away like a child, by making me the outsider, by smiling at him, by letting him think you're on his side like everyone else is. Letting him think he's won! They always—"

He grabs my mouth hard, forcing my cheeks together within his aggressive clasp. "You need a goddamn pacifier, girl. You need something in this mouth to stop your incessant thoughts."

Then his lips crash with mine, his tongue punctures between inside, and my entire body burns up. There is no other thought, not a single fucking rational direction only a foggy abyss of sensation.

I close my eyes, fist the sheets beside my naked body, falling helplessly into *invincibility. God,* I never want to forget the texture of his mouth, fierce and warm, the domination of his lips taking mine like they want to swallow me, the taste lingering as his tongue plunges into my mouth, eating my moans and whimpers.

He kisses me hard.

He kisses me deep.

I know my mouth is inexperienced, but he seems to want it anyway. My mind reels. My lips exist for him to consume. Take. Bruise. I gasp for breath, so he gives me his, purposely exhaling into my lungs, filling me with everything *him.* It's too much.

Tears surface, clinging to my eyes. The raw possessiveness behind his mouth forces the muscles inside me to pump uncontrollably, begging shamelessly with each pulse. I lift my hips off the mattress, needing pressure, needing *him.*

He growls. Dragging his hand from beside my head, he balances on the other. He cups my pussy, pushing down, slamming my pelvis back to the mattress.

But the weight of him...

God, the authority in it.

It twists desire into a hot ball inside me. My hips buck inadvertently, fighting against his hold. Barely able to move under his mass, I enjoy the crushing feel.

His hand pins me down.

I rub into his hold.

When my pussy grows wetter, leaking onto his hand, he bites down on my lower lip, provoking startled yelps from me. Whimpers seep through my lips, shame circles, but I can't stop my hips from grinding against his scorching hot palm.

He rumbles in response. When teeth seem to pierce the skin on my lower lip, my body freezes. His tongue laps along the burning flesh before he leans back. My eyes widen at the sight of crimson gloss marring his lips. I'm bleeding. He bit me. And I've never seen anyone look so feral and wonderful all at once.

He glares at my flushed face.

Works his jaw muscles.

Venom and warning ripe behind his eyes.

Something wars within him.

"*Fuck it,*" he hisses, yanking open the top button of his pants, dragging the zipper down, the sound resonating inside me like a drum counting down.

My eyes widen.

God... this is it.

His steady gaze never wavers. His face would seem cruel if not for the genuine want and vulnerability in his endless blue irises.

As he pulls his cock out, fisting the root roughly, he parts his lips, exhaling in a rush, relief tumbling down his breath.

I rip my eyes away from the intensity in his, panning down to watch his fist working his cock in long, firm strokes.

Oh. My. God.

I pant as he drags his tight palm three lengths worth up his dripping shaft. The throbbing muscle is thick and hard, long with a perfect upward arch. Three aggressive veins create bulging blue channels up the length. The black lines from his torso tattoo lick down, finishing at the root.

Just like him, it's larger than life, so perfectly formed, steel-like and menacing.

He watches my throat roll slowly.

It's going to hurt. If he fucks me like he just kissed me, he's going to rip me in two. I shake my head to argue, but no words leave my arid mouth.

He drops his cock. The length of it strokes his shirt, the weight of it swaying and bobbing.

It happens fast. He handles me, pulling me to the edge of the mattress where he stands and pushes my knees apart, exposing me, spreading me open like an invitation. My heels slip off the mattress, my backside nearly on the edge.

Wrapping my legs around his back, he straightens to study the length of my form as I grow wetter and wetter, preparing for him. How does he do that? My body reacts to his instantly. It's so wrong. So animalistic.

I hold my breath, and we both watch as his fingers touch my slick pussy lips. "So pretty. Do you want me to stretch you with my fingers first? I'd very much like to do it with my cock." Wide-eyed, I peer up at him, a looming muscular physique unhidden even within his clothes. "I'm already completely possessed by you, and I haven't even been inside you," he states. "I need you to know that as soon as my cock enters your body, you belong to me. Not as a lover. Nothing that trivial. In every way. You won't like what that means... Tell me to stop." He nudges his cock at my pussy, still using his fingers to touch the outer lips. I wriggle against them, and they slide around in my wetness. His eyes darken, his tone dangerous with warning as he says, "Tell. Me. To. Stop. Fawn."

I can't. Words are hard to find, while air is thick and impossible to draw in. "I... I... Will you fit?"

He lets out a deep growl and bands my small waist with his big warm palms. I can't move as his face tightens under the sensation of watching his cock part the flesh. *"Yes."*

Then he drags me down the steel-like length of him. I cry out as I'm slowly impaled on his thick, long erection until he has to force himself further in on a throaty groan.

He's halfway sheathed within me when a smile crosses his lips. I gasp for air under the dark inference.

My pussy burns, utterly stretched at where he enters me. My core protesting. The muscles enveloping him pulse like they are broken, stalling. My cheeks flush, heat from the embarrassment over the way he must feel them, too—kneading him—feeling my body gripping his. Shame spirals through me. It's not in my control. I don't know if that's normal.

I try to stop the contractions, but I can't.

"You feel so good, sweet girl," he says, his words blanketing my concern in warmth. "You're strong inside. I had a feeling you would be. And you're the prettiest thing. Too pretty. Don't fight me. You belong to me now."

My hands fly up to grip the taut muscles on his arm as he

stretches my sensitive insides open to take him to the hilt. I can't move, impaled on him, so utterly full.

He stills when he hits the end of me, dropping his head backwards, his twitching muscles waring with his restraint. Lifting his head again, he glares down at me. "You will be a good girl for me, little deer. Do as you're told, and everything will be okay. You will let me fuck any part of you. You will take me like a good girl. And you will thank me when I kill the boy who put this baby inside you while you were too high to consent."

I keep whimpering; he keeps smiling, seemingly awash with release already, relenting to an urge held captive.

What? Kill—

Impatient, he doesn't wait for me to comprehend his words or the sting. Doesn't wait for my body to relax around his before he tightens his hold on my hips and starts to fuck me. My pussy convulses uncontrollably, and all other thoughts and sensations flee. I am overwhelmed and embarrassed by the feel of him pumping in and out of my soft pulsing flesh.

"*Fawn*." My name comes through a strained growl as he drags himself out and pushes back in again. "Fuck. *Mine*." He squeezes my hips, angling me, lifting me, using me as he thrusts into my body.

"Not that boy's."

Thrust.

"Not Dustin's."

Thrust.

"Mine."

I chant. "*Oh God. Oh God.*"

He watches his cock drive in and out, his eyes glued to that private part of us as he slides me along him. "Good girl, you are taking me so well." He then murmurs to me in another language; his rumbling cadence, twisted and desperate, soars over my body as he fucks me.

And even though he is relentless in his domination, making my small frame take him over and over again, I have never felt so completely safe. I don't know what that says about me. I don't want to think about it right now. I listen to him groan in that sensual language. And I don't know what he is saying, but the sentiment behind his deep timbre carries security into my heart and soul.

While he takes what he wants, watching closely so he doesn't miss anything, I squeeze my eyes shut, unable to handle all the stimulation, needing to block out the sight of him so carnal I'll explode if I keep looking.

It comes on fast.

It's not a subtle rise of sensation like when he spanked me, or a shy unpredictable orgasm like when I touched myself. This pleasure builds with the same brutal force as the pounding of his pelvis between my legs. I open my eyes to see him still feral with pleasure, watching my body take his punishing thrusts.

His eyes snap to mine as he meticulously tilts my pelvis, rolls his hips, hitting the buzzing muscle inside me, once, twice, and then fire ignites in my abdomen. Exploding through the rest of my body, the bolts of pleasure and heat reach my fingertips and drop to my toes.

Fuck. He knows what to do with my body to make it break with agonising bliss. I cry out as he punctures me through my orgasm, as my pussy clings onto his cock, as my muscles become so twisted, like a rubber band, they hurt.

"I'll let you off this once, little deer. But if you ever come again without screaming my name, I'll fuck your tight arse-hole until you need my cock inside it just to feel normal—" He loses his words in a groan, and I writhe on the mattress as he angles his hips differently, losing a few beats of his merciless rhythm.

Then he grows inside me, the sensation almost startling as he comes, fucking me while his orgasm rips through his body. He pushes into me harder, seemingly aggressive with his desire to get as deep as possible while hot fluid spills within me, around his shaft, and drips across my thigh.

It's a beautiful sight.

The moment he loses control.

I never want to forget the way his brows pinch, his mouth parts, the sound growling from him in a primal and feral timbre. I know he said I belong to him. I'm his dark possession. But people lie. Everyone in my life lies. Eventually, they give me up. But I'll never forget that my body can bring this king of a man immense pleasure, if only for a minute.

He stills, breathing deeply. A mist of sweat coats his neck and forehead, while beneath his shirt, I can still see godly physical potential bursting from his powerful physique.

He withdraws from me, the sensation hollowing me out, striking me with bliss on the withdraw and with pain as the tissue inside me is left quivering and tender. Tucking his still semi-hard cock away, he squats behind me. I can't even move. When his fingers touch the aching flesh at my lips, I gasp on a whimper.

"Are you in pain?"

"A little." I lie—it hurts more than a little, but I think he knows that as he strokes me gently. He's huge. I'm not surprised it hurt. More cum slides from inside me, and I feel it drip from my pussy. My cheeks burn with embarrassment when his fingers slide around in the fluid that left me, a blend of his release and mine, before he smears it over my backside and thigh, painting my skin.

"So pretty. Don't shower until I tell you to."

"But I'm covered—"

"In me. You think I somehow forgot such a thing?" He stands up, slides over me, and scoops me up. Carrying me a few steps, he settles my head on my pillow.

I look up into his blue eyes. "You're leaving, aren't you?"

"We are not going to spoon, little deer."

My mind is dazed. "That was like..." *My first time. Can you stay? Please.* I stop on the sentence I was going to say, not able to force the pathetic pleas through my lips. He doesn't care. He doesn't feel guilt for fucking me and leaving. He's infallible. My eyes bat slowly, lashes waving like heavy fans, the weighted upper lid wrestling with my will to open them again. I win, meeting his soft blue gaze. "Will you tell me what happened with Landon?"

He leans down, forcing me to close my eyes again as he presses his lips to one eyelid. Then the other. "Sleep," he orders, his tone a rumbling timbre carrying emotion with it.

This time I'm unable to force them open again.

I can feel his hands feed the sheet around my frame.

Hear his heavy footsteps and the sound of the door closing. I tuck my knees up a little, forming a small ball. Slumber drags me out with it.

THE SHEET SLIDES down my body.

I spread my legs. Even in deep, peaceful slumber, I can feel his palms pushing my thighs open. Fluttering my eyes, I instantly meet his. I blink at him, taken aback by the sleek black suit, the smooth, freshly shaven jawline.

He leans up, planting a palm beside my head, to hover over me. Searching eyes roll around my sleepy face, as though he can see through the layers of cells to the feelings I conceal beneath. *You left. You left when I needed to be held.*

His other hand cups me between my wanton spread thighs, his long middle finger coaxing entry between swollen flesh. A little high-pitched whimper leaves me, and his brows pinch in response.

In the back of my mind, a black spot beckons me to reach for it, a question or event we are meant to be discussing, but the energy around us won't allow me to.

Snared by his eyes, messages of confusion and intimacy I cannot comprehend gloss mine while his usually dark, hard stare seems to soften. It is a new look, I think. His hand leaves my core, finding my chin and angling it as he studies my lower lip. The small cut in my flesh hums and prickles, but I don't mind the sensation at all.

He exhales hard. "I lost control yesterday."

"I don't want your practised smiles," I whisper, wishing he would pull my jaw towards his lips and let me feel their commanding dance.

His eyes meet mine again. "And I don't want yours." As he scoops a piece of ice from a glass on the wooden bedside table, plopping the cube in his mouth, his expression shifts to one racketed with hunger.

Then he crawls over me, his strong body moving down to settle between my knees. The man is all action, fully suited for business and yet, I lie lax and mouldable and exposed...

"No." I touch the hand holding my thigh to the mattress. "I haven't showered."

He ignores me. When he kisses my puffy outer lips, my reservations dissolve and I melt into the sheets on a long moan.

Completely vulnerable.

Completely at his mercy.

Completely safe.

His cold tongue laps up and down my sore, tight lips while the cube he introduces slips between them. Soothing the skin, his tongue and the ice work in unison, building a steady simmer of pleasure just below the surface of my arousal. My muscles unravel to the gentle stimulation.

"I like this," I murmur to the air, closing my eyes.

I arch, lifting my backside inadvertently as he groans his response into my flesh. A sound so primal it stokes the simmering bliss, keeping it perpetual and even. Perfect. Comforting, yet completely carnal.

My body shudders with gratitude as he dives in deep with the cool, strong muscle of his tongue. His mouth is dreamily chaste, kissing me in an almost romantic way that has me swooning and arching and whimpering with sensation.

When the ice melts, he reaches for another cube, until they are all gone. Water and my own arousal coat my lower half, puddles of melted ice collecting in the blanket below my arse.

He licks me diligently.

Sucking my clit so softly.

Until I can't ride the light simmer of pleasure anymore, and I climax around his gentle attention. The rolling orgasm more subtle, longer, sweeter, a sensation I could crave at all hours of the day and not tire from it.

He sits up, licking his glistening lips. "You didn't say my name." He grins devilishly. "You know what that means."

Unwillingly, I float down. "What name would I use?"

He smooths my hair down my head. "Always, Sir. You are the only one who calls me that, sweet girl."

I move into his warm hand, liking how he brushes the

side of my hair with his palm, his fingers lightly skating through the strands. "Even when you're... inside me?"

He groans, a dark tic forming in the corner of his mouth. "*Especially*, then."

My cheeks warm. "Yes, *Sir.*"

"*Good girl.*" Lowering his hand, he makes me instantly mourn the way his gentle pats made me feel. I don't care to analyse it or dissect the feminist perspective. I liked it. I liked it because every part of me felt warm, safe, seen, and I'm not going to deny myself that bliss just because it's unconventional.

"And you slept like I told you to," he states. "You slept half a day and the whole night. I would have taken care of you sooner, but I know how much you needed it. I'm very proud of you for not fighting it."

I attempt to rise, but he nods to the bed, and I drop back down. "I slept through the night?" That hasn't happened since... the sight of Landon and Clay talking thrashes through me. "*And you will thank me when I kill the boy who put this baby inside you while you were too high to consent.*"

Landon.

I force my way up and he leans back, allowing me space. His brows draw in, eyes narrow—unimpressed, but I don't care, quickly asking, "What happened yesterday with Landon?"

His jaw tics. "Who?"

"Landon. My brother—" I say, my voice rising as uncertainty clutches at my vocal cords. If he didn't choose him over me, if it was a practised smile, then what happened. "You spoke. What did he say? What did you say? Why did you drag me away? Why—"

"Calm down. Ask me one question at a time."

"Why would you drag me away like that? I was humiliated," I admit, the talons of betrayal banding me. He's lying to me about something. "What did he say about me? What did you say about me?"

Within his eyes, softness dissolves into muted disdain... or is it *jealousy?* "Do I seem like the kind of man who shares well with others?" His tone is soothing, yet awash with warning. A hint at something dark lurks deep.

I shake my head at myself, staring at the ends of my hair as I coil the length around the tip of my finger. "I've been searching for answers. I need to know what he said to you."

Knowing I have said too much, I glance up at him, meeting scrutinising blue eyes. "What you need to know is that I dislike hearing your name spoken from that boy's mouth. And I dislike not having the information myself. You lied to me. How do I protect you if you lie to me? I'm going to need you to explain why you are here."

"To give the baby—"

"Fawn." He warns. "The truth. Now."

My admissions play with my tongue, wanting to fill the space between us. Is that what intimacy does? What an orgasm does? Makes you open and honest? The Spanish Inquisition would have gone very differently if they had caught on to this nifty trick. Relenting, I admit, "Okay, but I didn't lie to you... I came here to find my dad because I knew he was in the Mafia. Well, not knew," I correct with a sigh. "My mum said so, but she was crazy... " I get lost in the story, the order to tell him. "I don't remember the night I got pregnant. Just the next morning... *Benji*, my foster brother, he's dead. The leg of the table—" I swallow thickly. "It was through his stomach. The glass top smashed, shards glittering within the fibres of the cream carpet. Blood like a pool around him. I don't even remember where I was standing or sitting or if I woke up in the bathroom or on the couch.

Landon and Jake were hysterical, and it was like I was just plopped into this alternate dimension."

His eyes darken, sweeping down my body to the small bump and back up to my face. "Go on."

"I didn't come here to *just* give my dad the baby. I mean, I was going to offer him the baby, that's true. I needed to ask for help with getting a good family for him, at the very least. I didn't want him to end up in the system—"

"Like you."

"*Yeah*... like me." I exhale hard. "My mum never asked for help with me. I wish she did. I refuse to do that to him..." I shake my head. The concept of the Spanish Inquisition brings with it the main reason I'm here, in this house with a man who always carries a gun on his person and has more henchmen than Gru from *Despicable Me* has minions. "There is another reason, too. Something I thought only a man like him... well, like *you*, could help me with. I want the truth about what happened to Benji... and to me."

He listens carefully, his jaw set hard. "What did the police have to say about the dead boy?"

I lift my knees up and hug them, the ache between my legs basically gone, but the sting in my heart while remembering the way they dismissed Benji's death is present and screaming. They treated him like trash. No loss to the world. "He slipped," I state numbly. "They claim he slipped." It hurt for a long time, like a fist squeezing my heart. I imagined a future with Benji in those first few weeks after his death. A sweet reverie of a future where he loved me, where we would have raised this baby together... I take a big breath and continue. "I begged the police to search the room, look into his murder... I mean, death. They didn't believe me. My brothers said he slipped. My foster mother said he slipped. We were underage. So, it was a fucking accident."

"But it wasn't. You think something else happened, sweet girl?" He lifts his hand to rub the smooth skin along his strong jaw, a gesture I've often seen him do when deep in contemplation. "But no one cares." His words hurt, however unbelievably true. It is always the truth that hurts most. "And what did you expect from Dustin? To torture the boys. To kill the one who raped you."

That word scores as it enters my ears. "It wasn't rape."

"No?" That pure darkness that lives inside him so contentedly, so in sync, flashes in his eyes. "What would you call it then?"

"I wanted to be with Benji," I admit, reaching for the ends of my hair again, working them around my fingers as his body tightens further with each coil. "Someone hurt him. I feel it. And... It's dumb. It's ridiculous... *But* I want my first time back. I want some details. Was it slow? Did he kiss me?"

His lips ghost my ear now. Dangerous heat envelops me as a snarl of words spits from him. "I'm going to need you to stop right there, little deer, or we will have a repeat of last night, and your pussy is not ready to take me again the way I want to take you after hearing that... So, it's in your best interest to keep the romantic language between you and this fucker to a minimum." He leans back, his eyes blank and unreadable. "Go on."

A current of warning rushes down my spine. I suck my bottom lip into my mouth, the sting from his teeth reminding me of last night. Of his claim over me. "*Benji*... his room was in the basement. That's where we were. He has a camera set up down there. I think he was filming us. But when I confronted Landon and Jake the next day, they told me he took it out the day before, but I don't believe them. I remember while we were watching the movie, in the corner of the box, there was a red flashing light."

Thinking back on my last day in that house, the day I demanded they show me the recording, I shudder. Blood still stained the carpet, and like dye on a shirt, it seemed to grow over the week, seeping in deeper, expanding in a way it might had his body still been there to feed it.

I clear my throat, all the admissions now like water leaking from a dame, just wanting out. "I couldn't think. I remember my brain stalling, arrowed on that one truth—the recording must be here. I trashed the room," I admit, not proud of my temper—*my eccentric* behaviour. Those arse-holes are right. I am—can be—eccentric. "So, of course, my foster mother threw me out without a hint of guilt. She'd been waiting for the day I misbehaved, which I'd never done before. The foster board doesn't like uncommitted custodi-ans, even though I was of age at this time, but she didn't like me the moment I grew boobs so..." I laugh without mirth. "I wasn't surprised when she kicked me out for '*violent tendencies*.'"

Suddenly, he straightens to his full height. Cutting into my thoughts, he says, "I'll look into this."

Climbing to my feet, I follow him from the bed. "Wait...That's it? Are you going to get the recording?"

He smooths his pitch-black tie down, his face a thing of emotionless beauty. "Yes."

My heart ping-pongs inside my throat. "You believe me, then? That something else happened?"

Clay stares at me through several of my shallow breaths, his eyes studying my face, from my wide, uncertain eyes to my parted mouth. Stepping until his shoes skate along the tips of my toes, forcing me to arch my neck to keep his gaze, he lifts his warm palm to trace my lips with his thumb. "I will always believe you."

And it takes all my willpower to not fling my arms

around him. Tears burn around my irises. "And you won't hurt them, though? Will you?"

His hand twitches before dropping from my face. Emotional armour erected around his pristine black suit. He glances down at me through his dark lashes. I want to reach for his jaw and demand his gentleness return, but it's flittered away after my utterance of not wanting them harmed. "I won't hurt the boys... yet."

When he steps towards the door, I bolt after him, rounding his authoritative frame until I am in front of him. Halting him with my palms to his warm abdomen, I realise this is another place I haven't yet touched him. My fingers flex over his shirt where the hardness of muscles beneath act as a formidable wall. "Do you promise?"

He puts his hands on the tops of my arms, gently lifting me up and planting my feet on the carpet away from his path. "I'm not repeating myself."

CHAPTER TWENTY-THREE

Dear Benji,

We buried you today.

Everyone was crying over your fresh grave. All the girls from school were there. They cried, too. I know you will want to know that. I didn't cry, though. Fuck no. I'm too angry for you. For me, too. They don't really give a shit that no one remembers how you fell. They don't give a shit. But I do.

And something is wrong, because they lied about the recording, Benji. I know you were recording us, and I think it was because you knew something was going to happen between me and you... I, I don't feel right about this.

But they fucking buried you anyway, and all the truth and questions were buried with you.

You know what... I think we made love the night before you died. Maybe that is why you were recording because you wanted to keep the memory of our first time. Am I right?

I don't remember the act, and Landon and Jake told me that I fell asleep on the couch, that they did too, and we all woke up with you impaled on that table leg... But I felt you inside me the next day, Benji. I was sore. Why did your brothers lie? What the fuck happened? Did Jake get mad? Or jealous? Did he push you onto it?

God, I wish I remembered the way you touched me. I like to imagine it, though... Hey, would you like to hear a story?

This is how it happened: I imagine that you looked at me from across the glass table and you smiled—that smile. All the girls love that smile.

Our eyes met.

Something changed in that moment, and you saw me as more than what you did before. You saw me and you shook your head, like, how could you not have noticed it before? How much you wanted to kiss me. Then Jake said something stupid to me, and you stood up in a blind rage, and you ordered him to leave and Landon, too.

Everything was different. You knew you wanted me. Finally, you saw me. For the woman

I had turned into. You took my hand and led me into your bedroom. I was so fucking nervous. Even in my imagination, I'm nervous. You kept looking at my lips and I kept looking at yours.

We didn't kiss. We did that inches-from-each-other-without-kissing thing that you said you liked when we watched that movie. I forget which one but it's one of your favourites.

You undressed me.

I undressed you.

You helped me onto your mattress.

And lying on top of me, you told me where to put my hands, and yours went everywhere, like you had more than two and they were all touching me. I felt you all over. You were gentle when you pushed into me, and I watched as your eyes closed in that moment.

Then I kissed you.

I stole the first kiss.

You opened your eyes and smiled at me, shaking your head because I took it before you could give it.

Then we made love.

- Fawn

CHAPTER TWENTY-FOUR

MY SHOES RAP slowly along the abattoir floor. Striding between the cow corpses hanging from the railing, I reach for my phone and decide to check in on her just once, despite myself. I hit Bolton's number.

Two rings and he answers, "Yes, Boss?"

"What did she do today?" I ask, stopping outside the door to the processing floor, the scent of bleach and raw, clean meat thick in the air. I stroke the bristles along my jawline. This is all about her. This entire evening, this entire interruption is all about finding out who killed a boy I'm pleased is dead and who put that baby inside her so I can finish him too.

My fist tightens around the phone as her confession to seeking her father for help stirs in my mind. Help where her foster mother failed her, where the police failed her.

Frowning ahead, I recall her bowed, fragile frame sinking into the chair in the witness room while the officer sneered at her confused state. She needed someone to believe in her. No one did. Neither did I...

They won't make that mistake again.

The truth is all that my sweet girl wants.

Who took her innocence when she could not consent? Who came inside her pretty young pussy like a fucking invalid who didn't consider the consequences? They knew she had no one. Pregnant or not. Raped or not. No one would care, and no one did...

A smooth smile rests on my lips as venomous rage races the length of each limb, my Butcher fists aching immediately.

I'll be giving my little deer more than the truth. I'll be giving her bloody revenge. Despite her self-preservation to not call this incident rape, I can't call it anything else. And that thought is explosive—my Butcher head burning hotter than ever before.

"She has decided she wants to learn to cook," Bolton says, dragging me from my own rampant torment. "She was in the kitchen most of the day with Maggie. She's never cooked a thing in her life, Boss. Besides two-minute noodles, that is. She is just jumping straight into wanting to know how to bake a birthday cake."

My brows pinch in. "A birthday cake? It's not her birthday, Bolton."

"No, Boss. She wants to make a *kid's* birthday cake with little knights and a castle..." He clears his throat. "Her words, Boss, not mine."

An ache moves into my chest. "A kid's birthday cake."

"That's right," he says, meaning threaded into each word.

Is she considering keeping him? I inhale hard, exhaling the conversation even harder, needing a rational mind that isn't drifting to her making her son his first birthday cake in her new house, the house she bought with the money I'll give her in exchange for her father's death. "Make sure she has everything she needs." I lower the phone, ready to hang up, before setting it to my ear again. "Watch her around glass."

"Yes, Boss."

Hanging up, I slide the phone into my jacket pocket, straighten my black tie for my company, and stroll into the processing room. The breaking of bones under heavy-handed hacking fills the room with an ominous drum. Off to the left, Paul is dismembering a two-hundred-kilogram cow carcass. Each violent hit of the mallet to the bone makes the two boys tied up to their chairs tremble and whimper. The smallest of the boys, fucking Landon, wheezes with anxiety.

My brother, Bronson, sits on his chair backwards, his arms folded over the top of the backrest, his eyes glued to the boys, a chilling smile on his lips. I wonder if he remembers what that was like. I wonder if it plagues him to see them after— For a split second, the sight of him tied to the chair instead inundates me, but I clench my teeth, shove it away, stop it from allowing any remorse or guilt to tamper with the justice I am to serve. I haven't asked Bronson to work this side of the business since... Nevertheless, this is sensitive—a personal job. I didn't want to involve the rest of the Family in the District and have them ask questions about Fawn. Didn't want anyone to know anything about her now that...

Now that I care...

Vinny greets me at the door before falling into stride beside me as I close the gap between us and our guests. As he pulls out a chair for me, the sound of the back legs scraping the cement soars through the room, only interrupted by the mallet breaking bone. I nod my thanks but stay standing. Gripping my brother's shoulder, I stare at the bound and gagged boys in front of me, the whites of their eyes begging me to show them mercy.

Bronson's hand touches mine, patting lightly, never tearing his gaze from our guests. "Hello, beautiful."

"Bron," I say, removing my hand. "Do you know who I am?" I ask the boys, threading my fingers together and resting them in front of me. Vinny circles the young lads, removing their gags from behind their heads.

"Answer the Boss," he states, tapping Landon over the back of the crown, flicking slick blond hair over his forehead where it clings to sweat and dirt accumulated over the past twenty-four hours.

Landon nods, his eyes bloodshot and raw, a sign of last night's turbulent emotional state. "The mayor."

I smile smoothly as another bang from the mallet, cracking a bone in two, hitting the table beneath, echoes around the otherwise void room. The boys flinch. "Do you know who I really am?"

They both nod.

I direct my attention to Jake, the bigger and heavier of the two. Clearly, he indulges when given the chance. If he indulged in my deer, protected the fucker who did, or, *Christ,* even thought about it, I'll gladly be slicing off the parts of him that lured him into temptation. "I am here on behalf of Fawn Harlow—"

"That bitch? You serious? How much did she pay you? I can get you—"

I glance at Vinny, tightening every muscle inside me, so I don't inch closer and slice his lips from his face for calling her a bitch. Vinny nods at me, reading my every subtle gesture. His fist meets Jake's face to silence him, sending his head backwards, rendering it a circling lifeless weight for a

few seconds of blackout glory. Then Jake regains consciousness on a hysterical whimper.

His reality rains down on him.

"Fawn is the daughter of a very important man," I state
deadpan; it's not a lie. Dustin Nerrock is District royalty. A part of
Cosa Nostra for the best part of four decades. So, whether in life
or death, as my ally or my enemy, his name holds weight and
demands respect, or my whole goddamn concept of this institu-
tion crumbles. These boys should lie down at Fawn's feet, beg to
be the man she walks over, for being the blood of a boss. A
princess in the District. "Do you have anything to say about your
actions before I enter my office and watch the footage?" Bronson
and Vinny found the SD card in the side of Jake's laptop.

Fucker.

He must enjoy watching whatever is on there... I try to
control the raging current that sparks my muscles to react, to
beat and maim. "I will give you a chance to repent. Just one.
Please"—I widen my arms, holding my hand out to Landon
—"you first."

Landon's anxieties are full-blown attacks now, wracking
his body on the chair so violently it is any wonder it doesn't
keel over under the fitful motion. "She wouldn't have even
known," he gasps, "if she hadn't got pregnant," he pants. "It
wouldn't have mattered because she wouldn't have known."

A loud thud shakes the boys. The mallet delivers the final
blow to separate a heavy leg from the cow, dropping the
entire meaty limb to the floor.

"Shut up!" Jake barks at him, sobbing and growling, a
vibrating mass of attitude and stupidity. "Don't tell him
anything." *This one is dumb as shit.*

"Shoot that one in the kneecap," I state, and within
seconds, Bronson blows Jake's knee open, creating a fleshy

crimson crater. Guttural howling follows me as I stride steadily towards my office and close the door, already fucking certain what it is she wouldn't have known. Despite my desire to keep moving, to stalk back into the slaughter room and show them just how much it fucking *matters,* I slide onto the chair, the laptop already open and lit.

Beside the mouse is the SD drive.

Disregarding the heat firing inside my temples, I insert the SD drive, click on the only MP4 in the file, and lean back as the screen comes to life. Bathed in a light glow from surrounding dimly illuminated lights, the view of the room is visible through a sepia-style hue.

Directly across from the camera, a couch and a glass table are plain to see, but the low-light and poor-quality equipment cause the surrounding areas to be licked with darkness. Pixilated. I slide the bar across until I see a blur of people enter the room. I stop and watch my little deer in a pretty dress sit down in the centre of the couch. Her brothers: Landon, Jake, and the dead fucker, Benji, position themselves around her.

She will never be alone like that again.

My little deer.

My Cosa Nostra princess.

Mine.

Distractingly, my heart hammers against the bars of my ribs, an angry spike of adrenaline throwing it into a damn frenzy inside me, while outwardly I simply lift my leg and rest it on my knee.

Ball my hands into fists.

Tighten my entire body.

Watching the footage play out.

CHAPTER TWENTY-FIVE

THREE MONTHS *ago*

THE TELEVISION FLICKERS ON, *but it is one of those old-school boxes, thick and bordered in a kind of wood-look laminate. Static brings it to life, lighting the basement with flickering colour and then the glow of a black-and-white movie.*

The girl and the boy on the screen are naked, but the girl isn't moving, and then I realise it's because she's unconscious. It isn't in English. Despite the disturbing content, I find it hard to look away from the hypnotic way her body shakes as he takes her without consent.

I glance from the screen and meet Benji's soulful gaze. In my mind, I smile, and yet, my lips won't form the curve.

Still, I'm almost certain he winks at me.

Subtle. Just for me to see. And even in this strange state of intoxication, I feel my heart soar in response to that gesture.

When the girl on the television screams, my eyes cut across to watch as she wakes up with the boy inside her. It's not a nice film. But Benji likes cult movies, and I like him...

Dotted in light from the standing lamps and the monitor, his room in the basement looks plucked straight from the set of an 80s show. On his wall, retro pin-up girls pose, their pear-shaped physiques tightly covered in short jumpsuits, taunting my skinny frame. He likes his girls curvaceous, confident, and dominant. Everything I'm not. Marilyn stands on a drain, air lifting her dress, and she pretends to be demure.

A cough drags my attention back to my brothers, back to the cannabis and cocaine sprinkled carelessly on the glass coffee table. My eyes scan the faces, naturally landing on Benji once more, and he gives me that grin. I think I successfully smile back this time.

A whooshing fills my ears, my heart rate slow but shuttering, nonsensical. I go to stand but wobble, dropping back down onto the couch.

No one notices.

My mouth is suddenly dry.

I go to talk, but the words don't reach my tongue, yet I know they are in there. My bare thighs are like ice below my palms, and I wonder if I'm wet or sweating or if it's just the sensation of being cold.

"She looks fucked."

Benji moves beside me and wraps an arm around me. I lean into him, seeking comfort as the inebriation climbs into my consciousness and warps my reality. His scent covers me like a blanket fending off the awful helplessness my condition brings with it. We watch the horrible movie play.

My eyes shift from the rape scene ahead, slicing through the air to a blinking red dot...

... flash... flash... flash...

BENJI LAUGHS ON A COUGH, *thick, pungent clouds moving around the space between the four of us. They have moved now, and the credits are rolling... I don't remember when that movie finished.*

A hand settles over mine, and I drop my gaze, staring at the way my bare thighs press together. A short white dress. Benji likes it, and I enjoy being smiled at by him. I watch Landon's hand remove mine so he can touch my skin. It all feels the same, though. His hand. My hand. My thigh is so numb I'm not sure I'd feel a knife scoring my skin. Is that normal?

"Landon, man, give her another hit," Benji says moments before dropping his nose to the glass and sniffing loudly. He tilts his head back and sucks air in.

"What time is it?"

I glance at them questioningly, but they continue to talk, continue to smile—such huge smiles. Did they hear my question? I focus on my tongue resting on the roof of my mouth, my jaw locked together. Did I say it out loud?

I blink.

I blink again, and I'm on my back on the couch with Landon kneeling on either side of my hips, working his arms low, fumbling with something below my knees. Benji is behind my head on the couch now, looking down at me, and I meet his eyes. My heart feels like a slow bass in my throat.

My eyes sting.

His narrow. "It's okay, Fawn. Just breathe."

When did I lie down?

Landon groans. "I've seen nothin' so fuckin' sexy in all my life. Don't you think, Jake?"

"Perfect," he agrees. "Doesn't seem right for you to go to someone else, does it?"

I spread my thighs to see what he's doing, and he hisses. "So sexy. I bet you're tight. The tightest little thing."

God, I don't understand. Is he talking about me? Am I still watching that movie? His hand is on his cock. Needing to speak, I open my mouth, wanting to tell him I can see him, that he should put it away, but it all feels silly. I giggle, but I'm not happy. I want a scream to come from the place that giggle came from. My heart whooshes between my ears.

What is even happening?

I want... I want someone to walk downstairs, to see what I'm seeing so I don't overreact, misinterpret. The vision of him touching himself blurs, my eyes misting up with tears.

When I slowly turn my face, heavy and mechanical, I see Jake. Pleas fill my eyes with water. My lips refuse to move, but his smile is the biggest of all, sloped, morphed.

When I look back at Landon, my dress is bunched around my waist, and he is dipping down between my legs. Terror circles me. No. Something is wrong with me. Something... I'm seeing things. A whimper fights its way up my throat when a wet and cold sensation touches me between the legs.

"She likes it. Keep going," Benji says.

My mind screams for me to thrash around beneath him, summon all my strength, every muscle rigid with the need to fight... but my arse just shuffles slightly instead.

"God, she tastes good. Come here. Try her."

My brothers move.

Switch.

Benji is there now.

I can't keep track; they are like lines of black streaking the room. Back and forth. Back and forth.

I close my eyes to stop the lines from moving, but I can feel licking between my legs, hear them talking about me. It's not real, though, it's all in my head, and if I can just sleep, when I wake up, we will all laugh about my silly mind.

Darkness.

"THAT'S ENOUGH. *Her virginity is mine. You promised,"* Jake growls, his deep tone right by my ear, his breath gushing past like wind. My body is being touched...

Pain spears me.

My eyes open to him pinning me to the cushions, kissing my throat, panting, the smell of marijuana swallowing us both.

It doesn't go away.

His body is heavy, squeezing the air from my lungs. He's stretching me open. Crawling up inside me. My face is so wet, tickles, trickles, a rushing sensation from my eyes, pooling into my ears. The pain is excruciating. When he thrusts harder, rocking us both on the couch, the dotted lights overhead bob, fizzle in and out, and no one seems to notice.

It's my eyes.

They keep closing.

Open.

Close.

Jake groans. "Fuck. You're right. Oh, fuck me." *I reach up, grasping his shoulders, trying to see if he's real, convince myself that this isn't happening to me, but to the girl on the television. The pain is only a manifestation of my mind.* "She's tight. So fucking tight, boys."

"She likes it, man. Listen to her moans."

He gets rougher. His breathing gets heavy, strange, uneven. "Like my cock, our ... dirty ... little... slut."

Don't touch me. Stop it. Stop it. I don't want it. A violent grunt rattles between my ears. Jake stills on top of me, panting heavily, nuzzling into my wet hair, and I think he must have heard my screams, understanding I need help.

"My turn," *Benji declares.*

I manage to roll over onto my stomach. Or was I turned?

Vomit fills my throat, a mouthful pouring from me along with the heavy fall of tears and sweat. I grip the armrest, hauling myself up but my body is like lead.

"Where are you going?" Benji laughs. Fingers sink into my hipbones, pulling me backwards while I scratch at the couch to stay on my knees. I grunt as my torso is flattened, weighed down by someone sitting on the backs of my thighs. A hand presses between my shoulder blades, decompressing my lungs, squeezing the air from them. I wheeze for more as he starts to thrust inside me, using the body that I'm unable to control but cannot escape feeling.

"WHERE ARE YOU GOING?"

I tremble violently as I climb to my feet. My toes drag on the carpet with each step, the vision of the bathroom ahead guiding me. It's so many steps. My muscles ache, and parts of me that shouldn't hurt are on fire. Limping into the bathroom, I slide my feet along the tiles to the toilet. When my legs give up, I manage to pull my body up onto the bowl.

I sit, spread my legs.

A strange sensation leaves me, dropping into the water. Then I wee. I reach for the toilet paper, wiping myself, hissing as the paper feels like razors between my legs, but I'm not sure why. Pushing to my feet, I turn to flush, halted by the sight of red water and thick white blobs in the bowl.

The shaking of my limbs becomes hysterical. My finger freezes on the button, not wanting to flush it in case what I am seeing will be washed away and forgotten. Wide-eyed, tears stream down my face. No. It wasn't real.

I don't flush the toilet.

Barely alive, I walk back into the main room, head cast down at my feet. They seem to be working now.

"Flush the toilet, dirty girl."

I convince my head to rise. Grinning wildly, Jake stands opposite me with his thick brown hair mussed.

He steps towards me, and I shuffle to the side until the wall hits my spine.

He laughs. "What? Don't you like me now?" he says, approaching me slowly. "A few minutes ago, you were hugging me so tight with your pussy you didn't want me to leave."

My blood crystalises, freezing right inside my veins. No. "No," I mutter, hearing the word but it's not real.

This is the movie.

Jake doesn't stop advancing on me. When his eyes run the course of my body, smirking when they settle on my thighs, I peer down.

My breath catches, and I cover my mouth to silence the sound of the whimpers that follow. It's a horrible helpless cadence, and I can't stand it. My thighs are red, raw, and the skin is coated in pink liquid. "What happened? I'm bleeding."

"You don't remember anything?" Jake asks, and somehow his already big smile grows, becoming a gash of taunting horror.

"Stop smiling. I'm hurt," I whisper, my eyes bouncing around the room. Where is Benji?

Jake moves towards me, but adrenaline scorches a trail up my spine, forcing my legs backwards.

The sound of Benji snorting something snaps my eyes to witness him rise to his feet. He appears by my side, and I exhale deeply. "I'm bleeding, Benji. I'm bleeding."

"That's enough," Benji says to Jake. "Let her get cleaned up. You had your fun."

"Fuck your shit." Jake walks straight at Benji and throws him to the side; the sound of the glass table shattering pulls a cry from

me. Jake clutches hold of my elbow and throws me face down on the cushion.

I try to scramble up.

I try to move.

But there is pressure on my back. He's touching me. Keeping me face down. I twist my head to the side, tears sliding down my face, seeping into the cushions, and then I see Benji lying on his back in the glass. His eyes are wide open. His mouth parted, sucking in shallow breaths.

He doesn't look good.

I pan down to see a thick piece of metal impaled through his abdomen, a puddle of blood creeping out from under him. He's not moving.

He's dying...

I open my mouth to speak, "Help—" But a guttural groan rips from my throat when someone thrusts into me.

CHAPTER TWENTY-SIX

clay

FUCK!

My fist hits the laptop screen. Broken pixels explode in a kaleidoscope of colours around the shattered glass as it flies backwards off the desk, cracking in half, the monitor and the keyboard separating.

I flip the desk, sending everything to the ground. Small dots of blood from my fist spray with my jarring movements. I don't feel pain. Don't feel anything. Everything is submerged deep in a volcano of fury.

My mind roars.

Drawing my weapon, I point it at the glass panel opposite me and unload round after round after round, releasing all fifteen bullets into the air, needing the noise of exploding glass and gunfire to deafen the rage burning my brain to damn volatile psychosis.

It isn't enough.

It'll never be enough. I should have shut the goddamn thing down before I saw it all, before I saw them all take turns while she tried to crawl for safety, but I couldn't leave her alone in that room with them for a second time and closing the laptop to savour my rage was an act I would never abide.

I hurl the gun through the panel, breaking off the glass stalactites clinging to the top of the silver frame. My muscles twitch, every mass tight, as my heart pumps molten blood through my veins, frying the ends and my compassion along with it.

Creeping across my vision and into my mind, darkness finds a fixed place within me. A sneer curls my lips as I walk from the office to meet the ashen faces of the soon-to-be-dead boys tied to their chairs, I immediately lock eyes with Jake.

The fucker who stole my deer's virginity.

Who ripped through her and made her bleed.

Standing very still, I watch him and Landon scream, panic, their mouths hollowing and moving, pleading probably, but I can't hear a thing within the den of violent fury in my mind. The butcher has taken parts of the carcass and left the room. Vinny is still a shadow blanketing the boys.

Bronson slowly straightens from his chair, tense and wary, staring at me like I'm the damn rapture personified. For a moment, my little brother, the one who will slice a man's face off and have a tea party with my niece all in the space of an hour, appears wary of what *I* might do.

He deadpans. "What did they do to that sweet girl?"

I don't respond. It wasn't a question.

Glaring at the boys, useless sacks of shit, a chilling calm greets me, as is the way with processes like this. "Is that the only copy?"

Vinny answers. "There are two copies, Boss."

"I didn't ask you," I say, staring at the boys.

"Two! Two," Landon says straight away.

"Destroy them both. She never sees them," I say to Bronson. "Hand me the pliers," I demand of Vinny, thinking about how this fucker tied to the chair licked her and groaned around her flavours, how he appreciated her taste before another man could. One who might have deserved her, as doubtful as that premise might be.

Gritting my teeth, I circle the boys slowly as Vinny hands me a pair of saw-like pliers, and Bronson gags Jake for the duration before heading towards the office to destroy the SD cards. They will never breathe life into her rape again.

I stare at Jake. He will get his turn soon enough—after watching, hearing, knowing what is to come. What I'll be taking from him piece by piece.

The boy's wide white eyes follow my every move, glued to me like a tether—like prey watching a predator waiting for the moment it lunges for their jugular.

"You're... you're not going to kill us?" Landon says, his voice is knotted with breathless hysteria. "That isn't... that doesn't really happen here."

The hooves and calls of cattle passing by the abattoir wall cause him to jerk in place, pursuing the sound. "Have you ever been to an abattoir before?" I ask. "My family owns five across the greater Western Australia region. It was the first business my old Don bought when he came here from Sicily. We like our meat. Sicilians, that is... Do you know who Fawn is?"

"I didn't know..." Fierce sobs break from Landon's trembling lips as he shakes his head over and over. "We didn't know."

"She is the daughter of a boss in the District, *Cosa Nostra*." I stop circling him. Stop behind him. "You raped the daughter of a very dangerous man."

He yelps as I squat behind him, flinching away from me,

even though I've barely breathed on him. When I cut the cable ties at his wrists, he freezes. Whimpers. Doesn't even try to escape. *Pity.* I would've loved hunting him down like the animal he is.

Making my way over to a chair, I pull the light metal seat to him until our closeness is intimate. I sit down, my knees a meagre inch from his, his stench seeping from his slick skin like waves of tangible adrenaline and endorphins.

His hands are no longer fastened behind his back, but he hasn't moved them.

I stare impassively into his petrified brown irises. Then glance over at Jake, panting around his gag. "I'm going to tell you a secret, boys. Fawn's father betrayed me. My father. My family. When I find him, I'm going to order his execution. As is *my* right, and mine only." I tsk. "But he is still a made-man, and in my world, that stands for something." I set the pliers down on my knee so I can retrieve the cigar tin from inside my jacket pocket. When I light the cigar, drawing in the silken smoke, his alarmed gaze drops to my knee. To the sharp pliers. "It has to stand for something," I say around the sweet clouds.

"More than that though," I continue. "You touched my property. You did not have permission. And you made her cry, bleed, and put a baby in her young womb."

"It's not mine!" Landon cries. "I'm not. I can't be."

I still. My eyes flick to Jake, basking in his terror, before going back to Landon. "And how would you know that?"

"I couldn't finish. Not with them watching. I didn't want them to know—I didn't want them to know, so I just pretended to come."

"Interesting."

"*Oh. God.* Don't kill me!"

"God is on my side, boy. And you have tasted her, felt her

inside, and that is damn unacceptable." I look at his eyes—misted in shock, glued to the tool on my knee. "Take the pliers." His gaze darts around the empty processing room, landing on Jake, then Vinny, and finally Bronson. Bronson grins, a dimple poking into the side of his menacing smile. I soften my eyes on the boy, the intent inside orderly, disturbing, punishment. "Take the pliers, Landon."

As he swallows, his throat rolling, he brings his shoulders forward, wincing through the atrophy. The bowed limbs, tight and sluggish, would ache. The sliced flesh at his wrists would sting.

With a shaky hand, red raw from fighting against the plastic tie, he takes the pliers from my knee. Drawing them quickly to him, he clutches them like a crucifix to his chest.

His savour.

Not likely.

I lean back in my chair, sucking on the cigar. "Now use the pliers." With each syllable, his panting becomes harsher, his lax form shaking under the extreme panic thrashing through his body. "Take your cock out." Guttural whimpers vibrate up his throat. "Remove it." His head drops forward, tears streaming down his face, filling his mouth. "And I might let you live."

While he sobs hysterically into his lap, Vinny rounds him, appearing over his shoulder. Reaching around his throat, he applies the sharp edge of a knife to his sweat misted flesh. Light runs along the clean metallic surface as Vinny presses the silver blade to Landon's rolling throat.

The boy freezes in horror. Slowly, he lifts his chin to recoil from the invasion. "No. No. No. No," he pleads while the knife lightly grates his throat over the vibrations his words cause. "Wait. No. I'll do it." He fumbles with his zipper, not looking down—*no*, he is locked on my eyes as I blow another heavy white cloud, hazing the air surrounding us. The knife drags an inch across his throat. Crimson blankets in rivulets from the warning incision. "No!" He grabs hold of his cock, howls in agony, preparing to do it, but his fist shakes violently around the pliers. He doesn't move.

He closes his eyes, sobbing, defeated.

"Are you sorry for what you have done?" I ask. "Are you sorry for hurting her? You won't be raping anyone again, will you? Tell me you're sorry, my boy. Tell me how sorry you are."

"God," he bellows, opening his eyes—red, raw saucers in a bloodless face. "I'm *so* sorry. I'll never even look at a girl again. I'll never—"

I throw my cigar to the ground. "Good boy." I smile, and nod at his fatty flaccid shaft. "Now show me how sorry you are. Prove you'll never do it again. Show me you deserve this, and it'll all be okay," I say smoothly. His eyes become vacant, lost in the trauma. "It's okay. You can do this, my boy. If you do it fast it won't hurt as much. We'll fix you up and send you on your way and you'll get through this."

I watch.

Vinny waits.

One snip.

Landon drops the pliers and gargles on his pain. I reach down and retrieve them, grab a hold of his cock, and snip into it. Clipping the final fleshly thread, I watch the fatty column slaps the floor. Landon passes out. I nod at Vinny, absent of even a slip of remorse. Vinny drags the knife along Landon's throat. Blood sprays through the webbing of veins as his carotid arteries are severed.

Then there is quiet.

I glance over at young Jake—his head rolls with nausea —and then back at Landon—his neck flaps open. But all I can see is a little deer, terrified and confused, as she stares at blood and cum dripping down between her pretty white thighs.

"So, Jake," I say, turning to smile at him. "Are you sorry for what you have done?"

CHAPTER TWENTY-SEVEN

AURORA LEADS me down the hallway towards double doors with fancy square grooves carved into the polished dark wood. She pushes the long silver handle down and steps inside, holding the door open for me. "You should sleep in here tonight, Fawn. Don't be nervous."

Immediately, I know whose room it is as the intoxicating scent of his cologne, sweet cigars, and warm male flesh wraps around me in a carnal way. My heart picks up pace. I stare at the wooden four-post bed, standing royally in the centre of the expansive space. A large private lounge area with black leather couches and a desk are in opposite corners.

My breath catches at the window, splaying the entire length of the west wall. It is too clear. I fear I may throw myself off the edge and land three storeys below.

I force my feet forward. "Why?"

"Your room is too far away from him. He requires you to be in here tonight."

"But this is..." I blink at his room, all dark, all masculine, all very Clay Butcher. Twisting to face her as she holds the door open, I say, "But you're his wife. Don't you—"

"I'm his business partner and, I like to believe, his friend. But we are not lovers, Fawn. Our relationship is based on the archaic truth that I am a woman and without Clay, I am nothing but a bargaining chip for the *Cosa Nostra*. With him, I am his partner. And I get a say in this empire my father loved more than me and my sisters." She sighs, shaking her head a little, seemingly exasperated by her own words. "Go to sleep. I wouldn't wait up for him."

Her words make me sad for her. "Why does he want me here?" I say before I can retract the question. Usually, I would just take the crumb that I'm offered, but for some reason, I know a crumb won't be enough this time. I know I want him. Waiting for my father or not, I want to stay here—with him. I don't have the luxury to entertain the idea that there may be a commitment on his end. Intimacy, yes. So much more than I ever knew existed, but this is another level now. Sleeping in his bed... it terrifies me.

Because... I think I love him.

"Perhaps you should ask him yourself," she says as she leaves, closing the door behind her.

Left alone, I strip off my clothes and change into my new white silk nightgown. It feels like heaven on my skin. When I switch the light off, the small downlights immediately glow to provide the perfect light-to-dark ratio.

I crawl into his bed—*his bed*—fanning my fingers out to touch the smooth black material, the mattress barely moving beneath my weight. All I can think about as I curl into a ball on one side, knowing it is his side, the scent of him on the pillow giving it away, is that this means something. Being in his bed, without him, means something big.

Suddenly, I bolt up, remembering my dreamcatcher. I've never slept without it. Jumping off the bed, missing its comfort immediately, I rush back down the halls and up the stairs. The passages seemingly go on and on, but when I finally get to my room, I pluck the dreamcatcher off the bedpost and rush back to his room, not analysing why I'm running.

In his room, I dangle the beautiful web on one of the posts and nest above the covers on his side of the bed. The ambient air is the perfect temperature. I close my eyes slowly, blinking the unfamiliar corner of the room from my sight until...

THE SPLASHING of water wakes me from my dreamless slumber. I bat my eyes open to find the same unfamiliar room, the same sleek sheets, the same perfectly firm mattress, but I'm not alone. I flip over to see a glowing rectangle around the bathroom door. The sound of water rolling off a body sails from the shower, hitting the tiles beneath.

My lungs fill with an anxious breath as I slide off the mattress and walk over to the door. I just want to test it. Twisting the handle to see if it is locked even though I am sure it— The handle twists in my tiny grip, and I push the door open, not allowing myself time to rethink this.

As I walk into the elaborate ensuite, the scent of sandalwood and citrus cloaks me. Candles, set up in threes on a deep ledge running the span of two walls, dance in the light breeze from the exhaust fan. His house staff must spend a lot of time creating this perpetual scene of luxury for him because I don't see a man like Clay Butcher wasting his time on lighting candles if only for himself.

The steam parts to reveal him under the faucet. Feeding his hands through his hair, dragging them down his face, his back to me, he is yet to notice me. The thick strands look longer and darker under the spray, deliciously so.

I should make a noise.

Look away, even.

But I can't.

I stifle a toe-curling moan at the sight of his taut round arse and his long, strong legs, compactly carved into valleys around each muscle. He's tall. Athletic. His muscles pulse as he washes himself, and mine tremble to behold him.

"Did I give you permission to come in here?" he asks without turning to look at me. When I don't immediately answer, he turns to face me. Icy-blue eyes find mine, his expression shifting from dark to outright carnal, as he strokes the inked grooves at his eight-pack. His abdomen twitches as he lowers his attention. My eyes pan down to watch him wash the length hanging between his thighs.

My heart pounds hard. My lips are suddenly arid. "I can't believe that was inside me," I whisper to myself more than to him, pressing my thighs together as I feel myself weep from my core. Clearing my throat, I say, "Are you turning me away, Sir?"

Something irrevocably sad passes over his gaze, a brief disturbance, a slight interruption to his otherwise controlled mien. "Take that little dress off. Come here."

Ignoring my body's predisposition to obey him, I ask, "Did you find the—"

He raises a finger, effortlessly wielding the control over my tongue, silencing my question. "I don't want your words right now, sweet girl. But I do need you in here with me. Agree or leave."

I don't want my questions blocked, but I want even less to leave and exponentially more to be what he *needs*. "Yes, Sir."

Gripping the hem of my gown, I slip it slowly up my body. The scorching heat of his gaze follows the seam's path over my thighs, pussy, stomach, and breasts, causing me to moan. The silken fabric caresses my flesh, putting a tangible sensation to his predatory watch.

I pull it free, flicking my hair free also. Standing naked in front of him, I focus on breathing through my endorphins, ignoring the damn butterflies.

Glancing down his body, I swallow as he grows until his cock is thick and bouncing by his navel. The pink head pokes out from his foreskin. It looks so smooth. Menacing.

I glance back, finding his eyes hovering on my beading nipples as I move to stand with him in the large shower. I used to joke I could hang a coat on my nipples, but truthfully when they pebble, they ache and buzz with discomfort. More so since getting knocked-up.

As I join him, he steps backwards, allowing me access to the downpour. The water glitters on our bodies while the steam hangs in the air.

Although he is the epitome of smooth, effortless control, his eyes flash with pain and need and something that twists my stomach. Something that makes my eyes burn. What could have affected him so?

I touch his cheek, and he closes his eyes.

I think I love you.

Taking the opportunity, I drag my fingers down from his cheek to the hard, flat planes of his chest and then caress the rolling slab at his abdomen until my fingers touch the tip of his cock's pink head. I gasp as it pulses, and I slide my hands back up and over the ridges and dips that form each muscle. He opens his eyes and watches me explore him.

There is very little youthful about him, in the sense that he is all hard edges, defined lines, every inch of him a machine of a man. Just another way Clay has utter control over every aspect of his life.

My hands slide in the soap at his abdominals and follow the thick muscles carving an angle down each hip. I trace the images laced in ink above his caramel skin. Three legs fanned out around a face, a heart and a gun at his right hip. In a straight line from his left pectoral to his left hip, words are written in another language. Across his collarbone, a subtle scar that looks old is weaved with an ink vine as if to make the mutilation beautiful, as well as draw attention to it.

I wonder why.

A tattoo was something I had never thought about. I might get one... maybe a butterfly, only because they live so erratically within me whenever he is around. Their presence will be a constant reminder of the weeks I spent being his...

When his big hands travel up my sides, I quiver under the all-encompassing attention. He is so much taller than me; he reaches right over my shoulder and retrieves a bottle of shower gel from the sill behind.

He lathers the gel into his hands, creating fragrant foam, before caressing my throat and chest with the suds.

He's washing me...

As he cups the lower curve of my breast, I tremble with emotion and yearning. With desire. Leaning into his palms, I urge him for more pressure. He works both handfuls. His thumb and forefinger flick my pointed nipples, and I cry out as the sensation overwhelms me.

"*Fuck* it," he hisses through his teeth. Then he drops to his knees, takes a nipple into his mouth, and sucks on it, long and thoroughly. I grip the dark wet hair on his crown, holding him to me as he gently treats my nipples, switching from one to the other. He is so tender tonight; tears sting the backs of my eyes, wanting to announce my emotions.

As he stands, his hands trail the length of my sides, stopping under my arms so he can lift me effortlessly. Placing me on the ledge inside the shower, he opens my thighs wide.

His gaze lingers on my body, and mine is on his heated, chiselled features as he concentrates on cleaning me. Rubbing soap into my thighs, his hands cover the entire breadth of each soft column. He is all hard. I am all soft and pliable, and it feels so right.

As his fingers near my pussy, I shuffle on the tiled ledge, tilting my hips slightly, invitingly. His fingers touch my lips, and then he strokes between them. I arch my neck back, my chin to the ceiling, moaning, the sound bouncing off the glass shower casing.

He slides a finger inside me, and I buck, clench.

"That's my good girl. *Fuck*...You're sucking me in, sweet girl. Have you been thinking about me?" He slides another long finger in and moves them in unison, stealing my breath with each rhythmic stroke. I join the motion of his skilled hand. "I asked you a question."

"*Yes,*" I pant.

"And what thoughts have you so deliciously wet that you are dripping all over my fingers?"

"Your mouth on my pussy..." I moan as he rocks his finger within my clenching walls. "The ice. The..." *The way you say 'mine.' The way you called me 'your belonging.' Your smell. Your lips. God, I want your lips.*

God, I think I love you.

"You are going to be a very addictive little thing," he says, watching me crumble under his attention. "You remember what I told you. You belong to me. Nothing in your past matters. I will be making sure you are spoilt rotten. The way you deserve."

God, his words...

The peaceful finality to his declaration ratchets up too many emotions. The tears I was withholding blink from my lashes, and I grip his hair as he focuses on my pleasure. Dipping to mouth my pebbled nipples again, his tongue laps gently, provocatively. The feel of his wet solid muscle on my sensitive beads rushes to where his fingers work at a methodical pace. I have never felt anything like it. Comfort and calm. Safety and bliss.

All about me.

Every act. As though he can read my body, my heart, what I need and didn't know. He understands the primal desires that I barely recognise myself, attuned to every shudder, every buck, all the rolling motions drifting me out to a place of overwhelming sensation. I close my eyes and swim in an ocean of pleasure, moaning loudly.

Then my pussy grips his reverent fingers, causing him to wrap his arm around my waist and cradle my rolling head moments before my orgasm pours through my cells. "What do you say, sweet girl?"

My head rocks back into his palm as I cry out, "*Sir.*"

He holds my small trembling frame to the hard slab of his, enveloping me in the safety of his powerful arm. As his fingers twist and roll against the muscles inside me, I am so consumed by him, by his words, by the throes of my orgasm, that I start to sob.

I think I love you.

SOMETHING IS DIFFERENT. He's different. Resting my head on the thick swell of his bicep, I struggle with the emotional turmoil inside my mind. I want to dive headfirst into this blissful moment that is him and me, but lurking under the surface is utter fear and the lingering sense of my impending rejection.

Grab opportunity by the balls.

On our sides, my small body in the long commanding cocoon of his, I can feel his heart on my spine, beating away like a powerful, sturdy drum. Slung over my waist is his thick arm, banding me to his torso, and over my calves is his long heavy leg, while his hand cradles my barely noticeable swollen stomach. The emotion hurts. What happens when my dad comes? Will he care that I've been intimate with his associate?

A man twice my age?

Slut. Slut.

Grab opportunity by the balls, slut.

I clear my throat. "Can I ask you a question, Sir?"

His breath warms the top of my hair as he murmurs, "What would you like to know?"

I twist to face him, coming within an inch of his lips, the same lips I am dying to feel again. "Do you think my father will help me with the baby?"

He blinks slowly, a mask of indifference setting firmly on his handsome features. "It matters little."

My brows pinch in. "It matters to me."

"It shouldn't." His nose touches mine, and he draws small circles on the tip. It is so tender. So sweet. "Work on that."

A man like him couldn't possibly understand the weight

of poverty, of having no skills to offer the world. "I can't look after him alone."

He leans back, eyes like blue diamonds, flashing seriously at me. "I have already confirmed that you will be looked after. I don't make idle comments."

My heart grows, but I want to take a pin to it, to deflate the hopeful naivety with which it expands. My head hasn't forgotten the past eighteen years of lackless offerings turned betrayal. "By you?"

"Yes."

"But what about my dad?"

His eyes narrow. "As far as I'm concerned, I'm your everything. Your teacher. Your lover. The only person responsible for you. For your health. For your happiness. For your orgasms. Do I make myself clear?"

Lover... The word sings in my mind. "My lover?"

He sighs roughly while I'm seemingly missing some point, a petulant child chanting, *'But why.'* The tiny seafoam-blue freckles in his irises seem to glow as he says, "It isn't as romantic as it sounds, little deer."

I touch his cheek, the small bristles coarse under my palm but undeniably virile. "No?"

"No." His large hand swallows mine before removing my palm from his face, and it feels like an icy wall is being erected between us. Is it to keep me out? Or to keep him in? "I won't be yours, but you are mine. That is already settled. You will handle this better if you forget about your father all together. The man is not worth your consideration."

I frown, thrown by the way his teeth gritted around each syllable in that last sentence. "Wait? I thought you were friends."

"I said nothing of the sort. We are associates."

"So you don't like him?"

"*Fawn*," he warns. "One lesson you need to learn, sweet girl, is that there is pleasure in acceptance and submission. You came to me. You *trust* me. So let me decide what is best for you." His irises become thin blue rings around a consuming dark pupil. "Now, you need something in your mouth to stop those lovely lips from asking questions you don't need to worry about anymore. Lay with your head towards the foot of the bed and suck my cock."

Air locks in my throat. "What?"

"Your ears work perfectly fine." His thumb comes up to my lower lip, folding down the flesh while his gaze skims the inner pink depths. "You are overthinking. Anxious about things that you don't need to be—not anymore. I need to redirect your troublesome thoughts. Suck my cock until you don't feel the need to ask so many questions. Until you stop worrying. Until you understand that I am here to take care of you. I will do the worrying for you. Let me protect you... even from yourself."

He doesn't mean... like... to calm myself down by sucking his dick... surely that can't be a thing. My eyes widen with realisation. A provocative curve plays with the corner of his mouth. "Do you trust me?"

I nod slowly. "Yes, Sir."

"Then do as you're told."

"Yes, Sir." Pulling the sheets back, he reveals his semi-hard cock. As I move around the bed, he lays on his side and I lay down on mine with my knees curled up and my head in line with his beautiful, engorged erection. "I don't know how to—"

"I didn't tell you to make me come, little deer. I told you to suck until you feel better about your place with me."

I open my mouth, taking the clean, salty tip between my lips without any expectations to actually perform. He hisses

246 · NICCI HARRIS

his satisfaction, and a warm pool of sensation rushes through my entire being. It's nice pleasing him.

Mouthing the tip clumsily, I flick my tongue around the knotted base of his head to the smooth curve at the top. I suck lightly, close my eyes, and breathe through my nose. When a little salty fluid comes out of the tiny slit on top, I moan my enjoyment. I play with him, focus on him, and the questions just... *stop*.

"You are such a good girl." His fingers nestle into the blonde strands at my crown, gently combing through them. "You belong to me. I take great care of my belongings. I know you're stressed about the baby, sweet girl. I am very proud of how seriously you are taking this responsibility. There will be things in your life that only you can control. For everything else, trust in me. I will make sure you never go without. You never *just* survive." He strokes my chin as I work the tips of his head. "You can come up here now."

The hard, smooth tip of his cock slips out from between my lips, and I turn, then slide up the bed to face him again, immediately hit with lust-filled blue eyes.

I shuffle slightly, feeling his cock knocking at my stomach almost like he is demanding further attention, screaming his neglect. "Does it hurt when you... get hard?"

His lips twitches with a grin. "What a sweet question."

"You haven't... you know." I avoid his calculating gaze, forcing the word out. "*Come*."

"It does," he groans, in a way that seems to stifle a powerful, primal urge, "hurt to be anywhere near you, sweet girl, and not be inside you."

I smile a little. "But you operate best under a level of duress, right, Sir?"

"What a promising addition your mere presence will be to my peak condition." A full-blown charismatic smile sweeps across his breathtaking face, and I think my heart just ballooned to the point it will need a new body to reside in. I wonder if he'll share his.

"Well, I am glad to be of assistance to you." I laugh while willing my heart to regain a steady pace as he looks at me with that stunning smile and those soft eyes.

He chuckles once, but the moment of easiness, a slip in his typical calm unaffected demeanour, dissolves as he narrows his eyes on me, as if everything about me is a puzzle and if he squints hard enough, the pieces he can't quite place will slot into place. "Tonight," he says, smoothing a piece of hair down my head, "wasn't about me. Now, I've already let you stay up and ask questions. Don't get used to it. Roll over and go to sleep."

As I turn to face the other way, he pulls me back into the cave of his body. I try desperately not to let that bliss, contentment, and safety flood me. A little is okay. A whole ocean of it, though, will probably result in my head submerged and my reality saturated in everything Clay Butcher.

I failed. I am already drowning in him.

I know nothing about relationships. Of love. From a mother or father or lover or friend. I am a blank canvas without appropriate conventions and healthy dynamics to measure my experiences by... but I know whatever is going on between us isn't what everyone else has.

It is more.

It is everything.

He is *everything*.

He is walking, talking sin. He is patronising and controlling and has emotional amour so comfortable around him it has formed another layer of skin. Condescending. Dangerous. Secretive. Lethal, most definitely. He has blatantly told me he isn't mine but promises me a future with security.

And I am in love with him.

Irrevocably in love.

Invincible.

CHAPTER TWENTY-EIGHT

WHEN I SIT up in the morning, well-rested and surrounded by nothing but the light hum of the air-conditioner, a sinking dissonance slides over me. This is the second night I have slept through without having anything to record in my notebook. This morning, rattling around in my brain is a vast content of nothingness. I drag my hand down my face and sweep my hair over my shoulders.

I blink ahead. Above Clay's desk is a clock, ticking away, with the little hand happily pointing to the nine. I slept in too. Presumably, Clay will be in the City Building, cutting ribbons with big scissors or signing important documents, or whatever a mayor does on a Wednesday before lunch with Jill from marketing. I slide out from his bed and shower. I don't know if there is a Jill from marketing. Maybe her name is Robin or Jennifer. No matter her name, I'm jealous she gets to spend time with him.

"I won't be yours."

His words lay facts down inside my mind before I can

even toe the line of jealous girlfriend. I'm not. He's not. We are something else entirely.

After the shower, I wander naked into his huge dressing room. The moment I step inside, sleek downlights in the recessed ceiling build a perfect glow above the racks of clothing.

"Woah," I mutter, moving between the rows of garments to sit on a black leather ottoman large enough to sprawl out on. To the left of the impressive space hangs suits and shirts, organised by colour and style. In small cubicles below the outfits are his shoes.

On the right—my breath hitches—are *my* clothes... "What the fuck?" More than I bought the other day at the boutique, too. Also organised by colour and style. Despite his procurement of the items, they all still seem to be in my usual bohemian style, but somehow...*not. Boho-chic*, I would call it. I drop to my knees and touch the cute dusty pink slip-on flats in a little black box. Then the tan ones. And then heels. I pick them up, inspecting the thin wrap around leather. "So beautiful," I whisper, a sudden Everest of dizziness rising through me.

"I will be making sure you are spoilt rotten."

A little chuckle slips from my lips.

He is so fucking bossy even when he's not here.

I slip into a cream-coloured lacy shirtdress, with henna style embellishments, and just long enough to cover my upper thighs and slide on the pair of pink flats.

For the rest of the day, I watch Maggie cook and learn a little as she goes about her usual routine. As soon as she finishes baking brownies, I spring from the countertop and search the entire house for Jasmine, eager to share them with her, to hear about her day, to tell her about mine, but despite Bolton having mentioned she is rostered on, I can't seem to track her down. The way things are headed, it is as if we could one day have a kind of friendship, and for the first time in my life, I want to explore that. Be honest. Unguarded.

And although I am surrounded by people, her absence transforms the mansion. It seems larger, and I feel myself getting emotionally lost in the vastness and the hustle and bustle of it. Wincing when I recall that awkward conversation about Cinderella and pumpkins, I realise I haven't seen her since the night of the party.

My heart is slow and a little low, when I retire for the evening, not having found her. Entering his bedroom, I glance around without my awe-goggles on and find it to be equally as soulless as it is beautiful. Wandering around the room, I circle each perfectly exquisite piece of polished blackwood furniture.

My heart sinks lower still.

The only sign this is a permanent residence and not a hotel room is my dreamcatcher swaying under the air conditioner's gentle current. Sighing, I make a mental note to create a pillow stack with his cushions every morning.

Glancing up to watch the clock tick past the notch at the eleven, I frown, knowing he's been gone all day and most of the evening. *Unless...* unless he's here in the house somewhere.

Striding from the bedroom, I head towards the office I saw him in last week.

As I approach the door at the end of the hall, music entices me to stop by another instead. I push the double doors open and see a bespoke television screen spanning the entire length of a wall and two rows of leather recliners set on a small incline.

A fucking theatre.

"Woah," I mutter.

As I walk down the centre, taking the little steps to the lower level, I notice Xander at the front; he's not watching the show flashing in the soft lighting but is highlighting pages in the thick document on his lap.

"Hi," I say, and he twists his head to see me. "Sorry, I didn't mean to interrupt."

"Fawn," he sings, letting a wide, charming smile transform his serious expression. "Not at all, girlie. Come sit with me. Oh, wait, shouldn't you be in bed? I know my controlling big brother has some serious rules in place for you."

"Well, I can't sleep, and he isn't here." I shrug. "So, what's he gonna do." I move over towards him, sitting on the edge of the cushion. I realise the last time I spoke to Xander was in the heat of a breakdown. That he was just trying to help. "I'm sorry about last week, Xander. I was rude."

"You were not." He hands me a stack of papers, and his grin is a thing of beauty, but it doesn't gentrify the sight of bruising below his jaw and the barely healed black eye.

I take the papers on a kind of automatic response, but stare at the colours flaring below his caramel skin. "What's with all the bruises? You don't strike me as the kind of guy who gets into pub fights."

"Only on Wednesdays," he jokes, then nods at the documents clutched in my hand. "Wanna help? Highlight every mention of damaged property due to the fire."

"Is this for Sir's campaign?"

He drops a highlighter down on the paperwork. "You could say that. We need reasons to evacuate the people around the docks. There is a lot of attention in that area now and well, we don't—"

I raise an eyebrow at him, continuing his sentence. "You don't *want* attention in that area." He snort-laughs but doesn't answer, so I point at the television and say, "You're working and watching television?"

"Yeah, I seem to focus better when there is background noise..." His eyes skirt along my face for a moment. "The bruising is from boxing, Fawn. I'm not getting into bar fights in big bro's city."

We talk about all sorts of things, and I'm pleased to find that it's easy to be myself around Xander. He's less regimented than his big brother, although I wouldn't trust him with anything personal. Not like I trust Clay. I'm not sure I have ever trusted another person the way I trust him.

After a few hours, the time must be close to one a.m. and my eyes flutter. The show we ignored the entire time slowly fades from sight. I curl onto my side on the recliner and allow slumber to drag me away from the theatre and out to the nothingness I will my unconscious state to bring me.

CHAPTER TWENTY-NINE

clay

I LOOSEN my tie as I turn the corner, mild impatience rolling up my spine; she isn't curled up in my bed. Bolton texted me with her whereabouts, so I'm not surprised as I pull the theatre doors open and see her asleep on her side with her knees up, bowed in tight like a kitten on the recliner.

Stepping over to the dial on the wall, I dim the lights, drowning the space in near darkness. Only the movie streaming on the opposite wall lights up the area with sporadic hues of colour. The colours bathe her face.

Collecting a grey mink blanket from the back of Aurora's usual spot, I stroll over to my little brother and lay it over him. He groans, flopping his head to the side, his face to the wall but not before I can make out the subtle deformities across his jawline. I grit my teeth, stroking the bruising before brushing a piece of his dark hair from his face. I should kill them all for agreeing to spar with him, but that would only send him to the illegal pits to beat out whatever demon has him eager to give and receive the blows.

After removing the papers from his lap, I twist to my little deer in a ball on her side. Her knees are high by her chest, her arms around them, looking ripe for the taking.

Mine to claim.

This girl makes me want to fuck her perfect pussy until it's swollen and plump from the friction of being mine. Makes me need my cum inside her, dripping down her thigh. Need my teeth marks on her mouth. There should be no mistaking who she belongs to.

I tilt my head, gazing at her white knickers as they flash at me from beneath her hiked cream dress. I never want pain for her again. Not like she has been through already.

Hovering over her, I slide my fingers up her leg, her skin prickling and dancing under my touch. She is mine. I cast a shadow over her petite form. Following my fingers with my gaze, I explore from her ankle to her hip, caressing soft, pale flesh. My cock grows quickly under the sight, touch. I run two fingers between the valley where her legs lay on top of each other until I meet her pretty pussy. The shape of two softly formed lips outlined beneath thin white material. Stroking her plump folds, I watch her hips circle my meticulous movements. Dustin's daughter likes it when I play with her pussy.

Awareness slowly seeps into her muscles, her body reacting to my touch, and then her mouth joins the waking world, releasing sweet, feminine moans.

I clasp my hand over her mouth.

When I dip my fingers beneath the silk that scarcely covers her and tunnel them between her tight lips, her eyes fly open, finding me leaning over her. My fingers in her.

Arousal and a hint of fear blankets her irises before they drift closed again and she takes my thrusts like a good girl. She trusts me. The vibrations of her moans against my palm have my cock so thick in my pants it throbs within its confinement.

Gritting my teeth, the need to feel her squeeze me as I fuck her burns through my muscles. She should be in my room.

So I can take her the way I intend to.

I press myself against the armrest to ebb the beating in my erection while I fuck her with my fingers. Her little pussy weeps around my thrusts, making each inward drive and outward pull easier than the last. My fingers are deliciously coated in her silky wetness. Her tiny hands circle around my forearm, nails digging into my skin as I work her.

I glance quickly at Xander. He is unmoving. Silent.

Looking back at my deer as she takes my fingers to my knuckles, I growl, angry that I must wait to feel these muscles milking my cock. Her pussy pulses and grips at me, holding me in and fighting against me, squeezing me out.

As I pick up pace, scooping and twisting, rubbing her walls as I draw out, her eyes open again. Wide like a doe blinking from above my hand. I narrow my gaze on her, and her chest pounds with nervousness. Sliding my thumb between her arse cheeks, clamping around what's now mine, I press the pad to her arsehole, feeling it pulse. *She likes that.* Still working my fingers, I keep up my thorough exploration of the deepest, tightest parts of her pussy.

Her moans get louder, and I lower my face to the gap between her white-blonde hair and her neck. "*Shhhh*, sweet girl. Don't wake up my brother."

Her dual-coloured eyes glaze over as she rides me. She is close, and so very beautiful when gagged. With her cheeks puffed beneath the tight grip I have on her mouth. Muffled moans. Tears clinging to her lashes under the onslaught of waves of pleasure. Submissive. Curled up.

258 · NICCI HARRIS

I like it a great deal. I watch as my fingers slide inside her through the delta below her arse, the way her knickers hook beside my penetration and grow wet from her arousal. "Your dress was hiked too high when I came in. Lay a blanket over yourself next time."

I lick a tear from her cheek. "Come for me, little deer." On command, her orgasm flares through her, forcing her entire body to tighten and lock onto my fingers. Her back arches. Her nails drag along the cords in my forearm. Her muscles quake. And I keep giving my good girl what I want, reaping all her pleasure from her, wringing every shudder and spasm from her fatigued little figure.

Her muscles slowly loosen.

She sobs with emotion into my grasp. A spike of something similar hits me in the chest.

Goddamn it.

This girl.

This little addiction.

The only temptation I allow myself.

I lean down and scoop her lethargic body into my arms, cradling her lax, weightless frame to my chest. Accepting me as she should, her slim arms flop around my neck and she buries her head into my shirt. Blonde hair falls around us as I carry her up the steps and through the double doors, back to my room.

She is nearly unconscious, but I am so fucking hard my cock is dripping in anticipation. So I lay her on her back in the centre of the mattress, and she turns her head to the side, moaning in sleepy, pleasured delirium.

I undress and crawl up her body, dipping to drag my tongue along the smooth, creamy flesh of her legs before biting the seam of her pretty dress, dragging it up as I climb.

She aids me as I remove her clothes, rolling and moaning

as her new cream dress comes off, her lacy bra and matching knickers, too. My erection swells further, smearing her thigh with my precum.

"*Sir,*" she exhales the word, half-awake for me.

Trailing my fingertips up the sides of her quivering body, over her hips and along the small tracks at her ribcage, I get to her face. Cupping her flushed cheek with one hand, I thread my other hand between our bodies and notch my cock at her entrance.

Her breath hitches.

She pouts her lips with intent, her eyes still closed even as her mouth eagerly begs for mine. For gentleness. Intimacy. Not something I usually offer... but *fuck*...I let her have what she wants. Leaning down, I touch my lips to hers. Kissing her open mouth, I lead our lips in a slow rhythm. Her mouth is carefree, careless, and so sweet, slanting around mine as though she doesn't care about rhythm, only to taste me and have me taste her.

She's dessert.

"Are you ready to take my cock?" I say into her mouth.

She circles my breadth with her slim legs, resting her heels on the backs of my thighs, pushing slightly to encourage me. "Yes..." she moans, husky and airless.

"Good girl. Only breathe my breath, sweet girl. Nothing enters this body tonight unless it comes from me."

A rough groan escapes me as I sink into her, and she arches and curves her spine on a cry, taking me to my balls like the good girl I know she is for me. A young girl I should have never touched, but even God wouldn't dare take her from me now.

The relief of being sheathed within her tight pussy is damn blinding, dark tendrils of desire breaching the edges of my vision. *Madonna Mia.* My hips work methodically between her thighs, pumping my cock in and out, but I keep my mouth tender on hers while she mewls around, gasping every time I hit her cervix, moaning each time I withdraw.

I don't know how she takes me so deep with this small pelvis and that tight hole, but she does. And I know—relish —that each night when I fuck her, I can guarantee she'll be walking slower, sultry, still feeling my deep, thorough thrusts throughout the succeeding day. "*Yes.* You're doing so good, sweet girl. You're taking this really well."

My sweet girl.

My vulnerable girl.

Mine.

I breathe hard, laboured, into our kiss, and she relinquishes all control to me, inhaling my air, sheathing my cock, accepting my kisses, gripping my shoulders like my presence tethers her to the Earth, as though I'm her gravity.

She clutches the tight contracting muscles either side of my neck as I roll and angle but still give her that precious intimacy she so desires—no, deserves—even if it is hard for me to give. I give her my kiss.

She gives me herself.

As our lips move together and her body writhes, I force her to accept me deeper still. Awareness of my feelings, of my fear, of losing her or failing her, sweeps into me like blood on a shirt. My pulse thrashes in my neck, heart punching my ribcage, not unlike it does when I wake from the vision of Bronson tied to that chair. *Violent fear...*

I don't like it.

She drags me from my concern with the movement of her lips... the way they slide over mine, sucking my heavy exhales between them, accepting my command that she will need me like her next breath... is indescribable.

Needing to be closer somehow, I slow down my thrusts,

steady the roll of my hips, and curve her little pelvis as I stay deep. I cup both her cheeks and rest on my forearms to give her mouth more attention.

She whimpers with emotion, and I groan with something similar. The full length of my body touches the entire smooth length of hers—both of us sliding together in our perspiration.

These lips... These fucking pretty lips... I eat at her mouth, the sweetest mouth, with the sweetest questions.

She is utterly soul commanding.

I won't let her go.

I'll keep her even if she hates me after what I do. After the lies. I'll keep her anyway.

With that thought, my balls contract and tighten. Heat bubbles in my abdomen as I tense, thrust faster, milking myself on her clinging pussy. As I angle myself just right, she screams, pulsating with her own orgasm, and at the same time I fill her with cum, groaning and growling because I'm pissed she has made me feel like this.

I can't let her go.

And I can't stop kissing her, slow and soft. Her lips are like—*fuck me*. They are like peace and comfort.

Fucking comfort.

AS I STARE at the ceiling with my hands cupping the back of my neck, Fawn lays beside me, her arm slung over my waist, head resting on my bicep. This is not good. Nothing good can come from my feelings for her. Lead weights sink inside me, as if she has found her way into the very heart pumping for this cold stone soul. I will still be using her when Dustin shows up. I will... She won't be harmed, at least not physically. *Dammit.*

"Did you speak with Landon?"

Her question hits my temples, but I don't react. "Yes. I paid him to leave town," I say smoothly, running the tips of my fingers through her pretty blonde hair. I'm not partial to blondes... *Fucksake.*

"Did you find the recording?" she asks, her voice mouse-like, seemingly aware she is poking the bear but risking it anyway. A wolf, my deer.

"Yes."

"What?" She sits up, her hair dropping down around her shoulders, the long length cascading over her pert breasts. I brush the strands away from her nipples so I can see the way they pebble like bullets. "Where is it?" she presses.

I swipe my thumb over one and she catches my wrist. I scowl at her hand. Raising my gaze, I glare at her through my lashes. *That's mine to play with, little deer.*

She shrinks slightly as I reach for her hand. Frowning, I unclasp her fingers from my wrist and palm a handful of her small breast with smooth authority.

Leaning forward, I take her bulleted nipple between my teeth. She trembles and moans, both a protest and a plea. Feeding her hands up my neck and into my hair, she cups my head, holding me to her.

"*Please.*" She whimpers, and it's both a sweet feminine sound that provokes my cock to want to fill her and a broken desperate sound that contracts my muscles, wanting to protect her from everything. Her own self-discovery.

The truth.

I lick her nipple before releasing it, the tiny tube more red and flushed from my attention. When I sit back, her hands slip from my hair and drop to her sides. "It's gone," I state. "I destroyed it. All that mat—"

"*No*," she gasps, and my fists ball in tight. She covers her sound with her hand and shakes her head slowly. "*No*. I wanted to watch it."

Outwardly stoic, I say, "As far as I'm concerned—"

"What about what concerns me?"

Blood simmers through my forehead, and I grab hold of her jaw to silence her. "If you interrupt me again, sweet girl, I'll lay you over my knee—" Releasing her quickly, I lean back and focus on her incredible dual-coloured eyes as they puddle with tears. *Fuck.*

Sighing my agitation out, crumbling my composure under her sweet gaze, I ground the only truth she needs. "Benji fell. You don't need to see that."

Nodding, the information settles into her gaze, and then another spark of inquiry flares through her. "And the father?"

I grind my molars, jaw muscles pulsing under the pressure while I will that Butcher head of mine to calm. I touch the soft white skin on her cheek. "The man who raises him is his father, Fawn. You will accept that."

She blinks at me. Her line of sight shifts over my shoulder, eyes losing focus as thoughts sweep across them.

I stare at her. "*Can* you accept that, sweet girl?"

She doesn't waver; her eyes are fixed within a memory. "Was it Benji?"

Fuck it. Gritting my teeth, I tell her what is best for her, what will keep her at peace. "Yes."

She looks at me, and I bite back a growl when she says, "Was he gentle? Did he tell them to leave? Did he kiss me?"

Fuck! I have never wanted to tear the entire fucking world apart with my bare hands, bring the houses and mountains and forests down. Reap all the peace and fucking happiness from others merely to offer them all to her on a shiny platter.

She can have it all.

Every damn thing.

This lie scorches. It'll scar. But I'll take it all for her. "Yes," I hiss, the words singeing my tongue. I lift my hand to sweep her blonde hair over her shoulder and imagine how I might have taken her the first time. Had I been young and in love with her at the time. Had I been emotionally available. "He told his brothers to leave. That you were his focus now. Only you. He wasn't always gentle because he was too over-whelmed by you, little deer, but he took you thoroughly. He was never going to let you go, so he held you all night, still inside you." The words come out easily because I'm no longer talking about him.

Her eyes move to meet mine, green and blue and filled with trust and vulnerability and, *Christ...*

She squints, panning her gaze over my face in a seeking kind of way. As though she knows I was talking about me. "I wish he was yours," she says, and my heart aches inside my chest. Aches for her.

And I bite back a wince. "*He is.*"

Fuck.

I don't know what that fucking means, but I said it, and I meant it. *He is mine.*

She is mine.

Needing to redirect her from this concern, I say, "I've taken care of everything. I will take care of you. Both of you. Are you worried?"

She doesn't answer, so I shuffle and cup the back of her head, gently cradling her. "Do you want to please me, sweet girl?"

She swallows thickly and nods with hints of uncertainty that instantly make me hard. I stroke my erection.

Her shoulder blades roll as she crawls down my body. I keep a grip on the root of my cock and pump gently as she encloses the tip with her soft inexperienced lips.

I squeeze my precum up with my fist, the rush of sensation making me groan. She hums and licks, enjoying the hint of what I could give her. *Madonna Mia.* I need this.

Need to control this situation.

She shouldn't have to worry.

I don't want her concerned about anything. I gently trail my fingers along her shoulders and down her arms, her soft muscles responding, twitching with delight. Finding her crown, I brush her silky blonde hair with my fingers. "You have been through a lot. Too much. And you have done it all by yourself. You didn't let life break you, but you also won't allow it to embrace you. You're scared. I need you to trust me, little deer. I will do the worrying for you. Let them all go now. All the questions and concerns about that night. Let them all go."

As her mouth gets keener, my breathing becomes heavy, and I drop my head back, stifling the need to growl her name. "You're doing really good," I pant. With one hand in her hair and the other meeting her wet mouth as I jerk myself, I have her completely submissive.

And content.

Closing my eyes, I pump my shaft while her exploratory lips do more for me than any skilled mouthfucking ever has.

The sweetness of this girl... *Madonna Mia.*

I open my eyes and see a sparkling blue and vivid green gaze staring up at me while she mouths the tip of my cock as though my girl is eager for more flavour. I release my shaft so I don't get too close, too feral over the sight of her contently sucking my erection. "You're so pretty. These eyes,"—I use two fingers to brush down her forehead, dropping below her brows, forcing her eyelids shut as I travel over them with my fingertips—"are a thing of enchantment."

I watch her hold me in her mouth for several minutes, exhaustion slowly creeping into her eyes. She rests her head on my abdomen, batting her weighted lashes with her mouth still enclosing my cock. Perfect. She's perfect. "That's enough. Come up here."

CHAPTER THIRTY

A TORRENT of pain blazes through my lower back, and I cry out, rolling over to get away from the cause, but it's inside me. In my mind, I know it's happening *inside* me. No matter how hard I fight to get away from the perpetual stabbing at my spine, it stalks along in my wake, like a man hovering over my crippling body with a knife, plunging it into my back.

There is no such man.

I crawl to the bathroom on my hands and knees. Pressure bloats around my lower spine, sending shooting stars into my vision, while the need to get to the toilet keeps my tireless knees and hands sliding along the floorboards.

Muscles inside me spasm.

Nausea fills my stomach.

And I'm no longer on my knees but lifted. Flipping in pain as strong arms carry me into the shower, I'm so confused by the moment. All I can feel is the devastating agony.

It is all I have room for.

Sir...

The spray of the water hits my head, and he slides down to the marble tiles with me in his arms. My legs folded like a pyramid over his, my head in the cup of his elbow.

I writhe.

Cry out.

Another burst erupts, and I scream so loud the sound continues to beat off the walls long into the next stabbing sensation, and the one after that. Or maybe I haven't stopped screaming. I don't know what's happening.

"Help." Is all my throat has the energy to say between bursts of guttural sobs and screams. *"Help."* Trembling hands that belong to me reach to cup the pain.

Then my back rips down the centre and my body opens. I reach for my core and bring my hand back. The sight of strings of blood drags another scream from me.

As I wail at the viscous rouge fluid webbing my fingers, Clay pushes my hand from view. He cups my cheeks, directing my pooling eyes to his piercing blue orbs, a stark sight amidst the dread blurring my vision.

"Don't look, Fawn." My name. *Don't look.* The combination of those words twists my heart.

I sob. *"Sir."*

His brows draw in, and he grits out, "It's going to be okay, little deer." He pulls me in tighter, and my back convulses again, my thighs forced wider by contractions. Pressure detonates at my core, in my sides, all across the nerves attached to my body. They fire all at once like rockets inside my central nervous system.

"Goddamn it, Fawn! *Fuck,* I've got you. Breathe for me. *Breathe.*"

Blinded by the pain, I squeeze my eyes shut, panting, and howling through the agony, the immense pressure. My hands fist. My nails stab my palms. And I can't control the tightening of my muscles. Clay pries my fingers apart, placing his arm into my grasp, so I can shred his skin instead.

Then I feel the swelling inside me drop. *Leave* me. And the pain ebbs to a dull throb. The finality of it... of that *passing* sensation, of less pain, hurts so much more.

I wail as the reality of what just happened slips through the gaps between my dwindling pain. The cramping now like broken promises and the ruins of possibilities.

Clay buries my face into his chest. "Don't look." My nails are embedded in his forearm, while his big, warm body lulls me, rocking with me back and forth. "This is the last thing, Fawn. I swear it! The last thing. I will drag God himself to Hell before I let you hurt again."

The feel of being so empty and hollow assaults me, and I dare not glance between my thighs because I know what I'll have to witness, what I'll have to acknowledge. Fourteen weeks of delicately constructed life reduced to a blob, a crimson mass. I didn't want him anyway...

Clay's warm hand pushes my wet hair from my face as the warm spray soaks us, mingling with the blood puddling around our bodies. I didn't want him anyway...

Clay presses his lips to my forehead. "It's okay, sweet girl. Everything is going to be okay."

I didn't want him anyway.

Bad things come in threes.

Her suicide: number one.

His murder: number two.

My miscarriage: number three.

CHAPTER THIRTY-ONE

THE MINUTES FADE INTO HOURS, each and all passing by like seconds. The agony. The miscarriage. His arms. Sirens. An ambulance and this hospital bed, wheeled from one room to another under the strip lighting, a stream of glowing yellow to my unfocused gaze.

Shadows of people lean over me.

Muted conversations.

They give me a sedative; I know that much is true, and I give in to its loving pull, embracing the darkness that swims directly into my bloodstream.

Then there is just him.

With my eyes still shut, my mind balancing on the cusp of consciousness, I feel his fingertips slide across my forehead. The soft scent of his cologne, the earthy musk of his skin, and the subtle aromatics of cigar smoke fill the room with his presence.

His touch trails down my cheek, igniting my skin. After he traces the shell of my ear, he tucks a piece of hair neatly behind it. The sedative is strong as it drags my mind back.

And.

Forth.

From blackness.

To his gentle strokes.

And back again.

His fingers find me in the abyss once more. They caress down the side of my face, replaced quickly by his knuckles continuing to stroke. His thumb flicks out to run the course of my lower lip, and his touch is so... chaste. I love him. It's not a small, blooming love. It's explosive. Tremendous. And devastating.

His touch burns with this unrequited love.

With my eyes still closed, I mumble, "You have a family, Sir." My mouth strains around each word while my mind refuses to settle on a state of consciousness. "You say you weren't home, that you didn't grow up with them, and that is your excuse for..."

I don't know if I'm even talking aloud or if I'm dreaming this verbal heave of insight.

I chuckle. "*Straight lines* and *pressed shirts* and *three meals a day. No cake without dinner.* Don't say sorry unless you mean it. *Conventions.* And, yes, Sir. No, Sir... but what I think, Sir, is that you don't *want* a home because you don't know who you are outside of business. You don't want to have a family around because you don't know how to behave unless it's *Big Mafia Boss Butcher*. Sir, you're institutionalised. You don't know how to be... just Clay... just, *iddy-biddy* Clay Butcher." I hum my amusement again, still talking in a kind of sleep and drug-induced stupor. "Xander wants to impress you, ya know? He is dying to be noticed by you. Do you see him? I see him trying *so* hard... I think those bruises, the fights, they are for you. To get you to notice... I see myself in him. I know what it's like to beg for attention. I have spent my whole life trying to get noticed and no one did until I got pregnant with an important man's grandson and now... You don't appreciate what that means, Sir... to a girl like me. I was hoping my dad would notice me... I was hoping he would take me, too, ya know? *Take us.*"

Only some words reach my tongue, the others lost to the grasp of the sedative. "But now, now I'm your burden, Sir. And you will push me aside, too. For business."

My head rolls to the silence.

To his reverent touch that hasn't left my cheek, warming the cool skin with his worshipful caress.

That is all that passes me by.

Then, after seconds or minutes or hours have passed, his words meet me somewhere in my deep world-avoiding slumber. "You want me to be *just* Clay?" he says softly, as though he isn't sure if I'm conscious, and perhaps he'd prefer me not to be. "Okay, sweet girl. You asked me once why I couldn't sleep." In my mind, I frown at the sound of his strange tone. Detached. Chilling. "I told you I was afraid of failure, sweet girl, and you looked at me like I was out of my goddamn mind. A man like me clearly doesn't fail." Within my unconscious state, I hear his desolate chuckle. I don't like it. "Truth is, I fail a lot, little deer. I fail everyone besides myself. I'm a selfish fucker like that. The woman I have spent most of my life with is a prisoner of the *Cosa Nostra*. *My prisoner.* She either leaves and loses everything she has a right to, or she stays for the scraps of her legacy. It isn't my choice.

"My brothers... I was never there for them. I don't know how to make that up to them. I don't think there is a way. Xander has pain that I know nothing about, and I'm too stubborn to ask or allow him to dwell on such a thing. The Butcher in me wants to knock it from his skull and tell him to toughen up. I know that's wrong, but I can't change the way I am.

"Max. He closed off a long time ago. I barely even know the man he has become.

"Bronson. I left him with the weight of being what I should have been. I left him to look after them even though I promised him once, many years ago, that I would get him out. But I never did. He lost part of his sanity to this business because I couldn't keep my promise. And he nearly died tied to a chair while I drank whiskey and laughed at my own brilliance. I thought I had it all figured out. I didn't. I failed them all.

"And you, sweet girl. I have failed you now, too. If I wasn't such a selfish bastard, I would have organised another ultrasound so you could see the heartbeat that I saw. I should have twisted the screen that first time. I should have... Perhaps we would have caught something. And if I didn't owe my brothers so much for my absence, perhaps I would have taken you and the baby and left the city, little deer. Given you everything that a beautiful, resilient girl like you deserves from a man like me who has it to give. Perhaps I would have left this life for you. Been comfortable, being comfortable. With you. And him. Perhaps... but we'll never know."

I COME to on a hard mattress with a needle channelled beneath the skin on the back of my hand and the sound of beeping and shuffling feet. There is a bit of pain. No more than my monthly period. No lingering reminder of the baby.

Just nothing.

No Benji.

No baby.

Both are just gone.

Awareness spills into my heart; I was going to keep him. Maybe I could have gotten a job just like Jasmine did, find a little house on a cul-de-sac where he could ride a green bike with the tassels on the handlebars. I could have learned to bake. It doesn't matter what. Cakes. Scones. I'd have taught him, too, when he was big enough to crack the eggs for me. I could have done it. I don't feel useless anymore. I don't feel unworthy. I think I felt optimistic... resilient.

Just like Clay said.

Now though... No baby. No recording. No Benji. The whole event bled from me in that shower. The only sign anything happened is the thick pad I can feel between my legs and the cramps reminding me I'm soon to be even more hollowed out.

It is as if Benji and I never had a relationship, never made love, never cuddled after, no memory or consequence to hold on to. Now that I know it was him, that we made love the day he died, I try to imagine his smile when I told him I was pregnant. That we are connected in a very special way. And then I imagine him feeling this loss, too. So, it isn't another death, like my mother's, that I am left to feel the loss of alone.

Maybe wherever he is, he's sad, too.

With a reluctant sigh, I blink in rapid succession until my eyes adjust to the room. The sun cuts through the space, slithers of rays lighting up the dust as they float in the air.

Through the window, I can hear the soft coo of birds and the low drone of the normal humdrum world. Circling the back of my skull, a recent conversation, either a dream or—

"Little deer." Clay's deep timbre carries across from my right, and I roll to chase the sound. He straightens from his chair, his white shirt rolled up to his elbows beneath a black vest. After he moves to my side, the look in his eyes as he studies my face can only be described as shattered blue glass, shining as if wet. "Do you need some water?"

"I don't need my dad anymore," I mutter, although I know that entire idea was redundant and stupid for a while. When I stepped through that gate two weeks ago, I had no idea what would become of me. I never knew who he would become *to* me. I might have avoided falling, drowning in him, tumbling helplessly in love with the most unattainable man in the world.

What right does a girl like me have to be anywhere near a man like Clay Butcher, anyway? I know what it was... a sense of responsibility and pity on his part that tethered us together. That and my pretty body. And since love can't be found in pretty things alone but in lasting connections— ours washed out in the shower—it is only a matter of time before he casts me aside like everyone else does. I won't be cast aside—I'll step aside.

I roll away from him and face the window, cuddling my waist. "I don't need you either, Sir." It's a strangled lie. But I refuse to be his pretty little burden.

"Clay," he grounds from behind me. I blink at the beam that slices through space like an ethereal light, taking with it another piece of my existence, another piece I didn't know I wanted until I had it. And him, too.

Closing my eyes, I breathe deeply and feel my mind swimming in the past months of fatigue. I pretend to sleep, and my heart slows to a steady, boring beat. I hate it.

I hear him move and sit down on the chair on the other side of the bed. I wonder if he has slept at all... although I know the answer is *no*. After all, he operates best under a level of duress.

Over the next few hours, he doesn't force me to speak or

move or acknowledge him, letting my meek tantrum go unpunished, leading me to believe he has already started to care less...

Doesn't feel the urge to call me out on my behaviour. On my lie that I don't need him.

A whooshing sound precedes gentle footsteps and a hushed voice. "Here." Aurora's gentle cadence dances around the room, pulling me from my half-slumber. "I got you a coffee. Has she woken up at all?"

"On and off," he states, disembodied.

I hear her sigh. "You can bring her home, you know? The doctor said she doesn't need to be here."

"We will leave soon."

"She'll be more comfortable in your bed."

"I doubt that."

"*Clay*," she drawls, his name soaring with sad understanding through the air. "It wasn't anything you did—"

"That's enough."

My throat tightens. Does he blame himself for my miscarriage? It didn't even cross my mind that he may harbour guilt, and for what?

"Jasmine has packed a suitcase for her," he says, and I suck a sharp breath in, feeling sadness like a swamp rising around my feet. I was going to leave anyway, so it's good he has made this easier. It's really fucking convenient, actually. Now I don't even need to pretend I am here for any reason other than the pregnancy... I don't need to pretend... Defiant tears rise behind my eyes, and fill my throat, tightening it. I want to scream into the pillow, but he continues, "I've told Vinny that you will lead discussions with—"

"What have you done?" she cuts in, and I can almost hear the steam bursting from his ears at the audacity of being interrupted. I don't care, though. I wish I could fall asleep; wish I didn't have to listen to him discard me like—

Strained exasperation leaves him on an exhale. "I am delegating, Aurora. Isn't that what you advised me to do?"

"They won't respect—"

"They damn well will respect you, Aurora!" he snaps, and I don't think I've heard his voice break in that manner before. Not steady and measured at all. Twisted like a live wire, sparking at the edges of his resolve. I want to shuffle from the mere sound of it, feeling acutely awake now, but I'm nervous my movements will bring a fresh wave of pain.

His voice deepens and lowers as he says, "You are *my* wife and *goddamn Cosa Nostra* royalty. That stands for something. You need to stop this nonsense. Jimmy is dead. You are his legacy. Demand respect from them."

"Where will you take her?" Aurora asks with a sigh.

"I'll be taking her away for a few days," he states, and I sit up immediately, twisting with wide eyes to face him, finding his sharp, knowing gaze already trained to mine. "You breathe deeper when you are asleep, little deer."

"Where are you taking me?"

Aurora risks a quick glance at Clay before looking at me again. "I'll take my leave," she says, smiling softly. "I'm sorry for your loss, Fawn. These things are never fair."

"I didn't want him anyway," I mutter, but the strangled sob that breaches my throat betrays that obvious deflection.

"Tough little thing, aren't you?" She walks through the door, saying, "You would have been a force to be reckoned with if you grew up in our world. Where you belonged."

Where I *belonged*? "*Belong...*" I whisper, playing with the syllables, the phonetics.

I set my eyes on Clay once more. My heart skips a beat, no, an entire track, at the sight of him. He's leaning forward on his knees, hands clasped together, cradling his chin, blue flakes in every hue glowing within his eyes. I'm not sure if my heart will find its way back on the same tracks when he is gone. Forever hurtling through the wasteland inside me where he used to reside. A glimpse of affection—a*t every-thing.* "It's only a matter of time before you tell me to leave. Why can't we just get it over with?"

He rises to his feet in one smooth movement, and I hold my breath as he approaches me with those powerful, measured steps. "I won't be asking you to leave."

"*So...*" A sad derisive laugh breaks from my lips. "You're married to the business, Sir. Not to mention literally married. What am I?"

His knuckles stroke lines down my cheek, and I close my eyes to fall further into the intensity of that sensation. "You belong to me, sweet girl."

Belong.

I remember when I thought that belonging to him would be the sweetest of existences, and I was right. A girl like me should be content just having tasted such sweetness, but it makes little sense. And I'm a survivor first but tumbling helplessly behind that is the dastardly trait I inherited from my mother—hopeless romantic.

"Why?" I hear myself ask. I flick my eyes open, crashing with the intensity in his. "Why? I have nothing to offer you, and you have everything. I get you felt responsible for me before, but without the baby, I just don't buy it. What do you want from me? Because I'll be honest, Sir, I won't survive much more of this. You're saying things you don't mean and making me stupidly hopeful for a future with you in it. You are making me weak. Reliant." My throat clogs up with tears, my voice stuttering, emotion rising to a panicked crescendo as the truth falls from between my lips. "I won't survive the

280 · NICCI HARRIS

day you drop me, Sir, because my entire world is starting to centre around you, and I'm fucking scared that I'll have nothing left inside me once you pull yourself out! So, tell me. Tell me why! Why me!"

Possessiveness ghosts across his eyes as he lifts his hand to clasp my jaw, before leaning down and pressing his lips to mine, soft, warm, safe; a lingering kiss that seems to branch out to every cell within me. His deep, rumbling hum pulses through me. His mouth feels like a gift.

Even after he breaks away, straightening, I'm left with waves of dizzying euphoria. "Do you remember what you said to me when you were sedated, sweet girl? The way you *mocked* me." I swallow down the lump that forms as his eyes shift dangerously over my face. "I told you that if you didn't like something, to use your voice. You did. And you were right. I don't know who I am outside of this business. I've spent my whole life on one path, with one destination. I have known exactly what to do and where to be. I knew every turn." His brilliant blue gaze softens, and I see him... I see *Clay*. "*Fawn*. Why you? Because when I'm with you, my sweet girl, I'm lost. And I quite enjoy that."

Sentiment holds us entranced until a man wearing a white coat and one of those bouncing rubber pocket watches strides through the door. I break eye contact to peer over Clay's shoulder as the man suddenly stops, seeing Clay towering over me. "Sorry. Should I come back, Mr Butcher?"

Barely heeding him, Clay keeps his eyes locked on my face, saying, "No. Now is fine, Price."

The nervous-looking doctor approaches my bed, stopping at the foot and resting his hands on the railing. I cuddle my waist protectively, not having pleasant experiences with men in uniforms. Clay's brows furrow as he assesses my defensive response. "How do you feel, young lady?"

"Miss Harlow," Clay states, a subtle bite to his words.

The doctor laughs once through his nerves. "Sorry, of course. Miss Harlow, how do you feel today?"

"Fine," I say with a sad shrug, but it is just a little drop in the ocean of all the emotions I am awash with now. "Normal."

"I'm very sorry for your loss. We looked at the boy. He was small. It was nothing you did, and nothing could have been done. Our bodies know when things aren't right," he says, and I try to fight the roll of my eyes. It is such a line. So, my baby wasn't right? Cool, thanks for letting me know. I feel so much better now. "You'll be bleeding for a while. Ultimately, you're just having a heavy period. Do you have supplies?"

Clay answers, "Yes," and I try not to glow crimson. God, please tell me he didn't buy me tampons. Aurora bought them, surely. I can cope with that. Flashing behind my eyes is the image of Clay Butcher purchasing tampons like he does stocks or illegal weapons, with effortless authority. Well researched. Tested. Measured. I inwardly cringe, turning towards the window as my embarrassment creeps up my neck and envelops my entire face.

"I'll leave you to it then," the doctor says, offering Clay his hand to shake, but when Clay ignores his gesture, turning his attention to me, the doctor pretends he didn't and walks from the room.

Worrying my bottom lip, I peer back up at him, meeting the blue gaze of the most powerful man in the city, maybe the country. "You brought me tampons, Sir?"

"Pads, actually." My hands meet my face as my cheeks engulf in fire, but he doesn't allow me to dwell, saying, "You will let me take care of you how I see fit. That isn't a request."

CHAPTER THIRTY-TWO

MY ABDOMEN COILS AND THROBS, never letting up with the reminder I'm having my period for the first time in months. Skipping along with the discomfort is the fact that my bags are in the boot, and we have been on this country road for an hour, heading to an unknown-to-me destination.

I've never even left the District.

I might have been excited if I could feel more than the sadness clouding my mind, sitting heavily atop all other thoughts.

As I look down at Clay's hand on my thigh, his fingers dipping into my skin in a gentle, commanding hold, I reach for happiness, for excitement. I remember wanting this moment, wanting to feel someone strong and dependable put their hand on my thigh. An indication the relationship is real. It *is* real. I wish I could appreciate it more but the swing of my mood only sways from sad to guilt and back again.

I peer back out of the window, trying not to let my emotions show, trying to veil them in a mask of fatigue. Clay stares at me; the feel of his gaze is everything and so much more, but not enough to ebb the hormones firing through me.

The road is hilly. I have never seen trees so high they weave above the road, creating an organic canopy, only breached by strobes from the sun. It's so fucking beautiful, and as we veer left onto a dirty road, a bespoken wood and stone house stands in the distance.

We cross from dusty red roads into lush greenery and manicured gardens, and I can't silence my mother's voice in my head as she lectures me about sustainable water protocol.

"What is this place?" I ask, my knees pressed against the passenger door as I gaze through the tinted glass. We are approaching a lavish manor-style homestead that looks like it's plucked straight from the country in England and dumped in the District's outback. Through the vast glass frontage, a fire dances from within a floor-to-ceiling stone hearth. "Do you own this house?"

Following my gaze out the window, as though to check the subject of my inquiry, he says, "Yes, sweet girl. I used to come here when I needed to get away from the District. I haven't for many years, now. Do you like it?"

I sigh. It reminds me of a house I saw on this renovation show, where the owner was a carpenter, and he made the entire thing out of trees from his property. It took him ten years, but the house was so detailed, so unique. Luxury meets charm. I like it. "Well, yeah. I do. But it doesn't scream Clay Butcher. It actually looks like it might be comfortable —*shock horror*. Quick get the kids into the shelter because the world must be coming to an end."

He hums his response to my joke. The car pulls into a large garage with stone cladding, the roller doors on automation, opening before us and closing behind. "*My world, perhaps—my work cannot end in the city,*" he says, unclipping his belt just as his door opens, his personal assistant, Que, on the other side. "And as you so eloquently pointed out, all I am is business. Well, I rarely have anything more important than the business to prioritise."

He steps from the car and the door closes on his shadow. It's suddenly quiet. And even a metal sheet separating us fills me with an urgency to get out and into the same air as him.

Breathing deeply, I watch him circle around the back and open my door. He leans across me, enveloping me in that scent that is all *him*, and unbuckles my belt. "And now you do?" I ask as he straightens outside the car. When I step out, I come within an inch of his formidable wall of muscles.

"And now I do." Staring down at me with undeniable affection and flickers of immense possessiveness, he entwines our fingers. Leading me through the garage, he guides me into the house. Flanking us are two of his henchmen carrying our luggage. I really wish I knew their names.

Awe arrows through me when we cross the threshold, stepping into the cavernous space adorned with polished wooden walls, floors, and exposed rafters. It reminds me of a log cabin, only on steroids. It's wondrous.

On his haunches by the flickering fire, Henchman Jeeves places a log within the hearth. The wood below cracks. He jerks to his feet when he sees me, his face solemn, his brows drawn in as his eyes meet mine. "I'm so sorry, Fawn."

"Miss Harlow," Clay demands, and I feel his fingers tense around mine. Not a twitch of restraint. Dead still.

"No." I squeeze his fingers between mine. "Fawn. Fawn is fine. I can choose what people call me."

Clay darts his eyes between us while Henchman Jeeves

seems to shrink a few feet. I think I'm taller than him now. Clay's gauging gaze levels the situation, the disapproval ripe on his chiselled face. Then he drops his attention to my lower abdomen. His jaw pulses. "No, you can't. But I'll allow it when you're alone."

Unlacing our fingers, he moves towards the kitchen. His signature nod directs my gaze to a golden-haired lady rolling dough on the wooden countertop. "This is Julia. She will make you anything you wish to eat..." He pauses and turns that tall, powerful physique to face me. "Even cake, little deer. Anything you want."

"*Fuck.*" I half-smile. "If I'd known the baby was keeping cake from me, I would have..." I trail off. The joke burns my tongue. My smile slips. "Too soon."

Glowing eyes the colour of the ocean on a bright still day soften on my face, and although they are no less command-ing, they're filled with deep sentiment. "Humour is how you deflect, but it's just as revealing as if you were to cry. I see you, sweet girl. Whatever you need to say or feel will not be judged. By anyone... if they wish to keep all their fingers."

My heart grows as his words inflate it with that hopeful-ness I fear. But I don't want to take a pin to my ballooned heart today. I think I'll let it float—full of him—for a while. "Was that you deflecting your affections, Sir? With maiming fingers?"

"Such a sweet question. No," he states, walking towards a wooden door with carvings of a grand Marri tree. "It was a very clear warning for my staff."

I look at the lady leaning over the kitchen counter for the flour and then to Henchman Jeeves as he stacks wood. They are both going about their business. I'm not at all surprised. I'm sure there is fear circulating this level of compliance and nonchalance; however, there is undeniably also respect.

He nods towards the open door, and I wander through, sensing his soft commanding eyes as they track my movements around the master bedroom that is finished in wood to match the rest of the house. Our clothes are hung in a walk-in style wardrobe, our shoes placed like tiny soldiers below them. A small smile tickles my lips when I see my dreamcatcher hanging from the left side post of the bed. He misses nothing... or was that Jasmine's idea? I wonder if she knows what happened, I wonder why she hasn't tried to reach out to me.

Still at the door, he says, "A bath is waiting for you. Take your clothes off and I'll be in shortly."

When he closes the door, I do as I'm told, skating my fingers along the wood as I make my way into the bathroom. In the centre is a free-standing bath with shiny claw feet.

Breathing in deep, I strip and step into the warm pool of water as steam drifts from the rippling surface and hangs in the surrounding air. Sinking down into its depths, the water rising to just over my breasts, I lean my head back on the lip and close my eyes. The warmth and buoyancy lessen the pain in my abdomen. I hum my enjoyment.

Hazing through my mind are sparring emotions, wanting to both be in awe and love but also curl up in silence until I don't feel so raw about everything that has transpired.

The baby was Benji's.

No butterflies at all.

I haven't felt a single flutter since before writhing in pain on the bathroom floor. Butterflies, dead. Benji, dead. Baby, dead. "You're a survivor," I mutter to myself.

It is not long before I hear the wooden door rattle on the hinges as it opens, and footsteps move in that graceful, measured way that only Clay Butcher can pull off with a six-foot-five physique.

"I was going to keep him," I say, opening my eyes and sitting up to find him pulling a chair over to the bathtub. He is still in his neat pants but has lost the tie and jacket. His shirt unbuttoned and casual, the sleeves rolled up to his elbows, revealing cords of veins, curves of muscles, and scratch marks from when I clawed him in the shower.

"I know, sweet girl." He picks up a loofa and lathers it with soap scented like coconut before brushing it gently down my shoulders and chest.

I shake my head in confusion. "How did you know, Sir? I didn't even know."

"You knew."

He's right. I did. As he washes me, I can't stop noticing how I used him as a scratching post and how he has more evidence of my miscarriage than even me. I reach out and grab his forearm, inspecting the gashes that would have wept with blood. He holds still, letting me look. "You look like a feral cat attacked you."

"A sweet little deer, actually," he says, his voice deeper, more gravely, while afflicted with fatigue. I presume he hasn't slept for days. It's an incredibly sexy sound; sleepy Clay Butcher. Gruff. Husky. Yummy.

"A *stray* deer," I mutter, releasing his forearm.

His hand dips, breaching the warm surface, sinking to cup my abdomen. Even as tiredness moves in waves through his irises, they are no less controlled, no less attentive. "Is that self-deprecating behaviour going to return?" he says. "I thought we were making progress. Do you need a repeat of what I did in the car?"

His hoarse tone, wrapped in sleepy huskiness, reaches deep inside me. I think about the sting as he spanked me. Shook my body. Sent waves of sensation to my already beating clit. Then I remember the way I felt in the wake of that moment. The subtle burn. A feeling of safety. Accountability. The way I trusted him that little bit more... "Do you think I need it, Sir?"

He strokes my empty abdomen as though his tenderness can fix the hollowing of my womb. "Perhaps. Are you cramping?"

"It feels better in the water."

He lowers his hands and massages my thighs, deep tissue pressure that loosens and comforts. He's strong, dominant in the way he touches me, but in no way rough or overstimulating.

My eyes bat close, and I melt beneath the meticulous hands of the most intense, dangerous, and beautiful man I have ever met.

While his hands slowly work around my entire body, he talks to me. "When I say you belong to me and that I will take care of you, this is what I mean. You are not a stray. You are owned. I warned you once to tell me to stop. I warned you what it meant to belong to me... True, I didn't plan on keeping you then. I do now. There will be times when you hate me. For what I have to do. I am sure of it. That will change nothing between us. I want you to know that if you try to leave, I will hunt you down. I want you to find comfort in the fact that you have no choice. You are mine. Because ever since I laid eyes on you, sweet girl, that is the only place they have wanted to be."

I look at him. Moaning as he palms my breasts gently, I feel my nipples pebbling against his palm. "You will hunt me down, Sir? Why would I want to leave?"

"I am a sinful man."

"A dangerous man," I agree, pridefully, without a hint of care for the rest of the world because what did they care for me or Benji? No one cared. The system left me with a foster mother who made me feel worthless. The police didn't care enough to investigate Benji's death, to find the recording I now know existed. It must be intoxicating not being the victim. I swallow hard. "I wish I was a dangerous person."

A grin coasts across his lips. "My affections for you make you the most dangerous girl in the country," he states seriously, and I exhale, a flitter of contentment moving into my chest, finding comfort in his darkness. It is potent, that flitter, spreading out like stems, curling into each cell.

I remember my mother talking about reincarnation. About how we turn into a vibrant, uninhibited butterfly after this harsh existence as a weak, humble caterpillar. I pretended my mother was a butterfly the day she shot herself.

But I don't want to wait until I am dead to experience my own reincarnation. I want it right now. In a cocoon of Clay Butcher. I hope that in my second life, I am a monarch butterfly.

They are graceful.

Beautiful.

And poisonous.

I CURL IN, clutching at my lower abdomen as it cramps in an intense droning rhythm. Clay isn't behind me on the bed, but my body screams that his proximity is close. And he is watchful.

I squint at the corner of the room, where a shadow of a man sits, eerily motionless and stiff.

"Are you watching me sleep?" I ask, my voice twisted.

He lets out a rough sigh. "I can't *not*... watch you."

"*Clay,*" I say his name and it feels right in this moment,

because the tormented heat rushes from him is smouldering
—concentrated. He needs something. I don't know what. I
doubt he'll let me be the person who comforts him—if there
is such a position in his life... but I want to try. I blink at the
formidable shadow in the corner. "The doctor said there
was—"

"I don't need your reassurances, sweet girl. You fell from
the bed writhing in pain."

I force a small smile. "*Can't fall off the floor.*"

He continues, unamused. "You managed to crawl
halfway across the carpet before I woke to take you into my
arms. I—" He pauses, and the silence that follows feels thick
and ominous. "I sleep too contently when you are in my bed.
Too comfortable. I should have never let this happen."

"You're not God—" A moan leaves me, and he immediately rises from his seat, moving to the bedside. The mattress
dips, rolling my body towards him.

Clay collects me in his arms, cradling me as he sits to rest
his spine on the headboard. I snuggle into his large embrace,
surrounded by him, enveloped in his long, muscular arms.

He opens his legs, and I slip sideways between his solid
thighs, my legs a pyramid over him, my back supported by a
thick, powerful bicep. My head flops to the side, meeting his
chest, relaxing as I feel the sturdy, commanding drum
within. The arm I am resting on hooks around my waist,
sliding across my quivering abdomen and down to the seam
of my underwear. I catch his wrist, and I feel the rumble of
his growl.

"Little deer, that is the second time you have stopped me
from touching you where I want. I tolerated the first. I'll take
you over my knees this time as soon as you're feeling better."

I blink up at him, meeting his endless blue eyes. "I have a
pad on. It's covered in blood."

"And you think I somehow forgot such a thing?"

I release his hand, and he continues its descent. He grips the thin strap on the side of my knickers, and I shuffle in his lap so he can slide them up over my knees with the pad still stuck to the inner lining. I kick them off quickly, wanting to get the sight away from him, away from me. *God... this man.*

He settles my backside on the mattress between his thighs, opening my knees wide. I let my legs fall apart, provoking a satisfied groan to leave his lips at my submission.

My embarrassment lights a furnace below my cheeks, yet I hide it well, nestling into his chest. His fingers trace my lips, and I'm so sensitive there I begin to mewl.

I peer up and watch his heated gaze follow the exploration of his fingers. When he strokes the smooth skin, he says, "Who did this?"

I look down at his fingers. "Did what? Shave?" A nervous sound leaves my throat, a chuckle waving into a scoff. "I did it. I do it. I always—" I clear my throat. "I've always shaved ever since I went through puberty."

"What colour is your hair?"

I swallow thickly. "Blonde. Light."

"I'd like to see it. Leave it for me, and I'll shave you from now on, the way I like." He hums, deep and husky. "You're just as beautiful here when you're bleeding as any other time. Do you think your blood makes you less appealing? It is very feminine." His breath becomes deeper, carrying a groan. I feel his cock like a steel rod under my thigh. "I'm hard just thinking about sinking my cock inside you."

His forefinger parts my lips, sliding inside me easily within the slick of blood, while his thumb creates little circles around the bud above. I whimper my enjoyment and flush with the unavoidable awkwardness this act brings.

"Don't be embarrassed," he says, his voice strained. I recognise that twisted cadence. It's the same sound he made when he said it hurts being near me and not inside me. It's arousal. "I've had a lot of blood on my hands, but never in such a way. Your orgasm will help with the cramps, sweet girl."

I roll my head on his chest as he worships my inner muscles with thorough, deep thrusts. Massaging the sensitive walls just as he did my body in the bathtub, he adds another finger to better increase the pressure. "That's my good girl. Your pussy sucks my fingers in so beautifully."

I tilt my pelvis to join his motion, and he groans, kissing a trail down my forehead until he meets my eager lips. Cupping the side of his neck, the taut muscles cording beneath my palms, I open my mouth for him, taking his tongue inside me as it mimics the thorough rhythm of his fingers.

Our moans and groans spiral together in a combined symphony. Our bodies work together. Mine, lifting to meet his penetration. His, kneading the aching walls, loosening the muscle inside me, ebbing the contracting.

I love you.

I become breathless in his slow but boundless kiss, in the twisting and scooping of his fingers, in the dull throbbing at my womb. It all heightens the pleasure he is building through me, and I can't decipher one sensation over the next, but it all feels *good.* So good.

"I want to fuck you, little deer." His hot breath blankets my face as he groans into our kiss. "But you're too sore. Your pussy won't be able to take me after what you have been through." Not stopping his repetitive motion between my thighs, he threads his other hand down to release his cock from his pants. "Would my sweet girl like to see me come?"

He hisses into our kiss, his mouth becoming clumsy for a moment as he jerks himself off.

"*Yes. Yes.*"

Then the sharp pull of desire drags me over the edge. I squeeze his neck. My back suddenly seizes and arches with a roll of warmth that continues forever, spreading up to my heart, causing it to gallop within me, all the way to my toes, tensing them into balls.

"*Clay!*" I scream his name. *Clay. Clay. Clay.* I take his tongue, his fingers, his everything. I'll take it all.

He growls his own arousal out as he pumps his erection with brutal force, fisting it and drawing upwards until he shoots hot fluid over my legs. Convulsing beside me, his fist creating friction against my thigh, the liquid slapping my skin, he works his cock until he is empty.

Still holding his neck, I deepen our kiss as he breathes gruffly into my mouth. I tremble with sensation while his muscles slowly relax, but both our bodies melt together.

When he breaks the sultry dance of our lips, he leans his forehead into my hair, and it's so vulnerable that for a moment, I want to scream, '*I love you!*' For an endless moment, I want to whisper, '*I understand I belong to you. You won't be discarding me. You won't let me go. You'll hunt me down. I agree. I agree to it, Sir. I'm yours.*'"

He lifts his head, his eyes hooded with ecstasy. Licking my kiss from his lips, he looks down as he pulls his hand from between my legs, his fingers and knuckles covered in pink juices and thick red fluid, and I don't care.

He cares even less.

After he has cleaned me up, we lay down in bed together, and I clutch onto him. As my mind rolls, delirious on a cocktail of everything *him*, I murmur softly, "I love you, Clay."

CHAPTER THIRTY-THREE

THE SOUND of feet rapping on the wooden floorboards pulls me from my state of peaceful oblivion. For a few moments, I bask in the serene haze of waking from a restful state. And I realise that even my subconscious trusts him—Clay Butcher. I no longer have the nightmare. I no longer fall into the television... or is this my body's way of letting go of what was growing inside me?

I crack one eye open, wrestling with my mind's intent to stay asleep a while longer. Yet, the weight over my waist and the heavy calf hooked over my feet causes both eyes to widen on the polished wooden panels opposite me. He's still in bed with me.

He slept. Through the night...

Closing my eyes, I breathe him in, the earthy, rich scent of masculinity with lingering hints of cologne. I love the way he smells. Not like a boy. Like a man. Staring at the back of my eyes, I recall last night like a mirage of flashing images: the bathtub, the massage, his kisses. Touch. *"I love you."*

Behind the door to our right, the footsteps continue,

heavy steady ones followed by small pitter-patters and then a young girl's voice quickly hushed by a man. Blinking my eyes open, I adjust to the ambient yellow hue that the sun has gifted us this morning. The hour seems late.

I roll over in his arms, but they tighten immediately, making it hard for me to manoeuvre. Within the cage of large, warm muscles, I manage to get around to face him. His breath fans down my face, heavy and warm, with tones of his port cigars. He hums. As he fights against the world trying to wake him up, his brows weave, creating a slight ridge between them. His long dark lashes fan below his eyes. *Why do some men have the most spectacular eyelashes?*

I lift my hand to his chiselled jawline, mapping the dark bristles lightly peppered with grey. Beneath his caramel skin, I see the pulse of his jaw as he clenches his teeth. Everything about this man is firm, serious. Even as he rests, he is a formidable presence. So, I lean forward and press my lips to his before licking the valley between, coaxing him to wake up and relax his jaw.

I'm his...

I belong.

He growls in his chest, and I smile softly at the grumpy response. "You slept through the night, Sir. I'm so proud of you for not fighting it," I tease.

With a start, he jerks me onto my back, holding me captive beneath him. I lose my breath as his lips crash against mine in a punishing rhythm that sends blissful stars soaring around my body.

My ballooning heart rests comfortably, warm and full, within my ribcage while my lungs strain below his heavy weight. It is a pleasurable sensation. Being so close to crushed, but not close enough to hurt or suffocate. Enough to feel the epitome of *secure*.

I moan into our kiss as the length between his thighs presses into my hip so hard it could bruise me with the right pressure. Rubbing his shaft on me, he groans. To experience this man, raw, feral, animalistic and without his practised façade, fills me with warmth. I moan when his mouth attacks my chin and jaw, ravishing my skin.

His hips begin to move in a sleepy way, chasing a sensation, an ebb to his erection, I am overcome with the desire to please him. Like he pleases me. "Are you under duress?"

His lips smile at my neck. "Somewhat."

"Can I please you?"

He drops his forehead to mine, his breath a tumbling wave of heat. "Would you like to?"

"Yes," I whisper.

Rolling onto his back, he pulls me with him, his blue gaze holding a dare, a warning. "I'm going to come in your pretty mouth then. Am I correct in saying you have never done this before?"

My nose brushes his as I nod. "Only with you."

When he raises his hand and pushes two fingers through my lips, a small grin curves the corner of his mouth. He pushes them inside, down my tongue, to the back of my throat, where he pokes hard at the end. I gag a little, my throat closing around his penetration. He retracts his fingers. "What you did before isn't the same thing, sweet girl. Do you want to suck my dick anyway? Gag around it? Would that make you happy?"

I nod, worrying my bottom lip. I really want to make him feel all the intensity I do when he pleasures me, and I think I can do it. A wisp of a nod shows his approval, and with that, I crawl down his body. For the first time in two days, my stomach flutters with excitement and nervousness—my missing butterflies.

Stopping at the first protruding two-pack, I find it too lick-able to resist. I wanted to lick him weeks ago and, dammit, now I'm going to. *If I lick him... does he belong to me?* I lap my tongue out to roll it over the hard grooves shaping his abdominals. The slab of muscles tighten.

As I get to his thick cock, it bobs.

His fingers comb through my hair before he leans up to scoop the blonde curtain into his fist so he can hold the lot in a ponytail, offering him the view he so desires.

Inhaling courage, I take him into my mouth, and he releases a deep, encouraging groan as I flick my tongue around. I peer up to see his blue gaze hooded, his jaw clenched. The breathtaking intensity in his eyes forces mine to close, and I concentrate on pleasing him, on pleasing my man.

I'd like him to belong to me...

A small amount of salty precum slides into my mouth, mingling with my saliva. I use it to further wet his shaft. Exploring the long, steely muscles with my tongue, I flick around the silken skin at the head to the bunched foreskin below. I lap a line up the tight cord beneath before travelling further, tonguing the slit. He bucks slightly when I do that, so I do it again. And again. I feel his thighs tighten. The hand gripping my hair urges me deeper, reassuringly, not forcefully. "That's it. Let me slide down your throat. *Relax.*"

I try to take him in. The veins below his skin pulse under my attention. Halfway down the solid muscle, I hit the same spot he poked with his finger, gagging slightly. Sliding back up his erection, I immediately dive again, this time getting a tiny bit deeper.

He hisses. "Good girl. You're doing so well."

A moan leaves me with his praises. A rumble of my

enjoyment reverberates around his cock, provoking his pelvis to thrust upward.

After a few bobs of my head, I get a rhythm, sliding down with pressure and dragging my tongue along the lower knot of skin on the withdraw, while his fist causes a sting on my scalp.

Tears stream down my face.

His groans become grunts.

His muscles tighten, contort.

"I'm going to come. You're going to swallow every drop I give you. Then lick me clean... That's it... Oh. *Fuck*. More...That's a good fucking girl." He jerks my ponytail back and pushes me down, controlling my head in a brutal way that causes my throat to contract and whimpers to soar around his thick cock with the battering sensation. "*Good... good girl.*"

Then he explodes in a violent rush, flooding my mouth with his cum, shaking and pulsing through the moment, never relinquishing his control over my head. I swallow, but it's thick and powerful shots of hot fluid. I love the indecency of it, the virility. The rawness. I love bringing him that kind of pleasure. I want to do it again.

He groans softly, his head dropping back on the pillow. My powerful man, sated by my mouth. Satisfaction and pride flitter through me as I lick his cock, wiping all the saliva and cum from it with my tongue.

"*Christ*," he mutters. "Your inexperienced little lips fuck me up, sweet girl."

I rise and crawl up his body, settling down in the crook of his shoulder. Peering up at him, I find his eyes closed and his chest expanding and falling in deep movements. "I did good?"

"Yes. Very good."

"Will you ever belong to me?" The question spills from my lips before I even think about it. His eyes snap open. "I mean...It doesn't seem fair—" His brows draw in as he stares at the ceiling. "I belong to you."

A long, slow exhale leaves him, stoking the kindling under my heart, forcing it to ignite with frantic little beats. He gazes down at me through his lashes, a softness to the piercing blue rings. "Not in the way you want, little deer. But much more than anyone else."

I let those words sink in, down to my chest, settling around my heart that expands just for him. *Much more than anyone else.* It's a sweet offering and one a girl like me can accept. More than a crumb. Much more. "I heard small feet before you woke up," I say, gently. "And they definitely aren't Hench— I mean Bolton's."

"Small feet?"

"Yeah, like a kid's."

He sighs his displeasure, sliding me gently from his chest and rolling over, leaving me in the bed.

Pulling the blankets up, I watch him stroll over to the closet, retrieve a pair of faded blue jeans and throw them on. They are slung low around his hips, directing my eyes to the sharp muscle-arrows at his lower abdomen, and *God*, they are sinful. They make me silly, make my butterflies manic. His torso is long and cut to the fine definition of a sculpture.

"You're so handsome." I sigh dreamily.

He sits on the edge of the bed, his eyes meeting mine, whirling with severity. "My brothers are here, sweet girl. They must have found out I came out here and took it upon themselves to join me. Such is their nature." When he presses his warm hand to my cheek, I rub into it, nuzzling, loving the gentle attentiveness. His voice drops when he says, "And my niece and nephew will probably be here too. Will you be okay with seeing them?"

A little ache moves through my chest, but it's not intense, just a meek reminder. I shake my head in his palm. "I'll be fine," I say. "I've never really been around children before, but my tastes are pretty similar to a kid's, ya know?" He smiles, watching my filter-less mouth roll. "Cakes. Cartoons. Pizza. Unicorns. Butterflies... I'll stop."

With a charming grin, he stands up, his hand dropping from my cheek, the warmth missing immediately, and any distance between us right now reminds me of loss. Then he disappears through the bedroom door. His absence brings waves of nervousness. Will he tell them who I am? Do they already know? How many brothers does he have? I know they are like '*the District Kardashians*,' but I sure as hell hope their wives don't behave like them. On the wave of nervousness, outright anxiety follows.

What if they don't like me? Will it hurt seeing his niece? A baby? What if they take one look at me and laugh at the ridiculous couple we make?

CHAPTER THIRTY-FOUR

I SWIPE my hand across my bare abdominals, feeling the muscles twitch and pulse, still loosening from that mouth-fucking my little deer performed. She sucked the sin out of me and then asked, *"Will you ever belong to me?"*

Fucksake.

That, and her *"I love you, Clay,"* have me twitching and animalistic. Possessive. Volatile, and not me at all.

Not careful.

Not fucking neutral.

Knotting my brows, I stride meaningfully to find my family and assess the situation before she wanders out here and into a full-blown Butcher gathering.

Passing the kitchen, I see Julia preparing a platter of fruit and filling carafes of bubbly orange liquid.

Please, make yourselves at home.

Mussing my dark hair with my fingers, I wander, barely dressed, towards the rear sliding doors. Already in view through the glass panelling is my four-year-old niece throwing a bucket of water on Bronson and Shoshanna's

Staffy, Crixus, who is completely covered in mud, probably from the dam half a kilometre down the hill.

He brought the fucking dog?

He can't leave a single member of his family out for even a moment. Hovering near, Max and Bronson watch young Kelly spill more suds on the grass than on the bouncing Crixus.

Bronson, of fucking course, is also drenched from his dark-brown hair to soggy boots, his black shirt and jeans dripping from being submerged. I'd guess he dove in to drag their unruly Staffy from the muddy depths. That dog is free-range… just like Bronson.

I sigh my annoyance, approaching the alfresco, catching sight of the four women in the wooden gazebo to the left. Apparently, it's a fucking family affair. Further waves of frustration billow through me.

As I pull the sliding door open, Bronson's eyes meet mine. "Hello, darling. You slept in. Oh, no—" Bronson laughs, not caring that I'm clearly not pleased by his presence. "Look out, big brother looks cranky."

"Uncle Clay! I'm washing Crixus!" Kelly shrieks over to me, her squeaky little voice vibrating with excitement as the Staffy bounds around with energy rivalling her own. "He was trying to catch the fish in the water down the hill."

I find a smile for my niece. "Throw some of those suds on your uncle Bronson while you're at it, sweetheart."

"It's not our fault we have to force ourselves on you, you grumpy prick." Xander's voice finds me before I twist to see him lighting the barbeque on the porch while my half-brother Konnor unwraps sheets of bacon.

He's not lying. I've taken more on than any other Don to keep this scene, this concept of family normalcy for my brothers and their partners, their children. For the past twelve months, since Jimmy's death, I have kept our business running with minimal disturbance to their otherwise normal existence. Only bringing them in on the Dustin issue, Bron in on the incident with my little deer—a *Butcher* issue.

This legacy is my right and burden.

Konnor tips his chin. "Sweet pad, Clay."

I nod politely at him, before muttering to Xander, "I would have appreciated a text." I stroll across the lawn to the gazebo, smoothing my frown into a polite smile for the women in my family. The absence of Aurora in this moment is tangible; she would have been among them, offering greetings and conversation, smoothing the path for me to follow suit. But my wife is where she belongs, where she really desires to be, managing our business while I manage mine.

I don't *need* to worry.

Although, I do.

I've not made even two steps in their direction before Cassidy's large black and taupe Bernese Mountain Dog appears behind her chair, approaching me at a stalking pace.

Fucking crazy animal.

Clara raises her hackles, her eyes assessing my intentions from her lowered head. We stop in front of each other. She levels me while I dare her to the challenge.

"Clara," Cassidy calls, and the overprotective mutt strolls back to lie beside her owner. I'm surprised Max doesn't have disputes with Clara over her claim on his wife.

"What a beautiful sight you all are." I circle the table until I'm behind Stacey, who is the closest thing I have to a sister. With her rich chocolate-coloured hair and tanned skin, she could pass for Sicilian too. Well, with the time she spent with my brothers when they were teenagers, I imagine she knows them far better than I do. Growing up, there wasn't a single family gathering that Xander's best friend didn't attend.

I kiss both her cheeks.

"Nice smile," she teases, her eyes coasting over mine, apparently aware I'm not impressed by the impromptu visit.

Cassidy has already twisted in her place, her strawberry-blonde hair swaying in the wind, her slim arms wide and inviting an embrace. "Me next!"

I pass Shoshanna as she nurses her son, Stone, gripping her shoulder in greeting. She returns my gesture by patting my hand. "You look different," she points out.

"That's because I'm not dressed," I say, leaning down to take Cassidy into my arms, kissing the freckled skin on her left cheek and then her right.

Clara makes a small humph sound at my feet.

"It's been too long," Cassidy whines. "Kelly misses you."

Releasing her, I straighten. "I highly doubt that."

She feigns shock, her hazel eyes wide with mock offence. "Are you calling me a liar, Clay Butcher?"

"A fibber, Cassidy Butcher," I retort. Not wanting to overlook Konnor's girlfriend, Blesk, the Marilyn-Monroe-style-blonde beside Cassidy, I kiss her cheeks too. "Nice to see you again." She smiles softly, but the slight rise of her shoulder may indicate she's not keen on the Sicilian custom.

Noted.

I know little about her, but she is family all the same. The sliding door running along the tracks strikes a sense of urgency through me, so I turn to see the epitome of a deer in headlights, frozen at the threshold. Her long blonde hair hangs down the back of her muted-pink shirtdress that exposes long perfectly formed legs shuffling with nerves.

"Clara, no!" Cassidy scolds before I even get a lead on the large dog now rushing at Fawn.

Launching towards the beast, I relax somewhat to a steady pace when I see Xander step in front of Fawn, creating a blockage with his body. Clara screeches to a tumbling halt, peering around my little brother's thighs to see the new arrival.

My sweet girl doesn't even flinch in the face of the dog eyeballing her and standing at above waist level. Over Fawn's shoulder, Bolton is a meagre few inches from her back, glaring at the fluffy dog, ready to wrestle it to the grass if needed. He cares about my little deer. I appreciate that. Money can buy a lot from a man, but no currency is superior to affection. I nod at him, and he respectfully takes a few steps backwards.

"*Woah.*" Xander holds his hands up to Clara. "Seriously, you guys need to tie her to a post or something."

"If I tied her to a post, what use would she be? She wouldn't have hurt the girl," Max states plainly, grabbing Clara's pink collar and dragging the hefty dog back to his wife. "She'd just keep her away from Cassidy."

As he passes me on my way to collect Fawn, I fight the urge to growl, talking through clenched teeth instead. "Last chance, then she goes on a damn lead."

Xander sidesteps from my path when I get to Fawn. I cup her soft cheeks, and she flutters her eyes closed, seemingly unable to hold them open when I'm so close. So sweet, my deer. "Do you feel up to meeting my family, sweet girl?"

Her eyes open, wide green and blue, fluttering up at me through lashes like golden fans. "Are they ready to meet me? How will you introduce me?"

"I don't need to. They know who you are."

"Oh." Her brows weave. "Because of my dad or... do they know about... *us*?"

I curse inwardly. That familiar sensation ignites through

me—fear. Fear of *her*. Of my affections. Of what will happen between us when I kill her father. "They know now."

Her eyes flash from mine, darting to the right and then left, meeting the eyes I know are glued to my back and this situation. I watch the slender column of her throat roll under their attention before she finds my gaze again. "Yep, they'll definitely have a few questions."

I drag my thumb over her lower lip that is still rosy, still a little swollen from being such a good girl for me.

Mine.

After everything she has been through, I want to throw her over my shoulder, draw my Glock, and put bullets through anyone who tries to influence her. I want her deaf to outside voices, blind to every manipulative face. I want her ears honed to my timbre, her smile provoked by my mere presence, because she knows I'm the beginning, middle, and fucking end for her and I'm all that matters.

I want complete control.

CHAPTER THIRTY-FIVE

THE ALFRESCO and lawn area is dotted with overhead fairy lights, while the dense darkness of the bush creates black borders around the space. Anything could be within that black abyss, but it's not menacing. It's beautiful and wild.

Music soars around us, "This Town" playing through the speakers. The melodic voice of Niall Horan singing about love. The words remind me of Benji, being children and never saying the things I wish we had.

"*Everything comes back to you.*"

Konnor and Blesk are dancing under the twinkling lights; her high ponytail flicks around as she giggles, not taking him seriously. He tries to teach her the steps Cassidy showed them earlier, but she's not as graceful as Cassidy. He seems to like that more, though, somehow.

I peer across the lawn at Shoshanna and Bronson tangled together in the free-standing hammock. She throws her head back laughing at something he says. He's animated as he talks. I've only known him for a day, but I'm sure whatever he's going on about is ridiculous or completely mad or both.

In the gazebo, Cassidy has fallen asleep in Max's lap, cradled in his big arms like a toddler. Beside him is a baby monitor, but he's fixed on his wife's face. His eyes, stormy grey, study the girl in his arms as though he has just in this moment fallen in love with her, as though he is helplessly *falling*.

"Butterflies, they come alive."

Clay's furrowed brows and tight assessing lips roll into my mind. I smile. There is no doubt that Benji's memory hovers around me; regret and uncertainty do that, keep the memories lingering instead of laying them to rest with him. But... the parts of me responsible for loving aren't his anymore. If they ever were.

My heart is big for Clay

My hands shake for him.

My breath catches for him.

"Everything comes back to you."

At the sound of Shoshanna's laugh, my throat tightens around a knot of jealousy. I sigh, wanting moments of laughter in a hammock, wanting peaceful sleep in Clay's arms, wanting to dance on his feet like Blesk is doing right now with Konnor. They all look... *comfortable*. Maybe I'll have that with Clay one day. But Clay Butcher is at odds with comfort. And I'll take whatever that brilliant man gives me with the knowledge it's more than he offers anyone else. That's enough.

It has to be enough.

The sound of the sliding door breaks through the trance Niall Horan has me in.

"Get back inside, ya, boofheads." Xander blocks the dogs from coming outside with his leg, then sidesteps the tumbling canines, exiting the house and joining us. He walks across to me with a soft smile on his handsome face. "You okay, girlie?"

I nod, pretending it's just a passing question, but his trained eyes can't be missed even in the dim of the gathering night. He means it on a deeper, more visceral level. *"Are you okay?"* They all know. It was in their eyes all day.

Pity.

Deflecting, I say, "I bet Stacey passed straight out."

"Too much beer. She had three pints; that's a lot for her." He plonks down beside me on the bench. "She's usually not a beer drinker."

As the memory of my miscarriage being number *three* throws a rock of sadness into my stomach, I mutter, "Three is the *magic* number."

"What number is that?"

Cringing at my context-less comment, I dismiss it with a wave of my hand. "It's just one of those things people say." He arches a brow at me, not allowing my digression to take root. I roll my eyes. "Okay, *my mum* used to say, *'bad things come in three.'* Do you think that's true? It seems to always be the case."

"*Nah*, girlie." He scrunches his nose and shakes his head, a sweet kind of amusement, that isn't mean, rides his tone. "That's called a self-proclaimed prophecy. It's a dangerous thing."

I frown. "Huh?"

He twists to face me, and I mirror him. "It's like when you think don't trip, and then you trip. Your mind makes it happen or finds a pattern in the sequence of events. When they are just random. Shitty and random, buddy."

I collect up my hair, pulling it down the shoulder furthest from him so I can see his face without strands curtaining him. "I didn't make these bad things happen to me."

"No. Of course not, Fawn. But the number..." He stares across the yard at his brothers, not observing them but contemplating his words for several moments. He looks back at me, an idea dancing in his blue eyes. "Say, if something else happens, does it blow this conspiracy out of the water? Or do you restart? Start from one and just count to three again?"

I keep restarting... I snort-laugh. "It's silly, I know."

"Try this—" His grin widens, a flash of those perfect teeth dazzling me. "Good things come in threes. I guarantee it, Fawn." He hails two fingers, saying, "Scout's honour."

I feel his comment warm my heart, the awakening of that organ wanting one person and one person only. I nod towards the sliding door. "Where is he?"

A sigh leaves him. "Where do you think? His office."

I stand up and walk to the sliding door, opening it and holding it like that as I peer back over my shoulder at Xander. Sitting alone on the bench, he watches his brothers with a soft smile on his face.

For the past eighteen years, I have scratched at the surface of what a family looks like. I've ripped my nails from their beds trying to get to the core of it. Feel it. It's more than dinners and movies and conversations. More than sharing a space. It's effortless togetherness. Laughter on a hammock. Cradling your wife. Dancing. It's in the resting smile on Xander's face as he sees their happiness.

"Hey, Xander?" I call to him, and he slowly turns to look at me, not caring that I'm still hovering near, watching him. "Thanks."

"Anytime, girlie."

It isn't hard to find Clay. I'm used to the never-ending

corridors and hallways of his mansion in Connolly which makes this large five-bedroom dwelling a piece of cake to navigate.

I push the office door open. It slowly swings to reveal him sitting at the desk, watching someone on the screen talk. The burly Italian man addresses him as boss. Clay nods. He must be in an online meeting of sorts. Dressed in jeans and a shirt, he looks casual, but that does nothing to gentrify him. The power he wields is unmasked—obvious. Effortless. It is in his mannerisms. In the easy way he sits. In the graceful beauty he displays. In the unaffected twinkle within his eyes that warns and swoons in equal measure.

I shuffle my feet, contemplating what to do, hesitant to interrupt him, but the music riding the air at my back makes me desperate for his attention. His reassurances that we have *something,* not the same thing, but something that if you squint resembles what his brothers and their partners have together.

"Come in here, little deer," he says without moving; I should really be used to his X-Men abilities by now. "No, Vinny. When have I ever called you little deer? ... Yes. Keep looking into it. Keep the warehouse surrounded. I'll check in soon." He shuts his laptop and turns in his chair to face me.

I look down at my feet and then back up. "Will you dance with me?" I ask, still glued to the doorframe. "*Can* you dance?"

He grins, his piercing blue eyes rolling up and down my body in easy slow laps. "Dancing when you're six foot five is problematic." He looks at his desk and then back at me. "You're too far away."

I take a step towards him, disliking the space between us, too. "Have you seen Konnor and Cassidy dance? They're *incredible.* Like something off *Ballroom Dancing* or *Dirty*

Dancing or *Footloose*." He nods to his desk, and I take that to mean *'slide up here and sit in front of me'.* "Do I accept nods as a response?" I tease, using his words, and the corner of his lips twitch to curve further. I continue, "You know I'm not your employee. I'd like your voice not your nods." I contradict that entire sentence by doing as he silently commanded. Sliding along the wooden desk, I position myself in front of him, and plant my bare feet on his thighs.

He leans back, eyeing me. "Cassidy is a professional ballerina. That's why she can dance."

"*Woah.*" A nasty twinge moves inside me—envy. *What have you tried, Fawn? Well, sweet fuck all.* I just survived. "That explains it then," I say sadly, feeling the sting associated with my lack of talent or skills. "And Shoshanna is a doctor?"

His eyes soften on me. "Yes."

"Wow. Quite a family," I point out stupidly, an unwelcome sour taste pursing my lips. I hate it. "And you, you're—" I open my arms, wishing I would just shut up and not draw attention to the way this is making me feel shadowed. A little grass flower amidst delicately cultivated roses. "The most powerful man in the city. The man who nods and things happen. And I'm... just *Fawn.* Is it okay to be unspectacular? Ordinary?"

"You couldn't be ordinary if you tried."

My eyes want to bounce anywhere but to his face, want to hide my average existence as though he doesn't already see it. I'm impressed by *him.* That turned into a crush and that turned into love. I want to impress *him* so the same chain reaction can occur. "Is it okay to simply find my accomplishments in being a good mother one day?"

He grips my ankles. "It is."

"And that would be enough for... for someone spectacular to *love... one day*?"

He pauses for a moment, and the silence stretches an arm to me, an invisible hand turning my chin until I hesitantly glance back to his knowing smile. God, why am I so needy? Why am I so transparent? He finally says, "I imagine that kind of person would need someone to be ordinary with, sweet girl. I imagine a man who is always striving might only survive by having the *comfortable* presence of someone who grounds him."

"You hate being comfortable, Sir."

His hands slide up my legs, resting on the outer swell of my bare thighs. "I'm beginning to *love* it, little deer."

My heart balloons again, and I try not to laugh as I say, "You know something that's real and ordinary and beautiful and unspectacular?"

"What?"

"Dancing... *badly.*"

His assessing eyes switch. He leans forward, sliding his hands around my waist and down to my arse. Gripping my backside, he lifts me to straddle him. "I'll dance with you."

I tighten my arms around his neck and my thighs around his waist. My heart is so snug in my ribcage, bursting with *him* and *love* and *the moment.* The low hum of the music moves around the room, and he dances with me in his arms.

"I'm in love with you," I whisper into the crook of his neck. "I know it's a stupid word. An *unspectacular* and *ordinary* word, but it's the one that means what I feel. Can I say it to you? Can I say it as much as I want?"

His breath is hot on my neck as he says, "Yes."

On the other side of his chest, I feel his heart hammering at the same pace as mine. I wonder if it's also swollen, like mine. "How do you feel?"

He kisses my temple; it's too chaste, too much for me to

handle. Tears quickly flood my eyes when he states defini-
tively, "*Comfortable.*"

And there it is. *This* moment. *Him.* It wasn't an 'I love
you' or 'you're my world' or even 'I like you a lot.' It was one
word with limited sentiment twisted through the tone. But
from his mouth, it was fucking *Shakespearian.*

Good things come in threes. "You're my number one," I
whisper to myself before burying my head in his neck,
closing my eyes, and feeling his body sway us around his
office.

CHAPTER THIRTY-SIX

WE SPENT two nights at the Log-Cabin-On-Steroids with his family. I can't believe he doesn't spend more time with them. I can't believe how much I laughed, given the dull spasming of my lower stomach all but kicking me in the teeth to remind me every second of every hour that I'm no longer pregnant.

Bronson is a complete mystery to me. On the surface, he's tall and muscular, with tattoos everywhere, but his actions are both goofy and charming. Then Shoshanna says something or does something and he's staring at her. Watching. There is this darkness, this danger, and it's right there below his charming disguise. It is sweltering intensity. Like he'd jump from a cliff, hit all the rocks on the way down if he thought it would make her smile. So, I think, if the Butcher brothers were desserts, Bronson would be Rocky Road —crazy.

Crunchy and gooey.

Sweet and creamy.

Just an enigma of an experience.

It's hard not to like them... all of them, actually. Usually there is that one person who eyes you, who gets jealous—a girl mostly, but that didn't happen. Even the big guy who barely smiles, Max, is hard not to like.

Max would be a toasted marshmallow.

He looks like he could blacken anyone who gets close, like he's dark and hard all over, but then, his wife or daughter catches his eye and he's smiling because he doesn't rule his lips when they are around.

I saw it happen many times.

Xander... he'd be a Ferrero Rocher. A kind guy in a rough world. Covered in a hard layer, dented with bruises, maybe a self-inflicted construct to disguise and protect the softness of his heart.

I don't know what dessert Clay is. I think he's a cheese-board... formal and neat with those tiny dried berries that were once soft and juicy but are now hard and tight.

Sadly, it was apparent he is the outsider, or maybe they have put him on a platform, and he remains there. Always. Like he won't allow himself to be just... *Clay Butcher.*

It is the first day back at the mansion, and Clay is at work, and I'm sitting cross-legged on his bed staring at the onesie with the dreamcatcher on it. I could give it to baby Stone, but I think he's already outgrown it.

It hurts to think about my first and only present to my son being neatly folded, meticulously placed in a seal-lock bag, stored away somewhere safe, sentimental, and... *forgotten.*

I can't bear it.

You'll never be anything.

You'll never be anything other than a heartbeat.

Sighing, I recall Cassidy mentioned her little girl, Kelly, has recently started having nightmares. It's a developmental

319 · HIS PRETTY LITTLE BURDEN

thing, apparently. I wouldn't know, but I might have known soon, might have had some insight one day. Right now, though, all I have is my mum's remedy... a dreamcatcher.

I trace the stitching with my finger, deciding what to do. I will cut the image from the onesie and give it to Kelly the next time I see her. She could put it in her pillowcase or clutch it like a blanket when she tries to sleep. She could throw it in the bin, but at least for a second, when I give it to her, it would have been *something*.

Unlike him.

Needing a distraction, I slide from the room, immediately rendered to a standstill by Jasmine, who is darting away from the door, shying away at the sight of me. I twist to see Henchman Jeeves standing watch a few doors down, his feet a shoulder-width apart, his head following the blur of white and black Jasmine creates when she bounces past him.

He sighs, a message rolling down his breath.

"Jasmine?" I call after her, trailing her down the hall in her wake, but she keeps turning corners. "Jasmine! Please stop."

Then she abruptly halts, and I bump right into her. "You're not the pumpkin!" she spits out, a gust of meaning leaving her but no further context. I step back from her. It takes a few moments to register her words. "You're not a pumpkin. He is going to keep you. You're *his* ... I don't know. But you're not my friend. You're my boss."

I shrink back. Her words tighten my throat. "I *am* your friend... I... I want to be your friend."

"But you're not, Fawn. I will clean your room. And pack your clothes, and I'll help you dress when he takes you out, and I'll pro—"

"Well, quit then!" I throw my arms in the air, hating the fort she is erecting because I was going to demolish mine for her and like hell am I going to just let her suddenly build one. "You only did this to fill your time, right? You were bored. Just quit and be my friend instead."

"I lied," she murmurs, shame and regret set ablaze by her jealousy. "I lied to you. I didn't think you would be around long enough to know that I did... My parents *aren't* travelling. I've never even left the country."

"What?"

"I'm not rich!" she blurts out. "I've never met the *prime minister*. I don't have a boyfriend. My dad works for Mr Butcher. This is the family business. Que, my dad, he worked for Jimmy Storm for thirty years, and now he is Mr Butcher's personal assistant."

My forehead tightens. "Why would you lie about that?"

"Because you were like me," she says. "And I just wanted to impress you or just, like, be someone different."

Confused, I stare at the ground as her words seep into me, but they soon ignite below my skin, annoyance taking hold. "But I wasn't like you, though, Jasmine." I fix my eyes on her again. "I didn't have a father or a family business to fall into or a place to sleep. I didn't get to eat cake and have food spread across the kitchen to feast on all hours of the day... Don't you get it? Your life was—*is* impressive to me, just the way it is. Do you know what I have been through? What my life has been like until this house and Clay. *Hell*. It has sucked arse! You lied to me about your life, when all the while I would have sold my soul for it. And I wanted a friend. I needed a friend... I lost the baby, Jasmine. Did you know? Did you know and still not bother to come see me?" Her face falls, and I shake my head as disdain hurtles through me. "I have to go." I dart off down the hall, only hoping my feet will find their own way to the kitchen, where I can convince Maggie to let me watch her cook.

WORKING THE FONDANT, I use what Maggie calls *'the taffy method,'* drawing it out and kneading it back in, conditioning it. It goes from a crumbly mess to smooth and stretchy and usable. I smile, liking the control I have over it, the pastel red colouring, the sweet scent.

It reminds me of his cigars.

Wiping some powdered sugar from my forehead, a few ribbons of blonde hair stick out from under my hairnet, getting in the way. I channel my mind into the perfect fondant. Grabbing the rolling pin, I flatten it to about 300 millimetres.

"Constantly move it in the sugar, sugar, so it doesn't stick." Maggie chuckles from beside me, her black hair pinned inside her hairnet, her thin but strong arms working on the fondant for the *real* cake. Not the one I'm playing with. This is the first thing I've ever baked, and it doesn't mean I am going to be a *spectacular* wife or mother one day, but it means I have a chance at both.

Either way, I'm occupying my mind by grabbing opportunity by the balls, as Clay so eloquently said. And Maggie doesn't bid my mind much time to wander. Not to the fact Jasmine lied to me or my empty womb or even to feel the double-tap of my heart every time I imagine his long fingers inside me.

I simply don't have time for those thoughts.

Maggie's shoulder touches mine. "*Good,* Fawn. Now lift it using the rolling pin. Just like you practised. And lay it over the cake like a skirt."

The sound of a perfectly confident rap vibrates within my ear, causing my chin to jut to the side in search of the owner of those powerful footsteps. My heart rattles in my chest as he strolls through the kitchen with his eyes level and neutral, focused on the fridge and the beer he is now pulling from inside the door. He twists the top and turns towards me, leaning on the fridge door. I clutch the rolling pin handles while his eyes measure me from the hairnet to the apron to the pink shoes covered in white sugar dust.

"How is Jill from marketing?" I ask breathily, and he pushes off from the fridge and strolls towards me. The rolling pin drops from my hand so I can twist and follow his movements.

I press my lower back to the bench-top, and he stops in front of me, leaning in to grip the stainless steel either side of my waist, barring me in with the formidable wall of muscles commanding his body.

"Who is Jill from marketing?" he asks.

I peer up to meet his eyes. "The girl you have lunch with when you're in the City Building."

Smooth.

I clear my throat under his smirk. "Um, I made this cake. And we made cupcakes, too. Pink for the girls and blue for the guys, even though I think they should be allowed any colour they want, purple, black, red." I swallow my nerves. "Want one?"

Maggie makes a small sound of amusement, saying, "Oh, you'll never get him to eat something sugary like that."

He leans in, nestling his nose between my hair and neck, and inhales. I turn my face, gravitating towards his warmth. "I seem to be rather addicted to sweet things these days. You smell like dessert, little deer."

"It's the cakes, Sir." My legs buckle as my words spill out with a breathy exhale.

He growls by my ear, the gravelly tempo resonating

within my core. His sweet, smoky exhale cascades over the side of my face. "No, sweet girl, it's not."

I reach for a cupcake and slide up onto the counter, putting a tiny bit more distance between his encroaching tightly packed body and my small, shy one before his rumbling cadence forces me to spread my legs for him right here in the kitchen. "Try one." I hold it out. An object to separate us while Maggie is mere metres away, while he's making me feel as if I need him buried inside me just to gain a sense of... comfort. Any other state isn't enough. "I made this one. This one right here."

A whisper of a grin falls to a corner of his lips. "This specific one? How do you know?"

I laugh at him, and his grin grows. "'Cause it has the little channel on the side where I tried to push the batter in with my finger."

He watches me through his lashes as I squirm. Rolling up his sleeves to his elbows, he grips either side of my body again, the veins and definition in his forearms provoking a strained breath to escape me. It's loud; that breath. And he looks at my lips as though he sees it still vibrating from them.

Kudos, whoever made you.

Slowly, he leans down, his lips arrowed towards mine. But then grins, twisting to wrap his lips around the cupcake in my hand, his blue eyes never leaving mine. They narrow on my sheepish face as he circles his tongue inside his mouth, and it is seriously indecent.

My temperature spikes.

"*Shit*," I mutter before clearing my throat. "Is it... is it good, Sir?"

He hums around the bite, the sound familiar to the way

he hums when he is touching me, fucking me, looking at me. I'm delicious, and so is my cupcake. "It is."

Without tearing my gaze from his searing blue irises, I realise Maggie's quick exit from kitchen, muttering something about "tapioca."

I chew on my bottom lip as I place the crumbling half-eaten cupcake on the counter.

Two of his long fingers stroke the little valley where I have my thighs pressed together. "Open for me."

As I open my legs, he moves his hips between them, pressing his hard body to mine and squeezing my breath from me. Placing both palms flat over the black shirt, casing his tight, trim chest, I skim down the muscles pulsing beneath the lush fabric. He dips until his mouth travels down the side of my face, his lips coasting to my ear, a hum reverberating from him as he licks the shell.

I moan, dizzy from his attention. Dragging my fingers over the ribbed muscles on his torso, I realise I can't stop touching him, and he won't stop mauling my neck and ear even though we are in plain sight to anyone who enters. I don't know why that fact rises to my attention. I presume what we have is private... or inappropriate.

"Are you my good girl?"

"Yes, *Clay.*" Getting lost in the way his lips roam around my throat, I release a long whimper. I want him. I can feel the heat spread all over my body like an acute fever. "You're like a virus."

I feel his smile slide wide at my throat, and there is this surreal moment where I'm not sure that this isn't a dream. Like, am I really being kissed by the most powerful man in the District? In his kitchen?

His lips move on my skin as he says, "A virus?"

Fucking full of smooth comments today. A blush warms every inch of my being. "Yes, a dangerous one."

Just as his tongue flicks out to taste my throat, his lips freeze. Gradually, the clip-clop of heels grows in volume. He leans back, and his eyes are cutting blue rings of unbridled lust and heat. He drags his thumb along his lower lip in a menacing gesture that leaves me panting at the impure message.

In my peripherals, I see a blonde woman walk in and stop when she sees us. Quickly on her heels, a middle-aged man appears, his expression bordering on panic. "Boss, your—"

"I don't need a forewarning, Que." She stops on the other side of the large marble island bench, sighing as if her life is a perpetual disappointment. She sets her purse down. "Well, who do we have here?"

For a moment, Clay doesn't tear his eyes from mine, then finally twists, clasping his hands in front. I close my thighs. "My business," he answers smoothly. "We discussed you would call ahead. I'm a busy man."

She waves in my direction. "Yes, well, it appears you are very busy—"

"Mother!" His voice is curt and unyielding, carrying across to her with absolute warning.

I wince... And *fuck me,* she's way too young to be his mother. Aunty, maybe? But at least now I know who to congratulate for making him... *kudos...you?* I should ask for her name or introduce—

Clay cuts into my thoughts as he says, "You forget yourself. You will call ahead next time."

I suck a breath in and divert my gaze to the powdered sugar on my thighs, relenting that now is not a get-to-know-the-maker-of-my-man moment. Electricity crackles around us, almost audibly, as the silence lingers longer than comfortable.

She sighs softly. "I'm sorry, darling. I was in the area—"

"And you're drunk." He nods at the fridge. Then at the man dressed in all black. Without a word, Que grabs a shiny blue bottle of water and sets it down in front of Clay's mother.

Her red lips purse, silent, but her eyes flash with displeasure. "Oh, Clay." She slides onto a stool. "I am not drunk. I had a few wines with lunch."

"And you're avoiding the house because everyone is there. Am I right? You were not in the area at all." He exhales roughly, taking a step towards her. "I want to put an end to this feud. You will try harder or there will be consequences. Now—" He holds his hand out for me to take and I slide from the countertop with his assistance. "You should stay here until you sober up. Go outside and sit by the pool. I will have Que bring you anything you please. Then go home and try to get to know Cassidy, Shoshanna, and your grandchildren. They are not going anywhere. You best get used to it."

Holding his arm outstretched in the direction of the staircase, he signals for me to walk ahead of him, so I do, but I can feel his hot, dominant energy blanketing my spine.

What the fuck was that?

I chance a look at her as he steers me away. Meeting her sharp narrowed gaze immediately, I jerk back to face forward. It seems she is as interested in me as I am in her. If the prickles on my spine are anything to go by, she is still watching me leave. My mouth moves with the greeting I wish had been uttered. *"Hello, I'm Fawn. It is nice to meet you."* A normal introduction to the mother of the man who was pressed between my thighs on her arrival.

He has a practised smile for everyone but not for her. At

least, not today. Instead, I watched him belittle her in front of a stranger—me.

Does he have issues with his mother? She drinks, it seems. There are worse things in life than that, and given his *business*, I find it peculiar that it's such an issue.

We enter his bedroom, the room just light enough to see but dim enough to shift the mood, darken it.

He closes the door behind us. I still, facing the bed, but feel him moving around behind me. I want to ask about his mother. Mine wasn't great either. I stare at the dreamcatcher hanging from the bedpost and then at the onesie folded on the side table. "You don't get along with your mother?"

I hear a lighter flick open, a spark, and the sound of crackling smoke being inhaled. Turning to face him, my breath catches. He is cloaked in darkness, sitting on the sofa. Tie loose. Suit still pristine. He grits a cigar between his teeth and inhales and exhales without even holding it in his hand. The cherry burns like a flaming heart, blazing every time he sucks and darkening as he exhales.

Scoring a trail across my body, his eyes make his intentions perfectly clear.

My knees shake under his heated gaze. "Clay?"

He pulls the cigar from his lips, pinching it between his thumb and forefinger. His eyes are watchful. "Are you still bleeding? Have you been in any pain today?"

I shake my head. "Light bleeding. No pain."

A ghost of a grin touches his serious lips. "Take off your clothes, little deer. I have a gift for you."

My hand finds the ends of my hair. Soothingly, I twirl a blonde strand around my finger. "What kind of gift?"

"Take off your clothes."

Between the walk from the kitchen to his bedroom, his mien has flipped from playful and passionate to dark and intimidating. I like them both, but I can't help but think about how his mother's presence has affected him.

He leans back expectantly, laying one of his powerful arms over the back of the chair, the other holding the cigar to his lips as he draws in the sweet scented smoke. His eyes, *God*, they are so narrow, so arrowed on me, it's a surprise they don't feel like knives cutting deep, getting beneath my flesh.

With trembling hands, I remove my clothes, and then turn to lay them over the bed. With my back to him, I take a deep breath, willing my resolve to stay strong.

I stride over to him, completely bare, the light breeze from the air-conditioning dusting my hair around my face. My nipples pebble and ache.

His eyes are blazing blue rings that glare at me as I stop in front of him, my breasts in line with his penetrating gaze.

I run my fingers up the back of his head, through his dark-brown hair, and lean in until my nipple brushes his lip. He opens his mouth, and I slide my nipple through the slant, but he doesn't suck it or lick. "What do you want me to do, *Sir*?"

He talks around my nipple, his mouth defiant in giving me the attention I need—I'm desperate for. "Lay over my lap."

"Can I see my present before I lay down?"

"No. You can see it after."

"*After.*" The word falls through a heavy exhale. It wasn't a question. My lips just found the word both terrifying and exciting, and my ears wanted to hear it again.

He places a cushion on the other side of his lap. His blue gaze tracks me as I slide onto the couch, pressing my knees beside his left thigh. He widens his legs so when I lay down, my pelvis is on his thigh, my arse raised, my torso supported by his hard quads, and my forearms and head are resting on the cushion he positioned earlier.

His black suit pants are smooth, but at my navel his hard cock bruises the soft, supple flesh. I'm so aroused by being bent over him as he casually smokes his cigar. My heart is a steady little pulse in my neck. My pussy throbs. My hips shamelessly circle on his thigh.

I press against him with more force. Rub. Moan when I feel his defined thigh at my core. The intensity sends shivers along my spine, activating my skin, prickling the small light hairs all over my body.

"Are you humping me, sweet girl?" he says, the sound of his inhale and exhale the only way I can tell he's still smoking his cigar. Then a cloud of sweet vapour tumbles down my face.

I moan my response, stilling my hips but feeling as though they are a rubber band wanting to spiral free. I press my thighs together to fend off the pull, the tug of desire.

"Don't stop," he commands, his voice deep, husky. "Keep rubbing your pussy on my thigh. Can you make yourself come? Let me see you try."

I do as I'm told. Sinking my fingers into the cushion below my head and dragging my body along his thigh. I spread my legs and grind against him. It's dark enough that I don't feel much shame, a dim hue to slightly veil my wanton motions. But it is light enough that I know he can see everything, know he'll like it. The pressure is light, not centralised, not enough, but I'm dripping all over his pants with need.

He sucks on his cigar.

I grind on his thigh.

When he leans forward slightly, I twist to see him blunt out his cigar in the ashtray on the table and retrieve a wooden box about the size of a book. *Is that my present?*

He places it on the curve of my back. "Now. Close your eyes. I didn't want to blindfold you. I am very fond of your eyes, of your lashes, but don't defy me. This is about trust. Do you trust me with your body?"

"*Yes.*" I close my eyes, waiting. Acutely, I listen to the box open, to the contents being moved. I hold my breath until his fingers, wet and authoritarian, slip through the valley of my arse cheeks. His fingers slide around as if in a thick fluid... *wait.* I'm not holding my breath anymore. I start to pant. The thick pad of his finger presses to the hole between my cheeks before massaging the tight rim of muscles. A groan from deep inside me rolls up my throat.

"*God.* Sir. Please."

When he pushes the tip of his finger through the taut muscles, I claw at the cushion, arching my back as a raspy sound leaves me. I grind on him harder.

"This will become your favourite time of day," he states. *Oh. My. God.* Is that his voice? It's thicker, deeper, with a trace of an accent. The same timbre from the night he first took my body for himself, whispering to me in another language. He continues, and I swear his voice alone could make me come. "Every night, when I get home, I will lay this pretty body over my lap, and we will stretch your tight hole until you can take me the way I like. Hard. Deep. You'll soon come from just the feel of my finger on your pretty hole. It'll be visceral."

I shudder over his thighs; emotions war inside me. I'm not afraid. I love him. I love what he does to my body... but I'm intimidated and nervous, and my butterflies are not at flight but instead trembling.

While he explores my little hole, sinking deeper, savouring the motions, delivering me pleasure in slow movements, I twist internally with ecstasy.

God, it feels so indecent in all the best ways. I never liked decency anyway. I never fit in with *decent* people. Right now, I want him to pop his finger out only to sink it back in. And out. And in.

"*Please*," I hear myself beg while my knuckles go numb, losing sensation from the killer hold I have on the cushion.

"Deep breaths, little deer." Something cold touches my sensitive rosette, and I squeeze my eyelids together, wrestling with the innate response to widen them.

I breathe through the pressure as he stretches my quivering rim, and then... I'm full. There is no movement, and that makes it somehow worse. And better. *God,* I don't know. The pressure, lingering pleasure, unnatural and erotic sensation, is a constant.

Still.

Perpetual.

He hums his approval, lifting his hips, his cock bashing my navel from beneath his pants. "Fuck. This looks so pretty inside you." He removes his hands from my body. "Climb off me and have a look in the mirror, sweet girl. You'll like it."

On unsteady limbs, I crawl backwards from his lap. He assists me, stands with me, and leads me over to the mirror. I can feel it moving inside me, and I'm desperate to pull it out, to allow the muscles tautly hugging it to shrink back —relax.

I stop in front of the silver panel and stare at the naked girl with blonde hair hanging far too long and nipples standing like hard peaks.

Clay Butcher stands behind me so I can see his towering physique, a wall of muscles inside a black suit—his armour. He grasps my shoulders, encouraging me to turn.

I do.

Then I peer over my shoulder to see a shiny white crystal

poking out from between my cheeks. It's beautiful, and I look beautiful wearing it.

I gaze up from the sparkling crystal to his heated gaze. My heart shudders. He is staring at the little gem, and I'm gazing at him.

"I need you to fuck me," I whisper.

His scorching gaze rises to my face. "Say please."

"Please, Sir."

"Crawl around the bed while I take my suit off. Stay on your hands and knees," he says darkly.

Fucking hell. The mattress dips as I climb onto it. Winces contort into moans and flip back again as the plug inside me shuffles as I do. Now I understand why he wants me to move. I flutter my eyes through the contradictory sensations. The sound of his clothes coming off is all I try to focus on as I slide around the mattress, pacing the square fabric on all-fours like a kitten trying to find the softest spot to curl up on. My desire drips down my thighs. The walls inside me work around nothing, and I'm not ashamed of that sensation anymore. Unable to be embarrassed by anything while the plug somehow sends secondary tingles to my clit. I moan, halt, having to stop as the stimulation becomes too much. I close my eyes and arch my back, thrusting my arse into the air, angling my pelvis to ebb the pulsing around the plug.

I open my eyes when the room falls quiet. He stands at the end of the bed, his cock beating forcefully, pre-cum leaking already from the bobbing head. "I am so proud of how well your body has responded to my gift. Come here, my little deer. Bring me your pussy and I'll make it all better."

Scurrying over to him, I press my backside to his cock, and a deep growl leaves him. "Would you like that punishment now? For grabbing my wrist. Would you like to feel my gift move inside you while I punish this"—his big, warm palm strokes my bare arse cheek— "flawless skin."

I moan at his words. "Can I please have your cock?"

"Such a sweet question."

I'm already sweltering at the edges of my composure when he caresses my pussy with two fingers, travelling up and down the slick channel. *Fuck. Fuck.*

He hums. "Is there any pain? Any at all? You need to be honest with me. I'll still give you attention if you are in pain."

"No. Please. Please, I need you inside me."

A rumble of warning soars through the air. "Tell me to go slow, beg me to be gentle with your pretty pussy, or I'll take you the way I want, and it won't be either of those things."

Then a zap of pain fizzles through my body when he slaps my arse cheek, the crystal jerking within me, hitting the clinging walls, and resonating in the little buzzing knot above my trembling lips. "Tell me to go slow, Fawn."

He spanks me again.

Whimpering sounds leave me as my orgasm trickles through, teasingly, from that attention. My arse locks around the plug. My hips rock back into the fingers denying me the hard penetration I desperately desire.

I rub my pussy on his cock, pleadingly, as I mewl, arch, and beg with my bowing spine. *Take me.* I rub the length of him with my swollen lips, working towards that sensation. "Please, Sir. I don't want you restrained."

It's true. I want him real. Raw. Carnal. Whatever he needs to do to my body, I volunteer. I want my body to be the place he finds solace, the vessel that gives him pleasure, the heart he wants beating frantically alongside his.

"I'm going to ride this little body into my mattress. Are you ready for me?" Then his big warm hand spans my hip and part of my arse, and his cock slams into me, taking me from empty and wanton to stuffed and stretched before I can breathe. "Oh, fuck. *Fawn.*"

I burst into tears, overwhelmed but not at all sad. Throaty moans fall from my open mouth as he starts to fuck me. My mellow orgasm flares into a wild, unruly current.

He holds me still with one hand so I can take his hard drives; the other circles the small crystal while his pelvis hammers me hard from behind, impaling me repeatedly, at a brutal pace that drags yelps from my lips with each punch.

My orgasm doesn't stop.

One rolls into another. Never ending. My forehead hits the mattress. He holds my arse up for him to take. My body rackets. The climax of sensation shifts from my pulsing rosette to my battered pussy and back again until all the stretched, supple flesh detonates with further pleasure.

And he fucks me for so long. *So long.* My body is a numb mass. My legs trembling from fatigue; I'm unable to brace my hips as he takes what he wants from between them.

I moan into the mattress while he fingers the crystal and fucks me thoroughly. He twists the plug. Then finally presses down on the muscles beside the glittering gem, releasing it from the suction of my body. At the sweet agony of my hole being emptied, embarrassment drives through me, riding the explosion of another orgasm. This one, though, I can't handle. Can't take anymore. I'm useless against the onslaught, becoming completely limp, my backside held up by his hands.

"*Fawn.*" He grunts, and I know he's wracked with his own impending high. With each smack of skin to skin, a growl of pure animal intent rumbles through him, and he thrust two more times, flooding my pussy with his cum.

He pants behind me.

The moment coasts by.

His strong arms band around me, hauling me upright, pressing my back to his sweat-slicked chest. I flop against him, the back of my head hitting his chest. He holds me on my knees with protective dominance as his hand travels down my stomach to where he enters me. He touches either side of his cock as he withdraws, cum slipping out, dripping over his fingers, and down my inner thighs. As his laboured breaths fan my hair, he smears his cum across my pussy and up my stomach with his fingers. I'm weak all over.

Claimed.

Marked.

Owned.

His forever—he's going to keep me.

His breaths slow, returning to a steady pace. Then he collects me into his arms. Tucking me in bed, he soon slides in behind me on the mattress, locks my back to his chest, and rests his head above my crown.

I hum in the clutches of my fatigue, but I hear his heavy exhale. My hair wisps around, tickling my skin. "Tell me those tears were from pleasure, sweet girl."

I barely stifle a sleepy laugh; my ballooning heart loves the hints of concern he tries to smother. "I orgasm best under a level of duress, Sir."

He chuckles, deeply, and it is the best damn soundtrack to accompany the humming of my body. It's emotional intimacy. It's being *comfortable*. "You impress me, little deer."

I beam, even though my smile goes unseen. He has no idea how much that means to me.

CHAPTER THIRTY-SEVEN

I SLICE through the centre of the chicken, creating a pocket for the cheese to go into. The heat from standing near the oven while Maggie bakes bread has formed a thin coat of perspiration over my skin. I wipe my forehead with the back of my hand. Behind me, the pool is like a siren—all welcoming and seductive.

"Can I go for a swim?" I ask hesitantly because I hate offering to help and committing to something and then flaking out. "I just want a little dip and then I'll be—"

"Sweetie, you do not work here. You can come and go as you please. I love your company, but you should enjoy your-self too. You're so young. Go shopping. Go to a movie or read a book."

"A book." I glance across the pool and think about sprawling out like a kitten, soaking up the warmth, reading something smutty all day long until the sun descends, spilling colours through the trees. Then he'll get home and I'll tell him what I was reading. I wonder if he'll be happy about sharing me with book boyfriends. "Sounds so luxurious."

"Can we talk?"

I twist to see Jasmine with her chin cast low, her eyes on her scuffing feet. She looks uncomfortable in her own world, which I don't want at all. "Sure." I follow her through the French doors and stand on the grand stone veranda where I first met the Devil's prototype.

My Clay Butcher.

She peers out over the pool for a few contemplative moments before turning her solemn eyes to meet me. "I'm so sorry you lost the baby, Fawn." Shaking her head with regret flickering in her glossy eyes, she says, "I didn't know. I would have come to see you. I swear I would have."

My hair tussles in the dense warm draft. Hooking my finger around a strand, I pull it from sticking to my lips. "It's okay. I'm okay. It wasn't meant to be."

"That's a line." She sighs. "It still sucks. You can say it."

I tip my shoulders, a defeated little shrug. "It sucks."

"There you go."

"Should we start again?" Holding my hand out for her to take, I say, "Hi, I'm Fawn. I've never had a real female friend before. Girls rarely like me. Or they used me to get to my brothers."

Her hand wraps around mine, and we giggle as we shake them. "I'm Jasmine, and I think it's their loss for not using your brothers to get to know you."

We slump down on the steps and talk for a while before she heads back to finish her shift, and I wander down the steep decline to meet the pool's edge. Enjoying the breeze even though it is warm, I close my eyes and breathe in deeply.

Then I hear a sound coming from the bushes—a shuffling or a sprinkler or—

"Psst!"

My eyes flash open, and I spin to face the dense gardens surrounding this section of the pool. Squinting through the vast webbing of trees and shrubbery, I make out a black figure crouching behind a hedge.

"Don't look straight at me," the voice says. "They will be watching you through the cameras."

I square my shoulders, stepping backwards to put more distance between me and the boundary. "Who's in there?"

A hushed voice says, "It's Lee."

My stomach churns, and while part of me wants to apologise for being the reason he had a gun shoved in his mouth, another part of me—a strong, loyal part that belongs to Clay —just wants to tell him to go away. "It's best if you leave. You don't know what he'll do."

The foliage in front of him rustles when he adjusts his stance. "What did I do wrong?"

"Fine then, come out. But don't hide," I say, peering around the greenery to get a better view of his hiding spot.

"Don't look over here! Just look at the flowers."

My heart picks up pace at the startling strain in his voice. "I'm telling Clay you're back," I say, turning.

"Wait!" he calls, and my foot stops mid-step when he says, "I have a message from your father."

The blood in my veins chill to a frosty stream at the mention of my dad, at the inference that a message from the man I have been waiting for is a secret affair, a secret that needs to be kept from the people in this house. A secret that is whispered through trees between strangers. I don't like how I feel. Cold shivers run up my spine.

Slowly turning back to the hedge, I narrow my eyes on

the dark figure between the lightly swaying leaves. "I call bullshit."

"Just turn your back to the house and look at the flowers, pick them, act like you're counting them."

My breathing becomes shallow, air drawn in through my nose, my mouth purses, teeth clench—discomfort like a literal entity winding itself around me while intrigue keeps me rooted to the grass. I don't speak. Can't. I squat down and pick a small grass flower, my eyes losing focus as he talks.

"He's coming for you."

I don't understand.

"He's coming to get you out."

I'm not trapped.

Swallowing hard, I fight against the knot in my throat. I pick another flower and whisper, "But I'm not trapped, Lee."

"Really?"

No. I pick another flower.

"Look around... You couldn't leave if you tried."

I pick another flower.

"Clay and Dustin are enemies, Fawn. You're fucking bait! He's using you to get to Dustin."

No. "I'm not."

"You are!"

I stand with a handful of flowers that I don't want and will my knees to cease shaking. "He wouldn't lie to me." I dump the flowers on the ground, a pile of white, yellow, and green, creating a tatted mound by my new strappy shoes.

"Really?"

I rub my chest, feeling pin pricks hit my heart, deflating it. His words creep into me like demons spawning, seeping out with long black claws to change things forever. Infect my feelings. Ruin the first good thing in my life. My new *every-*

thing. I trust him. I trust him, goddamn it. That isn't something I do easily. It isn't...

What is Lee saying? That Clay is using me to get to my father? Like the girls used me to get to my brothers, like Benji used me to make them jealous, like Jasmine used me to make herself feel better... "*No.* I trust him."

"I didn't want to have to do this, but if you don't believe me, then, fine"—he throws something at me, the small black rectangle hitting my left shoe—"take this."

It rests vertically on the lip of my leather sole. I don't lean down. I don't pick it up because I know what it is, but I don't want to touch it in case it is what I know it is. *Fuck.* "What is it?" I say, my voice wobbling with my encroaching despair.

"The recording you have been looking for. Your father acquired it for you. He wants to look after you, Fawn. He wants to be your father. And he thinks you deserve the truth."

I know the truth. "I know the truth," I mutter with curt adamance, but my voice sounds fucking awful and obvious and... breaks on the following exhale.

"Do you? Where are your brothers?"

With that, my heart lurches into my throat, shuddering within the column, making it hard to breathe or swallow or *think.* "I'm leaving." I whirl around.

"Listen, just watch the recording!" he pleads, and I still with my back to the garden. "Then, if you still think Mr Butcher wouldn't lie to you, fine. But if you want the truth, more answers, answers you deserve, Fawn. To be in control of your own decisions in life, then meet me between the left hedge and the tennis court netting. There is a blind spot, and at 2:47 a.m. they switch guards. They talk and catch up for several minutes before they sit down. So, they won't see you running through the house or even get to that spot. You'll have maybe five minutes to get there. Then we won't be in view. I made sure of it. I used to smoke there. I made a tree barrier, and if we stay low, they'll never see us. And then I'll take you to your father... You'll be safe with him."

I close my eyes, focusing on the ominous humid air filling my lungs. Gritting my teeth and cursing myself with every step, I walk to the black SD card and snatch it from beside the pile of ruined grass flowers.

I spin and stride away from Lee as his words follow me. Burn within my skull. I curse outwardly, fighting with my doubt, with my faithless mind. Drawing Clay's deep, smooth timbre front and centre, I try to find the strength to ignore what was just uttered so convincingly. Forget it, even. Harmful lies from a scorned employee should hold no weight when our connection is so strong.

You are scared. I need you to trust me, little deer. I will do the worrying for you.

I *am* scared.

I'm scared Lee is telling the truth.

I ball my fingers in tight, digging my nails into my palms, feeling the sharp object inside, hoping I crack it by accident.

Hoping I render it defective.

CHAPTER THIRTY-EIGHT

I LEAVE THE COUNCIL BUILDING, heading towards my Chrysler idling by the curb. Even now, amid a busy weekday, my soldiers are stationed in the vicinity. Across the road at a coffee shop. On the rooftop. I'm a target, but that has always been the case, and it barely concerns me... usually.

But now I have Fawn.

A wave of blunt pain spindles through my chest.

Now, my concern is for the sweet girl who I have taken as my own. If something were to happen to me, an occupational hazard I was somewhat at peace with, who would take care of her? Who will teach her about her worth? Hold her accountable for her actions? Touch that smooth skin that prickles with soft blonde hairs? Play with her body? Shower her with attention? And the way she looked at Kelly and Stone. *Madonna Mia.* It is like a screwdriver to my guts as she is mourning her baby, quietly yearning to be a mother again —someday at least. I never wanted to be a father, but I won't deny her a damn thing. So, who will put that baby in her stomach? No one else will, because even in death, she'll be mine. Maybe I should visit a sperm bank... What a fucking absurd thought, given where my focus should be. Death has never been a fear. Now, I fear losing her, which can only happen in death.

My little deer.

My sweet girl.

She has worn down a part of this stone façade, inserting herself through the formations of my armour. It wasn't another stone that wore me down. It was the persistence of a little flower that wormed its way through the gaps.

Que opens the passenger door seconds before I reach the vehicle. I duck under the roofline and slide along the leather upholstery to the opposite window. Staring at the city, beating with life, I prepare myself to switch roles, prepare for another dark inquisition.

We head towards the docks, and the closer we roll, the denser a dark-grey haze from the bushfires gathers around the vehicle. I pull out my handset, and my eyes sail to the app for my home security system before I ignore the impulse to check on her, opening the text message from Vinny instead. It says:

> We have the arsonist at the warehouse.

We park outside the warehouse, and as I step from the car, two black vehicles file into the parking lot—my soldiers.

This part of the dock glows in an orange hue, being so close to the flames that ash falls onto my black suit like a dusty downpour. I peer out across an angry black ocean that would usually be littered with residents, boats, and fishermen but is now ominous as the shadowy clouds gather along the surface.

Vinny appears in the doorway to the warehouse, so I smooth down my tie and stride to meet him.

"What does our arsonist have to say for himself?" I ask, passing him, absently noting a strange grin on his lips. I head towards the back room where I know our guest will be waiting.

Vinny falls into step beside me. "*Her*self, Boss."

I abruptly still, understanding his ridiculous boyish grin. "What?"

"She's a girl, alright," he states, smiling wider, which can only mean—"Attractive, too. I have got nothing out of her yet. We were waiting for you. I don't feel comfortable hitting her, which left me a little fucked with what to do."

"I see." My forehead tightens as I continue at a steady pace to the end of the cavernous warehouse. The rap of shoes hitting the decades-old, creaky floorboards echo behind me as my employees join us inside.

Entering the room, I nod polite acknowledgements to Vinny's team and somewhat ignore the young girl sitting on a foldout chair with a wet gag in her mouth. Her fingers are entwined, the pink-tipped nails folding over her knuckles like delicate claws. Her wrists are bound with a three-stitch rope and fastened to a rail beneath the seat. She mumbles something around the white cloth between her lips.

I come to a stop a few metres from her and clasp my hands in front of me. Contemplating this situation.

Pretty blue eyes widen with my towering presence. I drag my gaze over her, measuring this girl up. Brand new white converse sneakers. Faded designer jeans. I tilt my head, observing the facets in her studded earrings as they flash a kaleidoscope of colours beneath the industrial warehouse lighting. *Diamonds.* Not my product, but good quality.

A thin film of perspiration collects on her forehead. I

frown at a small chaffing burn on her knee peeking out from between ripped denim, where she has obviously tripped, but she is otherwise unharmed.

As I stare at this misguided rich girl, Vinny leans into my ear, offering the rundown on her. "Her name is Kaya Lovit." My brows pinch with recollection. That explains the diamonds, the styled, long brown hair, and the healthy physique. "*Yes*, Boss, as in Lovit Industries. She's the youngest of the offspring. Nineteen. We got reports from witnesses that saw her in the area before the blaze, and Constable Jarvis gave us everything the police had. She did it alright, Boss."

Interesting.

"Bored with shopping?" I ask, a grin tugging at the corner of my lips while her eyes seem to search for something within mine. As though I'm under interrogation, as well. Vinny rounds the girl and removes her gag, gently so.

She shakes the sensation away, releasing a little cough and working her jaw in circles. She jumps straight in with, "What are you going to do, *Mayor* Butcher? You can't dispose of *me*. People will look for me if I go missing, and I'm sure my dad will have Stormy River raked for my body. You'll go to jail."

"Which is where you belong," I state plainly.

"You can talk."

I like her.

This is an interesting development. I smile, amusement floating through me. "You have me surprised. I'm very rarely surprised. But I'm far more disappointed in you than surprised by you. You see, the people I typically have bound to a chair don't have silver spoons up their arses. They are struggling. Their poverty makes them weak. Stupid. What's your excuse for burning down homes and threatening lives, Kaya?"

She locks her jaw, tight-lipped, seemingly withholding something while her narrowed blue eyes attempt to defy her transparency. "Just like you said." She shrugs, but it's a bullshit gesture because her chest has picked up pace—she cares. "I'm bored with shopping."

Not convinced, I study her face for any tells. Then drag my gaze down her body, halted by a thin necklace hanging between her breasts. I walk towards her. She shrinks back in her chair, even as her pretty, blue eyes narrow and follow my movements. She's playing at being tough, but not very well.

I hook the shiny silver chain with my finger and pull the pendant from between her cleavage. I display the piece on the pad of my fingers, smiling as I read, *"Princess."*

"Well," I say smoothly. "Are you going to tell me the truth, girl? Or am I going to have to get it out of you?"

She speaks through clenched teeth. "I *have* told you the truth. I'm bored. Like you don't know the truth already."

I drop the pendant, the slinky chain falling back between the mounds of her chest. Turning my back to her, I hear her gasp at the abrupt action, at the dismissal. I walk to Vinny's side. "Go to her father and tell him he'll need to pay the damages to homes and keep—"

"No!" she cuts in.

I smile at Vinny, who grins in return. Slowly, I turn to face her again. "What is it, Kaya?"

She leans forward. *"I'll* pay it back."

"It's millions of dollars."

"I'll"—she reaches for a plan—"I'll work for you."

I laugh. "Whatever could you offer me?"

"I'm smart."

"So am I. Look, Kaya, your father has plenty of money.

Just let him save you from this mess your boredom has gotten you into. You might not get any prison time at all. It all matters little to me."

"I don't understand. You're serious?" Her brows weave in, and I don't quite understand her question, her apparent confusion over the situation, but I don't show that fact. "You seriously don't know? *Fuck.* Don't involve my father."

"Why?" I ask. Heavy waves outside the warehouse walls beat through the following seconds of silence. A small smile creeps across my lips as I say, "*Princess.*"

She sneers at me, realising I knew her father was her weakness all along, but alas, what I don't know is why the hell she thought I was playing at my inquiries.

The petite brunette shakes her head in a way that shows her stupidity taking root inside her young brain. She looks at her bound wrists, muttering, "They blackmailed me into starting the fire."

"Speak up, girl. I can't hear you."

She peers up from her clasped fingers, meeting my unaffected gaze. Within her blue eyes she portrays less fear than men have drowning in theirs given a shared situation. "You won't bring my dad into this, then?"

"You are in no place to make demands."

"*Please.*"

I level her with my gaze. "I will consider it."

She sighs. "He has some... *tax issues.* I can't believe you don't know... This bitch from the news was going to go public with it. He'd do time. We'd go broke. He won't handle prison; he's too old now."

I stare, deadpan. "Keep going."

"That's it." Kaya looks around, her gaze coasting between Vinny and me. "That's all there is to say. I did it to keep the stuff about my dad out of the press."

"*Fuck*," Vinny bites out, knowing what I know, but I need to hear it from her and not jump to conclusions.

"Who blackmailed you?"

"I don't know her... A lady."

Irritation rolls up my back, hitting my ears, burning them. "What did she look like, girl?"

"Red hair. Stuck up. She never said her name."

Lorna.

Vinny scoffs, saying, "Why would she want to start a fire in the boss's city?"

"I don't fucking know. I thought he was behind it the whole time..." Her eyes bounce around my tight face, searching for a hint of the truth she believes I'm withholding. "Aren't you? I mean, you got a lot more attention after the fire, *District Daddy*."

"Vinny, stay." I nod at Vinny's associates. "You take the girl home." I walk to the warehouse window, taking in the wild ocean sprawling beyond the glass. The thick smoke from the bushfires hazing the horizon, making the stretch of coastline nothing more than a grey abyss.

Fucking Lorna.

She's taken this campaign to another level with this one. Risked lives. I knew her morals were rickety, and I've never denied mine are, too, but I have held on to the last slither of humanity in this business of mine, in me, that we—I—don't hurt innocent civilians.

I retrieve my phone from my pocket, calling her cell. It rings several times and then she picks up, her voice breathy as she says, "Lord Mayor, what an honour."

I cut to the chase. "I have the girl," I state monotone, and where her deep, husky cadence used to stir my cock, knowing what the lips that produce that sound can do to it, I feel nothing at all. This relationship is over.

350 · NICCI HARRIS

She isn't pleased by the end of our conversation, leaving me with a "Fuck you" after I suggest we re-evaluate our relationship. That it has been beneficial, suitable, and appropriate, but has run its course entirely.

All the while, I think about a far sweeter cadence, a soft voice that murmured, "Will you ever belong to me?" Outwardly the reason to end this sporadic engagement with Lorna is the fire, the lies, the arrogance, but stoked low beneath those situational facts is a little deer who wants all of me for herself.

I slide my phone back into my pocket, turning to find myself alone with my capo. His face tells me he's not sure that was in my best interests, as if I don't already know this. "I know."

"This is why I'm single, Boss." He smirks, though something in his expression betrays that display and I wonder what it is. Perhaps he's concerned about her leaking information to the news.

"She won't do anything too stupid. I'll have my wife smooth things over with her," I assure his silent protest. The distance between us creates an echo every time we speak, so I walk to meet him in the empty room. "They are very close."

He nods, knowing the dynamic between my wife and my lover—*ex-lover*. "Feminists."

"Indeed." I stop in front of him and reach into my pocket to retrieve my tin. He flinches before realising that I'm drawing a cigar and not my Glock.

"*Jesus*, Boss!" He rubs his chest. "You ask me to stay back, and then you act all shady," he states, and I chuckle.

"Shady?" I contemplate his misused word. Not shady... peculiar, yes, given I just released young Kaya with a slap on the hand and cut ties with a dangerously powerful women who is respectfully a large part of my campaign. I had no choice. "Tell me—" I light my cigar, sucking the tension-releasing essence into my lungs and speaking around my exhale. "In all the years I have known you, you have never had a relationship. Was there ever a girl for you?"

He sighs. I hand him the tin and watch him light his own. As the cogs in his head churn, he smokes it. "Well, there was a girl. Yeah. In Timor. I met her when I was serving. She was the most beautiful islander-looking girl. No English at all. Thank fuck. She had no idea how dumb I was."

I laugh once. "Did you ask her to marry you, and then she said no?"

He shakes his head. "She said yes, and then she took a bullet to the back."

My smile falls, and I have no further words for him. There is nothing to say to a man in his position; any small phrases of sympathy would be an insult to his experience.

We smoke our cigars in comfortable melancholic silence. I drop the roach and blunt it out with my shoe.

Looking at my capo, I nod my condolences, grip his shoulder and squeeze before heading out of the cavernous space, even more driven to get back to my little deer.

CHAPTER THIRTY-NINE

MY PALMS SWEAT, the perspiration gathering between them and the polished wood of his office desk. On the computer in front of me, the recording plays like a cult film I saw once; only the girl in this movie looks just like me. Same blonde hair. Same small figure. Same nervous tick as she twirls her near-white blonde hair around her finger.

The boys... they look like my brothers, one fat and smirking, one nervous and eager, one cunning and handsome.

No.

Why aren't you smiling at the girl who looks like me, Benji? Why aren't you smiling sweetly at her?

The boys take turns licking the girl between her legs while her head rolls with sporadic consciousness.

A pounding begins in my brain.

Why aren't you asking them to leave, Benji? So you can be alone with her? Why?

The girl who looks like me passes out, and the fat, smirking one thrusts into her so hard her entire body pulses up the couch. So hard her eyes fly open with the force of it, and the first whimpering sound escapes her contorted, hopeless throat. I hate her... Hate how weak she is.

"LIKE MY COCK, *our ... dirty ... little... slut?*"

WHY DON'T YOU CARE, *Benji?!*

The pounding in my head becomes a physical boulder of sound and pain, slamming from one ear to the other. The word *no* on repeat. A chant. A cry. A plea. I want to save her. I want to climb inside that monitor and drag her the fuck out.

"WHERE ARE YOU GOING?"

NOW THE GIRL is trying to get away, and she's so weak. So utterly *useless.* Her body isn't working at all, not for her at least, but it is working for them...

I shake my head slowly, whispering, "*No,*" before begging the girl on the monitor, "Get up. *Please.* Please get up. Don't let them hurt you."

But it's too late.

Because the cunning, handsome one that looks like Benji is pinning the girl's chest to the couch and fucking her from behind.

No. No!

I burst into tears, the current flooding my face, making the vision of the girl who looks like me, who is being fucked by her three foster brothers, a blur of gyrating fierce movements.

Their grunts are clear and haunting. I'll hear them

forever. In my head. In my nightmares. I'll hear the grunts like a battle drum, the last sound before a willing walk to death. I cover my ears as the drum beckons me to silence it forever, to do anything to stop it.

My heart twists.

But it's not me.

I shake.

But it's not me.

I feel hollow, painful helplessness.

It.

Is.

Not.

Me.

But the sound of their pleasure lingers inside the cells in my brain, a broken neuron on repeat. A sound that imbeds itself in deep.

"I'M BLEEDING."

NO. *No. No.* Bile rising in my throat, I throw my head to the side, expelling the entire contents of my stomach: three meals, cake, and ice cream.

A stomach full of lies.

My eyes are dragged back to the screen again as the fat one pushes the handsome one onto the glass table before taking hold of the girl again. Slamming her face down on the couch, he starts to fuck her again while she watches the other boy slowly bleed out all over the carpet.

My lungs shrivel inside me. Oxygen impossibly thick. I feel dizzy. Hazy. Airless. She looks just like me...

No.

It's not me on the screen.

It's not me who was raped.

It's not me.

"Fawn!"

The grunts from the screen, in my head—in my cells—and the pounding between my ears are all interrupted by a weak, useless name being called. Someone is calling *my* name from outside his office. I look up to see the office handle shake and shake and shake, but it's locked and I'm alone in here. With her. And them.

My body keels over, and I drop to my knees, press my palms to the carpet, and heave for oxygen.

It's not me.

CHAPTER FORTY

SOMEONE KICKS the door from the lock, splintering the plasterboard, dusting the air in small white fragments.

"Fawn, are you sick?" Henchman Jeeves says, panic an ever-ready entity, making his words pitch higher. Am I sick? Am I sick?

As I stare at the carpet, sucking in air—sharp, hot, thick air that doesn't want to be inside my tiny, shrivelled lungs, I see him kneel beside me. He reaches for me—his hands and skin and warmth hurdling me further into despair, and I jolt away from the horrible feeling.

"Don't touch me," I gasp, my mouth filling with tears around each sharp desperate draw for air.

He sinks back. "*Fuck.* Talk to me, Fawn."

I hate the tears. I fight them, but the wrestle forces a broken groan from my throat. I don't want to cry in front of him, in front of them, for them or because of them, but I can still hear the grunts that are now a part of my soul. A blemish in my brain.

Fuck.

My shoulders.

My fucking shoulders and chest won't stop shaking, and air won't flow freely into my lungs.

"Fawn? I've called Mr Butcher. He's on his way."

When I curl my fingers into the carpet, fending off the tremors, shooting pain rushes beneath the nailbeds like electrical currents, warning me they are bending the wrong way. I revel in the pain.

It's real.

Pain is truth.

Undeniable. No one can keep the pain from me, and I'll decide what is too much, what is enough.

It's my body and I'll decide!

I don't want to cry as I force the words out. "I'm sick." *And sick people cry, Bolton.* They howl and try to rip their nails from their flesh because they feel so terrible inside.

I'm sick.

"Can you stand?" he asks, but I haven't looked at him, focused on a spot on the carpet that has a tiny black fibre thread through it. A tiny imperfection. I couldn't see the fibre before; it is so small, but it's hard to unsee now that I'm homed in on it. I reach for it, plucking at the strand that is imbedded so tightly, this little imperfection in his otherwise perfect office space. A tainted blemish.

"I need tweezers," I say, gritting my teeth as the defiant black thread only moves deeper into the cream-coloured strands around it. "I need tweezers!"

Within a few seconds or maybe it's ten or twenty minutes, I don't know or care because Bolton is handing me tweezers. I need them. I tear the fibre free from the carpet. Sitting back, I hold it up. Squint at it. Air fills my lungs as I stare at the crinkled little strand between the pinched tips of my tweezers. I inhale relief, but the air is caught in the back of my throat when my eyes land on another.

And another.

Little black fibres everywhere.

No. No.

I don't like them. My cheek muscles start to ache from the lock I have on my jaw. As I begin to rip them all out, I become a vessel expelling grunts and growls. Removing the threads. One by one. "I need to get them!"

I don't notice Bolton stand and move away, but I'm suddenly lifted into the air.

Hands on me.

Hands on my body.

My heart beats painfully, threatening to hammer right through my ribcage, crack me in two. His hands scorch my skin, melting the flesh away from my bones, leaving only the shrivelled, sick essence of me inside. Touch hurts. I cry out and flail around in his grasp, kicking and screaming, eventually managing to gyrate free from his arms.

The burning stops when my feet touch the floor.

My pulse is a drone now; it sounds in time to the grunts and groans in my mind. Suddenly, the room presses in on me. It is too small. There are too many bodies. I don't see who. Just the shapes. All around me. So many. I snap my head around, needing an exit, an escape, a way out of this space—*this body.*

"Step away from the door," Clay orders, and even though I register his words, register his tone, and everything him, my legs bolt for the newly revealed exit.

I fly from the room, but not before hearing him roar, "Search the grounds!"

A blur of people dart from my path. Henchmen bracing their weapons in two hands, ready to unleash hell, pour out into the gardens. Ahead, I see the pool glowing, drawn to it. I sprint harder. My lungs sting. My muscles ache from being thrown around. Dragged along the couch. Thrust into. My body remembers as my mind churns the images, the sounds of being fucked, curdling them through my reality. Tumbling back to me, hitting me like the sky falling, is the truth.

My body remembers.

My skin set afire by the truth.

I run straight into the pool.

The cool water hisses as it coats the phantom of their touch, the scorched skin that didn't remember but now acutely blisters under every ghosting caress, every lick between my legs, every bruising squeeze of my thighs, every heavy breath.

The water soothes it. Swallows it. Holds me. Under the water, I'm free from the sensation of my body. Free from the weight of it. The burden. Under the water, *I'm free.*

With my heart so loud, so intense, it's presence inside me is violent, I fight to keep myself from the clutches of the world above. Feeling a straining sensation in my chest, my body wanting breath, I fight it. I'll burn in the air. My skin isn't my own when I can feel their touch, their breath, them—

No, I can't.

I have to fight it.

Strong.

My lungs burn.

I'm resilient.

My chest aches.

A survivor.

I fight it, oxygen-deprived and willingly losing consciousness, but then the water changes, pushes me up, and I'm dragged from the pool's hold.

Dragged into the air.

My flesh ignites again.

I fight to get back into the water where I don't hate the feel of my own skin. I fight in the arms around me, slapping his face and beating my fists into a wall of muscles. *Don't fucking touch me.* "Don't touch me! Don't touch me! Don't touch me!" Screaming, I savagely attack him, scratching the plane of his handsome face, his soaking wet shirt, ripping the scene apart, fighting back. I'm fighting back.

He grabs my wrists, singeing my skin within his palms. "It's me, little deer."

I release a long, throaty cry, "You're burning me!"

Don't touch me. The voice in my head from that day, the one they couldn't hear, the one that froze in fear on my tongue, howls in my mind.

Don't touch me.

Don't touch me.

Don't touch me.

I'm suddenly dragged to the floor, smothered in him, locked against him. "Stop, Fawn! You're going to hurt yourself." He's suffocating me. A snake made with scorching human flesh. My skin bubbles. But then his lips hit my temple, his voice saying, "*Shhh.*"

His hushing timbre soars through the grunting, the chanting, the little voice, the groans, through all the fear reaching me somewhere inside. Bringing with it the memories of the past few weeks while I have been his.

Mine!

The gun to Lee's face.

The way people part for him.

The deadliest man in the city.

The man who lied to me.

Protected me.

"Shhh."

It goes deadly quiet in my mind. The burning stops to the sound of him, and I go limp to his deep perpetual white noise. "They can't touch you. You're mine. You're mine."

I'm his.

My knees collapse, my body a decaying mess he supports in his arms. And I let go. Cry. I cry so hard my brain seems to detonate, bashing at my skull under the pressure of my violent sobs, of my racketing mind. I cry for every night between that one and this, becoming nothing but a vessel for every unshed tear. He holds the tattered pieces of me. He doesn't press for answers. *Who gave it to you? What did they say?* He doesn't ask me what he can do or what hurts...

He knows the answers.

Nothing.

And *everything.*

CHAPTER FORTY-ONE

CURLED on my side in *his* bed, with my knees up to my chest and my cheeks tight with tracks of tears, my body trembles like a pebble.

Clay's arms are banding my legs, pinning the little ball of my body to his. His fists are clenched, working, the sound of his knuckles cracking under the pressure, not unlike a direct promise of carnage.

Clay...

The most powerful man in the city is holding his pretty little burden. It's pathetic. The feel of him, though, douses the painful prickling of my skin. The skin that seems to have evoked the feelings from that night—the incident. It seems to have remembered, showing me, now that my mind has caught up, just what it feels like to be in that room with those boys. To have been alone. To have a dissonance with my own flesh. It has manifested to life in my reality.

My.

Reality.

I whimper. My entire body is shuddering and sore,

emotionally burnt out and confused.

So confused.

Debating with my mind, which wants to cower, to hide in a dark place inside me, and with my body which wants to drown or... *Fuck.* To feel something intense that doesn't burn. To remember, it's *mine.*

Because right now, my body only feels the incident. Like it has only just been dragged along the cushions, has only just been punctured so brutally I've bled all over my thighs.

It is clinging to all the gruesome details that my mind forgot, or maybe it's filling in the blank spaces that were lost forever. Either way, I'm experiencing the aftermath. Right. Now.

The pain.

The ache.

The recall.

"That's enough. Her virginity is mine. You promised."

You promised. You promised.

As those two words poke at me, I bunch in further. Clay's fist tightens harder. I am here for Benji. This is all for him. In Clay Butcher's house, having been on a mission to bring him justice and all the while, he... *he—*

The deceit expands in my throat. The naivety stabs my empty womb. The agony fists my heart. Did they bet on my virginity? Spoke about it. Discussed it. He *promised* Jake my virginity as though it was his to offer up with the chips and beer and marijuana they used to trade amongst themselves. Was I worth a car? A bike? What was my virginity worth to Benji? If I had loved him for his smile, for his charm, and for the moments he handed me the popcorn, that 'love' has collapsed into piles of debris in my heart. I could draw the lines of his smile, but now I want more than anything to take an eraser to his entire memory.

I hate him.
Bad things come in three:
Her suicide: number one.
~~His murder.~~ *The incident: number two.*
My miscarriage: number three.

And those things shine a blinding fiery light on everything about my existence. No matter how hard I try, no one wants to choose me. My mum chose death over being my parent. Benji chose whatever item was worth more than my virginity, and my body... it doesn't even want to grow, to create, to offer the world something special for all my suffering.

Nothing in my life... *works* for me.

Nothing chooses me.

Lastly, of fucking course, my dad. The man who doesn't know me. The man who I came here to see, to seek shelter from. The one who *'is not worth my considerations.'* The one who sent a boy to give me a recording of my trauma detailed in visual nightmarish horror with the knowledge I would watch it. He didn't choose me either.

He chose himself.

He chose to hurt me—*us.* Chose to leave me a grass flower instead of being my thorns.

My eyes widen on that harrowing truth, staring broken, swollen, sore, at the leather sofa against the far wall. All the fairy-tales I have told myself, the moments where I twisted the crumbs of affection into mountains, where I accepted handing over the popcorn as a sign of love, where I saw a dreamcatcher as a visual representation that my mum cared...

It.

All.

Fractures.

CHAPTER FORTY-TWO

STEADILY, I stalk towards the garden shed, eyes focused ahead, while in my peripherals Lee is being hauled across the lawn by Vinny and two of my soldiers.

She'll be okay.

She's fast asleep.

She's safe.

It isn't enough. I want—dammit—I need my eyes on her at all times. Need my hands close. My Glock drawn. I need the world to stop turning, to freeze so I can give her every inch of attention. Every inch of me.

I need to fix this.

I can't fix this.

Can't kill the ghosts in her mind.

Holding it all in, a thunderous volatility stirring, I enter the garden shed. Flicking the light on as the laboured sounds of the fucker being dragged through the doors carry on behind me, I don't speak. I watch as he is strapped to a chair in the centre of the space.

"You okay, Boss?" One of my soldiers asks, but I don't

answer, just stare at Vinny as he begins to beat the fucker Lee to a pulp. I don't respond when the first tooth fractures or when they all start to splinter and litter the dusty ground. While the brutal scene takes place, I'm thinking about her sprinting into the pool, sinking to the concrete base, giving up. After all her fighting, after clawing through life to survive, for a moment, she was willingly drowning.

"Boss?"

A harsh cry drags me back to the vision of violence in front of me. "Enough," I order, but it's too late as Lee is already a bludgeoned mass. I don't care. I'm not thinking straight.

I was too late to stop her.

Too busy.

Vinny halts with his fist in the air before moving out of my way. I step forward and clasp my hands. "*Hello*, Lee. That was a very fatal thing you did today, my boy."

When he opens his mouth, blood instantly flows from the hole. *Fuck.* He rips a word across his bloody tongue. "*Please.*"

"It smarts, doesn't it? You get used to it. I don't know if you know this about me, but I used to box a lot when I was in boarding school." I drag a chair over the pavers until I'm close to him. "There was this large caged area behind the theatre for all the props and whatnot. And we would have underground fights Saturday nights when there was only a skeleton staff on. Mondays, we were black and blue." I reach forward and grab his jaw, pulling a guttural moan from him. I inspect his bloodied, gummy mouth, wanting to ram my fist down there and rip his tongue out, wanting to beat him to death myself.

Needing to move.

My body turns to steel against the fight inside me.

Exhaling roughly, I drop his jaw, lean back, and lift my ankle to rest it on my knee, but my foot jolts back and forth—a tic festering inside me—my restraint not reaching far enough with the sight of my sweet girl, my little deer, in so much pain. "Who gave you the SD card?"

He whimpers, his mouth moving like he wants to speak but jerking pathetically at the pain. I notice the large muscle within, bitten and swollen, filling the space.

I shoot Vinny a quick glance; he should know fucking better than to beat him within an inch of his life. "Where is Dustin staying?"

His head drops forward, and he gurgles the words as a thick stream of blood pours from his mouth. "*Please.*"

Fucking please.

Restless, I lean forward, onto my knees, getting closer. "He's in the District." I assume, feeling this information in my very gut. "I know he is. Just give me the hotel, the address, the people safe-housing him, and I'll make *all* this pain go away."

"J-*Jimmy,*" he chokes out, a flowing crimson waterfall gushing from his open mouth. I clench my jaw at the sound of Jimmy's name. At the sound of my phantom. A dark cloud that covers all.

"Jimmy is dead, my boy. What are you talking about?"

His voice is already halfway to hell when he murmurs, "Watched the girl."

My body stiffens as something I've missed opens me up, allowing the ghosts of inadequacy to fill me. Right under my nose. Treachery seeps into my muscles. My Butcher head roars within my well-mannered façade. Of course. *Always four steps ahead of me, even in death, old boy.*

I worked beside Jimmy for the past decade, his chosen heir, and I still don't know all his hands. All his influence. *I'm* the damn fool. "Who is watching her now? Who gave you the SD card?"

Lee passes out.

Bitter deceit prickles at the backs of my eyes, but I ram the pain of betrayal down my throat. Rising to my feet, I hover over Lee. I lift his lifeless chin and tilt his head backwards. Effortlessly, I hold it steadfast. He gasps at the metal ceiling. All the blood squirting into his mouth from veins below his teeth, from the webbing of them in his near-severed tongue, start to pour down his trachea into his lungs. He gasps again, guaranteeing his death. Drowning.

Like my little deer.

She's drowning...

She tried to drown herself.

I bare my teeth and tighten my hold. His body convulses, and I watch—*revel.* Watching bubbles of blood and saliva foam around my fingers, I narrow my eyes. *Her pain.* He should feel *her pain.* And so drown he will.

I should drown them all.

All. Of. Them.

Then the men around me seem to catch my attention. The man behind me. In Jimmy's shed. By Jimmy's house. Not mine... I lose focus in this dying man's eyes, feeling the entire scenario of my existence, my city, my men, burn up in flames. It was never mine. Not really. I should have fucking known better.

I speak hushed but firmly. "Dustin is alive because Jimmy wanted him to be. And here I am, working in the same model as him. In a world Jimmy made. In a city he built. I just continued what he started." I speak to a dying Lee. To my capo—Vinny—behind me, watching. To my soldiers as they try to hold their stomachs. To myself.

I remember when I thought that *if anyone was to rip the*

Cosa Nostra from the District, the entire city would bleed to death.
Well, fuck, I was wrong. Again. It's not the *Cosa Nostra* that
grows like weeds within the city. It's *Jimmy Storm*. And I need
to pull him out. Weed by weed. "Jimmy wanted the entire
city to bleed if he did. And bleed it will."

Vinny's voice is hesitant as he says, "What are you
saying, Boss?"

I think about how Jimmy never burnt any bridges. Not
with Dustin when the fucker betrayed us. Not with us when
we demanded his head. He knew everything and everyone.
And... he knew my little deer.

"Fuck," I growl. He knew her all along. Of course, he did. I
release my hold on Lee's chin now that he is a lifeless pile.
"This is not my city, Vinny."

"Yes, it is, Boss."

"No, my friend." I shake my head stiffly, turning to face
him. "These are not my men."

He looks at me as though I have gone mad, or is that fear
I see playing in his eyes? "What are you talking about?"

I laugh with derision. "No more alliances, Vinny. They are
not mine. I did not make them."

"What do you mean?"

"I want them all brought in. Every Underboss. Every
Capo. Every division. The Japanese. The bikers. I don't think
they know who I am, and I'd like to officially introduce
myself as the head of the Family. Anyone who is not with me
is now *against* me. Anyone on the *fence*, a *peacekeeper*, is now
against me." I step towards him, growling, "Anyone who
questions me. Is. Now. Against me!"

I watch his throat roll. "They won't like that."

Exhaling slowly, I try again to calm myself down, but it
isn't working because I am not Jimmy Storm. Not a cold,
unaffected man. I am a *fucking Butcher,* and I'm at the end of

my goddamn rope. Lowering my voice, I say, "Did you not hear me, my friend? I said bring them. *All*. To *me*."

"Boss,"—he clears his throat—"are you sure?"

Anyone who questions me. Is. Now. Against me. I go deadly cold. Deadly still. A smooth smile slides into place. I stare into the wide brown eyes of the man who has been beside me for the past twelve months, a man who has worked for the Family for decades. "The thing about loyalty is that it's black and white. You are either loyal or you aren't. There is no sliding scale in loyalty. I know this better than most, as loyalty is easy for me. I've only ever been loyal to the name Butcher. At the core of it, it will always be them." Stepping towards him, I cup his head and kiss both cheeks before leaning back and asking, "How long have you worked for him?"

He shakes his head in my palms. "I don't work for him. I work for you."

I release his face. Scrutinising him, I feel a pang of pain, the knife sliding between my shoulder blades, the shot to the back of my skull in the church, as I realise how he took my words. Took *him* to mean *Dustin*. Not Jimmy. Not. Fucking. Jimmy. For him to instantly think I meant *Dustin*.

So many tells. Now... and recently. How did I miss this disloyalty? How did I— He flipped the table in front of my Indonesian associates. Was that a diversion? Were the weapon crates even short? He was anxious when I asked him to stay back at the warehouse with me. My eyes land on Lee, rendered *useless—Fucker*.

Nothingness, not the cigars shared, nor the conversations had, not the love of his life who was shot in the back— none of it will protect him. I am *not* a merciful man when it comes to them, to her. I'm no longer that man.

For her.

Don't fuck with me.

Don't fuck with my little deer.

Don't fuck with my business.

I meet his rich brown eyes. "I want you to know that I respect your loyalty." I nod with a knowing smile and levelling eyes that I can't mask, don't want to. This is my friend. My capo. My enemy... He should see *me*. Clay Butcher. The Don of the *Cosa Nostra*. The blood of the Family. "I do. I knew you were a loyal man so I should not be surprised you still are."

He risks a look at my soldiers, shuffling backwards under their gaze and mine. "Boss, what are you doing?"

Those nervous movements twist that knife in my back, and I deadpan. "Only two SD cards?"

"I thought so. I thought so. I searched—"

"No one knew, Vinny. Just you and my little brother."

"Jimmy had someone watching her. They would have known everything. That can't be me. I'm always here with you, Boss." His voice spikes with panic. "You can't be serious."

I nod. *He's right.* There would have been another man watching her.

Another man to hunt.

To drown.

But this man... *this man right* in front of me—I exhale, the air hissing through my teeth. "Only *you* knew that *she* didn't know. For Lee to have given her the SD card, it must have been under the pretence that *she* didn't know what was on it... *Loyalty is black and white.*"

"Clay. *Please.*"

"At least it's not in your back." I draw my Glock and put a round between his eyes.

CHAPTER FORTY-THREE

"She has been through hell. So, believe me when I say, fear her when she looks in the fire and smiles." -E.Corona.

I DON'T REMEMBER FALLING asleep, but as I jolt from slumber, I'm immediately aware that I'm wet between my thighs. The awfulness of that has me whining softly into the mattress before I even crack my eyes open. I fell asleep for however many minutes or hours, but in that time, my mind was unable to watch over my body.

When I'm asleep, my body is *alone.*

And now I'm wet.

Why am I wet?

What does that mean?

Curling on my side, the agony in my bones, in my muscles, forces winces through the gaps between my deep hoarse moans. "I'm wet." I burst open with shame. "I'm alone and wet between my legs. *Oh, God, why am I wet?"*

"You're not alone. You'll never be alone again." His voice is dark and husky, carrying across the room. He isn't close, and I feel our distance like literal torture. His skin is a blanket that douses the prickling flesh I'm wrapped in. Flesh that doesn't feel nice, doesn't seem to *fit* my bones anymore.

It.

Doesn't.

Fit.

I sob, strangled. "I couldn't control my body. I fell asleep. What did I do? I don't want to be fucking wet. This isn't my body. It feels *horrible*." I groan, hating the sound of my own voice because it reminds me of how useless it was to help me. To call for help. To scream my pain. To fight back.

Opening my eyes, I feel the burn, the friction of life and light and trauma like sandpaper chaffing me. I stare across the bedroom, fixing my arid eyes on Clay's fists. He's sitting on the black leather chair, watching me. His frame is a solid statue of angry, tight muscles, both hands clenched to the point of bloodless intensity.

"I'm wet," I say again, desperate for his outrage, needing him to be sickened too. To acknowledge that I'm wrong. So wrong.

Training my gaze to his piercing blue eyes, I shake my head through my utter revulsion, betrayal rushing the length of my tongue as I feel a pull to ask him to touch me, hold me, and I hate that desire just as much because that need was built with lies. He lied to me. I lied, too. We both formed this alias, this relationship, based on ulterior motives, but I can't seem to focus on the deceit when the very flesh holding me together feels so horribly wrong. "I don't like the way my skin feels."

"Your skin is *perfect*. Your body is *safe*." He rises to his feet, walking over to my bedside, and I roll onto my back when he hovers over me. The ends of the shirt I'm wearing—his shirt —rest in the middle of his thigh. "With *me*." His eyes lock on mine, assessing me, reading me. Then he steps back and holds his hand out for me to take. "Come. I'll show you."

When I place my much smaller hand in his, I catch sight of red stains on the cuff of his shirt and the sight, meaning, implication stirs something inside me, something vengeful. My eyes dance around the dried blood. Around the crimson pattern. It's big enough to imply the blood is someone else's and that someone else is probably not alive.

He cuts into my thoughts. "I killed them, little deer. They can't hurt you."

My eyes widen at the word *them*. Not him or Lee or a someone—*them*. A strained whimper forces its way up my throat as my eyes stare at the blood on his cuff representing so much more than a stain.

"Don't be sad for them," he hisses through his teeth, and the noise startles me. My eyes find his, find them twitching with rage. Unleashed for the first time. A real smouldering pit of fury. Not practised. "Don't you dare give them a moment of your sorrow, Fawn."

Them.

My brothers.

I blink over and over, trying to digest the information.

Through the constructed despair, the societally learnt reaction to the news of their death, I feel something stronger, something sickening and *happy*... I wince at it.

That's not a crumb.

Clay breaks my focus when he drops his hand and strides away. "Bolton will be outside. You may not leave until I come for you." He moves towards the wooden door with the kind of rigidity that should terrify me, warn me, but I leap from the mattress to chase after him.

"*No.* Where are you going?"

"You have pity for them!" He whirls to face me, and my brain tells me to shuffle backwards under his predatorial gaze, but my heart tells me to fall at his feet. "I know you need me right now, sweet girl. But you have pity. For. *Them.* I need to leave before I scare you. I'm not in control tonight."

My eyes gloss over. "I'm not—"

He stalks towards me and grabs my face the way he does when he needs to press his point, but his fingers don't burn when they sink into my cheeks. His body's heat doesn't deter mine. It calls me. Coats me. Relieves.

Consumes me.

He glowers, but it isn't for me. "I wanted to protect you from this. And I will. From your father who gifted you this trauma, who saw to it that he broke you. That is what he does, Fawn. He did it to Cassidy. He did it to Konnor. I don't regret keeping this from you. Somethings you don't need to know. Whether you fight me on this or not. Whether you despise me for what I do. What I have done. I will still do it. I can't help the way I am. But if the choice is between your understanding, your affections for me, or protecting you —*Christ.* I will *always* choose to protect you. I will—"

Choose me?

I shove him away.

Only to then lunge at him. Cupping his tense jaw, which pulses angrily beneath my palms, I crush my mouth to his as he growls his sentiment into my lips.

His muscles relax. Clay's arms circle my body entirely, banding, then lifts me until I am on my tippy toes on his shoes. My entire being hums, and for a moment, my flesh, my thighs, and my soul aren't trapped in that room. Aren't stalling in the recall of it all. It has been interrupted by his body.

His skin soothes.

Like the water.

Like the depths of the pool did yesterday, coating me in fluid movements and comfort and protecting me from the sun and air. He does that.

Protects me.

I break our kiss and take his hand, nodding that I'm ready for what he has to show me. His eyes narrow. A strange yet potent feeling fills my body with enough strength to follow him over to the mirror.

As soon as I'm faced with my reflection I want to hurl. I lock my jaw. Tighten my lips. Squeezing my eyes shut, I concentrate on the sensation of air rushing in and out of my nose. I can't stand the sight of her.

"I'm going to take this shirt off," he says, and I turn my head to chase the sound of his deep, husky voice. "You can keep your eyes closed if you need." His fingers glide up my side, hiking the material of the shirt up as he goes. The air touches my skin, making it *crawl*. I moan from within my chest, squirming under the uncomfortable sensation. "Lift your arms." I do as he asks, and the shirt comes off completely.

Wrapped in disgust, too wrapped in it to think about much else, my eyes stay closed as I gasp his name, "*Clay.*" I shield my body with my arms, digging my fingers into the flesh at my sides. "Talk to me. I need to hear your voice. Please."

"You're the bravest girl I have ever met." He pries my hands from around my naked body. "After everything you have been through, I thought you would shut down, but you're still here, and you still trust me. You know I lied to you. I lied about the recording. I lied about your father. You know this now. But you still trust me."

"Because I'm dumb."

"Because you're *brave.*"

His front touches my back as his fingers coast down my arms to where my hands dangle by my sides. "It takes courage to trust what you feel inside despite what the world shows you. You could have tried to escape. Tried to get away from me. But you know why I did it. You know.

"I was being your thorns, little deer. And I'm not going to pretend to understand what you're going through. For once, I need you to tell me what you need, sweet girl." His fingers entwine with mine, and he guides them slowly across my stomach, the tips brushing my skin. I feel it...

My breath hitches.

The gentle touch scolds. Hot. Prickling. Unnatural. I squeeze my eyes together harder, forcing them to stay like that, fending off the sensation.

"This is *your* body," he states, his timbre twisted and rough. Covering mine, his fingers cup between my thighs. "I want to worship you. Every day. Let me show you your pretty body." When he pushes my middle finger between my lips, he uses his to work it against the internal soft flesh. I expel a soft sob. "*Clay.*" Nausea hits me when the walls grasp at our fingers. They seem to overwhelm me, muscles working without conscious effort. It's not my body. "*Clay.*" I groan his name, the tone a desperate plea to stop or not to. I don't know which. "Clay, please."

"This is *your* body. I'm here."

I drop my head back on his chest, staring at the black abyss of my eyelids. I try to breathe. To concentrate on him. Not me. Not *my* body. "You're wet because your body is begging for pleasure. It's looking after you, sweet girl. There is nothing prettier than when you come, than when you enjoy your body. When you live in it. When you accept it."

I lick my lips as they grow drier with each inhalation. Our fingers slip in and out of my pussy easily, and the sensation is heightened with no visual stimulation to draw me from the feeling. My mind homes in on two things.

His voice filling my head.

Our fingers working inside me.

I suddenly want more, balancing on the cusp, on a teasing edge. My finger is so short and small. I pull it out and place my wet hand over his, pushing his in further. I take control, scooping my finger against his.

"Now, open your eyes," he says, his breath cascading along the skin on my throat, tussling my hair. I open my eyes to my reflection. My man is behind me. His fingers are inside me with mine over them. "Do you see what I see?" He kisses my hair. "Tell me what you want, Fawn. I'll give it to you. Anything. Everything. Just name it. Do you want more revenge? The cop? Your foster mother? Do you want the world to fear you?"

I stare blankly at the naked blonde in the mirror with her skin flushed from arousal. Feel his fingers working my muscles gently. Hear his heavy passionate breathing.

Then I whisper, "I want someone to love her."

I watch as my eyes well up, blurring the edges of my vision, making the girl in the mirror dissolve within the pools. Dissolve and appear more visually accurate to the life she has lived; the one she has barely existed in.

Like nothing.

No one's choice.

Is it too much to ask?

Fuck! It's too much to ask!

There isn't enough moisture left in her eyes, the need to cry a throbbing sensation. She has cried too much. "I want someone to love her!" I say again, bursting bright red and shaking. He pulls his fingers from inside me and turns me to face him, cupping my cheeks.

I sob those soundless noises and shed those dry tears. "No one loves her." My voice wobbles, emotions forcing my feet backwards, desperate for space. His hands slip from my face. He would have never allowed me this wide breadth before, but he is now. "No one has *ever* loved her, Clay. I pretended for so long that Benji did. That my mum might have. That maybe if my dad just saw me, just spoke to me, I mean. I can be funny, right? I can be interesting? I'm—"

"I love her."

My eyes fly open. I slap my hand over my mouth, shaking my head against the tight grip, my mind and body and soul unable to process what he said. Unable to accept it. Not now. Not after all the lies and betrayal, a perpetual downpour of deceit.

The words play in my mind. *"I love her."* Has anyone ever said that to me? Ever? My mum must have... surely? "What did you say?"

My reaction causes his jaw to pulse, causes torment to fill his dark, dangerous eyes. "I love you," he says again. "And I want to love you so fucking hard there is no room for the past. Or the pain. And I will, sweet girl. I won't stand by and allow you not to like yourself when what I see is... *spectacular*."

No. I crane my neck, searching his eyes for the truth lying below the surface. *The truth.* But there is too much emotion filling me right now. My heart strains to balloon for this broken soul, petrified to stone, unable to pump hard within a crushed body. It wants to. *God,* it wants to believe him. "You love her?"

"I love *you*."

Someone loves you, Fawn.

I shake my head slowly. "*No*." My throat tightens with those dry contractions. "No. You can't."

My head moves violently from side to side. No. You can't. Not you. Not the most impressive man in the world. "You're just saying it. You have seen the absolute worst of me! You have seen all the flaws. You can't. I don't believe it. I'm just your burden. Your pretty little burden. I'm—"

"I didn't see any flaws, little deer. I saw you tearing down the middle. I saw you being mauled by life. I can't rip those fuckers from your mind, but I will rip them from this world. All of them." His eyes blaze. "I *did*. I will be your thorns, sweet girl. Your future is with me. You're *Cosa Nostra* royalty. Do you know what that means?"

I blink ahead because amidst the horror of the past two days, in the middle of all this trauma, he is saying everything I have ever dreamed of. They are the worst words to associate with this feeling, with this dissonance, self-hate, and the words that I most needed to hear.

To believe them, though.

I can't.

Can I?

After all I have endured, believing would be like jumping from a tree the moment I was gifted wings. Not trying them out. Or growing into them. Just diving headfirst and hoping they fit. They hold my weight. The weight of my past.

The whiplash of this decision wraps around me. I can't grapple with what to feel or say or organise in my mind because it's too much.

When I don't answer, his deep, commanding voice rumbles, "It means you aren't ordinary, sweet girl." I relent my internal debate, finding his eyes—piercing, fierce blue vortexes of sentiment. "You're *powerful*."

I nod slowly.

"It's in your blood, that power."

My mouth opens as his words sail around me, my chest pumping harder to draw in air.

"You're not my pretty little burden, Fawn." He lifts my chin. "You're my pretty little queen."

THE END
Continue Clay and Fawn's story in His Pretty Little Queen
Here
Or turn the page for chapter one!

"It can take two weeks to build the body of a butterfly, and while we enjoy the pretty creature, we often forget what it endured to achieve that form. We forget the weeks that saw it split apart, broken down, and mashed up. We often ignore the courage needed to escape their safe hearth, to spread their newly constructed wings, and to soar the heights that were once an impossible feat."

his pretty little queen - book five

Chapter One
Fawn

A friend of mine told me that good things come in threes.

Him: number one.

Him...

Clay Butcher—the man sitting at his desk across from our bed with the glacier look of importance, of power portrayed through pursed lips and two pinched dark brows. Blue eyes focus on his laptop screen. His chair is an iron sword and shield away from a throne.

Through the large full-length window, the morning sun sets a soft glow to the room, accenting the curves of muscles across his bare torso with light and shadows.

I'm glad he is still here.

This man is breathtaking. I've always believed in auras; my mum swore she could see colours around living things.

I wonder what colour she would've seen around Clay Butcher.

One thing is for sure, whatever the hue, it exists as thick, tangible supremacy that even a blind person can appreciate. So, when he is gone—at work or the warehouse—his absence makes my entire world cavernous.

My entire world... Well, that's him... This house. The maids. Jasmine. The pillow stacks. The new sofa lounge by the poolside and the old wrought-iron one that now sits as an ornament in the garden. As it should be.

My whole life... *this.*

I'm not allowed to leave it or expand it. Not until he finds my dad and... *kills him.* Of this, I'm sure. Death is what awaits the man I share blood with, the one I don't know.

I tuck my hands beneath my cheek and shuffle my legs along the sheets, settling in further. Unable to tear my gaze away from Clay Butcher's level of perfection, I simply watch him work. And while he hasn't acknowledged I'm awake, he doesn't have to.

He knows.

He always knows.

"Come here," he says to the screen, and my lips quirk into a little smile. I roll my shoulders, and the silk of his bedding slides down my naked body as I stand.

I'm always naked in this room.

That's how he likes me.

My bare feet pad over the floor towards him, and just when I'm within arm's length, he shuts his laptop, slides it to the side, and leans back slightly, making space on the desk in front of him.

An action that speaks volumes.

Smiling softly at his silent order, I perch in front of him on the polished wood with my feet swinging, my knees pressed together, my hair dangling in long straight ribbons down each breast. He considers me with a knowing gleam that forces both nerves and excitement to the tips of my toes.

I wiggle them. His gaze darts down to watch my toes and then back up to settle on my face.

"You slept well, little deer," he says in a husky purr that assists the gleam in igniting my pulse. "You didn't even move when I came to bed. That's very good. Did you dream?"

"Of burning Maggie's chicken pie." I chuckle, remembering when our lovely cook had to use the fire extinguisher. Then, blushing, I lay my hands on my bare thighs to hide the way my knees inadvertently squeeze together as I say, "And of you, Sir."

He reclines further into his big wingback chair, saying, "Show me what dreaming of me looks like."

My heart does a double tap, but outwardly, I only worry my bottom lip while I hike my thighs up and let my knees fall apart. His eyes are unwavering from mine, but his intent blazes within them. After a few seconds, he drops his gaze to between my legs.

I blush immediately.

He drags his thumb along his lower lip, his eyes trained on my pussy and the underside of my backside pressed to the desk. The heat from his gaze prickles the little blonde hairs I have newly grown for him.

A smirk tugs at the corner of his lips, and he raises his hot gaze to meet my apprehensive one. "I said, *show me*, little deer."

He watches my throat roll, noting everything. He's always made me nervous, always set butterflies to flight within me, but now this part of our relationship is both absolute intimacy and a test for me to pass.

Can I touch myself and be present?

Am I comfortable in my own skin?

Have I moved on from what I saw—what I know—happened to me?

No. It's an easy answer.

No.

He knows this, too, but I try to please him, lifting my hand and touching the lips between my legs that are already slick in my desire for him. The wetness is a point of embarrassment as my finger slides through the thin slick result of my deep arousal.

I open my mouth, ignore the echo of grunting in my head —the blood-curdling sounds of my foster brothers' pleasure the day they all took turns with this body—and part the flesh at my core for the man who lies to keep me safe, who protects me with unwavering focus.

Even from myself.

The man whose touch can drown the voices, the discomfort while everyone else's, including my own, still scorches like a fire.

I touch the inner bud, and my backside pulses off the table when sensation zaps through me. A reaction of both phantom pain and real pleasure. I groan from my throat, hating the feel of my body as it responds without my consent, but I mask the sound. Mix it with a moan that is visceral because I'm torn in two wanting closure, to please him, to play and show him how comfortable I am in my body but also wanting no one to lay a finger on my skin but him...

Not even myself.

Not my untrustworthy hands. The same ones that gripped Jake's shoulders when he thrust into me. That convinced him I enjoyed it... *Did I? Did I convince him? Did he honestly believe I consented with my hands that night?*

If not with that, then with my pussy. I consented with that.

Didn't I?

When I touch myself, the muscles inside me consent when they pulse. And I hate it.

My finger trembles on my slit as these thoughts flood me. I don't want to feel what Jake felt. *"A few minutes ago, you were hugging me so tight with your pussy you didn't want me to leave."*

It wasn't me.

I did want him to leave.

"So pretty," Clay says, a hoarse timbre wrapped around his voice. "You still don't trust yourself, sweet girl. Don't be fake with me."

I stop touching myself and deflate on a little sigh. "Is it trust?" I ask softly. "I just want *you* to touch me. That's all."

"You don't trust your body anymore. Your pussy. Your fingers. *Yes.* You still trust me, but I need you to show me what's mine. Open yourself up in front of me and show me what your pretty young pussy looks like, but you're not ready. " He rolls the chair an inch closer to me, reaching out to grip the wood either side of my thighs. Enveloping me is the scent I love more than cookies and bread and melting chocolate and all the mouth-watering luxuries I now enjoy daily because of him—the scent of his cologne, of sweet cigars, and warm male flesh. "Do you want me to play with your body, sweet girl?"

I nod. "Yes, please, Sir."

"Such lovely manners... But you have to do something for me first."

I smirk, thinking about taking his cock into my mouth, sucking him until he is the one who is raw with me. "I'll do anything for you, Sir."

A soft smile settles on his lips as he knows this to be true. I mean those words to my core. I'd do anything for this man.

I've forgiven him for lying. For using me as bait to try to lure my father out of hiding. For hiding the truth from me.

Because he is my thorns.

The only person in this entire world to believe me, to care for me, to hold me accountable, to *want* me.

His smile flattens. "You covered the mirrors yesterday, sweet girl," he says, and I cast my eyes down to hide my shame. "You forgot to take the sheet in the dressing room down before you left the room. How long have you been doing that?"

Fuck.   *Henchman   Jeeves*—my   personal henchman/butler/*rat*. I know he's meant to watch me, keep me safe, but he doesn't have to share all my fucking secrets.

I mumble, "HJ is such a dobber."

"*Bolton* is paid to be... *a dobber.*" His finger goes to my chin, and he lifts it until I'm anchored in his crystal-clear blue gaze. "And you know this." He suddenly stands up, a wall of muscles erected before me and so close, so perfect, I struggle not to reach out and roll my fingertips down the rippling plane. I crane my neck to keep eye contact. "Come," he orders, offering me his hand to take.

"That was the whole idea, Sir, but I'm still waiting," I say, my teasing cadence laced with false strength.

His lips tick in a corner, but he says nothing, turning to guide my defiant feet towards the dressing room.

What does he want?

For me to look at myself in the mirror?

I can do that.

I only covered the mirrors because there are so many, too many, and I'm stuck in this house, and they are like shadows following me around every room, and I'm constantly glancing over my shoulder and—

He sits me on the ottoman in front of the mirror, that

entire bullshit spiel halting on my tongue as I stare at the girl from the incident reflected at me.

My brows pinch into a scowl.

She's like a train wreck—I force a smile at the reflection of the breathtaking man towering over me in nothing but his black cotton pants because I can't trust myself to speak to him right away.

He drops down—the deadliest man in the city on his knees for me—blocking the mirror for a moment with his head. His eyes heat. "Now lean back on your hands, spread your pretty white thighs, and watch me worship you."

He slings my legs over his shoulders and dips his head. The mirror comes into view, the girl in the reflection already painted in the crimson glow of arousal just as his mouth sucks at my flesh.

Instantly, I mewl around, assaulted by my reflection and by the eating motion of his lips.

His touch soothes.

And I'm whole. *His.*

His tongue presses in through the walls clinging with needy desperation to the steady penetration. I want to squeeze my eyes shut so I can focus on him. Avoid the sight of me. I want to grab his head, but I can't stay upright if I don't brace on both hands.

My backside rocks and lifts, so he slides his hands beneath each cheek to control me as he relentlessly fucks between my folds with his tongue, as he mouths me, as his lips rhythm crash sensation with sensation. Plunging through and out. Then massaging the supple soft lips as he withdraws only to spear me again.

My nails dig into the ottoman.

I do as he commanded, watching myself in the mirror with Clay Butcher on his knees between my thighs.

My eyes grow heavy when he slows down, flattening his tongue and licking up and down, then dipping in, only to lap over that quivering flesh again.

It's meticulous.

Like everything he does. As soon as a part of my pussy wants attention he is there, reading the pulsing muscles like I'm connected to him through tangible waves of sensory information. Like I'm an extension of... *him.*

I'm so wet; I still shiver with shame for that fact—my response to him will be smeared and dripping from his lips and chin.

He growls into my pussy, his feral enjoyment vibrating for a moment through me as though he is ready to actually bite down and rip off flesh. He's dirty and carnal. This regal man is completely at odds with everything he shows the world.

My mouth goes wide, moans soaring through the dressing room as the sensitivity that has me weeping into his mouth turns into severe heat. My backside clenches in his palms, so he grips the plump globes, spreading them to deepen his kiss further.

I buck again.

He laps his tongue up from my opening to my clit, where he sucks the bundle of nerves between his teeth, clamping on and flicking, igniting fireworks within me.

I whimper.

My legs jolt up.

My body convulses. But his grip on my arse is unyielding, holding me to him.

"Oh. Sir." My eyes roll with dizzying pleasure. "I can't. It's, it's too—" A long moan rolls up from deep inside me as I'm hit with a bat of pleasure, blackening my vision for a dreamy moment.

I tense up as my orgasm continues.

My arms shake under my weight.

I pant his name like I'm conditioned to do, watching my reflection as I begin to come, my hips grinding shamelessly on his face to increase the pressure, to intensify each perfect lap of his tongue.

I bat my eyes until they close under the weight of arousal. The rough bristles around his jaw graze, easing the needy skin as he refuses to relinquish the suction on my clit.

"*Oh* God!" I cry out, my arms buckling. My back meets the ottoman while my hands fist his crown, my fingers desperately knotting his dark hair for control.

I arch my back as the final waves of sensation swim through me, and he keenly changes his pace to suit the flow of my orgasm.

Slowing down, he mouths me between the legs as if he were kissing me better after a bruising make-out session. And it is a ridiculous thought, but I instantly wish he would kiss my lips like he is kissing my pussy. It is something that still seems rare between us—a simple kiss.

I run my fingers through his dark hair adoringly, the light above us highlighting the sparse greys that drive me crazy. Flattening my body to the ottoman, I hum my enjoyment to the chaste motion of his reverent mouth.

My body warms as he worshipfully moves up, skating his lips between my hips, along the plane of my stomach and between my ribs as I arch into him.

His tongue slides out to taste the sweat between my breasts, and then I lift further, desperate to meet him.

Our lips connect.

He's kissing me...

My world explodes into stars as we kiss with his possessive groans mingling with my exhausted, sated moans that are wrapped in deep everlasting sentiment.

For this man.

I feel *everything* for this powerful man. There is no one else. Not a friend, siblings. *Nothing.* Only him.

My number one good thing.

Hitching my legs around the back of his, my naked body slick with perspiration slides along him. His hand moves up to grip the column of my throat, his thumb lifting my chin to direct and control our lips.

Cupping his jaw to deepen our kiss, I feel his arousal brazenly hard between my legs, bruising and teasing.

I wriggle until his erection is thrumming along the sensitive flesh between my folds. I begin to grind on him, needy and desperate for more. To pleasure him. To pleasure me. I rub along him. Back and forth with my hips.

His mouth becomes fiercer on mine. I keep kissing him even as it hurts, even as his teeth flare and his fist tightens, hissing air from me.

He locks his jaw.

Stops.

Stilling his movement, our kiss becomes one-sided as he says, "You want more? That's very pleasing."

I have come to learn he enjoys watching and feeling me as I move on his body. He could toss me aside if he didn't like it, but he doesn't. He likes me rubbing on him like a cat. Perhaps, he likes my desperation. Lifting my hips off the ottoman, I slide along his shaft, spoiled for more pleasure.

"Good girl," he growls, the twisted timbre revealing his arousal and restraint. "You try so hard, little deer. Can you have an orgasm all by yourself for me?"

I roll my hips shamelessly, chasing the sensation.

God, I'm tight all over, desperate for—*something*. Something is missing.

I become feverish.

After his mouth's assault on me. And now this. I need to prove I can, but I can't. I need him to finish it for me. "*Please* —" I let out the words through a tight moan. "Please, help me."

Clay's lips slide into a smirk against my mouth as I continue to kiss him clumsily. The taunting sensation burns in my ears. My pussy leaks all over his pants in anticipation.

"*God,*" I growl, reaching for my climax while it eludes me, feeling as though I will combust if I don't get off again.

Using his body to get there—

"Don't cover the mirrors again, little deer," he orders, lowering one hand to slide a finger inside me so easily a second joins almost immediately. "Oh, you're so wet. So tight. My sweet, sweet girl."

I close my eyes and clench around him, but when he thrusts in, he draws back out in quick succession. I buck to chase the deep penetration. "That's it. You're doing very good." He pushes in again. "Do you want another finger?"

"*Yes...*" I barely manage to speak, laboured breath beating hard against his mouth.

"You're so greedy."

"You make me feel this way."

There is amusement in his voice as he says, "I know."

"What about you, Sir?"

"Your pleasure is for me." He adds a third finger and it's unbearably snug inside me, so when he starts to move all three with the talent of a well-oiled machine, I'm blanketed in stars. "I need to stretch you. You're tiny. You have a little hole and a small frame. Every time I fuck you, you end up sore, and I need your body ready to accept mine. I need you weeping the moment you feel me, hear me, see me. I need you ready to take me. You will be shaped to fit my cock, walking around with my cum filling your knickers—"

My orgasm rips through me with a husky cry. "*Oh*." I pulse around his fingers as he rubs and wrings my climax from me. "Sir, *so* good."

His cock bucks with bruising need between us, but he is the master of control, ignoring his obvious arousal. With the gentle massaging motion of his fingers sliding leisurely in and out of me, he brings me down from my second orgasm instead of thrusting into me like I know he wants. He hasn't taken me in such a way in weeks. Not since I saw the recording and watched my body being used like a toy by my foster brothers.

I squeeze my eyes at the thought. Focus on him. He peppers kisses over my face as he says, "You haven't had many pleasures in your life, sweet girl. I promised to spoil you. I'll spoil your sweet pussy for attention."

I roll my head on the ottoman, groaning.

His kisses gently bring me down from the wave of pleasure I'm riding. They simmer with sentiment as my muscles unfurl and relax to the reverent affection.

Looking at him again, I tilt my head to see his are now closed, his dark brows pinched, his lips a tender rushing stream over my skin.

Then they are gone, and he is standing with me in his arms. A weightless extension of him. He walks me over to the bed and lays me down on the mattress, placing a hand either side of my head. And I know this routine.

"What will you do today?" he asks, and I deflate, knowing he'll be gone all day and I'll wait for him. "Don't look so sad, sweet girl."

I break our gaze, looking absently into a corner of the room. "What can I do?"

"Anything you want."

"You won't let me leave the house."

He grips my jaw gently, moving my face until my eyes relent and meet his—crystal-clear blue orbs bordered by dark lashes. Breathtaking. Commanding. "We have been over this."

"I know," I say, disappointment coiled around my tone. "I know. *It's not safe.* I guess I'll have more clothes brought up, or perhaps I'll cook that pork belly again or watch another movie or hang out with Jas—"

His brows weave. "This doesn't please you?"

"I should be grateful," I mutter honestly, although the humility is seemingly a tatted echo in my mind. I want to want things. I want to demand them. Yet, there is this voice, the same outdated voice, a small and breathy resonance, that reminds me to accept, to shrink myself, to fit in.

He steels. Then pushes off the bed, striding over to the dressing room, the lights growing at his presence. "I'm taking care of you, little deer." He speaks to the room as he dresses. "What do you want? Use your voice. Tell me."

I sit up and watch him. "I don't know."

His phone comes to life, cutting through the air like a knife severing our conversation. I frown as he stares at it. "Whatever you desire, I will do. Think about what you want." He grabs his suit jacket and the phone as it rings perpetually.

Then he approaches the bed, leaning down on his hands, his shoulders rolling, his chin dipping so his lips can take mine. His intent is a quick, firm, breathtaking kiss, but I know this, so I cup his strong jaw to demand more than a moment of goodbye. Deepening the motion of his lips, I channel all my want into them until a groan moves through his throat.

He breaks our kiss, his lips hovering close, commanding mine to stay still as he talks against them. "I want a list. Think on it. You will tell me what you want, sweet girl, and I promise to give it to you."

He vanishes through the door, and I'm left confused. I don't know what I want. Does he think I'm withholding something? Is that a thing? Like the charades of my intentions?

I don't know who I am.

How am I supposed to know what I want?

The water of the swimming pool ripples as I swing my legs through it and watch distractedly as the substance twinkles and moves below the sun.

What do I want?

I'm learning to cook, which sings to my maternal side, and I know I won't be locked in this resort-like gilded cage forever, just until he finds my dad... And *kills him.* I swallow thickly, clearing my throat as heavy footsteps pour down the path.

"*Fucksake,*" Henchman Jeeves pants, dropping forward with his hands to his knees.

My henchman/butler/rat...

Not happy with you.

He breathes through a kind of panic, having exerted himself to the point he's vibrating to get air.

Three guards are now halting from their run behind him, sighing with relief when they see me sitting unfazed by the poolside.

I blink at the dishevelled men. "What?"

Henchman Jeeves catches his breath before saying, "For the love of God, how did you get down here?"

And I know it was stupid and that Clay won't approve, but I don't lie when I answer, "I climbed down the fire escape on my balcony."

"She's going to get us killed," one of the henchmen hisses, spinning and sauntering off, curses soaring around him.

Henchman Jeeves slowly shakes his head. "*Why?* Why would you do something so dangerous and—"

I shrug, interrupting petulantly. "Looked like fun? The ladder is perfectly safe. It isn't like I climbed down a fucking drainpipe. I wasn't escaping. The ladder is right there on the side of the balcony. I just had to climb over the railing."

The remaining henchman grumbles behind him, wiping his rigidly set brow. "Don't tell the boss, Fawn, or..." His voice continues to run, but the words are mumbled through annoyed breath.

Henchman Jeeves frowns at him, scolding him with one snap of his gaze. "Miss Harlow." He turns back to me and offers me a faux smile. "It would be best if you don't tell the boss that you were by the poolside alone."

Fawn. I don't correct him and ask him to call me by my given name. He slips up often, but I know he must call me Miss Harlow now. I don't even know who Miss Harlow is, really. It doesn't seem like my name; I never felt like a Harlow. I was hoping to find my identity as a Nerrock. And I'll probably never be a Butcher... I sigh. "Would you get fired?"

Shaking his head slowly, he laughs without mirth. "I *wish* the answer was yes."

"He'd kill you?" I whisper as the other guards wander

back inside the house, clearly annoyed, leaving HJ and his fixed gaze that delivers an undeniable answer to that question. "I see." I nod towards the retreating backs of the other men. "They don't like me very much."

He sighs, pity tumbling through his voice. "You do talk to your food more than you talk to them."

"Clay told me not to talk to them."

"I'll have words with them. Don't worry."

My hero. "They don't treat me like they treat Aurora. They treat me like a ward. Like they are babysitting... So do you now. We used to joke."

He looks regretful. "Fawn. It's respect."

And it isn't his fault or theirs. I'm an eighteen-year-old unrequited daughter of a mob boss and the lover of his enemy. Bound in inadequacies and eighteen years of an orphan identity to boot. No idea what to do from one moment to the next or how this half of society lives.

Privilege is kind of boring...

So, I get it—they don't know how to treat me.

Just like I don't know how to behave.

Get book

our thing - book one & two

Blurb:

The city's golden girl falls heart-first into a dark underworld.

I want two things in life: to be the leading ballerina in my academy—

And Max Butcher...

A massive, tattooed boxer, and renowned thug. And my very first crush...

I may be a silly little girl to him, but he's intent on protecting, possessing, and claiming me in every way—his little piece of purity.

But there is more to Max Butcher than the cold, cruel facade he wears like armor. I know; I saw the broken boy inside him one day when we were only children.

So, even as I stand in the shadows with him, as people get hurt...*as people die...* I refuse to let him believe he's nothing more than a piece in his family's corrupt empire.

There is good inside Max Butcher, and I refuse to let him live in the dark forever.

Get book

the district - origin story

Jimmy Storm - 1979
Controllare le strade; control della citta
(Control the streets; control the city.)

MY FATHER WAS a *ladder-man* in the late 1940s. In the old country - Sicily. He was the boy the Family trusted with their money, for he was the one with the clearest vantage point. The expression *ladder-man* had come about back in the early gambling days when young men would stand on ladders on the casino gaming floors, watching and waiting for misconduct.

My father was the most trusted and feared man in Sicily - a complete oxymoron, I know. But it all depended on who was doing the trusting and who was doing the fearing.

The Family paid him ninety lira an hour, which was good money back then, and so of course, the crooks of the club - the ones on the gaming floor pocketing chips, counting cards, and winning too much of the Family's money - found death quickly. There was very little chance for rebuttal once my father had them in his sights. He was an adolescent then and rather engrossed in the power bestowed upon him, as would any young man be with the strength of many at his beck and call.

Things were irrevocably simpler back then. If there was a misdemeanour, it was handled quickly, quietly, and strictly; very few people lived to talk about it. Which is how it should be.

According to gossip, my grandfather was a 'likable type' and had no knowledge of his son's activities. Luckily for us, my grandfather had died when my father was sixteen, leaving him without any relations. *Luckily?* Yes, because there is little I can learn from a 'likable type' of man.

After three years of being the boy up the ladder on the most notorious gaming floors in Sicily, my father became an orphan. And an orphan he was for exactly two days before the Family picked him up and officially made him their own. They bought my father. They owned him then. It wasn't until then that he really understood what he'd signed up for.

He had married the mob.

When you marry the mob, as when you marry a woman, you are contractually, spiritually, legally, and emotionally bound to them. The key difference being, there is no such thing as divorcees - only widowers. That is where it all had started - humble beginnings and a life of servitude to the Family.

When I was a young man, my ego was larger than Achilles', rivalling my father's in every way. It would be fair to say I flexed my muscles every chance I could - at the boys at school, at the people on the sidewalk offering me less than obedient glances. . . at everyone. I was a *sfacciato* little shit, and partly because of that cheekiness, I learned to thrive on the sensation people's submission gave me. I'd usually be hard as a rock beneath my trousers in the midst of a power play.

I am Jimmy Storm, son of Paul Storm, and my name is legendary. Storm is not our real name, of course. My father named himself when he became a made-man.

Half of Sicily owed the Family money, which meant we owned half of Sicily and her people. We managed people with ease, for their lives were worthless to us and priceless to them. I grew up around the cruellest, slyest, dirtiest bastards in the country and they set the benchmark for my behaviour as an adolescent; they were my idols.

When I turned twenty-seven, my *zu* Norris and I left Sicily, taking with us blessings and funds from the Family, with our sights set on a new place of profit. We flew to an area of Australia renowned for its wealthy residents - a secluded section on the coast consisting of four towns: Brussman, Connolly, Stormy River, and Moorup. I recently learnt of an Australian idiom for this kind of unmonitored and isolated area - 'Bandit Country'.

I was out to prove myself at any cost.

Which brings me to today, and the reason I have my shoes pressed to a man's trachea.

"I am *Jimmy Storm!*" I state. The rubber of my heel presses very slowly on his windpipe, and when he tries to buck away, I know I have found the *puntu debole*. He tries desperately to claw at my foot, attempting to relieve some pressure. He can't, but that doesn't save my shoe from getting covered in fingerprints, and *that* is just so inconvenient.

My *zu* and I have been in this miserable part of the world for three god forsaken weeks and have found nothing short of disorganised, disrespectful, and inferior versions of la Cosa Nostra. The young man whose trachea I'm currently crushing is Dustin Nerrock, and he is 'the name' about these parts. A slightly hostile *parràmune* has taken place and I am simply establishing my dominance.

We'd met under casual terms, but this disrespectful man forgot his manners along the way. I've been told, 'What the Australian male lacks in brains, he makes up for in brawn' and I truly hope so. Since being here, we have found a lack of connections, a lack of muscle due to scope - all of Sicily is smaller than this area of Western Australia - and far too many new legalities to... manipulate without consultants to advise us. Despite my indelicate means of conversing, the end game is to get Dustin Nerrock and a few other big-name families in this area to work with us.

For us...

Dustin's father died last year, leaving him with businesses scattered throughout the area, but with no idea on how to utilise them. Money and dominance are the game. The man under my shoe has more money than sense, an ego that rivals my own, and a name people know. And soon, here, people will know mine.

"Do you have any idea who-" Dustin chokes, struggling to force words out while my boot is pressed to his throat.

Pity...

"*Oh scusari,*" I say, feigning concern. "Did you say something?" His face looks so feeble; I want to crush it 'til it goes away. Men who bow are ants, small and helpless, but infinitely useful when put to work. I've been told my temper is an issue. Apparently, it is obvious when I'm irate; I speak a mongrel version of Italian, Sicilian, and English, and my accent seems to thicken... *Personally, I don't hear it...*

"*Madonna Mia,* are you going to cry like a *paparédda,*

Dustin. You're the man about these parts. Stand up!" I yell, and then press my heel further into his jugular. . . so he can't. "*Alzarsi!* Stand up!" He can't. I won't let him, and the whole idea of that makes my dick twitch.

I find myself tiring of his weak attempts to fight me off. I remove my shoe from his neck, allowing him to gasp and drag some much-needed air into his lungs. And he does, sucking like a man possessed. His palms meet the pavement under the dimly lit street lights and I take a few steps back to allow him room to stand. His pushes off his hands and climbs to his feet, a scowl firmly set on his face. Dustin all but growls at me and then spits blood to the side, his body shuddering slightly while he regains air and stability.

I mock, "Are you okay, *paparédda?*"

"You're in deep shit," he hisses, coughing at the pavement.

The bitterness in the air is tangible, an entity apart. It is time to switch the play and lead the conversation in a more mutually beneficial direction. I've humiliated him, and now I shall woo him.

"Let's talk like gentlemen, Dustin," I begin, removing a handkerchief from my pocket and offering it to him as he coughs and clears his throat. "Please oblige me?" I wave the folded white material in front of him, a feigned gesture of a truce.

He takes it and uses it to wipe away the little pieces of gravel pressed to his cheek. "Talk..."

"Perhaps we can start again. *Se?*" This is my favourite part of conversing - switching the play, manipulating the conversation. "You know who I am now, and I know who you are. You also know what I do, *se?*"

He stares at me, his brows drawn together, his eyes narrowed. "Yes."

"Well," I say, clapping my hands and grinning widely at him. "That's an excellent start. May I recommend we take this little *parramune* to a more appropriate place? I know an establishment not too far from here. . . Will you join me for a drink? Put this *little* and unfortunate indiscretion behind us. . ."

***

It didn't take long for me to gain Dustin Nerrock's favour. In fact, it took less time than I'd imagined. The man is hungry, power hungry. I recognise it in him. It is indeed a trait we share. After three hours with Dustin, I'm even more convinced that this area holds infinite possibilities. To start with, there is a high crime rate, which, of course, is a huge benefit to my cause as protection comes at a cost. There are strictly governed gun laws, which, of course, means demand, and I am happy to supply. There is a vast class division, which means two things: an opportunity to clean up the riffraff at a cost, and addicts - I love addicts.

My father once told me to never choose a side, but to rather find out their motivation(s) and make them beholden to you. 'Control the streets; control the city.' I share this philosophy with Dustin. The final and most tantalising piece of information is that this country is bursting at the seams with minerals and is far too big to secure thoroughly. There is gold, diamonds, and unsealed access roads.

"I have never met a rich man I didn't like," I declare, clinking Dustin's glass with mine.

A grin stretches across his face. The grin of a man whose eyes are suffused in dollar signs. "Well, that said, there are others we need in on this. . ."

"Yes." I raise the glass to my lips and the smoky whiskey fumes float deliciously up my nostrils. "A man who my *Capo* told me about. *Big* pull in the old country." I use my hands to talk. My Sicilian mannerisms are hardwired. "*Big* pull. But he seems quite the enigma. I could not track him down. He has recently married some beauty queen from England and is probably just. . . How do you Australians say it? *Fucking* and *fucking*. No time for business when there is pussy. *Se?*" We both laugh and I play the game of equals; that is what I want him to believe. "So this man," I continue, "he is a half-Sicilian, half-Australian, mongrel. *But* the Family. . . They seem to love him. The name I was given was Paul Lucchese."

Dustin's gaze narrows, his amused expression slipping. "I know who you're talking about. . .We can't trust that bastard." And I'm immediately intrigued. . .

"He is very important to the Family." I feign a sigh, but I'm eager to meet the man who has inspired such a reaction. I have never liked 'likable people'; it is the unlikable ones I prefer. They have attitude and spirit. They make excellent soldiers.

Dustin seems to study my expression. "He will never agree."

"He will. I assure you-" My attention is redirected to a clearly inebriated character as he swipes a collection of glasses off the bar; the sound of them smashing rudely invades my senses. I tilt my head and watch from our booth as he begins to yell and threaten the bartender.

Well, this is a pity.

I was having such a peaceful drink, and I have my favourite shirt on. The inebriated man's grasp of the English language shocks me, and it makes me wonder whether it was his mother or father who has failed him so profoundly; perhaps both.

"Listen, 'ere," he starts, pointing a shaky finger at the bartender. "I ain't sellin' nufin. I'm just 'ere for a drink."

Interesting. . .

I shuffle from my seat and excuse myself politely. After walking slowly over to the man at the bar, I lean beside him and smile.

"Wah you want?" He lowers his voice. "I ain't sell nufin'." His mouth opens and expels words only vaguely fathomable. It is a damn pity about this shirt.

"*Scusa.*" I motion across to my table. "I was drinking over there with a very important colleague of mine and you're making it rather hard to concentrate. May I suggest finding a different establishment, *se?*"

It has been a long time since a man dared strike me, and it is apparent why over the course of the next few seconds. He stumbles backwards and then jolts forward, throwing his fist into my face. The smell of his breath knocks me harder than his knuckles do. My cheek burns for a short moment.

I shrug apologetically to the wide-eyed bartender and jab the bastard beside me twice in the throat. *Jab. Jab.* His knees meet the floor with a thud. My knee rises to connect with his chin. *Crack.* A guttural groan curdles up his throat. My knee rises again. Another groan. The back of my hand collides with his cheek. How *irrispettoso.* I can't stand disrespect in any form. As I stare down at his swaying body, I notice a small stain on my shirt.

"*Madonna Mia. Fare le corna a qualcuno,*" I hiss at him. "Look what you did."

***

Dustin's brawn most definitely comes in handy as we relocate my new friend to a more private locale - an old building Dustin inherited. He doesn't look quite as lively laying bound on the cold concrete floor. Although, my dick does like the bindings. . .

I can already tell that after this exchange, I'll be in dire need of a lady's company.

"Will you drag Mr. . .?" I stare questioningly at our bound captive.

"Get fucked . . ." He chokes on his own words.

"Very well, will you drag Mr Get Fucked so he is sitting against that wall just there, *se?*" I smile calmly in my new partner's direction, pointing at the rear brick wall. "Thank you, Dustin."

This disused warehouse would make an excellent abattoir; perhaps I will recommend a new business endeavour to Dustin. I ponder this as I remove a few items from my bag and set them down on the wooden workbench behind me: a blade, a bottle of aqua, and a Luna Stick. Pouring a small amount of water onto my shirt, I gently wipe at the stain. The chill from the liquid sends shivers down my spine.

"Such a pity," I mutter to myself. When I tilt my head to watch Dustin manoeuvre our intoxicated captive to a more suitable position, I feel serenity wash over me. These are the moments where I truly shine. In the grit. When others usually waver, I am at my most contained. Perhaps, it also has to do with my new partner's eager and obedient behaviour; after all, I did nearly squash his throat into the pavement a mere few hours ago. A sly grin draws my lips out. Who said money can't buy happiness? Money can purchase the most loyal of comrades, and fear has no limit. Empires have been built on the foundations of both.

"I am Jimmy Storm. You know me?" I query, though I know the answer.

"No," our barely coherent friend snaps, pulling away from Dustin's grip.

"Well, this is Dustin Nerrock. You know him?" I ask, once again knowing the response. Our inebriated friend glances up at Dustin and nods, appearing to exhibit a suitable level of unease. "Well, now you know me too. Jimmy. Storm. I would like to know who you work for."

"I'm not fucki—"

"*A-ta-ta-ta.*" I wave my finger at his rude interruption. "Before you say no, we found ten grams of heroin on you. Now, don't lie to Jimmy. Tell me who in this town supplies you. . .And then I will give you an offer you can't refuse."

"I'm neva snitchin'. He'd fuckin' kill me."

"I see." I sigh and turn to my assortment of items. "I respect that." As I pick up the switch knife and feel the cold metal in my palm, I run my finger over the blade, the rigid edge grating my pad. The excitement of what's to follow forces blood directly to my groin and I find myself in a state of impatience, eager to show Dustin how I assure success.

I spin on my heels and walk directly to my captive. I lean down. The blade slices through his flesh like a zipper parting fabric. The knife ruptures the nerves within. The deed is done. His eyes widen and his hand grips his left wrist. Blood trickles through his fingers and drips onto the concrete.

"Shit," he cries. "Wha tha fuck? You said you respected tha."

"I do, very much," I state adamantly. "I hope you live. Loyalty is my favourite virtue."

"*Christ,*" Dustin mutters from behind me. *Yes,* this is how we interrogate in *my* Family.

"You will die from exsanguination within ten minutes." I squat at the man's side and grin, watching his face pale and his head bobble on his neck as nausea floods him. I have seen this look many times. "I am a spiritual man. You would not know, but I am a Catholic. And I could swear to Mother *Maria. . .*" I stare at him as he struggles to hold his head up, narrowing my eyes to better study his. "I could swear you can see death take a man. The seconds just before. . . in his eyes. . . you see death enter him."

Something akin to a whimper splutters from his throat and panicked tears burst from the corners of his shallow eyes. This poor underprivileged street rat will not be missed and without any evidence, his disappearance will be stamped as drug related. Which, in a way, it is. "Now, tell me where I can find your boss and I will help you live."

"What? How?" Dustin asks me.

I laugh from deep within my abdomen; I just can't help it. "I told you, I'm a spiritual man."

My weeping captive tries to speak, "He is. . . he owns. . ."

"Can you feel that chill?" I ask him, moving so close my lips brush the shell of his ear. "*He* is near, my friend."

"He owns Le Feir. The bakery." He passes out, seven minutes before closing time. The smell of his blood, metallic and tangy, hits my nose. It pools around his outstretched legs, creating small glistening puddles. *Yes,* I think to myself, *this warehouse would make an excellent abattoir.*

Deciding to keep my word, I stand and walk briskly over to the workbench, retrieve the Luna Caustic nitrate stick - one of my favourite tools. While I roll up my sleeves and wet the stick's tip, I think about what a real shame it is that my captive won't be conscious to feel the burn. I hear it is quite a unique sensation. My dick is throbbing like a stubbed toe below my zipper as I approach my captive and squat by his side. I begin to cauterise his slit wrist. The blood makes it rather difficult, however, not impossible, and I've had plenty of practise. "So young Dustin," I call over my shoulder, my eyes unwavering as I work. "We will pay Mr Le Feir a visit tomorrow, make a deal. We don't want any product besides ours hitting these streets. This is now our *quartier,* our *District.* Why is this?"

"Control the streets, control the city," he replies, his nerves stammering through his voice. A chuckle escapes me. I think I may have scared my new partner; how quaint. It appears Dustin Nerrock doesn't get his hands dirty; he must be a proficient delegator. But as my father once told me, 'It is the dirt that makes the man appreciate the sparkle'.

"More importantly than Mr Fier," I say, "is organising a meeting with the man my *Capo* spoke about. . .You know him. Where will we find him?"

I hear Dustin release an exaggerated breath. "He doesn't go by Paul Lucchese anymore. His name is Luca Butcher and he lives in Connolly."

nicci who?

I'm an Australian chick writing real love stories for dark
souls.
Stalk me.
**Meet other Butcher Boy lovers on Facebook. Join Harris's
Harem of Dark Romance Lovers
Stalk us.**

It's taken three years into my author career to write a
biography because, let's face it, you probably don't care that I
live in Australia, hate owls, am sober, or that my husband's
name is Ed—not Edward or Eddie—Ed... like who names

their son 'just' Ed? (love my in-laws, btw). Anyway, you probably don't really care that my son's name is Jarrah—not Jarrod or Jason—to compensate for his dad's name *Ed*...

I ramble...

Here's what you really want to know. I'm a contradiction. Contradictory people are my jam. I am an independent woman who has lived her entire life doing things the wrong way, the impulsive way, the risky way... my way. I'm not from a rich family but I've taken wealthy people chances... I'm my own boss. I'm a full-time author, an Amazon best-seller, all despite the amount of people who said I couldn't, shouldn't, wouldn't... I'm that person.

So while I live a feminist kind of life... I write about men who kill, who control, who take their women like it's their last breath, pinning them down and whispering *"good girl"* and *"mine"* and *"you belong to me"* and all the red flag utterances that would have most independent women rolling their eyes so hard they see their brains.

I write about men who protect their women. Men who control them because they are so obsessed, so in love, they are terrified not to... Do I have daddy issues? *Probably.* Did I need to be controlled and protected more as a child and this is my outlet? *Possibly.*

So... if you don't like that... if you don't see the internal strength in my heroines, how they are the emotional rocks for these controlling *alphahole* men... then don't read my books. You won't like them. We can still be friends.

But I want both. I want my cake and to have a six-foot-five, tattooed, alphamale eat it too.

facebook.com/authornicciharris

amazon.com/author/nicciharris

bookbub.com/authors/nicci-harris

goodreads.com/nicciharris

instagram.com/author.nicciharris